Awakening

A COLONY FIVE NOVEL

DONNA MAREE HANSON

ISBN ebook 978-1-922360-08-3

ISBN Paperback 978-1-922360-09-0

Edited by DP Plus (www.dpplus.com.au)

Cover by Patty Jansen (https://pattyjansen.com/)

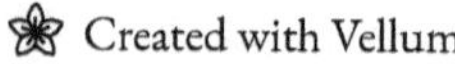 Created with Vellum

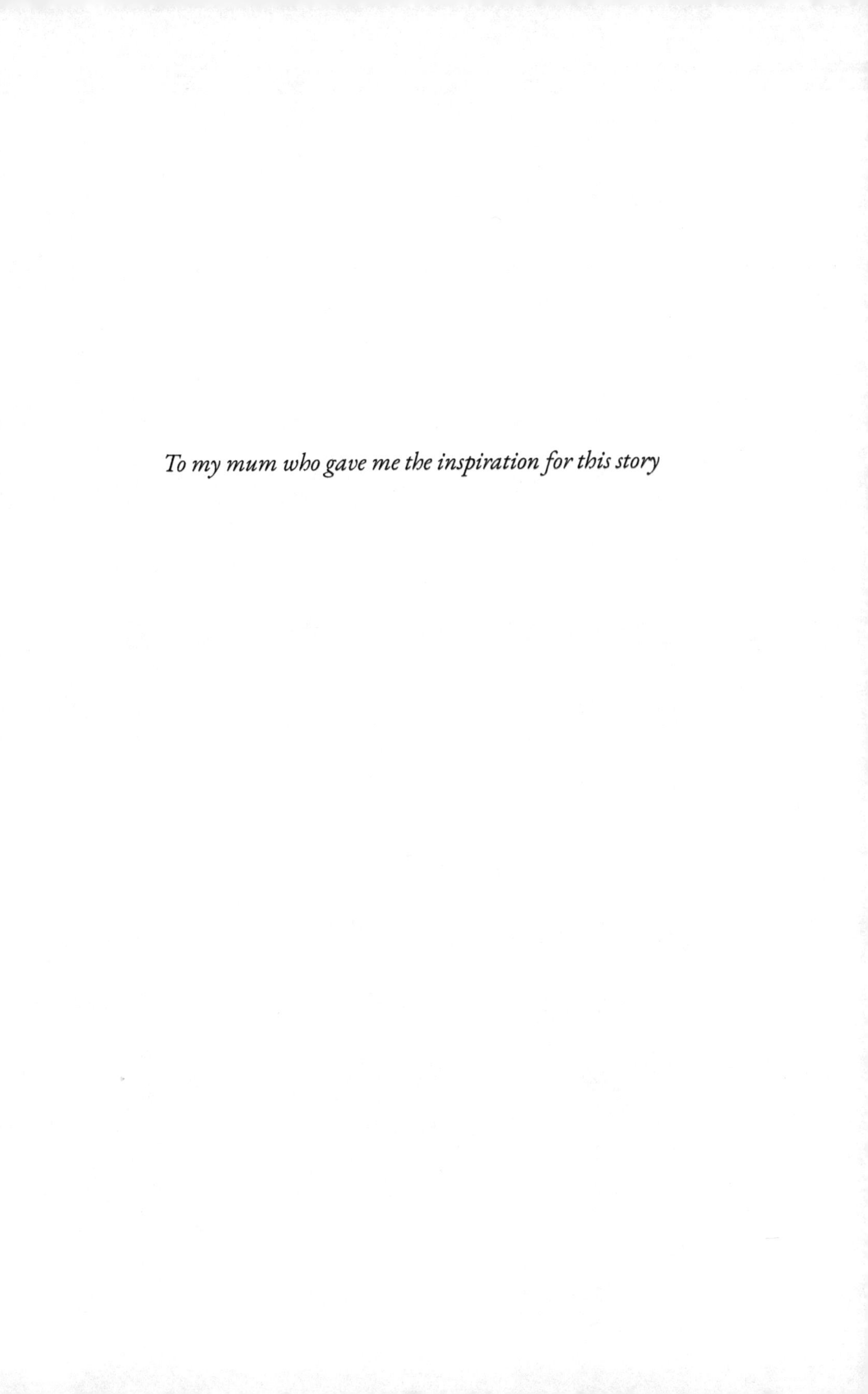

To my mum who gave me the inspiration for this story

Prologue

Year 15 from date of settlement

"I s it contained?" General Frank Milo asked, his dark brown eyes turning from the latest screen updates. Despite the chaotic situation, his short dark hair was perfectly in place and his uniform was crisp and clean. It was his duty to lead, set the example and make the hard decisions. As the commander of a colony ship, he did not expect to be facing the situation they were in now. Their precious embryo bank defiled, some stolen and altered right under their noses. His nose.

Major Freedom Maitland stood at attention waiting to report the latest news, his blond hair standing in tufts and his uniform crumpled as if he had slept in it. "As far as we can ascertain, the situation is under control, sir. We were able to recover some embryos from the clandestine laboratory that have not been altered."

Milo shook his head. "We still have issues to deal with. And we have to report back to Earth Colony Control about the situation. That's not something I'm looking forward to." He didn't want Earth Colony Control shutting the colony down, cleansing the planet of the genetic taint of altered human DNA.

As he spoke the last, Dr Siobhan McPhee walked in, lean and energetic as usual and snagging his attention in the unconscious way she did. "We do have to report, General, and we'd best discuss what we can say before you do anything that affects the future of this colony."

Milo swivelled in his chair. Siobhan was a vision—one he often saw when he closed his eyes at night. Dark red hair, wide, intelligent green eyes and full, red lips and white teeth that dazzled when she smiled. When this situation was under control, he had a mind to pursue her and convert his daydream to reality. If not for this current crisis he was sure he would have had things well in hand by now. His tension eased as he looked upon her loveliness. "What did you have in mind, doctor?"

"We can't let ECC know the full extent of the damage. They will shut us down. We've come too far for that to happen, invested too much of ourselves. Now that you have contained Lenane's illegal experiments, we can limit the damage and move forward."

Milo leaned back in his chair. "How do you suggest we do that?"

"Well, you used our security detachment to destroy the facility and the hybrids. They know, so we have to have some way of stopping them talking about it."

Milo looked to Maitland and frowned before forming a response. The special forces personnel worked as their security detachment and were his to command. His idle fantasy about her cooled as he wondered what she was suggesting. He turned back to her. "I'm listening," he said, even knowing he wasn't going to do anything to harm his men. They'd given up their lives to be what they were, and he couldn't betray that sacrifice. He'd even got dispensation for them to take up a place in the colony if they wished, despite their inbuilt tech. Although the technical details had not been determined as yet—keep the tech enhancements and nanotech or lose them?

Her face was serious as she met his gaze. "Well, you got them out of cold sleep. I suggest putting them back under immediately."

"For how long?" he asked, moving in his chair to hide his disquiet. Was entertaining this idea a betrayal of his men?

"Not too long. We know cryosleep can affect recall, but I suggest we back that up with a counter story, one that will disguise the events, as they go under."

Maitland coughed into his hand, and Milo lifted his eyebrows in an invitation to speak. "That might work on the security forces, but there are other members of the colony who know things and others who suspect something untoward and could guess at the truth."

"Haven't you heard of spin, Major?" Dr McPhee countered. "We can deal with the few who have suspicions or who start rumours."

Milo tugged his bottom lip as he considered. "My men will know the truth when they wake as it will be in Colony Five's history. You can't expect them not to check out what has happened while they were in cryo."

She gave him a nod of acknowledgment. "No, they won't because we will alter the records, the history. We can use the same story as we put in the spin we give everyone else. It will be close to the truth just not all of it."

Milo swivelled his chair and faced his desk, using a stylus to doodle on his electric note pad as he thought things through. Her idea had merit. It was better than losing Colony Five and being homeless because returning to Earth was out of the question. Indeed, they didn't have the resources to do that as their settlement ships has been repurposed for buildings. Besides, it had taken too long to get here, and they had come too far to go back now. The alternative would be to join one of the other colonies but with their different ethos, they would be outsiders, always interlopers. Why should the misstep of one misguided geneticist, who decided to go against the colony's charter and meddle in Human purity, be allowed to risk the colonists right to live here and pursue their hopes and dreams?

Yet, he didn't like subterfuge and doing as Dr McPhee suggested meant doing just that. He didn't want to lie to his men, didn't want to betray their trust. A few more years in cryo wouldn't hurt them and, when everything settled down, they could re-join society, take up a place in the colony and settle. He didn't like altering colony records, either. Dr McPhee, Siobhan, was right, though. Unauthorised genetic manipulation of the human seed stock was unacceptable and was sufficient reason to 'cleanse' the planet. Earth leaders were strict on that. Well, some factions were more extreme than others. Like everything, policy was a compromise. Who knew what the policy would be in the future, when bureaucracies changed? They had fifteen more years before they were able to apply to self-govern at which time they could make their own decisions, but right now, with supply ships and colonists still scheduled to arrive, they had to appear to toe Earth Colony Control's line.

He turned back to Siobhan, her lean body resting against the opposite desk making his blood burn. A memory of an encounter between them aboard ship surfaced. Yes. Fiery. And delicious. It wasn't just the attraction that made him accept her point of view. She spoke objectively and to the main issues. He knew she didn't like subterfuge any more than he did, and these crimes had happened in her own department and involved her colleague. "Very well, we will do as you suggest. How will you account for the missing embryos?"

She let out a long sigh and met his gaze. "Thank you, General. I know this is a big decision. As for the embryo bank, there is an allowance for losses caused through transportation, implantation failures and storage issues. I think I can put a report in and explain it that way." She rubbed her palms against her trouser leg and frowned. This was not easy for her either.

Maitland added. "I can look at what our records contain and do my best to obscure the truth."

Milo sighed. "Right then, I'll get my men ready to go back to cryosleep and prepare a pre-cold sleep briefing. Hopefully another five or ten years will pass quickly, and they can take up their place in the colony if they wish."

Maitland pulled a face. "But they have tech implants that aren't consistent with our colony charter."

Dr McPhee nodded. "I see that as a complication too."

"That may be so, but all my security team were offered dispensation if they choose to settle. That was a condition of their employment and non-negotiable. Some may opt to travel on to other colonies or return to Earth when we release them. There is also the option of removing their tech enhancements, but that would be voluntary. For the present we can't tell if we'll have an issue with nanotech in the breeding pool or not."

Siobhan rubbed her chin and was silent a few minutes. "Well, then, I agree, there's no point worrying about that now."

Maitland nodded as he caught Milo's eye and then left the room.

"I know this hasn't been easy. Let's get on with fixing our future," Siobhan said.

Milo stood up to move closer as she stepped closer to him, stopping just a hand breadth away. "I'll drink to that," Milo said, inhaling her light floral perfume. "Officers mess at close of First Day?"

Siobhan swished her red hair behind her shoulders, her green eyes sparkling. "I think I can manage that."

With a mischievous smile on her face, she pivoted and headed for the door, pausing on the threshold to look over her shoulder at him. "I think you are a sensible person, Frank. I appreciate you working with me on this."

Not able to help himself, he grinned. "Likewise. And for the record, I'm glad the worse of this crisis is over and I'm looking forward to catching up with you later."

Her answering smile was full of promise.

Chapter One

LET THEM BURN

Year 149 from date of settlement

Deleen Milo darted out of the administration building's front doors and ran along the short bridge to the maglev station. Waiting was a sleek glass and steel carriage, with a bullet nose and streamlined body. A ping of the alarm had her leaping inside as the door snapped shut behind her. Just as well she made it, she thought, as she puffed from exertion. It had been one hell of a day and she couldn't wait to get home. Being deputy head of security for the administration had its challenges, today being the biggest of all. A quick glance around and she groaned. The carriage that could fit forty people seated was packed with an additional twenty people standing. She grabbed onto an anchor strap, the heavy weight of fatigue making her ready to kill for a seat. Staring at the backs of heads and thinking mean thoughts helped. Maybe someone would vacate.

It was late in Second Day and the crowding was to be expected, she supposed, as the second shift were all knocking off work, too. Colony Five's rotation, and Central City's location on the equator, meant two work shifts per planetary day, commonly broken into First Day and Second Day. She'd been working more than fifteen hours a day for weeks, setting up the security protocols to cover the administration systems. That was nearly two complete shifts in a rotation.

What really peeved her, though, was that after all the hard work, she did not get the promised promotion and was then ordered to take leave with thirty minutes' notice. No *thank you*. No *goodbye*. A quick look at her wrist unit showed her that the automated message had come exactly thirty-one minutes ago. No wonder she was in a sour mood, as well as tired. After so much focus for the last few months, she felt untethered, adrift. What kind of holiday could she organise in half an hour? She ground her teeth as she thought of the injustice of it all.

The sun wasn't due to set for a few more hours, though, and she didn't like the prospect of facing an evening with nothing to do. Not after such a tumultuous day. She needed a distraction—a date or something.

As the carriage sped up, she leaned on the anchor strap and snarled at her reflection in the window. Her face was haggard. Definitely not date material this evening. Her normally well-groomed ginger hair was standing up where she'd been tugging it as each new directive sped across her desk. That was the other odd thing. A sudden change in administrator and rapid-fire policy changes and directions. No sooner had she asked what was going on than she was out the door on forced leave.

In the reflection even her natural tan, courtesy of one of her ancestors, looked faded. The combination of nationalities that had established Colony Five gave her some interesting traits that she was proud of —pale coffee-coloured complexion, hazel green eyes and stunning red hair. But this evening even her superior genes weren't coping.

Rumours of a change in Colony Five's administrator had been brewing for some time, due to leaked information about affairs and dodgy financial dealings. But Deleen couldn't shake the feeling that there was something off about today's happenings. Administrator Carlo Levington may not have been the brightest of leaders, but he was honest and too stupid to be devious. At least, Deleen thought he was, despite what the press said. Now, he'd taken retirement. Just like that. No forwarding address, no farewell speech. Zilch!

The new administrator was supposedly someone in Levington's

team. She pictured some bald guy, with pale eyes between red-rimmed lids. Not that she knew anyone who looked like that. Gossip was a powerful thing, though.

Wiping the fringe out of her eyes, she took in the commuters with bleary-eyed disdain. Like her, they were from settler stock, either direct descendants or products of the embryo bank brought from Earth. Each family had an obligation to gestate and raise one of the embryo to build up Five's population and fulfil the colony's obligation to Earth. The varying degrees of skin tone, hair and eyes among the people in her carriage stood witness to the settlers' vision for the colony. Her fellow citizens could trace upwards of ten different nationalities in their blood line. Nobody on Five was pure anything, except human.

Look at them, she thought, sitting on their asses, their minds numb to the magnificence outside the window. The sun shot shafts of golden light into the buildings and bathed garden squares full of flowers and shrubs, both native and imported from Earth. Central Park came into view with its tall trees, lush grass, recreation areas for adults and children, ponds and waterfalls, all to please the eye and ease the mind. She sighed and relaxed at the beauty of it all.

All of the other passengers were glued to their personals, a little square of tech that kept them up to date on everything they needed or didn't know they needed to know and what they really, probably didn't want to know. As she rarely went anywhere without her personal, she was being hypocritical. Then she groaned. She'd left her work personal on her desk. No way she was going back for it while she was on leave.

Her gaze flicked outside to the trees gliding past as the maglev's track circled through Central Park. Five's sun burnished the tree leaves with purple highlights. Orange glow possums swung from branches and vivid red parrots darted from tree to tree. A sigh escaped her. Maybe she should have walked to her apartment. It wasn't that far, she supposed. A walk through the park might have lifted her spirits and helped work the edge off her annoyance.

Central City was built to a standard design; an inner circle contained the admin complex and wedge-shaped Central Park, with the suburbs growing outward forming concentric rings. The main administration building had originally been one of their settler ships, which had been dismantled and repurposed for building materials. The maglev passed over Settlers' Square, signalling the end to Central Park and the beginning of the inner burbs. These buildings glowed faintly silver in the light. It really was very pretty. Not as evocative as the family homestead out in the wilds, but still beautiful. Her own apartment was in the next ring, mid-city, and as a result was constructed of home-grown wood and kiln-fired plastique.

Her gaze shifted to the carriage occupants again and she was arrested by something—something that made a cold hand clutch at her heart. After blinking once or twice, she tried to understand what it was that had caught her attention. Then she saw it. Everyone's personals had the same headline on their screens. She narrowed her gaze to bring the words into focus. *Bring out the cold soldiers who lie in frozen sleep.*

Her jaw fell open. What the hell were cold soldiers? The message dimmed then flashed up again with different words. *Do not wake them nor let their tranquil faces beguile.* She bit her lip, her heartbeat skipping. *They are purveyors of death.* Deleen swallowed as the screens refreshed again. *They must burn!*

Her teeth ground. *Damn!* She itched for her own personal. Leaning down, she asked the young man sitting in front of her. "Excuse me for bothering you. Where did that message originate from?"

The guy didn't even look up. "From the administrator's office."

"Oh?" she replied automatically, ignoring the cold hand gripping her heart. She mumbled, "Thanks." The carriage angled as the track curved around the inner city. Looking back, she glimpsed the central admin building where she worked. Something very weird had just happened and she found it hard to focus, as if her sense of reality had shifted.

On the Mid-City platform, she paused at a vending machine and waved up a serve of roasted Derry nuts and a protein shake before heading to her apartment. The nuts were hot and fragrant, but she had to wait until she got inside before she could dig a few out and munch on them. Her studio apartment was on the third floor. She walked up the stairs rather than riding the lift. She was too fretful and nervy to stand still and be shut in a box, even if it was only for a few seconds. Taking each riser aggressively, she worked a little tension out of her muscles and sighed a few times. It was no good. The bad vibes were still there when she opened her door.

A good sex session might be a cure for that. It would certainly take her mind off things for a short while at least. Once inside she keyed up the booking form for the local Liaisons clinic. Damn! Her favourite therapists were fully booked for the next three days. No free spots that evening. She didn't think reserving a time with anyone else the next day was going to help, so she declined the proffered slot.

That left the water therapy option in her bathtub. Luckily, Five had abundant water so she would feel no guilt. Not like on Earth, where the population had destroyed the environment so badly that water had been a luxury few had been able to afford. Spruce and a local minty herb went into the bath water, filling the air with a stimulating fragrance. She screwed up her nose, maybe stimulating wasn't what she was after. Too late now.

An hour later, she was relaxed all over and damp from her bath, draped in a loose robe. Her studio wall folded the bath way, and she walked over to the floor-to-ceiling window to gaze out over the street. She could see out, but no one could see in.

People walked below, maybe heading to bars or restaurants or just enjoying the evening. The equatorial weather was balmy, without being too hot. Down the street, she caught the news headlines flashing across the corner of Founder Building. It was a repeat of the earlier message she'd seen on people's personals, and it made her skin chill. That message would loop around to Settlers' Square, where most of the people out of doors tended to congregate during the evening. She caught the words "Let them burn" as part of the message and shuddered.

It was so out of character for this colony, which was built on tolerance, to advocate such an extreme action on anything. Apart from native rats and invasive vegetation, nothing was burned. The population was non-violent and embraced difference. Crime existed, of course, but not a lot of it. Everyone was mixed race. It was the First Settlers' creed. It was what they had planned—a society where everyone was equal. You only had to look at the manifest listing of the passengers of the first colony ship to work that out. It had representatives from ten Earth countries and over the years the interbreeding had blended them.

Her personal unit sat on the side table. She picked it up and scrolled through the announcement about the cold soldiers. It seemed cryptic to her. Apparently, some early colonists hid cryogenically frozen soldiers in the city, and they were deemed to be a danger. Deleen's eyebrow rose, wondering about her grip on reality. This was the first she'd heard of frozen soldiers. If they were hidden, she supposed it wasn't widely known. That thought did not help her sense of disconnection. There was no reason for soldiers frozen or otherwise to be hidden. There had been no wars, no military action. It made no sense. If it wasn't nonsense, then she should know about this threat, given her position as the city's deputy head of security. Now, thrust on leave, the new administration had decided these hidden cold soldiers needed to be eradicated—surely not a coincidence. Her pulse hammered and her mind raced. The announcement used words like *cleanse the colony, eradicate the threat and destroy the infestation*. Her feelings of restlessness returned, and she walked up to the window again, looking for signs of change in the populace below, or movements that indicated panicked behaviour, for some tell-tale sign that would clue her in to the sense of unease riding her gut. It was difficult to focus though, to think clearly. It had to be fatigue from working long hours for the last few months.

Finishing off her meal of Derry nuts and the last of her protein shake, she realised she'd never get any sleep. She tried dialling up a vid, but nothing grabbed her. Her call to her friend, Vi, went unanswered. No girls' night out for her. It was her own fault, of course, Deleen hadn't answered Vi's last five calls. It was due to her workload, nothing more.

Deleen's most recent project had been installing all the latest security protocols and access privileges into the administration's systems and the complex of seven buildings that housed the people who managed Five's affairs. No wonder she had no social life. Giving up on entertaining herself, she decided to try sleeping.

Before switching off the light, she toyed with the idea of reserving a spot at the Liaisons clinic with an escort she didn't know, then quashed the idea. Maybe she'd meet someone during her enforced holiday, someone willing to show her a good time. With a laugh, she thought about how she'd like to show them a good time right then.

* * *

On impulse, the next morning Deleen took a trip out west to the Yszti Plain to get away from the city and leave thoughts of work behind. Past the manufacturing sector, with its automated plants that supplied the colony's needs and some extra for export, the plain spread out as far as the eye could see, so flat that the light created mirages. First Day was enough time to explore, and she'd be back in time to do some socialising during Second Day. Although, she had some making up to do with Vi before she could organise that. After scouring the gift shops and selecting a few items for workmates and Vi, she had them designated for delivery and headed off for a long walk.

The plain gently undulated with soft mauve hills and cream-coloured grasses. Wildflowers bobbed their heads in the gentle breeze and bird song filtered through the sound of tourists. After walking fast, long and hard along the trail, she slowed and took her time, enjoying the shadows cast by the section of forest she was in. She wasn't sure whether this area was native or terraformed and didn't really care. It was pretty and soothing and that was all she was interested in. With a sigh, she turned to go back to the terminal and head home. Sweat was starting to build up, and she had paused to wipe her forehead when her personal chimed.

Drawing it out from its sling, she saw the caller was Vi. "Hi, Vi!"

Vi's smiling face filled the small screen. "Thank you for the gift. You shouldn't have."

Deleen wondered at how fast the delivery had been. "I'm sorry I've been neglecting you. I was busy." She shrugged seeing Vi's barely percep-tible nod.

"Hey ho! What're you doing in Yszti of all places, Del? That's a backwater."

"Just relaxing, Vi. I need ..."

"You need to stop working so hard and get some perspective in your life. How are you going to get a partnership going if you're away working all the time?"

"Partnership? I don't—" Vi cut her off before she went down that familiar path of denial.

"Partnership. And don't give me that bull about being a career girl. You have to reproduce, and I can't imagine you'd let a vat do your job for you, hey."

"Look, Vi, I know you think partnership is the best thing going. I can allocate my reproduction rights to someone else, someone who wants a larger family."

"But you have to pay lots to do that. Shirker tax, remember. Anyway, when are you coming back to Central City? I miss you already."

"I'll be back later, by the end of Second Day. You want to do something then?"

"Why, yes, I do. Leave it to me. I'll organise everything and send you the deets. Bye."

Vi's image disappeared from the screen. It was with grave misgivings that Deleen headed back to the transport hub to catch a ride back to the city. Vi's night outs could lead to lots of regret and a fair share of hangovers. Even with the drive for a healthy lifestyle on Five, a good night out on the town was something that had managed to stay part of the local culture, despite the First Settlers' efforts. The sense of unease in her gut made her crave the distraction of a carefree night out, to let her hair down, to forget.

Instead of catching a maglev back to her apartment, Deleen chose to walk home through Central Park, where the main transport hub deposited her, and enjoy the milder sunshine of Second Day. She lost herself in her surroundings, letting her mind wander. A pungent smell pulled her out of her reverie. The squawk of glow possums retreating made her look up. They were moving *en masse* towards the centre of the park.

Taking a deep inhale, Deleen tried to work out what it was. Something was burning. Ahead, the path curved, skirting a clump of Koli palms and she hurried her step to find the source of the burning. Out in the open, she saw orange light reflected in the sky as errant flames danced above some bushes. Her skin went cold and immediately she rubbed at her arms as if that would help in some way. A bonfire? Here in Central Park? Bursting into a run, she found herself confronted by a terrible sight. In the picnic area, next to the pond, was a huge conflagration. Bushes had been cut down and were being tossed into the flames, creating white, pungent smoke. In the centre were two large box-like things, with transparent lids. Larger than a coffin. A small explosion within the fire sent out a plume of smoke and sparks.

She stepped closer, casting wary glances at the onlookers. Two cops were standing guard. On closer examination, she saw that the boxes were more like sarcophagi, made with tech, and inside were bodies. Large bodies licked by flame. Hands and fingers curled. Charred and burning flesh. Deleen froze. Then the wind billowed a waft of smoke that sent her coughing and she covered her nose. The pungent fumes overwhelmed her. It was the smell of burning flesh.

Her mind flew back to the lines of text on the personals in the maglev. *Bring out the cold soldiers who lie in frozen sleep. Do not wake them or let their tranquil faces beguile. They are purveyors of death. They must burn.*

The crowd were chanting the words. "Burn them! Burn them!" Deleen could hardly believe her ears. They were burning people. Her brain went into denial, but she could see it with her own eyes, taste their deaths on her tongue. These cold soldiers had been burned without even being woken from their cryosleep. It was horrible. Eyes filled with tears, Deleen ran through to the front of the crowd. She screamed for them to stop. Abruptly she was shoved and thrown to the ground. She scrambled to her feet, wary of being trampled, and came up short as one of the cops blocked her way. The first flush of panic fled and she knew the situation was dangerous, explosive. "Let me pass. I want to go home." She thought her request was reasonable.

"You must wait until the burning is done."

Shocked, she blurted out. "I don't want to." Hysteria clawed at her throat. She wanted to scream and cry. The heat bathed her face and was starting to scorch. The crowd stepped back, and the cop took her elbow and guided her to the edge.

"It's required," was the calm, unemotional reply.

That got her attention, helped her focus. "Required?" she asked, unable to hide her incredulity.

The cop scrunched up his mouth as if her question annoyed him. "Give me your name and administrative number."

"Why?" Deleen was surprised. That was not part of the security protocols she'd been busting her gut on.

"All witnesses must be identified," came the stern reply.

Astounded, Deleen flashed her government ID. He blinked after reading it. "Thank you, ma'am. I didn't realise. You may go."

As the deputy head of security, she was this cop's boss. But that didn't give her much confidence. This security officer was acting out of character. She'd been placed on leave. *Danger signs*, her mind screamed. She needed to be circumspect until she knew more.

Deleen backed away. "Thank you," she said quietly and then turned for home, taking the bridge that would shorten the way. Before the path curved away from the pond, she looked back, sickened when she saw the outline of a burning limb. These people had burnt human beings. Human beings that were still living. How was that possible?

Back at her apartment, she looked up Five's history on her personal. The search term *cryostasis* didn't reveal anything other than a definition and the use of the technology to get the First Settlers to the planet. She looked up the term *soldier* and the search returned the standard definition, and then *cold soldier* came up blank. She wondered at that. Exhausted, she fell asleep with her personal on her lap. Bad dreams troubled her until a loud chime startled her awake. A call on her personal. "Vi?"

"Yes, it's me. Have you forgotten our date?"

"No, come up. It won't take me long to get ready."

Deleen's hands were shaking as she tried to put her clothes on. She was going to need that drink before she did something stupid and, possibly, dangerous.

Chapter Two

DREAMS

"He's kind of cute, don't you think?" Vi said in a slurred voice, using the booth they were sitting in to keep herself upright. Her makeup was smudged and her normally well-groomed blonde hair had fallen out of the elaborate coil around her head and was half down her shoulders. Her dark eyes narrowed, as if sizing up a bug instead of her drinking buddy.

Deleen leaned around her to check out the room. "I'm not sure. Which one?"

"Which one? You need another drink, woman." She lifted the bottle and green liqueur splashed into Deleen's glass. Deleen tried to take a sip and missed her mouth and the green syrupy booze dripped from her chin.

The next swig was successful, until the sting of the booze hit the back of her throat making her splutter and choke. Vi struggled to maintain a sitting position, then decided slapping her on the back in an exaggerated fashion was the most considerate thing to do. The guy she'd been sizing up cast them a disparaging look. "Oh, you've blown it, Del. You're too drunk. He's snubbed us."

Deleen let her head fall back against the padded booth wall and didn't like how the room swam. "Well, well ... he's probably clinic bait anyway."

Vi giggled, then her face crumpled as she burst out laughing. "Clinic bait? What the hell is that?"

"The male version of me," Deleen replied in all seriousness. If she could keep Vi in focus, she was sure the room would stop spinning. "Can't keep up a conversation long enough to get to the seduction part. Too busy to try, so just heads to the clinic for some sex therapy."

Vi screwed up her face and slammed down her drink, oblivious to how much splashed onto the table. "But you have to pay for that service and that sucks." She hammered her finger in the air at Deleen. "Sex should be free."

"I know. I agree. But sometimes it's just too hard to wrangle." Deleen leaned her head back against the booth seat and sighed.

"So, when did you last get laid?" Vi asked as she studied the now empty bottle of booze.

Deleen rubbed her hand across her face. Did Vi mean at the clinic or in the social context? She decided to fudge it. "Mmm ... been a while. Before my latest project began. Maybe three months."

"Three months?" Vi didn't bother to disguise the look of pity on her face. "That's not healthy. Promise me you'll go to the clinic tomorrow. You must be so ... so wound up." She rolled her hands to make a wheel.

Deleen tried to hold her head in her hands and accidentally knocked the bottle over. There were only the dregs left, but it was enough to spill onto the carpet. A slight whirring sound grew louder. Then she cocked a drunken eyebrow as a small, round cleaning bot came out to suck up the liquid and dry the carpet. She giggled, struck by a sudden absurdity as one did when intoxicated. "Now, if that little bot had a vibrator attachment all our troubles would be over."

Vi saw what she was looking at. "How do you know it doesn't have attachments?" She lifted her eyebrow in challenge.

Deleen's jaw dropped. "No, really?"

Vi waved a hand flippantly. "Of course not. I don't know, really. I don't let my appliances dally with my bits. I've got a boyfriend. A real live man."

Deleen frowned. "You do? When did that happen?" She'd been working too hard. At least now she could let her hair down and relax.

"Two months ago. We're thinking about filing for a standard domestic contract and a breeding permit."

Alert suddenly, Deleen jerked upright. Her stomach protested and she nearly puked, but managed to hold on to it. "Breeding permit?" She swallowed hard, hoping to maintain her stomach contents in place. "Are you sure? But I haven't even met him."

"You will if you behave yourself and stop working so hard. Maybe he has a friend."

Deleen lay back against the booth's seat again and put her legs out under the table to massage Vi's thigh with her toes. "Oh, please, not the matchmaking with friend gig. Don't do that to me."

Vi scoffed and smacked Deleen's foot before she stood up and yawned. "We should go. It's dead in here." She shimmied around the table to get out of the booth. "Hey, you can stay over at my place if you like and we can keep on gasbagging, just don't misuse my appliances."

Deleen laughed and laughed, unable to control it. Wiping tears from her eyes, she choked out. "Gasbagging? What kind of word is that?" Deleen waved a hand before her friend could reply. "You read too much in that library of yours. No, I'll go home. Don't trust myself." Deleen slid free of the booth and put an arm around Vi's waist. With a smirk she said quietly. "From memory, your cleaning bot is way too sexy."

Vi laughed and stumbled and then arm in arm they exited the bar. "You need to walk me home," Vi said, jerking her head as if trying to appear sober and failing.

"I know ... I am." They laughed and slurred verbal trash at each other on the way home. As Vi's apartment was in the same Inner-City building as the bar, it didn't take long. Deleen had to hold back the nausea in the lift. She didn't think she was going to escape the vomits, unless she took some remedy. She couldn't remember if she had any.

At Vi's apartment, they lurched through the door. Vi stumbled to the wall and hit a switch. Her bed rocketed out readymade and she fell onto it, face first.

"You okay?" Deleen asked, trying to orient herself to find the exit.

"Fiiiiine," Vi said, waving an arm vaguely. Then turning on her side, she managed to say coherently. "Lock the door when you leave."

Before Deleen left, the sound of snoring reached her. "Great,"

Deleen said as she struggled to stand up and gather all her paraphernalia together from where she'd dumped her stuff before they went out. She tried to remember if it was all there as, blurry-eyed, she studied the table: Personal. Shoes. ID card. Jacket.

About an hour later, she entered her own apartment a little more sober, but not by much. Her head was throbbing and her stomach was undecided. Either it was going to keep its contents or not. She didn't care overmuch. She hit the switch for her bed and tumbled into it.

* * *

At first, Deleen fell fast asleep, although her bed seemed to rock and roll like a boat on the ocean. A few hours later, she woke up with a terrible thirst and a hammer hitting the inside of her skull. Some painkillers and a tube of water later, she lay back down. The room didn't swim as much, but her stomach was still undecided. The meal she'd had with Vi was still there, waiting to pounce. Luckily, her cleaning bot was every bit as diligent as Vi's. She lay there in the dark mulling things over.

Vi had a boyfriend and was thinking of breeding. With a sigh, Deleen turned that idea over again. She didn't know if she'd ever do such a thing. Closing her eyes, the image of the burning in Central Park came back sharp and clear. She tried to dislodge the image, the memory, but it wouldn't go away. It was as if it had hooked inside of her, caught on something. Soon her lids grew heavy, and she tossed and turned trying to avoid the memory. She tried thinking of her favourite worker from Liaisons, but that didn't work. She tried imagining Vi with a child, and even that scary thought didn't stop the image from dominating the forefront of her mind. Eyes closing, she began to dream.

A first it was surface stress stuff: work, security password algorithms, her boss talking nonsense, which sounded sensible but was only dream fluff. The headline repeating over in her mind. 'Burn them, burn them' made her whimper. She tossed and turned, waking enough to realise she'd been dreaming before sinking lower.

A dark tunnel. Footsteps. Her grandfather walking into the shadows. Her following, crawling along behind him, hoping he didn't see her. Belly crawling, she kept to the darkness, unheard, unseen. Where was her grand-father going? Where was this place? The homestead where her grandfather had lived? The old bunker? The dream grew strange, colours and voices and quickly changing images. She remembered the door. The lock. Then as she tossed and turned, she remembered the face—the sleeping face. Blond hair cut close to the scalp. Straight nose jutting out. Pale mouth, bottom lip fuller than the top. Skin looking white and pasty. He was big. He was scary.

Waking with a start, she blinked away sunlight. She'd forgotten to shut the window. The city was there for her to see. Climbing to her feet, she pulled on a robe, groaning as she got up, hungover and heavy limbed. When she stood at the window to look across the city, she frowned. Plumes of smoke came from about twenty separate spots across the city. She shook her head and looked again, peering over through the row of apartments into the corner of Settlers' Square. Closer to home, two separate bonfires. A grey smoke haze hung over the top of the trees. Closing her eyes, she mumbled a prayer. There were people in the flames. Frozen arms charring. She fell back, hand to her mouth and vomited onto the carpet.

Dazed, her brain tried to understand what the hell was going on.

After some more painkillers, that muted her headache, and a shower that revitalised her spirits, Deleen was more in control of herself. She pushed the burnings to the back of her mind. There was nothing she could do. It shouldn't be happening, but it was, and she hated feeling powerless.

Vi had organised for them to meet for lunch during First Day. A mutual friend, Cheree, was joining them. A distraction was what she needed. She almost hadn't thought about work for five minutes. After a restless night, security algorithms jumbled together in her brain like the worst kind of stress dream. There was something else there in her mind. Something she didn't want to revisit.

Down in the restaurant in Inner-City, she was sipping arctic ice water and checking out the view of Central Park's lake when Vi and Cheree walked in. Dark complexioned, Cheree looked carefree and a bit smug, probably because she was expecting a child and doing it the natural way. Cheree rubbed a hand over her rounded belly and gathered her dark curls into a ponytail. "Del," she said, taking a seat. "What happened to you? You look like shit."

"Me?" Deleen looked down at herself. She'd dressed in a smart, salmon-coloured pantsuit and even had her hair coiffed for the occasion, fluffy curls bouncing free. Maybe the makeup didn't disguise the previous evening's indulgence. "Oh," she flapped a hand. "Just hungover!" Vi looked fine, which made Deleen decry the unfairness of it all.

Cheree shook her head. "You should take some neutraliser—that will clear your system of the ill effects," she shrugged and sat down before fixing Deleen with her dark eyes. "I haven't seen you in a while. You look older, a bit worn." Cheree eyed her carefully. "I don't think that colour goes with your hair."

Deleen fingered her ginger locks. She had thought the salmon colour would work, but obviously that was a mistake. She dialled the suit's tone to a rich green. "Better?"

"Oh, that's much better," Vi said, flapping a hand before leaning in to whisper. "What were you thinking?"

Cheree chimed in. "It was the colour of vomit."

Deleen turned and stared. "That sounds appropriate. I was alcohol impaired."

"Enough said," Vi quipped and began to peruse the menu.

Cheree shook her head, a tut-tut emitting from her lip-sticked mouth. "I don't know why you do it to yourself. You can drink synthetic booze and it just passes through without consequences and gives you a buzz on the way."

Deleen turned to Vi and waggled her eyebrows meaningfully.

Vi coughed. "Please, don't give her ideas, Cheree. It's hard enough to get her to party most of the time as it is."

Cheree nodded knowingly. "Of course, it's your influence, Vi. You nearly got me expelled from college on ..." She counted her fingers. "Let me see, five occasions."

Vi's chin shot up and she pouted. Her hair was long and straight, and she had dark freckles on the creamy skin of her nose. She looked so natural, but she was carefully groomed. "I thought it was six."

They laughed at this and then settled in to key their orders into the table. Cheree brought them up to date on her gestation and the habits of the father, whom she had started to cohabitate with to share the childcare arrangements. There were other perks, too, like sex at the ready, but mostly her story was a comedy of errors and misunderstandings. Deleen hadn't laughed so much in ages. Her head ached anew, so she slipped in another analgesic, not wanting to dampen the camaraderie by leaving prematurely.

Vi filled their glasses with no-alcohol bubbly and made a face. "To the future," she offered, lifting her glass to Cheree. They drank their toast.

Cheree checked the time. "I'd better go soon. I have to meet another friend. Terrible thing happened to her."

Vi leaned in, eyes wide. "Really? Like what?"

Cheree's expression changed; her mouth turned down. "Her family have been taken away by the cops."

Deleen raised her eyebrows. "Taken away? What for?"

Cheree screwed her face up. "Well, you know about the call out. To bring out the frozen soldiers?"

Deleen's skin went icy. "I noticed."

Vi sniffed. "I have no idea what that's all about. What soldiers?"

Cheree nodded in a knowing way. "Apparently there was an army here when Five was first settled. They were frozen when they were no longer needed, ready for the next time. I've heard that they were brutal, used only as a last resort by the First Settlers."

Not buying this story, Deleen sat forward. "I've never heard of them. Why bring them out now? Where were they kept? I don't recall that there are cryogenic facilities here in the city."

"Well," Cheree continued eyeing them both and leaning in to whisper. "My friend said they had a soldier in their basement, behind a false wall. A cousin blabbed about it and the cops came and took them away and the cold soldier was taken out into the street."

"And your friend?" Deleen prompted.

"She's in hiding. She was at work at the hospital when she saw her family being taken away on the newscast. She was smart enough not to go home."

"But," Vi asked, "what did they do wrong? Is it illegal to have these soldiers in your basement?"

Cheree gave her an incredulous look. "Yes, it's illegal. An edict came out yesterday."

"What?" Deleen said in a shout. She looked around. "Sorry," she whispered. "I didn't see this edict."

"It's in black and white on gov channel. When they first put the call out some people voluntarily surrendered their frozen soldiers. Only ten were burned."

Deleen repressed a shudder. "Why are they burning them? Surely if they are no longer needed, they should be revived and retrained so they can live among us."

Cheree tapped a finger on the tabletop. "I heard that some people tried to complain and just like that it's illegal to house one." She snapped her fingers. "The first sign of resistance and the law changed."

Deleen's heart thumped and she had to fight for calm. "How is your friend?" she asked.

"She's scared and she can't find out anything about her family. But I've heard they are going to be tried for treason."

"Treason?" Vi and Deleen said in unison. "But that's ridiculous," Deleen added. Freethinking was a right on Five. You could bad mouth the administration and, provided you didn't harm anyone, there was nothing anyone could do about it.

Cheree considered this. "If you think about it, I suppose it is a bit strange." She shrugged. "But the administration must know what it's on about, mustn't it? You work there don't you, Del? Why are you so surprised?"

Deleen nodded slowly. "I do work there, but I'm on leave. Forced leave." She switched her gaze between them and shrugged. "All this happened after I finished for the day. There's a new administrator. Perhaps he's a bit hardline."

"A new chief of security too. Felton," Cheree said. "Ace Felton. And you're right, I'm not sure I have heard of him before. He's quite distinguished in his photo."

"Felton?" Deleen shook her head, not quite sure what to make of all this. "But he's not in security. Besides, that was meant to be my job. They said it was going to Filipe Gado instead."

Cheree shrugged.

Administration must have worked through the night to implement so much change. She was out of the loop and right then happy to be so. What was going on was scary and a tad insane. How could someone commit treason? There was no foreign power involved. No threat to the colony, as far as she knew. And Ace Felton her new boss? No way. The man was an idiot and a lower-level liaison officer.

Cheree stood up. "I've probably said too much. I'd better go." She air kissed them both and left, waddling slightly with the weight of the baby.

Deleen turned to Vi. "That was a lot to take in. Do you think we can have real bubbly now? I think I need a drink."

"Already ordered."

After a couple of drinks Deleen experienced a nice relaxing buzz. Her world had been turned upside down and she had to admit she was struggling. Event after event kept her off balance. It was time she took control of herself and tried to come to terms with her new situation. She keyed up the nearest public link and began searching Five's history. She had her personal with her, but something warned her that she shouldn't use it for this search. What she wanted to know should be freely available in the colony archives.

"Stars, you're boring!" Vi complained as she refilled their glasses. "Doing homework?"

"Just curious about something," Deleen replied without looking up. "Have you heard of these cold soldiers before?"

"No. Not a thing, and I read a lot." Vi said and smiled and waved to a man leaning against the bar.

Distracted, Deleen saw who Vi was waving at and wasn't surprised. "Um," Vi said, meeting her gaze. "Okay if I ... you know ..."

"Sure, be my guest." Vi went off to chat up the guy and together the pair walked out into the mall area, chatting and window shopping. He had brown hair cut short, a strong jaw and pale eyes. With that build, solid arms, large chest and muscled thighs, she suspected Vi might forget about cohabiting with her new boyfriend.

Deleen studied the screen. There was no reference to an army in the early settlement chronicles. She checked the date of the entry and saw it had been updated recently. She rechecked the history of the colonisation of Five. According to the official record she was reading, it all went smoothly. There was a list of dates when things were built, and short biographies of the settlers, her ancestors included. She keyed off and replaced the device in its niche and sat back. Vi was no longer in the mall outside the door. She checked and there was a message on her personal saying goodbye. Deserted by Vi, Deleen went to pay the bill but discovered that Cheree had covered their meal when she left. The human waiter said that Vi had covered their bubbly and there was nothing to pay.

Deleen left the restaurant and made a beeline to exit the mall by taking the lift to the ground level. The itch of unease returned. That nagging feeling irritated her mind, and by the time she made the ground floor it was a lump of panic. When she exited the lift, she noticed two cops getting into the adjacent one. Deleen frowned. For some reason, she thought they might be looking for her. Shaking her head, she stepped out to the street. There was no logical reason why they should be after her. All she did was look up something on the public net. Yet, if she used the maglev, she'd need to use her ID and they could track her from the restaurant. As she hadn't used her ID to pay, they couldn't place her there. Maybe she was getting paranoid. Maybe she wasn't. Maybe it was booze-related paranoia. But walking through the park to get home seemed like the best way to obscure her tracks.

Chapter Three

REVELATIONS

Deleen had lived in the city for all her adult life, but her ties were to the land. The settlers built up their wealth growing crops and raising livestock, firstly to feed themselves and then to export to other colonies. As a child, she'd visited the Milo family farm and even lived there during the long summer vacations. Lots of her childhood memories were of that place, the homestead in the wilds. Her paternal grandfather, Melvin, who'd lived to be one hundred and twenty, had been born on Five. Her grandmother, Emma, had died early in life and she couldn't remember her at all. An accident out on the farm and medical help arrived too late. Emma had been born from the embryo store. Melvin's parents had been General Frank Milo, who was of African extraction, and Dr Siobhan McPhee, an Irish biologist. They were among the first to land on the planet and establish the colony.

Deleen's father, Devlin, had been born on the farm, but preferred the city. Her mother, Mara, had signed up to another partnership and went on to have another two children. By agreement, Deleen had stayed with her father. Unfortunately, he'd not lived as long as his father. Devlin, had eaten a poisonous plant on one of their visits to the farm. He didn't do it deliberately. It had been the result of a mutation. The plant had some inherent toxicity that had become concentrated on Five.

It hadn't been an easy death. The doctors hadn't known what it was. Only the autopsy revealed the cause. Funny how she found it hard to picture his face. Her grandfather she recollected well, but her father? She shook her head.

At her grandfather's knee, she had listened to stories. Some were hazy now. She remembered the stories about tilling the land and about the gene-bred beef cattle and the root stock for their grain. The Milo family was a First Family. She was proud of that.

The second wave of settlement expanded the colony and the third had boosted it even more, giving them a city and more domestic trade. With the natural increase in the population, boosted by the embryo bank, the colony now had over one hundred thousand people.

On her personal, she did a quick search of the early history. It was hard for her to picture those early days, even though there were lots of vids and still pictures of the first colony ships easily available. As she scrolled through, she noted that there was a big hole in the history of Five. Her search of the archives confirmed it. There was nothing about soldiers, frozen or otherwise.

She pocketed her personal and kept walking along the path, absently admiring the foliage. In the middle of Central Park, a scream startled her. Raised voices and shouts followed. She looked up and around and then nearly collided with someone who ran out of the bushes onto the path. Pulling up, the wild-eyed person mouthed soundlessly and then bolted into a clump of bamboo. It had been a middle-aged woman, maybe fifty years old. The skin on her face was red and bruised and Deleen thought she saw grazed knuckles. A growling noise grew louder, and Deleen soon discovered the source—a crowd appeared to be chasing the woman. They yelled and waved their arms, some carried sticks. They hadn't noticed her as she stood stock still, marvelling at this very strange behaviour. Hopefully, it wasn't Cheree's friend. She cast a look at the back of the crowd as they disappeared from view.

A sense of unease crawled across her skin, leaving her tense and scared. She had to leave the city. She had to get out of here. This place was turning crazy. It was time to retreat to the family farm, deserted now. She had time—on indefinite leave.

When she arrived home, panting and sweaty, a message vid was waiting for her. She clicked on it. "Del!" It was Vi, sounding panicked. She was calling from the restaurant. "Something weird just happened. I came back here to look for you and then cops came looking for the person who'd used the public link. They questioned all of us. I didn't give you away, but they requested the surveillance cam. You need to make yourself scarce." Vi looked to the side. "Gotta go. Love you."

Panicked, Deleen grabbed a bag and packed some essentials: clothing, food ration packs, credit slips—the non-identifying kind. She normally paid the Liaisons clinic with them because she valued her privacy. Luckily for her, she had enough for the trip to the farm. Within thirty minutes of listening to Vi's message, Deleen was at the transport hub buying a ticket for Everglen, where the Milo family farm sat on the outskirts.

* * *

Deleen didn't relax until the transport pulled away from the station. Dressed in a mint green pantsuit, she looked like a vacationer. It was a smooth ride and fast. Checking over her shoulder, she noticed three other passengers in her capsule. The transport consisted of two capsules, with large glass windows. The other had a family, three children and a harassed parent. Rolling her eyes, she was grateful the booking computer had seated her in this capsule away from the noise. At least, she could nap.

Closing her eyes didn't help her relax. Her heartbeat hammered and she had to breathe deeply, holding her breath in and letting it out slowly. Part of her mind said she was overworked and stressed and freaking out about nothing; the other part said she was doing the right thing and that something sinister was going on, that her liberty and her life were under threat. Would three hundred kilometres be far enough away from the city? It would be enough and it was time for her to get a grip. Paramilitary training helped to some degree to settle her nerves. Yet, given she could fight, shouldn't she stay and try to counter what was going on? Why did instinct drive her to flee back to the homestead? Was it safety, or something else? Something there, some memory like a dream hovered out of reach. "Refreshments?" The transport's serving bot said next to her ear. Her eyelids snapped open, breaths coming in short pants. She really needed to get a grip.

"No, thank you," she replied, as naturally as she could, hoping no one noticed her startled response. The android's pale face showed no emotion. It was only a low-grade model, built for simple tasks. It went up to the next passenger and had better luck.

If only this transport was at her destination already. She tapped her feet and looked out at the blur of scenery. Her eye could not catch a single thing. A blur of green, then a blur of brown and then another blur of green. She checked the time on her personal. Still forty-five minutes to go. She checked her ticket. They were due to stop at Fountain Spar in ten minutes. Deleen was tempted to alight there and make her way to Everglen under her own steam. That way if she was being tracked, even with the surveillance cameras, it would put them off the scent. Again, she battled the issue of paranoia. Was she being ridiculous?

Fountain Spar station appeared after a brief deceleration. The family in the front capsule had alighted and as it was now empty it was detached. One of the passengers in her capsule got out, also. For a moment, Deleen caught the scent of lavender on the air. Fountain Spar made perfume and lavender products. Nothing odd happened at the station. She stayed on the transport, glad that she had acted rationally. As the capsule gained speed, she was able to relax enough to doze. She wasn't sure how long she was out of it before they braked suddenly.

Jerked awake, she blinked away confusion. Outside the window there were fields of green and red grain. They had stopped. The two other passengers in the capsule peered out the windows and then looked at each other.

Deleen kept a close hold of her panic. Then an announcement piped in. "Please remain calm. Security will be with you momentarily." So it wasn't a malfunction or power outage. It was a security screen. They were usually random inspections, ticket validations and so on. Rarely would they need to go after anyone. With all that was going on, she was afraid that this feeling of fear was her new normal. Her palms began to itch, as she glanced casually out of the window, trying to estimate how far she was from Everglen and if she could reasonably make it on foot. Her footwear was highly inappropriate for a long hike, but she could get away with a sprint. She tried to calculate how long it would take to reach her luggage and change shoes.

One of the other passengers, a male, got out of his seat and started to pace. "Bastards! They shouldn't be making us wait!" He slapped his hand on the capsule door, which didn't even budge. Above his head, Deleen noticed an emergency lever. It was red and large and looked easy to engage. She stared at it. Should I? Could I?

Her departure from the city had been quick and quiet. Surely, no one could have tracked her onto the transport. She'd paid in non-traceable credit chips. But if they had her image from the restaurant, they could match it with any of the surveillance images. If they were looking for her, they'd find her. This quick? It depended on how desperate they were. She knew that the facial recognition would find her eventually.

The other male passenger lay back in his seat, apparently unconcerned at the delay or the pending arrival of security. He pulled his collar up, his hat down and went to sleep. The one by the door paced around and made sounds of disgust, grunting and groaning. Soon the roar of an air transport grew perceptibly louder with each minute. This decided things for the agitated man. He jumped up, snagged the lever and jerked it down. A sharp ring blared as the door opened. The man threw himself out the door, hitting the ground running as he headed into the fields.

Deleen sat up and watched as he left a trail of crushed grain in his wake. She hadn't thought about leaving a trail in her mental calculations for making a run for it. If she'd run, her tracks would have been obvious. Given her training, she should have known this and her not thinking of it was proof of how freaked she was. If she was going to survive, she needed to draw on that training, no matter how theoretical it had seemed at the time. A desk jockey didn't get out in the field much. Her own sense of alertness did not lessen. Security may not be coming for that man but for her. The other passenger sat up and looked out her window. "Not a smart move." His comment jolted her for he had not spoken previously.

"I guess not," she returned, but her gaze was still on the retreating man. The sound of the air transport grew louder, the whine of its turbines jaw-clenchingly irritating. The buzz sounded overhead and then zoomed past as they kept going straight after the escapee. The alarm from the emergency door stopped, leaving her ears ringing. "Stand clear. Door closing," a metallic voice said. The capsule gave a judder as it slowly built momentum, until they were at their previous speed. Deleen gripped the chair arm and saw the half-moon curves of her nails imprinted in the fake leather. Letting out a sigh, she rested against the head rest. Not running had been the right thing to do. Only because the other man had run. If the capsule stopped again that was a different matter. That didn't bear thinking about.

* * *

The capsule reversed behind her and sped away from Everglen station, which was a terminating stop. The other passenger was greeted by a man, who kissed him and held him close. Lovers, she thought. There was no one to greet her. It had been five years since she'd visited the farm. Not since she cleaned it up after her grandfather died. There were cousins, but she'd lost contact with them. They lived in North Bore, a couple of hours capsule trip to the north of the city. Most of Five's inhabitants lived close to the equator, due to the moderate weather and adequate rainfall. The orbital rain machines helped with the climate, keeping the farms and the colony well-watered. First Settlers brought machinery, so agriculture was mostly mechanised.

Looking around, she saw that there was no one else on the platform and put her small suitcase down. Transport hire wasn't looking good. She sat on a seat nestled under a tree and decided it was probably better that way. While she changed her shoes into proper walking shoes, she did a stocktake of the assorted vending machines ranged along the outside of the platform. Going on foot to the farm may be doable, but there were no supplies there so she'd have to take some food with her. Water, she could manage, as there was a well in addition to the water tank. It rained quite frequently so that wasn't going to be a problem. She checked her store of credit slips. Enough to buy some supplies, even at the vending machine's inflated prices. They were there to service the holiday makers, the ones that came out here to get out of the city for a bit. The residents would buy what they needed in bulk for regular delivery at half, maybe even a third, of these prices. But beggars can't be choosers she thought as she studied the vending machines. Using what remained of her anonymous credit, she bought enough prefab meals to last two weeks. Not that she was intending on staying at the farm that long, but as they would keep for years, she thought stocking up in case of emergencies was a good thing.

From her suitcase, she pulled out a thin slip and shook it. It opened up to a backpack. In this, she placed all the meals she'd bought. It was only half full, so she took another look at the machines to see what other necessities she might need. She had teeth cleaner, makeup and other personal care items and she frowned as she looked at the options. What had she forgotten?

Toilet paper. She fished around in her pocket for the loose credits she had and bought a dispenser. It would last a month. Tucking that into the backpack, she added her clothing from her suitcase, and she sealed it up. The suitcase folded down into a small purse. She put that in her back pocket and faced in the direction of the farm. It would take three hours to walk there. It was later in Second Day than she liked, but she figured she'd arrive just on sunset. Enough time to turn the power on and settle in.

There was a road of sorts on the first part of her journey. Not the modern flex seal, but an old-fashioned concrete surface. It was easy to walk on. Remembering the man on the train and his obvious trail, she wasn't going to trek through the crops to reach the farm more directly. She'd do that further on. If she was lucky, the fields close to the farm would be lying fallow. As she walked, she tried to remember what arrangements she'd made for the place after the funeral. A neighbour leased most of the land, but she couldn't remember if it was for stock or crops. She would find out soon enough.

The sun reddened as it lowered in the sky. The grain rippled in the light wind and the ears burnished crimson. This was the non-leased section of land, where her machines ran the planting cycle, which only required slight remote monitoring and adjusting from her. She bit her lip, realising she hadn't glanced at their schedule for years. Yet here was the grain, growing strong and tall. It was a magical sight. She'd forgotten how beautiful Everglen was. When had that happened? How could she forget something so wonderful and cherished? She loved the city, her job, but part of her always felt good out here in the sticks. Her personal was starting to weigh heavily, so she changed hands and adjusted the straps of her backpack.

Up ahead was an intersection. When she reached it, she took a left turn and kept walking. It was the half-way point from the station to the house. The rays of the setting sun hit her full in the face. She fished out her sunglasses and dialled up dimmers. Immediately her vision was clear of glare.

A hairy animal burst out of the grain to her right and ran past her. She started and let out a squeak. It was an Oomrat, one of the large, native rodents that plagued the region. Lucky there weren't Oomrats in the city—well not that she'd noticed—as they were perpetually hungry. Hitching the backpack higher, she checked her surroundings and her timepiece. Her shoulders ached and her feet were going numb. She hadn't done this much exercise in nearly a year, since the last security training camp. Looking at the wall of grain, she bit her lip. There should have been a pathway. Had it overgrown or was she lost? Walking on a bit further, she could see no sign of it. She dared not check the colony's direction finder, as it would ID her in a snap. She walked a bit further, racking her brain for familiar markers and instead came up empty.

It looked like fields of grain. The grain was taller than her, so she couldn't see the farmstead or even her neighbour's house. Standing there gaping, she weighed up what to do. Keep walking and then back-track from the road or cut across the fields. A buzzing sound grew louder. She turned around and then faced forward again, trying to work out the direction the noise was coming from. Up ahead a bright green harvester burst out of the grain, swivelled around in a three-hundred-and-sixty-degree turn and dived back in. It was unmanned, so there was no point in waving it down. It did, however, leave a nice wide path and in the dimming light she caught a glimpse of the homestead ahead. Her machines had ploughed grain over her track. Served her right for neglecting them.

The path through the grain was not as easy going as the track would have been, but judging by the distance, it would not be long before she could put her feet up and surround herself with childhood memories. A smile lit her face. She had made it and she was coming home.

Chapter Four

THE HOMESTEAD

The main house was musty after been shut up for a several years. Dust covers shrouded furniture and moths flew out of the linen cupboard when she went searching for bedding. The bookshelves contained old books, real ones with cobwebs on them. No auto here. No self-making bed. She'd have to do it the old-fashioned way, with her hands. This she managed with a bit of sneezing when she shook dust from the bed covers.

The water at least was plentiful and hot. The neighbour had been servicing the power cells and maintaining the filters to keep the water supply clean. As she ran the tap to fill the old-fashioned tub, and the steam rose, memories returned of the holidays she'd spent here as a child. At that time, the old-fashioned things were an adventure, a break from the ready-made lifestyle of the city. It not only made her nostalgic for the past; it made her realise, not for the first time, how dependent everyone was on technology. If there was a crisis in the city, a serious malfunction of machines or power, the farmers and their families in backwaters like this would be better suited to survival.

That said, it wouldn't mean they would be unscathed. They would have little access to markets and would miss out on luxuries, but they'd be able to feed themselves and manage the necessities of life longer.

After she shucked her clothes, she eased into the heat of the water and sank down. With a sigh, she lay back in the water, closing her eyes, thinking about the past, about her time spent here as a child and a teenager. The crusty, lined face of her grandfather came to mind with his tight, curly dark hair, sprinkled with grey and his dark eyes that always twinkled and the warm colour of his ancestors in his skin. Why had she stopped coming here after her grandfather died?

As she soaped herself up, she thought about that. She loved the place. Evidently she did, because she had turned down two generous offers to sell. Yet why didn't she come here, even for the peace and quiet? Closing her eyes and letting the steam caress her face, she understood it. There were memories here, and secrets, and staying away was the best way to avoid confrontation. Her grandfather had wanted her to take over the farm, but she had her head in the city and in technology. Her father had predeceased her grandfather and had had no interest in the farm in any case, even though he would have inherited it. He loved the city as well, though he respected the farm. City life is what she enjoyed, and she was well paid in her security job and good at it. It was a pity she couldn't have the best of both worlds.

Shaking her head, she laughed. She'd like to think that the old man blamed her, but he didn't. Not really. Her grandfather was just frustrated by circumstances—the lack of more grandchildren, the inability to get her to care about the land and the farm he had lived on all his life. He'd loved Deleen and admired her mother, even if she did pass on the flame-like hair and freckled nose. "Ah, Del, your mother was a soothing influence on this house, and she tamed your father. I nearly despaired of him until her met her and brought her home.

"For a while there things went so well. You were born and it got even better. Then something soured. I don't know what. I don't know why, but she went away and then you and your father went to the city and left me here with the work and the memories.

"Your father knew I couldn't let this place go. There's too much at stake, too much history and it's our duty to keep this place safe. It's a haven, Del. A haven. Remember that won't you?"

Later as she was sipping tea in bed, trying to read a book she'd found on the shelf, her grandfather's words bashed around in her head. Duty?

Haven? It was just a farm. Sure, he loved it out here, but why didn't he sell up and join them in the city? He'd never even visited them.

Giving up on the book and gulping down the last of her tea, she dimmed the lights and snuggled into the bed. Sniffing, she turned over, but there was no avoiding the mustiness of the old-fashioned cotton sheets. Tomorrow, she'd have to launder them. She blinked in the dark, a moment of panic. Then she remembered there was an appliance to help with that.

Breathing deep, she cleared her mind of worry, packed away the events and stress of the day, and drifted off to sleep. Some time later, she dreamed. A clear vision of the farmstead, of running out the door, hearing it slam and seeing the fields and the barn and the other sheds and outbuildings, which were used for machinery or storage. Her vision shifted. Once again, she was back in that tunnel, that dark space, sneaking along behind her father. No that wasn't it. Her father's visage changed and became her grandfather, and he was holding her hand. She wasn't sneaking that time. She'd been in that tunnel more than once.

"This is why this place is important, Del. Never tell anyone about it. It's a secret. A family secret."

And, then, in her dream, she was looking at a face, a stranger, lying on his back. In her dream, the eyes opened, and she screamed. Screamed herself awake.

Lying there in the dark, her breathing echoed around her. The dream was so real. That moment on waking when a dream seems real and then you realise it isn't, didn't happen. It was too real, and she couldn't rationalise it away.

Unable to go back to sleep, she put on the light. Her grandfather's belongings were everywhere around her. She'd never disposed of anything, not even his clothes. Obviously, she had trouble moving on as well. But what was it with that dream, with that face, that stranger who seemed so real? What was she doing here anyway? This was ridiculous. After an hour of self-talk and failed attempts at reading, she once again turned out the light and fell into a deep and dreamless sleep.

* * *

The laundry done, the house cleared of dust, and food eaten, Deleen still couldn't relax. She paced through the house, touching things, looking out the window, but it didn't help her sense of unease. Being in the homestead made it worse. There was a tunnel in her dreams. Maybe it existed. As the weather was fine, she went outside, shaking her head over the puzzle in her brain. Was there a tunnel? May as well check it out, she thought. If that tunnel existed, she would find it. If it didn't, then there was no use losing sleep over some non-existent man in a non-existent place.

An inspection of the main barn did not reveal anything out of the ordinary. Recent use by her neighbour was evident in the reasonably fresh animal manure on the ground. The shed was as her grandfather left it. Tools hanging from labelled hooks, all nails, screws and little things in containers, and in drawers were smaller hand tools neatly arranged. Nothing seemed out of place. Obviously, the neatness genes did not pass down to her.

A vehicle approached and she heard the grind of wheels on the gravel outside as it pulled up. She stilled, a bit tense after what happened in the city and on the transport, then went outside to investigate.

A four-wheeled vehicle stood in the drive. Not a new vehicle. The finish was dull and there were dents in places. A working vehicle.

No one was inside. "Hello," said a voice behind her.

She jumped and swung around, heart thumping ludicrously.

"Sorry," the older man said. "I didn't mean to scare you. I'm the local judicial advisor, Judd Haines. I heard reports that someone was here. I thought I should check it out."

Deleen's heart thudded. Shit. Officialdom. Someone who would file a report. "Hello, Mr Haines. You may not remember me—Deleen Milo. I inherited the homestead from my grandfather."

"You're the owner?" He seemed disappointed.

"Yes. Nothing to worry about. Just visiting for my annual holiday."

He looked her over. "Yes, I see the likeness now. I haven't seen you in at least ten years."

She pretended to recognise him. "Oh, I remember you." She put out her hand to shake, stating her name again. "Deleen Milo."

He grasped her hand and shook it gently, his eyes flicking around. "Yes, Miss Milo. I recall the name. You alone here?" he asked.

"Completely, except for the Oomrats."

His gaze assessed the farm again and she figured he was looking for something. Damn the man, he would probably put in a report after all. "I'll be off then. Glad you're doing okay. The homestead is a sad place with no one living in it."

"Yes, I feel it. I miss it so much." She kicked at the ground, watching a stone bounce and then looked up again, regaining confidence. "It's in the blood you know. Perhaps I'll relocate back here. Would we be neighbours then?"

He grinned and relaxed his stance. Maybe he wouldn't file a report now. "Not close neighbours, no," he said, pausing before climbing into his vehicle. "My place is close to Everglen station, on the other side."

"I hope to see you around."

He climbed into his vehicle and drove off, leaving her waving. Despite its appearance, the engine was quiet. A new motor in there, she thought. After he departed, she continued her inspection of the property. There was nothing unusual in the sheds. No secret doors, nothing that matched her dream. Or was it a memory? Turning, she caught sight of something and then paused. Some shape of the ground triggered a frisson of recognition. Closing her eyes, she tried to form the image, match it to her dream.

There was a grass-covered mound, a couple of hundred metres behind and to the side of the homestead and the outbuildings. She approached it carefully, sweeping her gaze from left to right. It wasn't that high above ground. She paused, but the memory wouldn't come. She paced to one side of the mound and the next, hoping some sliver of the past would shine through. But there was nothing.

Forget, forget, forget. The words whispered in her mind. She stopped and turned slowly, looking over her shoulder as she did. The image of the face came to mind again. And the lips. Had she kissed them or was that just fancy? But, she couldn't have kissed them because he was inside something.

Visions of the sarcophagi burning made her shudder. That couldn't be it. A man in a sarcophagus, with a clear lid? Hidden here? Her heart thumped painfully as she fought to control her fear.

What had Cheree said? People had kept them hidden. Soldiers that fought a war. A war the records didn't document anymore. That woman's family was a First Settler, like hers. Her ties went back to Five's first days. What had been talked about around the table when she was little? Why was it so hard to remember?

"You'll always come back, Del," her grandfather had said. "You have to come back. When the time is right. You'll be here."

Hands on hips, she was growing frustrated. Her feeling of being untethered was gone. Now she fought to focus her mind. "Damn you, Pops! What am I here for? Why can't I remember?"

Kicking a stone, it flew up. It made a clunk when it landed a few feet ahead. At first, she thought she'd imagined the sound. How could grass *thunk*? She went over, knelt down and touched the turf. The texture was like glass, rather than grass. Tapping the ground, she heard a dull thud. Sounding out the edges of it she realised it was a door, a trapdoor.

* * *

Once she had excavated around the edges, she was able to lever the door open. It was dark on the other side. Sitting down cross-legged, she leaned in. After blinking a few times, she made out some stairs. Swinging her legs around, she put her feet on the first stair. When nothing out of the ordinary happened, she slid her bottom onto the first stair and her feet two risers down.

A light flickered on, concealed in the ceiling. The ceiling and the walls were lined with grey material. She brushed her fingers along it. The material wasn't familiar. A sort of formed metal, like from a spaceship. Snatching her hand back, she eyed the tunnel again. Yes, it was material from a spaceship. One of the settler ships perhaps.

She swallowed spit and lowered herself further down. The tunnel opened out and she was able to stand once she was at the base of the stairs. Then she stood stock-still. It was the tunnel from the dream.

Closing her eyes, she remembered the sounds, the shadow of her father—or was it her grandfather?—walking along with her following unnoticed behind. She glanced back up the stairs, to the patch of sky revealed where she'd left the hatch open. Thinking better of that, she crawled back up the stairs and lowered it again. Best not advertise this bunker's existence. Not with a close neighbour and a judiciary investigator close by.

* * *

The corridor was dark and quiet. The air smelt strange, sort of closed in, but not stale. There was air ventilation happening, maybe it came on with the lights. Stepping cautiously, she moved down the passageway, fighting ghosts of memory and disquiet. *Forget. Forget. Forget.* As she said the words over in her mind, she knew she'd been here before.

Maybe she'd been a lot younger than she remembered. As she stepped over the threshold, wall lights set low down came on, casting shadows and memories of nightmares around her. Her heart trembled and she stood totally still again. A shadow had moved.

Letting out a slow breath, she realised the shadow was hers, distorted by the light in the wall behind her. Her hearing grew accustomed to the thumping of her heart and then other sounds intruded. The faint hum of a computer and, perhaps, a gurgle of liquid. On the wall was a switch. She palmed it on, and the overhead lights drowned out the lurching shape of her shadow. Wall-to-wall shelves held containers, supplies of food and she saw as she walked over to inspect a dull silver chest, at least one case of weapons.

Her brow furrowed. She didn't remember a stockpile of weapons or food. But the focus of her memory was very specific. Then as she surveyed the cache, she realised it was hers now. It was her inheritance. With the politics right now, she was in an awkward situation. She was the colony's deputy security officer and if this bunker was found by the administration she'd be in a lot of trouble, perhaps locked up and the key misplaced. Her breathing kicked up and her heart raced. She was in serious shit.

Shaking her head, she fought for some clarity. She needed to think this through. Was it her family's? Had someone else set this up in the years she'd been absent? No. She knew that wasn't the case. She'd been

43

here in this bunker as a child. Her family built it, maintained it; there was no denying that.

An archway beckoned her through to another room. Standing on the threshold, all doubts flew away. She swallowed as her gaze took in the sarcophagus nestled against the far wall. A large machine with a black metal base and transparent lid. She'd seen enough of them recently to know what it held—a cold soldier—a frozen man wanted by the authorities, preferably burnt to a crisp first.

Wiping the end of her nose on her sleeve, she sniffed—the dust circulating in the air was irritating. Still, she stood there, waiting for what she didn't know. How did she know this one was a man? Because of the dream. The dream that was a memory. His face arose once again, a strong, clean vision in her mind as if this bunker pried it loose from the buried confines of the past.

She knew if she looked down into his sleeping face, she'd see him.

Forget. Forget. Forget. She'd been programmed to forget. But not completely, because it was coming back now. Triggered by something. Closing her eyes, she recalled the burnings. Those frozen men and women. Those cold soldiers burnt when defenceless and betrayed by the families who were meant to protect them. But the cold soldiers were there to protect the colony. She had no idea what the soldiers were protecting them from, but the feeling of danger had been growing for days—from the replacement of the administrator, to the strange and sudden forced holiday she had to take. Then the pronouncements, the orders to burn. *Bring out the cold soldiers ...*

What should she do? How was she going to know for sure that he was real? She had to look, had to see for herself what lay sleeping in this bunker, protected by the soil and the name of her family.

The black metal skin of the sarcophagus was cool to the touch, but the thrum of energy teased the tips of her fingers. The top had a clear cover and she leaned over and recoiled, letting out a scream as she fell backwards onto the floor. The face was horrible, not the one she remembered. It was black and it looked like a skull. Her breath hitched and her heart slowed. She closed her eyes, trying to calm down.

After a few breaths, she thought it through and climbed up again. This time she examined the body coolly, and not from a place of fear. It was clear then that it was a mask sitting over a face—a death mask maybe. Probably placed there deliberately to deter an unwanted visitor. The monitor panel had three flashing green lights. One was labelled 'open'. With a shaky hand, she pressed it and the cover slid back, belching out cold, chemical air. Reaching for the edge of the mask, she tugged it off and tossed it aside, as though it was cursed. Then she looked down at the face, still as death. It was him. The blond-haired man, with pale full lips and a straight nose. The chin was strong and the jaw square. It was him, from her memory but more defined. She was older now and there was a familiarity to him that was pleasing. She'd never seen him animate. She thought back to those who had surrendered their cold soldier and wondered how they could have done that. Killed these frozen humans without even giving them the option to breathe again, to choose, to fight.

Her gaze flicked up to the control panel and she pressed the two remaining buttons in sequence and then she gasped. How did she know to do that? What the hell? Before she could begin to freak out at the prospect of setting off a malfunction, lights started flashing. Jumping off the side of the sarcophagus, she edged away to give the machine the space it needed.

A moment of terror struck at the thought that the soldier would burst out of the machine, guns firing and killing her where she stood. What if the administration was right, and these cold soldiers were dangerous? Maybe they should be destroyed, and she'd done a stupid and dangerous thing.

Waiting with her pulse racing, she grew curious when nothing happened. Shouldn't the soldier get up, climb out? A few more anxious minutes and she got up the nerve to creep closer. It was then she heard a whimper. Something was wrong.

Chapter Five

AWAKE

Rik Chesson inhaled. Every nerve in his body flooded with sensation, and pain. His system was overrun with blood, oxygen and hormones. He was hot and then he was cold. He detected movement and knew he wasn't alone. *Danger!*

Disorientation fudged his mind and he fought for a semblance of reality, for understanding. He'd been frozen. Why? He couldn't remember. He was on a ship? No. He'd been on a ship and in stasis before, as that was all part of the deal. He had no idea where he was or what happened before. Before what? His gaze flicked up but there was nothing but bland concrete ceiling. Planet? Possible. Unless he sat up, he wasn't going to see more. He wasn't going to be able to decide what danger he was in.

Another sound alerted him to a presence close by. He couldn't sit up. Not yet. His lower limbs were tingling and numb as he wasn't fully awake yet. He used a relaxation technique to steady his breathing and to slowly clench and unclench each muscle to bring the sensation of being unfrozen to life. Odd memories darted, a mixture of present and past. He tried to sort it out. He bit down on the scream.

A face hovered over his head. He controlled his reaction, his fear response. It was a young woman. A redhead, with freckles across her little nose. Her wide, astonished eyes were bright green in a tanned face.

"Are you okay?" she asked, eyebrows drawing together to crinkle her brow. "You cried out."

He registered no danger from her. His sensors were coming online, and she was not redlining on the aggression factor. He unclenched his jaw and was surprised when his voice slid out his throat for the first time in years. "I am alive." He paused, assessing his vitals. "Breathing. All systems showing green. Unfreeze in progress."

He hadn't quite assessed whether he was okay. The aftereffects of frozen sleep took a while to kick out of one's system. He remembered pain. His fingertips were fine now, but his toes burned. The pain would pass like pins and needles did. He just had to wait.

Hormones were sending messages to his cells. Some cells responded better than others. He had a rather painful erection. Damn those hormones. Not all men came out of stasis with a hard-on. Why did it have to be him? With a civilian woman looking on.

The last of the monitors retracted from his skin, leaving pin pricks of blood on the surface. He lifted an arm, examining the skin closely. The small wounds were already healing over. The nanos in his blood resuming their programmed roles.

His brain kicked in—a surge of memories, more coherent than previously. He was on Colony Five. "Year?" he asked brusquely. She had to deliver information fast. He didn't want to freak out.

"149S." She was quick to answer. Her gaze travelled over him in a clinical appraisal. One hundred and fifty years from settlement. No. Too long. "Status?"

Her eyebrows drew even closer together. "Which status?"

Fuck! What the damn fuck? "Why did you wake me if there isn't a problem?"

She studied him as if thinking up an answer. "There are multiple problems, but not easily explained with you half frozen. And I only just remembered that you were here."

"Remembered?" he echoed. Right. Who was this nutter? How could they forget the expeditionary force?

"I'm Rik Chesson, Expeditionary Force. Family name?" he asked.

"Milo. I'm Deleen Milo. I'm from a First Family."

He listened to that name and waited for his memories to engage.

General Milo's descendant, he surmised. Judging from the colour of Ms Milo's hair the commander had succeeded in winning the glorious Doctor Siobhan McPhee's hand in marriage. Good on him. But Rik was awake now after nearly one hundred and thirty-four years of stasis. It had passed without him really knowing or understanding the passage of time. He was in a new world with very little tactical input. "I know the name," he said through clenched teeth as he rode the unfreeze. "Why did you wake me?" he asked again, as his body was buffeted with the shakes.

Deleen pursed her lips, eyes narrowing. "You're in danger. They have been burning cold soldiers. I had a dream that you were here and found you." Rik found that statement hard to parse. Cold soldiers? Dream? Seriously? Then he absorbed the meaning.

"Fuck! Burning the Expeditionary Force?" His brain wasn't functioning at full capacity yet, but he recalled his team, every single one of them. Burnt? He tried to bury the anger, the fear and the revulsion. How could that happen, after all they had sacrificed? How could those gentle colonists with their grand creed of tolerance burn the soldiers who had protected them. He needed focus and damn if he couldn't get unfrozen fast enough. Frustrated, Rik flexed his toes and wished for a faster revive.

Deleen frowned and shook her head. "Expeditionary Force? You mean from First Settlement?"

Most of Rik's body was ready. He needed to move. "Help me out. I need to find out what's going on."

Rik had been fighting fit when he volunteered for stasis, but his system was taking a while to adjust to life. Deleen steadied him as he climbed out. "Clothes?" Rik asked as he sat up. He was stark naked, and it wasn't that he was shy, but the woman was clothed and there were other things to think about than getting her naked too. Damn that hard-on.

Deleen went to the storage unit behind the sarcophagus and rummaged. Soon she came back with some drawstring trousers and a large shirt. Not the uniform he was expecting, but enough for decency. As he pushed his legs into the trousers he asked, "Food? I'm starved."

The woman frowned and went back to the storage unit. Soon the aroma of hot meat and vegetables reached his nostrils and his stomach rumbled. She brought over a tray. "I'm not sure how old this is but it's been in a stasis unit, so I think it's okay to eat."

Rik took the tray and lifted the fork, shovelling the food in faster than he could chew. When he saw the portion was nearly gone, he said simply. "More."

Deleen cocked her head, nodded with a puzzled expression, and went to get another serve.

Once his need for food was satisfied, he needed a bit more information. "Are we secure?"

Deleen, who had been sitting on the floor, stood up and looked over her shoulder. "I'll go check that the entry is locked from the inside. As for the exterior I'm not sure it will stand up to scrutiny, as I had to dig around the hatch to get in. That's got to be visible if there is a fly over or if someone comes snooping."

"Is there anyone else here?" Rik asked, his gaze now assessing the stores. His memory was coming up bright. He knew what was meant to be there for him when he awoke. His tech assessed and quantified. The Milo store looked solid.

"I'm on my own, but there is a neighbour who uses some of the sheds and I had a visit from a justice, who lives near the transport station.

Rik tilted his head. "More detail. Where are we?"

"Oh? Right. We're about three hundred and fifty clicks from Central City, in a sparsely populated rural area. There are way more cows than humans here. There are no military installations that I know of in the area."

Rik nodded. Not a perfect sit rep, but he didn't have much choice. He needed to assess the equipment and then find the closest of his team and wake them up before something bad happened. That this Deleen had saved his life, he was certain. One hundred and thirty-five years was a long time and if there had been peace in all that time it was no wonder they had been forgotten. He made that excuse up so it was easier to bear. A time limit had not been set when he went into cryo, but one hundred and thirty-five years was a very long time. He wondered what was out there, what waited for him. It was going to be different to what he had known.

"I need to do an inventory."

Rik began and it took hours.

* * *

Deleen woke up some time later, finding herself covered with a foil blanket. How she was able to sleep was beyond her. Footsteps echoed along the bunker's concrete floor as she sat up. Rik strode up, and now she could see the enhancements more clearly. He was seriously rigged with tech and probably had nanotech on the inside. He was dressed in what looked like military-style fatigues and he had pulled back a fake wall revealing a bank of machinery, which he was presently studying.

Running her hands through her hair, she tried to tidy it. Somehow, she had lost the tie for her ponytail. Next to her was a bundle of clothes and a portable bathing unit.

"We are moving out," Rik said. "Get dressed in those."

"Wait. Moving out? I'm not going anywhere." She'd already broken the law, and what about her job?

Rik turned. "I need you, and we don't have time to chat about it. Get dressed in that gear. You'll be more comfortable that way."

Deleen studied him, the firm set to his mouth, the bright glitter of tech in his eyes. "You know where some cold soldiers are ... don't you? Can we save them?"

Rik nodded. "Yes. If we move quickly. Will you help?"

Deleen studied what was beyond the fake door. Her grandfather had stored all this gear for a purpose. Now that purpose had to be her's, if she valued anything her family stood for. "I will."

Rik left her, so she took off her pantsuit and turned on the cleaning unit. It cleansed and refreshed her body. Next was the clothing, which was like Rik's, a combination of maroon and beige heavy fabric. Screwing up her nose, she shook them out. She reached for her bra and adjusted her breasts. There was no underwear in the bundle, but she could live without it. After slipping on the clothes, she folded the blanket into a neat square and left it on the floor. Walking up behind Rik, she studied what he was doing. Looking further into the bunker and what the secret wall had concealed, she could see there were more shelves, stacked with supplies, clothing and weapons.

She angled her head to get a better view. Lots of weapons. Big and small ones. "What the hell? That's some serious weaponry. How did grandfather manage it?"

Rik turned his head. "Give me a moment and I'll tell you about it. Right now," he said turning back to the readouts he was reading, "I'm trying to understand the situation. Things have changed since the war."

Deleen started. "War? What war? There was no war."

Rik looked back at her over his shoulder, eyebrows raised. "What are you talking about? Of course there was a war."

Deleen wasn't going to argue. If her grandfather had made this military stockpile, it was for a reason. If Rik was saying there was a war, then it was likely there had been. "Obviously ... um none in the official records. I suspect they have been tampered with. When was this war?"

Rik glowered, the tech in his eyes glinting. "15S. It was a short conflict, and I went into cold sleep just after we won."

"Right," Deleen said in a bewildered voice. *Forget. Forget. Forget.* She frowned as those words came to the forefront of her mind again. She knew something, or had known something, and had been made to forget. Did forget. So much deceit.

Rik finished what he was doing and came up to her. "You mentioned other cold soldiers being brought out and burned. Where was that?"

"In Central City. A couple of days ago, as a new administrator took control, then messages started coming out of Central Admin and then I saw the bonfires. I heard about people being arrested for treason for hiding cold soldiers. I escaped out here."

"Describe the messages, the words ..."

This was going to be hard to relate and she wasn't sure how he would take it. Her grandfather had been a military man and from his tales she knew they were very bonded to their fellow soldiers. "'Bring out the frozen soldiers' or something along those lines. 'Do not wake them' and then orders to burn them."

His eyes widened and his already pale skin went pasty. He swallowed but remained calm. "How many did they burn?"

She saw his cool anger and quaked a little. She felt guilt, too, because she'd done nothing. "I don't know … I didn't know … I saw one and I heard tens of them had been burned. I didn't know you were here. They made me forget. I came here because they were after me, I think. For searching for information about cold soldiers and then I dreamed, I remembered … I'm not sure and now I have one … I have you …"

He took a breath, visibly relaxed and said in a softer tone. "When did the burnings begin?"

Deleen gulped and fought for calm. "I saw some yesterday. Lots then and a few the day before. Two days. From when I was forced to take leave."

He turned back to the console that he'd been studying. "That explains the readings I'm getting."

"Readings?" Deleen tried to peer around him to the console.

"Our cryo machines give out signals to our location. I can detect only two close by."

Deleen frowned at the two glowing icons on the console. "How many were you expecting?"

Rik turned to face her. "My company had one hundred and fifty soldiers." Turning away, he keyed the console again. "You mentioned an edict. What was that?"

Deleen stood and chewed the edge of her thumb. "Well, I haven't actually seen it, but I heard it was now illegal to have a cold soldier and anyone found with one would be tried for treason."

Rik turned from the console and grabbed a pack from the shelf to the right. His movements were sharp, precise and angry as he started thrusting food packs in. "Fuck!" He grabbed another pack, shoulders tense and actions jerky.

"What are you doing?" she asked. She was not prepared for this, hadn't thought beyond waking him up and trying to understand. Something was seriously wrong in Central, but now this curve ball. What she understood about the past was obviously wrong as well. There had been a whole company hidden in the colony and she didn't know what it meant. It made her feel afloat, as if reality had pitched her sideways.

Rik looked up and frowned, the tech in his eyes glinting again. "It means we must move quickly if we are to save the rest of the company. And I fear there is an insurgency, and the insurgents will win if they take out all of us in cryo before we've had a chance to even fight."

Deleen bit her lip and considered. "So these orders coming out of Central are from insurgents? Someone has taken over the government?" She rubbed her chin and paced, finally nodding. "I think you must be right. Everything I've seen runs counter to Colony Five's philosophy. I've been so off-centre that I couldn't see it. No wonder I was put on leave just as the administration changed. I didn't get my promotion and that job went to someone unqualified." She paused and faced Rik. "I could try to contact someone in my team," she ventured.

Rik made a cutting motion with his hand. "No. Don't try to contact anyone. Not until we know the details. We must find the other two soldiers who are nearby and liberate them straight away. Then we plan the attack."

"Attack? What or whom are we attacking? The government? I know most of those people."

He spun round, eyes widening. "You really don't know who the insurgents are or who they could be?"

"I think I've made that clear. Explain yourself. Otherwise, I'm going to start believing the messages the administration is putting out."

Leaving the series of backpacks he'd been stuffing half open, he came toward her. She backed up and put up her hands. He was a big, tech-enhanced soldier and this close he was scary. "Wait. I didn't mean that ... but you must understand I don't know who these insurgents are or what is motivating them, or what they want. But you know something, or you suspect, so before we go anywhere you have to fill me in."

He paused, shook his head slightly and relaxed his posture. "In 15S we had a war with the Gogola. At first, we thought it was a territorial dispute, but that wasn't it. Their motives went deeper."

"The Gogola?"

"You haven't heard of them?"

She shook her head. "Some kind of non-humanoid life form?"

"Aliens, yes."

"And they look like what? A pile of mud? A bowl of gruel?"

"How can you be so ignorant?"

She folded her arms. "I woke you up buddy, so I'm not all that ignorant. And the records have been altered, if what you say is true. There was no war in 15S according to our official records. Nor at any time in Colony Five's history."

He sucked in a breath and then let it out slowly. "I agree there is a reason for your ignorance, if what you say is true. In one hundred and thirty-four years people can forget or be made to forget as you imply. The Gogola have some human aspects, but they also resemble animals."

Deleen's heart thumped and a queasy feeling filled up her belly. "Animals? What kind of animals?"

He shrugged. "Felines, monkeys, some rodents maybe. I'm not sure."

Deleen considered this and drew a conclusion. "Not aliens, then. Gene modification?"

Rik stared at her blankly, then shaking himself, resumed stuffing supplies into the packs. Deleen needed to sit down, and she groped for a bench and lowered down on to it. The colony's charter did not allow gene modification, other than to correct genetic defects. It couldn't be true. But the pieces of the puzzle were shifting and rearranging. Why change the history of the colony? If it had been aliens, then why hide it. Only something against Earth's colonial charter would risk the colony. Gene modification would be a reason to hide things. She nodded and swallowed. That was an awfully big secret to hide.

Rik looked up and their eyes met. "Perhaps," Rik tentatively agreed. "I heard rumours, though who did the gene splicing, if any, is anyone's guess. Renegade humans or an alien species. We didn't know and it didn't matter. The Gogola were a threat."

Deleen grimaced and then stood up. Walking around helped to settle her nerves, allowed her thoughts to calm. "How were they a threat?"

He lifted his head, assessing her. "They killed indiscriminately."

"Killed indiscriminately ... but now it's targeted at the cold soldiers ..." She walked away from him, trying to take all this in. "Back then, were any of the other eleven colonies attacked?" Astronomically speaking the colonies were in close vicinity to each other. Twelve ships sent out to colonise, to make new worlds and economic opportunities and a better life for them all. As far as she knew, no aliens had been encountered. Not yet. Not in this sector of space. Hence her concern about the physical attributes of the 'aliens'. She had a sneaking suspicion they were more likely genetically altered humans.

Rik watched her. "My knowledge is old and second-hand. It was reported that Colony Seven was attacked and wiped out. We were tasked to protect Colony Five."

Deleen took that information in and filed it away. She had not heard about attacks on Seven either. So, it was possibly true, or it was a way to leverage the soldiers to fight on Five. Since when did she get so cynical? When the government she worked for went crazy, she supposed. "Okay, so you saved the planet in 15S and then you and your buddies were frozen. Why?"

Rik leaned against the wall, arms folded, his eyes never leaving her. Deleen found the scrutiny uncomfortable, but bore it. He could probably tell whether she lied or not through changes in her blood circulation or body heat. She didn't know for sure because the kind of tech Rik carried was not allowed on Five or any of the colonies. It was a remnant of old Earth, the Earth they left behind to create something new.

"We did beat the Gogola," he said, as his eyes surveyed the bunker. Deleen let out a deep breath when he stopped studying her. Those eyes returned. "But we did not annihilate them. They went to ground and we could not find where. At the time, it was suspected that they would try again in future. We didn't know when. So, we were frozen until we were needed again."

Appalled, Deleen said,. "so, you could have been frozen forever, like a thousand years, maybe longer? That's terrible."

"It was not meant to be so, but if as you say we were forgotten by the populace there was a risk of that. So far it has been one hundred and thirty-four years, still in living memory, but for some reason you don't remember us. That took planning, action and cunning. The Gogola would not have forgotten us. They hate us, but they would have needed help to do this."

"I agree. There's a conspiracy here. I didn't remember and most people don't either, but someone obviously did. It was more than a memory lapse, though. I was programmed to forget. Only, some things leaked through." She tapped on her chin as she paced. "I started remembering, dreaming of you, when I saw the phrase 'cold soldier'. It's like it triggered something."

His eyelids flickered but he gave no other response.

"Why were you hidden in people's houses?" Deleen could think up a few reasons herself. Lack of infrastructure at the time, dispersed soldiers meant that they couldn't be wiped out together unless the whole colony was taken out.

"Each family group took us in. Some of us were kin, others just assigned."

Deleen's head jerked up. "Hell, are we related?"

"No." Rik shrugged. "You weren't born when I was frozen. I did not have any children, so I assume that there is no blood relation between us."

"And?"

"Dispersed, we were protected."

"Makes sense. But the rest doesn't add up. Someone wanted us to forget about you and the war. Someone wiped all knowledge of you from the colony's archives and maybe the other colonies' archives. Now someone is taking you out. A different someone, I'm suspecting." It had been too many years for it to be the same people, but they were connected. The offspring of the original Gogola perhaps?

Without responding, he returned to his packing, going to the shelves and selecting more equipment. "We need to get out of here and get the others."

"Now?" Deleen was thinking about logistics. She had no personal transport here and they couldn't use the main transport line.

"Yes, those two signals are transmitting for now. Their lives are in danger; we need to move quickly. When we find them, I hope I will find more. My range here is limited."

"We?" Deleen's heart leaped. "There's no we. I said I'd help."

He turned, dropping the bag he had been stuffing back onto the bench. "You're coming with me."

She backed up a step, not quite liking where this was heading. She had freed him, surely that was enough. "No. I'm not. I'll help you—maps, information, whatever—but I'm staying here."

"It's no longer safe for you." He turned back to the bench and latched the last backpack, then went to the weapons' locker. Small items went into pockets. Ammo and chargers went into another carry all. Some he placed on the bench.

Her stomach knotted with anxiety. "Why do you say that?"

"My indicator is likely to be flashing on two or three other units. If any unit is compromised, it could lead them here."

Her stomach dropped and she was suddenly sweaty in her lower back and on her nape. "But ..."

"A better reason is that you know this place better than I do. I need your help."

She frowned at the ground, trying to get her mind thinking straight. She'd come out to the homestead to keep safe. No, she came because she knew about him, even if it was buried deep in her mind. "I'm not up to this," she said looking back at him, meeting his stare straight on. She was happy to wake him up, but hadn't thought about the rest. "That would put me in direct opposition to the government. I work for them."

"Good, then your inside knowledge will be useful. What is your occupation?"

"Security."

He nodded in acknowledgement. "Hand-to-hand combat?"

"Some training only ... rusty."

His eyebrows lifted, questioning. "Weapons?"

She eyed the pile he was assembling on the bench. "Most of those, again rusty and only in training, not actual combat. I may not be much use in a fight. We are normally peaceful on Colony Five."

What she thought was a grin flashed onto his face and disappeared. "You just need to know how to stay alive. What do they do with traitors?"

Her head jerked up. She steeled herself. "The grapevine says they are never seen again. Not that I've actually heard about traitors until now. We have a criminal justice system, of course." She thought through what he was suggesting. "Hey, I'm not a traitor!"

"You know what you are. You've said yourself something is wrong. I'm sorry, you don't have many options. I can't leave you here."

Rik was so big, so controlled as he stowed equipment in the packs. Confident. Able. Still, she hesitated. It was a big step.

He was right, though. If they came for her, she'd be taken. Confined, or executed for treason, she would have no hope of restoring order or fighting this unknown force. All of Colony Five could be in danger. It was becoming clear; she had no choice but to go with him.

He watched her. "I need you, Deleen Milo. Please come with me. I'll do my best to protect you with my life." And that appeal from him slapped the door shut on saying no.

Her cheeks grew hot and possibly red. She could look after herself, but this was about more than self-preservation. This was about the Colony, its people and its charter, a charter she believed in. "I don't need you laying down your life for me, buddy. I do have some ability to look after myself and, as you say, I know this place." Deleen looked him in the eye and nodded once. "I'm with you," she said. "What do you need?"

"Pack food into two more packs." He pointed to where he had been filling packs.

"On it," Deleen said and grabbed a box full of meal portions. These she noticed were not one hundred plus years old. The dates were more recent. Ten years. She glanced at another one. Five years. Most were between those years. Her grandfather must have cycled through the packs all these years. She heard a click and looked up. Rik was checking weapons, storing ammunition and charge packs into pockets and latching them to his belt. Again, his movements were economical, controlled and precise. Such expertise inspired confidence in their chances.

When the packs were full, she sealed them up. Standing, she faced Rik, who tossed her a belt already loaded with power packs, projectile ammo, and a small shooter. She strapped it on. "I don't know if I can hurt anyone. I've never been in actual combat with real people before. I know the drill and all, but ..."

"We will train on the way. You have the basics, now you just have to hone your skills so that fighting is a reflex."

She strapped it on. "Do we leave now?"

"Shortly. I need to do a sit rep."

He went to the bank of machinery, and she saw there were some surveillance feeds. One in the front of the bunker entrance, the house and the access road.

"It looks clear to me," she said. "I have a neighbour fairly close. He leased some of my land."

"Wait. I'm switching to infrared."

He studied the images for a few minutes. "Nothing but a few rodents. Sunset in fifteen minutes. It would be better to leave under the cover of darkness."

"Where are we going?" she asked as she came up behind him. He changed the screen to a topographical map. Although the farm was situated on a plain, the land was not all flat. It undulated here and there, with low hills and shallow bowls where erosion had made its mark. "Here," he said, pointing.

"Mmm ... how far is that?" She checked the readout. "It looks like it might be the MacKenzie's ranch. That's about a thirty or so clicks away. I have no idea how we are going to get there. I don't have a vehicle."

"No vehicle. Understood" He jerked his chin at the screen. "We trek on foot."

She glanced at him sideways. "You mean walk?"

"Yes," he replied with a sharp nod. "Walk very fast."

* * *

Rik engaged his inbuilt night vision, guiding Deleen around a clump of undergrowth and warned her of the sudden dip in the terrain. He grinned to himself, remembering her cussing him out when she realised that walking didn't include using the roads. While she understood the reasons, after he explained it, she was begrudging, and also funny in her commentary. She'd give Mac, his corporal, a run for her money. That is if they got to MacKenzie before anyone else did. Bates would be next. If Deleen thought he was big, then she was going to be surprised by Bates.

They'd been walking four hours. Deleen hadn't said a word in the last three. Rik looked back and took pity. She'd explained she was city raised, despite owning the homestead. It would take her a few days, maybe a week, to toughen up. She had spunk with a side order of whine.

"There's a clearing up ahead. We'll take a break there."

"A break," she replied with a pant, trying to disguise the optimism in her voice. Her hair had come loose from the ponytail she had secured it in. Infrared showed him her face was overheated. "How long is a break?"

"An hour, and that's pushing the limits. We need to get far away from the homestead during the night, in case your administration comes looking for you. We'll find safe shelter before dawn, then you can sleep." He lifted an eyebrow and grinned. She couldn't see his expression and that was probably for the best. A light humming sound tickled his enhanced hearing. "Stop and drop," he hissed sharply.

He dropped, threw his pack under a tree and crawled to where she crouched down. From the outer pocket of her backpack, he pulled out a thin, camo cloak, put it over his shoulders and leaped on top of her.

"What the ...?" she yelped, voice low. She turned her face to the side so she could breathe as he pressed down on her back.

"Quiet," he rasped in her ear. "Flyer. It could have sensors. This cloak hides our heat signatures. Stay still."

He kept his weight on his hands, but still their bodies touched. Keeping their breathing in sync, he minimised the gap between their camouflage and the ground, pressing her flat. Heat escaping might give them away. As he pressed against her, he found his hormones hiking up a level. It was a known side effect of the cryosleep revival process. He did like Deleen, and found her attractive, but hoped she could not feel his hard-on pressing against her backside.

The hum grew louder, and he could sense the moment she heard it, too. Her breath halted and she waited with him, listening. As it faded away, she let out a long breath. He stayed pressed on top of her a few minutes more, until his sensitive ears no longer detected the drone. He got up, flicked the cloak and folded it up, while looking around, detecting nothing nearby but some small mammals. His enhanced eyes were reliable, so he let his tension drop a notch.

Deleen pushed herself into a sitting position and scraped her hair and vegetable matter out of her face. The backpack she threw on the ground beside her. He thought she should really cut the hair, but he wasn't going to suggest it. It was too beautiful to lose. "You should tie your hair out of the way," he commented gruffly.

"I lost my hair tie," she said, patting the ground to look for it. "I did have it tied up." She located the little clip and pulled her hair back again.

Annoyed that he couldn't stop looking at her, he grunted. She probably thought he was a sex fiend. While he had been described as such over the years and hadn't minded, it wasn't actually how he wanted her to think about him. He could see her quite well in the low light. Lucky she couldn't see him.

After the war in 15S, he'd into cryo and he'd been out of things for one hundred and thirty-four years. Although recollection was fuzzy, it was a strange dislocation because his body felt as if it had just woken up from a long sleep. Like he'd been among the living yesterday. The way Deleen spoke was a little off from what he was used to, some language drift he expected. He had no trouble understanding her. It was the other things that he was finding challenging. He'd lived closely with the members of his unit, fought with them and been through hell with them. He'd die for them. Being in close quarters with this civilian and all that it entailed was daunting: conversing, smelling, touching, worrying and caring about them. It wasn't just the time that had passed that was different. He was reacting to her in a different way. It was new territory and that was unnerving.

He'd gone into cryostasis to be of service to this colony and now he was doing that. It unnerved him to know that the colony had forgotten about him, about all of them. That was not part of the deal. They were meant to be heroes forever. Deleen hadn't forgotten though, not completely, and that was his luck. He owed her his life and that made up for the loss of time asleep, but not about being forgotten. He was pretty riled about that and wanted to get to the bottom of it. It was the Gogola, he was sure. Unless there was a new player.

Before they left there hadn't been time for her to fetch any personal items from the house. He'd brought her along in the fatigues he'd issued and nothing else. She hadn't complained about that, which surprised him. She climbed to her feet. "Better."

"You have dirt on your nose," he commented and touched his own in the corresponding place.

Drawing her head back in surprise, she wiped at it and then glared at him. "That nanotech in your eyeballs is a bit cheeky." She narrowed her gaze. "I suppose you can hear my stomach rumbling.

He grinned at her quickly. "You'd be surprised at what I can hear." He stood back to let her walk in front of him. "Come on, we better get moving."

"I thought we could have a break, seeing we have already stopped."

He shook his head, his expression no-nonsense. "That flyer could be looking for us or going to your homestead. We need to get farther away."

"Okay." She stamped ahead of him and picked up her discarded packs while he went to fetch his where he tossed them under the trees. Then he took long steps to get in front of her. Now and then he detected her light touch on his belt and realised that she couldn't see. The night was close and dark. He kept look out for hazards, guiding her in a quiet voice. They reached a section of land that sloped steeply into dark woods. He took her hand. "The terrain is tricky here. Follow my instructions. I'll guide your feet. Understood?"

"Yes, sir!" she said in a fake obedient voice. Her sass made him smile.

She clung to him, hand warm and dry, as they made their way down the slope. "Have you been here before? Do you know this place?" he asked.

"I don't think so, even though it's still on my property. I'm finding it hard to picture it. Is there a stream at the bottom?"

Rik's scanners created a three-dimensional graphic. "Could be. Yes, although there's not much water in it."

Still clinging tight, she responded. "Then this is the gully that separates the homestead from Fiddler's Ranch." She was quiet for a few minutes as they gingerly stepped from a rocky outcrop to a jutting clump of weed. After a while she added, "I'm not sure where we will be able to shelter on Fiddler's Ranch. He runs deer and large running birds, ostriches and emus, from memory. It's pretty flat, with some wooded areas."

"We'll make do. I have the means to hide us, but let's get there first. We have two more hours before we make camp."

"Two hours?" she drew the words out with a groan. He took it back. She could whine like a first-day recruit on a forced march.

* * *

Rik noted the last hour of their tramp passed slowly. Deleen had stopped whining and only made intermittent grunts as she put one foot in front of the other. He imagined she hurt from the tip of her toes to the roots of her hair. He pushed on, urging her on when her paced slowed, taking her hand when she stumbled. They had to make the distance and as they trod on, he started scanning for a suitable place to pass the day. Currently, they were on flat grassland, ahead was a heavily wooded section that looked like a likely place to set up. "Not far now. We'll camp there." He pointed ahead. Deleen didn't even lift her head to see where he indicated. A bud of pity filled his chest. He could carry her the last of the distance. He checked the distance on his inbuilt scanner. If he did that then he would be more fatigued and not alert enough during the day, whereas she could sleep.

"Give me your hand," he said to her. Deleen grunted. At first, he thought she didn't hear him, but then she lifted her arm and her hand flopped about as if she didn't have the energy to do anything else. She really was tired. He grabbed on and pulled, giving her some extra momentum.

Half an hour later, he stopped. "We'll camp here."

Deleen looked down at the ground and then lowered herself in a controlled collapse. Rik helped her off with her packs, rolling her back and forward until both were off. As she appeared to be in an exhausted stupor, he left her there while he set up the shelter.

Night clung to the branches of the trees. He chose one that had a solid central trunk and a protective crown of robust branches. After stomping on the ground to level it and kicking away dropped twigs, he chose a spot. The compact domed tent sprang up when he engaged it and he stepped back.

Sunrise was on its way, golden light starting to penetrate through the branches. Damp air held the scent of grass and some herb he couldn't identify. Methodically, he placed their gear inside the shelter, before going over to where she lay very still. Rather than trying to wake her, he knelt, picked her up in his arms and placed her in the shelter.

Next, he set up the sleeping space and unpacked two meals. Before he could make Deleen more comfortable, he had to scout for some camouflage for the exterior. Something that would fool a casual observer at ground level. The shelter provided screening from infrared, and would blend in with the terrain from the air. But if someone walked up to it, they would be able to see it was artificial. He found branches and leaves and arranged them so the outside of the shelter was obscured. He also muddied their path so that it couldn't be seen from the air. When he was done, he returned to the shelter, knelt down and shook Deleen awake.

"Come and eat."

She lay there like the dead. "Ms Milo? Deleen?"

Her eyes flickered open. A moan issued from her delicious mouth. Stop with the sexual attraction, he admonished himself silently. He peered out the opening of the shelter. The sun was not yet fully up but red filaments of light streaked the horizon that framed the trees. Bird calls increased and insects started to buzz.

"Come on, eat. Then you can sleep."

Her bloodshot eyes glared at him. "I want to die." Her voice was low and slow.

Rik repressed a grin. He was tired, but nowhere near as fatigued as she. His nanotech not only gave him enhanced hearing and sight, but it also supercharged his metabolism as required. After a couple of hours shut eye, he'd be alert and ready for anything. Unfortunately, Deleen did not have his advantages.

"Come on. I'll help you decide." He picked up a meal. "There's fake chicken curry." He picked up the other meal. "And fake chicken casserole. Mmm ... yum."

She didn't select an option. He opened the curry as that sounded the nicest and held it out to her. She closed her eyes.

"You need to eat. Come on. Then you can sleep."

Her eyes opened and then narrowed and her mouth snarled. "I want to sleep and maybe not wake up ever. I ache all over."

Rik had to remind himself he was dealing with a civilian. He let out a pent-up breath. "I know you're tired. I'm sorry for that. You need to eat and then you can sleep. Promise. You can sleep the whole day."

She shook her head, then rolled over and tried to crawl in the direction of the bed.

He placed a hand on the flat of her back and she collapsed. "I'll feed it to you if I have to."

Rolling over, her eyebrows arrowed together over a militant stare. Mulishly, she looked at him and he thought she would refuse after all, but then she nodded. Pushing into a sitting position, she held out her hand. He watched as she ate the food mechanically. She appeared to revive after the meal, enough to look around the tent. "Where are you sleeping?"

"Here." He scooped the last of the casserole into his mouth. He hadn't bothered to savour the taste.

"With me?"

He looked around him. One set of bedding was made up. There wasn't any room for another. "Looks like it."

Her indrawn breath should have alerted him. "I want a separate tent."

He paused.. She hadn't thought this through. That was extra kit to carry. "Why? I can protect you better from here."

"I don't want you getting any ideas. I want to sleep."

"What ideas?" He found this amusing. He was fatigued himself and this was his first outing out of stasis, so he was not in prime condition. "Besides staying alive?"

"You know what I mean."

So, she had detected that hard-on earlier. "You have not consented to sexual intercourse. Acknowledged. Nor have I offered any services. Despite appearing in my prime, I need to conserve energy to best protect us. Now go to sleep."

Deleen glared at him for a few minutes longer. He looked for some additional snacks, and ate some nuts and drank a protein drink. Eventually, after a few minutes, she crawled to the bedding, undid her boots, and then flopped down, not bothering to even cover herself or remove any clothing. Within a minute she was asleep, her deep breathing giving him the hint that she was out.

He shifted her boots to near the entry and unclipped the gear from her belt so he could slide it from under her as he rolled her over. He clipped the chargers and ammo and knife back onto the belt. He studied her for a moment, before reaching out to unbutton her overshirt and tug it off. He then folded it up and placed it over next to her shoes and belt. He undid her pants and tugged them off, folding them up with her other belongings. She was left wearing shorts and a T-shirt, so he covered her up with a blanket.

Before he turned in himself, he checked on the signal from MacKenzie. It was blinking steadily. That was a good sign. He hoped they made it to her before anyone else did. Then he stripped off his outer clothing, down to his jocks and joined Deleen in the bed. He knew he would give off a lot of heat, as his nanotech did their work while he slept. It was the reason he removed her outer clothing. It would help him keep cool and she would be kept warm.

He lay there next to her, listening to her breathing. Her light scent teased fantasies of sex. He stopped that line of thought. She had saved him and he owed her.

He'd been alone for a long time now, as he was unattached when he'd volunteered for deep sleep. In this last stint in cryo, he'd slept away so many years on the colony and, barring the action he'd seen in the war, he'd been asleep way longer before that during the journey to Colony Five. The colony ships had been full of the frozen as they made their way to this sector of space. The world he knew was far behind him, changed by time. There was no going back, only going forward. The future would be what he could make of it.

He turned on his side and studied Deleen's profile. A short, straight nose, lips red and cheeks pink and so warm and human. This is what he'd volunteered for. Protecting people like her. She hadn't been born then. But looking at her now, he hoped she was part of the future, his future and a future he would die to protect.

Chapter Six

A TENT ENCOUNTER

Deleen was horizontal. Every bone she had and more beside ached. Her feet were like lead and fatigue weighed her down. If Rik hadn't forced her to eat something, she didn't think she'd have the calorie load to wake up again. She had never, ever, ever walked so far and she had carried two packs. Hells! Who carried one pack these days, let alone two?

Time went in slow motion until her head hit the pillow, then felt like it didn't stop but sank into the earth. Her consciousness was swallowed up in a dreamless sleep.

Some time later, a noise brought her up through the layers of consciousness. Warmth radiated around her, and she was drawn to it, snuggling up close, she sighed as she rubbed her face against the hot skin next to her cheek.

The sound repeated and her eyes flew open. Light filled the tent. It was daylight and, judging by the ambient warmth, the day had progressed some. A hand touched her shoulder; she sucked in a breath and met Rik's gaze. He had a finger to his lips, motioning her for quiet.

He closed his eyes and she understood that he was linked into a surveillance feed. She waited patiently, not daring to breathe. When he smiled, she knew there was no danger.

"A deer," he commented.

Releasing the tension, she relaxed against the bedding and eyed him. Her face heated as she realised he'd been the source of warmth she'd been snuggling up against. Now that she was fully awake, the various aches and pains made themselves known. How was she going to face another march across country? She didn't think she could. Yet, she couldn't let Rik down. He had been frozen and now he was a warm, breathing human being. She closed her eyes against the memory of those she had seen burned. They would have been living and breathing if they had been revived rather than burned. They'd been murdered. Heart beating fast, she gazed at his face and knew she couldn't let another cold soldier die. That led to more thoughts about what was going on in the city and who really was in charge. These Gogola that Rik had talked about? If they were aliens or something else, they were still dangerous. Her mind shot to Vi and all her friends. If she copped out now, they would not be safe. No one would be safe. Her duty as deputy security chief was to keep the colony safe and that wasn't just the administration building—it was the colony.

"How do you feel?" Rik asked softly, almost a whisper.

Stifling a groan, she silently dared him to poke fun at her weariness. "Tired and sore."

"I have something that might help with that." He rolled away from her and foraged in the pocket of a pack. He held out a small tab in the palm of his hand.

"What is that?" she asked in a whisper.

"Analgesic. It will help with the pain. We need to get moving in a couple of hours."

He'd just turned away again to pick up a flask of water when a loud report sounded and a hole appeared in the tent where Rik's head had just been.

Stunned, Deleen swallowed a cry of surprise. Then she saw the hole and knew it had been a bullet. She was thinking of screaming in delayed reaction when Rik dived on her. Near smothered, she froze and then he hissed in her ear, warm breath leaving a moist trace. "Don't make a sound."

Another shot sounded, but this one didn't hit the tent. Rik closed his eyes, breathing slowly and calmly while Deleen hovered on the edge of hysteria, her screams held in check. The trembling began in her hands and after a few breaths her whole body was a quake.

The sound of voices drew close. Deleen closed her eyes. What if they were discovered? It was broad daylight. Their camouflage wouldn't stand up to close scrutiny.

The outside voices were clear for a few minutes. Deleen listened over the sound of her heartbeat. Hunters. They'd been shooting at the deer. After a few minutes where Deleen really wished she could scream, the echoes of the hunters' voices melted into silence as they moved away. Leisure hunting wasn't outlawed, but it was certainly looked down on. Out here in the sticks, she supposed it went unnoticed.

Rik stayed on top of her for a few more minutes. He wasn't heavy. He had curled himself over her to protect her and he'd been holding up his own weight. When it was quiet, he let out a slow breath and lifted himself off her. They lay side by side, facing each other. After looking at each other for a few minutes, Deleen said, "Thank you."

Rik's mouth twitched into a smile. She blinked. Was that the first time he'd smiled since he been unfrozen? The smile did really change his look; it softened the lines of his face, and she could imagine him relaxing and talking with friends. She wished she had the heart to smile.

"You're welcome. I'm sorry I misjudged the danger with the deer. I should have suspected there would be hunters, too." He gave her some water and she swallowed the pain meds.

"Not your fault. As far as I know, there isn't supposed to be hunting going on. It's not part of the First Settlers' creed."

"Nevertheless, I was careless."

She opened her mouth to argue, but he lifted an eyebrow and asked, "Are we going to argue about this?"

She shook her head. "I'm too tired to argue. I'm just glad that neither of us got our heads blown off. What about the hole in the tent?"

His dark eyes lifted to the hole. "It will repair itself by sundown, I think."

"Is there any more food?" she asked, suddenly starving.

He rolled away from her and she noticed his naked back. She blinked and then focused on the flask and the food packet he held out.

"Coffee and a muffin?" He examined the packet. "Well, I think it's a muffin, could be a cake of some kind."

She took the self-heating can of coffee and the packet and elbowed herself a little higher in the bed, but not too high just in case there were any more shooters out there. "Thank you. You're well prepared."

He was still watching her, but he shrugged. "It's the training. And ..."

"What?" she asked, after swallowing some hot joe. Her eyes closed as it slid down her throat. It tasted like heaven.

He shrugged. "I figured you would be hungry. You hardly ate anything before you crashed out."

"Yeah, I'm sorry about that. I left you to do all the work."

He laughed softly. "You were done in. You did well to get this far with so little complaint."

She frowned at him and bit into the muffin. She mused over his words while she chewed. "You're not patronising me, are you? Because I distinctly remember whingeing a lot." She moved her head to the side and considered him. "Well, until I was too exhausted to complain. I believe the expression is 'beyond words'."

Lying facing her, he rested his head in his hand. "I've heard worse."

Disbelieving, she lowered the muffin. "Heard worse?" She narrowed her eyes. "I can't tell if that's an insult or a compliment."

"A compliment. I like the steel in you."

"I have steel? What makes you say that?" She knew coming from him it was a huge compliment. He may have just been out of stasis, but he was fit and enhanced with tech. She had not maintained her fitness and training as she should have and had been desk-bound for three months on top of that.

His gaze lowered and she finally noted she was wearing only under-wear. He must have undressed her. Hell, why did her face have to heat up again?

Flicking off the bed cover, he shifted to a low stool and started rear-ranging one of the packs. "What are you looking for?" she asked.

He looked up. "Something more substantial than a muffin. Here, bacon and eggs." He lifted the packet and tore off the seal. Steam wafted out and the salty, tasty tang of fried bacon hit her nostrils. "You want?"

She gave a quick nod and then took the packet he held out. He put his hand into the pack and pulled out another. They ate in silence and when her hunger was dulled by grease and salted pork, she lay back.

Rik finished off his meal and then lifted his gaze to hers. His eyes contained heat and when their gaze met—a zinging sensation raced down her spine. "Are you having trouble with your hormones again?" she asked archly, because she thought her own endocrine system was malfunctioning.

"Maybe." He shrugged. "Some. You should rest up. I'll wake you when it's time to move out."

She sighed, because he was so right about that. Her body still felt like a lump and they had more trekking to do. She flopped back down and pulled the cover over her head to block out the light.

Chapter Seven

MAC

Deleen started awake. The silvery inner lining of the tent arched overhead. Outside it was night. Lit by the glow of a small LED, Rik sat fully dressed and had most of their gear either packed up or broken down for packing. She blinked at him, confused at first and then sat up.

Catching her eye, he tossed her a food pack. When she opened it, a rich gravy smell wafted out. As she ate, she noticed her clothes were neatly folded and on top was the portable bath.

It took a while for her to come fully awake. The food helped. Rik was obviously ready to leave, but didn't try to hurry her along. She ran the bathing unit over her body, noting that she did not feel as tired as she expected, given her near exhaustion that morning. Her head was slightly fuzzy after sleeping during the day.

She handed the portable bath to Rik, who packed it away efficiently. He tossed her a small packet, which turned out to be disposal underpants. He left the tent as she tugged these on, along with a T-shirt, camo trousers and an overshirt. When she climbed from the bed covers, Rik knelt to pack them up too. While she squeezed her feet into her boots, Rik stored all their gear into the packs. Once dressed, she strapped on her weapon. All that was left was the shelter, which would easily fit into an outside pocket when collapsed.

A faint buzzing made itself noticeable. Rik tensed, then went to the opening. He had placed a small sensor there that fed him the surveillance feed.

"What is it?" she asked hesitantly. "A drone?"

He lifted his forefinger to his lips, his eyes unfocused as if he was monitoring something internally. After a couple of minutes, he spoke. "Yes, a drone. I think they're looking for something, judging from their methodical flight pattern. Maybe for us."

"What will we do?" They couldn't stay put, as that wouldn't help them recover the other cold soldiers. Eventually they'd be found, which wasn't an option either.

Rik opened one of the packs. "Wear these," he said, passing her a small triangle. She watched him press the corner and the thing inflated. He put it on his head. It looked like a small umbrella.

Deleen looked at hers warily. "What does it do?" She had not seen old tech like this previously.

Rik cocked his head and explained. "It's a thermal screen, made from the same fabric as the shelter. It will mask our heat signature from the air."

She frowned as she looked around at the landscape and remembered the hunters. "Not the ground though."

"Correct. We'll be visible, including to infrared, if encountered from ground level."

She opened it up, moved it front and back before donning it. "It looks ug ..." she started to say and stopped because if it was going to keep her safe, she'd wear it.

As if he hadn't heard her, he held the packs out to her. "Are you up for carrying these?" He handed her three packs.

She took them from his grasp. "Good morning to you, too." She shouldered the larger pack on and strapped a small one to the front. She turned so Rik could attach the other to her backpack. He had about six of packs, a large one with the others tethered to it and two flat ones strapped to his front.

"It's evening," he said in serious tones, all soldier at that moment. As the sound of the buzzing drone faded, he opened the shelter and stepped out.

Securing the thermal screen with a tie under her chin, she followed. The woods were quiet, a light wind brushing against the pale green foliage and rustling the golden weeds that coated the ground.

Mist lingered in the branches overhead as a light rain began to fall. If the operators of the drones were searching in that soup, they were definitely looking for heat signatures. Thank the stars they were using drones that were easily fooled.

She moved out of Rik's way while he packed away the shelter. She scanned the forest, keeping a wary eye on the surrounding greenery. The sounds of small animals and insects grew louder the more she listened. The combination of cries and chirps was a comforting backdrop to the night.

Rik joined her at the edge of the clearing, turned and visually scanned the campsite and the air above their heads. "Ready?"

She checked the straps on her packs, shook out her legs and arms and nodded.

He stepped out of the clearing, pushing a path through two larger trees and kicking down some smaller shrubs. As he walked, his head keep moving, ranging over the landscape with his nanotech-enhanced senses. Not that they had discussed such things; she was basing that on observation and the reading that she'd done on earlier eugenics and tech enhancements undertaken by the military on Earth, well before the colony missions were sent out. The colonies were meant to be free of human-altering technology that was not directly related to improving quality of life. It appeared that principle was not followed as religiously as most people expected. But Rik was from Earth, so maybe the colony's laws didn't apply in his case.

Rik paused, whispering to her over his shoulder. "Careful. There's something ahead on the right. Stay behind me."

Deleen drew close. After another twenty paces or so, a small clearing emerged. Blood stained the grass with dark smears. Deleen blinked at the sight. Work of the deer hunters most likely. Skirting Rik, she saw what they'd left behind. They'd taken the head and left the carcass in the open. Trophy hunters. They had no respect for the life they had taken. Disgust churned her gut. This shouldn't be happening on Colony Five. That deer had died for nothing, its meat left to rot.

A bird dragged a piece of raw flesh away from the large wound on the carcass where the head had been hacked off. Large grey worms were visible through the holes they left in the hide. It looked like they had kept shooting at it even after it was down. Rik motioned with his right hand, indicating she move around the kill. He followed but checked everywhere. "What's wrong?" she asked, after they left that scene behind.

"Predators might be drawn by the scent of death."

Deleen eyed the bush. "I'm not sure there are any large predators, except humans and Oomrats and maybe Nightworms. Those little buggers can get quite big and aggressive." She wiped at a stray hair and shook her head. "What a waste of a deer, though. Grandpa would have been so angry about that. He always said you hunt for need, not for sport. He didn't like that hunting was frowned upon but complied with the restrictions. This though, well, he'd be wanting to kick some butt."

Rik glanced at her. "Yes, that is a good principle to follow. But do your people need to hunt for food?"

Deleen studied him and then looked away. "Not really. The deer is bred for export. I believe they are shipped live but I'm not sure if it's for food or just ..." she shrugged. "I suppose I should know."

Rik said nothing and turned his attention to the path they were following, which appeared to be an animal track. He glanced down at his wrist monitor, which was blinking green. "What's that?"

"It's telling me that Mac is still alive, but Bates is ... is blinking."

"Oh." What else could she say? So many of the cold soldiers were dead and she had stood by and done nothing. People who were like Rik when revived were living, breathing people.

"Mac is not far now."

"Your deputy? Is Mac as big as you?"

"I've worked with Mac for a while now. She's solid muscle and a bit shorter than me, but she'd dwarf you."

Deleen blinked. "She?"

"Yes, MacKenzie prefers the pronoun she."

Deleen had an odd reaction to this news about Mac. Territorial perhaps. Was she attracted to Rik? That was a new experience. They kept walking while Deleen digested that. "Is she a close friend?"

Rik peered over his shoulder, his expression not changing. "What are you asking me?"

"Oh, nothing. Never mind." Deleen's face heated. She was not jealous, she told herself. No way. She didn't go in for jealousy or ownership or partnerships. That's why she used the clinic, Liaisons—because there was no ownership or feeling of relationship. She had her favourites, but that was preference. Some people, men, she meshed with better than others.

"We have never been lovers," he said, watching her. "I'm not her style."

"Oh? It's good to know, to understand the relationships between ... er ... people." She said this in a straightforward way, hoping it came across as intended.

"Yes, I agree."

They walked on for another hour or so.

"So, how are we going to revive Mac?" she asked.

"The normal way," he replied as he pushed up a branch so it didn't brush against his umbrella head piece.

"But what if the person who is ... I mean the owner of the property where she is stashed, I imagine in a bunker ... what if they don't know she is there? What if they warn us off or call the administration?"

He was quiet for a moment. "We'll assess the situation when we get there. My parameters do not include harming civilians, unless there is a demonstrated threat."

"That's a relief. Does your tech let you sync with Adnet? We might be able to find the layout of the property." The universal network held all the colony's information.

He was silent for a minute or two. "Attempts at access have failed."

"I could try my access code." Deleen flashed a grin. Her access would give them lots more information than was generally available with public access. Her personal was in the pack, fully charged and switched off.

"I wouldn't recommend it. If they can identify you, where you are, then they can track us."

Deleen considered the handshake protocol required and agreed. Her link up would be traceable if they were looking for her. If they weren't, it wasn't too much of a hassle as the buffer where access attempts were filed would be flushed in a day or two depending on the number of times access was requested. "Could they detect your attempts?" she asked.

"No. I used a piggyback signal. Not traceable, unless the security protocols are set to look for that."

"They aren't."

He glanced at her. She shrugged. "I'm the Deputy Head of Security. Currently on leave. I know the computer and network protocols because I manage them. At least I'm hoping I will still be deputy head when whatever is going on settles down."

"If you have an infestation of Gogola it may take some time."

"Infestation?" She did a double take, a sudden quiver of fear in her gut. "They sound like insectoid aliens."

He glanced her way. "No, but they are fierce fighters. If they have taken control, it may take a while to dislodge them and it will be at a cost. From what you have told me, they have taken out most of the colony's defences by stealth and infiltrated the administration."

"Yes, except for the cold soldiers which they are targeting now."

He looked her in the eye and nodded once, definitively.

"I still don't understand why we didn't know about you or these Gogola or a war. It is unnerving to say the least and makes we question everything I know and have learned about our history."

Rik shook his head. "I agree it's strange. Someone must have purposefully altered the records and interfered with the culture to do that. Like I said before, we should not have been forgotten."

"But that interference must have been going on since the establishment of the colony. There has to be a reason someone would cover it up back then. Someone high up in the administration."

They'd been walking for hours. Her feet ached, her calves twitched, and every muscle rebelled. Anger overrode her fatigue. She was having a hard time understanding the scale of effort required to carry out the machinations that could allow a coup to occur. And why she, as Deputy Head of Security, had missed them.

As they walked through the night, she mused that nothing strange had occurred until she was forced to go on leave. She felt stupid and betrayed and scared. The appointment of the new administrator had raised alarm bells, a faint tingling in the mind. But the calls to bring out the cold soldiers and the burnings? It had happened so quickly. It was madness. The people had lost their minds. Sheer, utter madness.

* * *

After another all-night trek, according to the map they would reach the next bunker within the hour. Rik's enhanced vision had picked up nothing untoward. Ahead were signs of habitation—outbuildings, fences, livestock and fields of grain. The distant whine of a motor indicated that the farm was currently inhabited, which crushed his hopes of it being deserted. It would have been easier to recover Mac if no one was in situ, with the risk of exposure and resulting casualties much lower. If the owners were home, he'd have to negotiate with civilians and there would be witnesses, putting them in danger. Then there was the unpredictability of civilians; he may have to use lethal force to secure Mac if the situation required it. Although he would rather not against a farmer. These kinds of moral dilemmas annoyed him. He had to protect the colonists, but he needed Mac to do that. She was his second in command and a fierce warrior. He needed her to help recover the rest of his troops.

He couldn't expect all civilians to be as helpful as Deleen. She hadn't known why knowledge of him stored in the bunker was hidden, but she had worked out she had been programmed to forget. That she remembered and had the courage to revive him, made him grateful to her. To be burned, assassinated while still frozen and helpless, was not how he'd want to go. When the time came, he wanted to look death in the eye and face it straight on. He'd like to know what he was dying for, to know that his sacrifice had meaning. A wave of anger and despair filled him momentarily when he thought about the demise of the others, his comrades in arms. He punched down on the memory of Deleen recounting the sight of burnt sarcophagi, charred bones, bonfires.

Those he had held dear had been murdered and he had to stop further killings.

The sun was beginning to peep over the horizon, burnishing a light smattering of clouds amber. The *rat-a-tat-tat* of a machine echoed through the trees.

As Deleen moved past him, he grabbed her arm. "Wait up a moment."

She paused and turned. "What is it?" She was looking worn out, but at least had stopped complaining about it.

"Just a tractor. There are people in residence, so we need a strategy," he said, nodding to the buildings ahead.

She looked him up and down and then glanced over her shoulder at the farmstead. "Right. Best I handle this. You stay out of sight. I can talk to the owner, tell him I'm a neighbour in trouble. Do you know where the bunker is located?"

"Far side, about two hundred metres behind the main building."

She turned around and studied the landscape, her hand shielding her eyes from the rising sun. "Well, as the land around the house is cleared and in paddocks or corralled, there's no way to sneak in there without being seen. If I distract them, you might be able to sneak into the bunker."

As the sun rose higher, there would be too much light for stealth and he didn't want to spend the day in a shelter, not when they were this close to reviving Mac and could be discovered in any case. He thought through alternatives. They could try it at night, but would have to backtrack to the woods a few kilometres or take cover in one of the buildings. He glanced down at his wrist and saw the green light of Mac's unit. Bates was faint now. He didn't know yet if that was because he was too distant or whether something had happened to him or his cryo unit. They had to go with Deleen's plan.

It grated on Rik to have her go into danger for him, but he didn't think his other options held water. Her plan was sound. She was a neighbour after all. He could not pass for a colonist, but he could cover her in case of trouble. There were two lives at stake here, or three, if you counted Mac.

"Okay. You go in, but if I fire a warning shot, you drop. Read me?"

"Yes, sure," she said, her face dropping as she took in his weapons. "You won't have to shoot."

He shook his head. "Be prepared. Any sign of trouble. Yell and then drop, take cover and I'll come in."

She nodded, squeezing her hands together. "Try not to kill anyone. They are innocent in this."

He nodded, acknowledging her point. After taking off the umbrella hat, she shrugged off her packs and placed them on the ground. Wiping her hands on her trousers, she shook her shoulders and then walked off, straight to the homestead. She was dressed in fatigues but that was not that unusual, or so he hoped. He watched her climb through the rail fence, her head tracking to both sides. Good, she was being careful. Next she started walking in a wide arc and he wondered why. A dog's bark and growls filled the air, and he understood her caution. As she walked, he changed positions and he saw the animal, held back by chains, straining to get to her.

The front door opened. A tall, thin dark-complexioned man stood there. He couldn't hear what was said, but Rik could tell the man was tense as he watched the body language and the changes in his heat through infrared. He wished he hadn't agreed to this plan. The man was scared, wary. Deleen might be a civilian, but she was his civilian.

* * *

"Stay where you are," the man said to Deleen as he blocked the darkened doorway. His left arm was in view, the right appeared to be gripping the door jam. She couldn't see into the darkened hallway behind. There could be no one there, or a pack of aliens. She resisted the urge to look back to where Rik was watching.

She slowed to a stop and peered at the man, who was shadowed by the front porch. Sunlight hit her in the eye, but she squinted rather than move her hand to shelter her sight. "Hi," she said with a smile, keeping her arms at her sides. She was wearing a side-arm, but hoped that wasn't obvious. "Sorry to bother you. I'm from Milo ranch. I'm Deleen. Deleen Milo."

"What do you want?" he said, not showing any recognition of her name. He didn't offer his name. She couldn't quite recall it either.

"I'm in a bit of a bind and I could use some help."

The man tensed. "Why are you coming around here bringing trouble with you?" This came on a shout.

She bit her lip, understanding the man's fear. "I'm sorry. Trouble is coming anyway."

"So you say." He lifted his chin. "Who's your friend?"

"My friend?" Itchy sweat trickled down the small of her back.

The guy lifted his chin, jerked it to the scrub where Rik waited. "Yeah, him I saw on the surveillance footage."

They hadn't noticed the surveillance and wondered at it. "He's been helping me, Mr ... um."

"Okafor," he supplied and lifted a gun into view. So that's what the right hand was doing. Now he had his left there, securing the muzzle in her direction. She nodded and smiled a little, but kept her gaze on the farmer. The weapon had surprised her.

Keeping her voice steady she answered. "I wouldn't have made it this far without him."

"He's one of them frozen soldiers?" He lifted the gun, aiming it at her.

She looked him in the eye. "Yes. He is. He was in a bunker at my farm. He's been there since First Settlement, hidden for a reason. To be awakened when the colony was in danger."

Okafor's expression paled and he licked his lips. She could see the sweat sheen on his brow. Something other than her made him nervous. "How do you know there's danger?"

She pursed her lips, studied him a bit longer and then relaxed. "Why are you pointing a gun at me?"

He lowered it in response to her question. "I'm sorry." Then he shifted the gun back inside. "They came here."

"Who?" she asked, quickly scanning the yard for evidence there were others there.

"Government officials, they said," his shoulders were shaking. "Looking for something."

She nodded slowly, acknowledging his words. "Did they hurt you or your family?"

He cocked his head, studying her. "They threatened us, roughed me up some. And then next day you show up here. Why?"

She held her hands to the side. "We don't want to hurt you or make things worse. We've come for your soldier. There is one in your bunker."

He reached for the weapon, but didn't aim it at her, just had it ready. "I told them and I'll tell you the same. There is no frozen soldier here. No bunker neither." He lifted the gun again.

Her hands went up. "Please, lower your weapon. I won't harm you." Okafor was jumpy. She hoped that Rik wasn't trigger happy.

He looked at the gun in his hands, then lowered it, put it back behind the door jam. "Sorry. But they said the same thing. Looking for bunkers. They didn't find one and I knew nothing about it. They believed me in the end."

There was a dark stain on his cheekbone. They'd hit him. Bastards. "But there is a bunker. We've come to take ..." She didn't want to reveal MacKenzie's gender. "The soldier away."

"Away? What do you mean?"

"We will be quick. You won't notice a thing." Deleen checked the sky wondering if a flyer would emerge before this negotiation ended, then wondered if the man was stalling. He seemed too nervy for that.

He shook his head. "I grew up here. I haven't heard of a bunker. Never seen anything that looks like one. My father bought this place from the MacKenzie clan and there was no sign of any on the plans."

Deleen relaxed a little. "I understand that you don't know about it. The bunkers and their contents were disguised. I only found mine because of a buried memory. Please, we don't have much time."

Okafor nodded vigorously, his gaze flicking up. "They took the plans away. They said they'll be back."

"Then I have to hurry. Do you mind if we try to find the bunker?"

The corner of his eyes turned down in sadness. "I don't have a choice, do I? It's either you or them." He stepped back inside and made ready to shut the door. "What I don't see, I can't tell."

"Hey, Okafor," she called before he shut the door. "You best get ready."

The door drew back and he stuck his head out. "Ready?" he said. "Ready for what?"

A whimper leaked out of the house, and she realised his family were there, hiding. "Leave. Go into hiding. If they're coming back, they won't leave witnesses." She was guessing here, but she had a gut feeling that this man's safety and that of his family were in jeopardy.

His shoulders sagged and he nodded slowly. "No choice then. Just do what you have to do and leave us in peace." He shut the door and she signalled for Rik to come in.

The dog barked, a loud and deep woof. Rik came into view, his muscular legs eating up the distance. He marched past her and, with a shake of her head she ran after him.

Rik insisted on leading the way as they skirted the main house and headed to the rear of the building. He had the tech, so Deleen didn't mind. An extensive park had been built there, with a formal garden and maze, as well as play equipment for children. She looked back over her shoulder, hoping the children would get out safely. If the flyer had visited here and searched the place, Okafor was quite right to be rattled. Her security team was quite small. It made her wonder who was manning those flyers. Who were these people?

Past the formal garden, there was a small hill topped by a tree and an ornate swing.

"The bunker is below that." Rik lowered his wrist with the blinking indicator on it.

They skirted the bottom of the mound, obviously man made. It was too regular to be natural. She thought that from the top you could probably see all around. A good lookout to see if they were going to get flyer company. She suggested it, but Rik shook his head.

"No point. I think we know they'll come. Best to spend our effort on getting Mac out."

She ran her hands along the grassy sides of the hill, as she'd looked along the ground for signs there was a road or other structures under the soil, but her inspection had drawn a blank. "Okay, but I can't see any doors, or evidence of doors."

Rik stayed close, performing his own examination as they travelled towards the rear of the mound. The green grass blocked out a view of the house.

"I'm going to engage LIDAR." Rik explained, scanning the base and moving his head from side to side. He stepped further around and then came back. "Looks like the door is here, beneath the turf."

She bit her lips. The thought of digging through was not a good one. She looked down at her hands. Her manicure was pretty destroyed as it was. A noise beside her and she looked to Rik. He'd taken out a weapon and was checking its charge.

"Stand back. I'm going to burn it off."

A queer feeling in her gut at the sight of the weapon, she took a lot of steps back. Luckily the rear of the mound was skirted by some woods, a bit more ramshackle than the formal garden. Their activity was less likely to be seen by an approaching flyer or casual observer. But from above everything would be visible and vulnerable.

The day was growing quite warm and the shade from the nearby trees cooled her. They'd not stopped to rest after traveling all night. It was surprising how little fatigue she was experiencing if she didn't count the fuzzy, heavy head sensation. Too much adrenaline, she thought. Mac needed rescuing and the other one, the one with the irregular flicker on Rik's wrist. The longer they delayed, the less chance for success.

Rik initiated the weapon, which emitted a low heat pulse and a surge of air. The focus point of the pulse pushed away grass and earth and dissolved any residue. Within a couple of minutes, the bare metal doors of the bunker were exposed. She wondered how long they had been shut up. It looked like a long time. The farmer had not been the original landowner, unlike her own family's land. The bunker wasn't on the plans. No one had been tending the bunker. She shook her head slightly, wondering what they would find inside.

The door looked sealed shut. "Can you open it?" she asked.

He looked it over with his nanotech-enhanced eyes. "It needs a code," he commented after a while.

She blinked at him. "A code?"

"Yes, I am trying various versions of known codes in use by the unit and transmitting them."

Nothing was happening.

"But my door opened."

"It was gene coded."

"Oh," she commented, filing that away for later. "Then how will we open it?"

"There would be an alphanumeric code as well as the DNA recognition but none of the standard codes are working."

Time was slipping by and that made her nervous. More time for the farmer to have second thoughts about them waking a cold soldier and contacting the administration. More time for the flyer to return seeking them. "This was the MacKenzie farm."

Rik cocked his head. "Yeah, and that's strange because MacKenzie had no family connections with Colony Five. Hers had travelled to Colony Twelve. "The custodial family was Parsons, I think."

"Try that," she suggested.

He glanced at her and gave a slight shake of his head. "That doesn't work."

"Try combinations. Mac Parson or something like that."

Rik shook his head. "We don't have time for this shit. I'll have to blow it."

She stared at the stubborn door, nodding slowly as she agreed. "Looks like it will be the only way. Unless they used a numbering system."

Rik turned to her. "Like our unit numbers?"

She shrugged. "Maybe."

Rik paused, transmitting a code she could neither see nor feel.

A minute later the doors shuddered and then parted. Rik flicked his eyes in her direction, and she didn't even blink. The stakes were too high to point score.

A dark rectangle on the other side was all they could see of the corridor. A musty stink rolled out to greet them, confirming her observation that it had been untended for many years.

Stress lines furrowed Rik's cheeks. He was clenching his jaw and she guessed he was having the same thoughts. Only that steady blink of green light gave them hope that Mac remained untouched and frozen.

Rik crouched down and stepped into the unlit corridor as she followed close behind, using the glow of his tech to light her way. She didn't want to be kicking her heels on the outside while he woke up his colleague. There was no way she was waiting for the flyers to come searching. He didn't appear to want her to stay back either, looking over his shoulder and jerking his chin to encourage her forward.

"Does MacKenzie have a first name?" She'd like to use it when they met.

"Mackenzie, or Mac."

"Her name is Mackenzie MacKenzie? That's not very imaginative of her parents."

"Don't say that to her face?" Rik warned mildly, his voice drifting over his shoulder as they traversed the dark corridor.

What was this Mackenzie MacKenzie like? Would Rik change because of Mac? Would she be jealous, or Mac of her? *That's ridiculous.* No emotion required or needed. She lifted her chin, her lips firm. No emotion at all, her mind whispered back at her. She didn't do relationships. Besides now wasn't the time.

The dark passage opened into a room. The overhead lights flickered on, not all of them, but enough to reveal a large room similar to her family's bunker. She blinked as her eyes adjusted to the blue-tinged light. Ahead was the now familiar cryo unit up against a bank of metal cabinets. Rik scanned the room then gave her nod. "No one has been here."

Deleen looked at the floor and saw only their footsteps had made an impression in the dust. The dank smell wafted strongly from the left and she could see the wall and part of the floor bubbled with damp stains. Water leakage, she assumed.

Rik made a beeline for the rig, stepped up to it almost reverently and peeked through the lid. Then he placed his weapon flat on the ground by his foot and keyed switches in rapid succession. The unit, she noticed, was slightly different from the one Rik was in. A later model perhaps.

As the machine hummed to life, Rik darted over to the bank of cabinets, hitting one after another until he drew out sealed packets of clothing. He ripped them open, the packaging sending dust into the air, revealing a T-shirt and shorts. These he placed at the foot of the unit. He was making sure Mac had something to wear. There was something tender and sweet in that action.

Deleen wanted to watch Mac emerge but knew herself to be a potential intruder in the moment. To distract herself, she looked around her at the bank of cabinets. On opening some doors, she saw the supplies were stashed haphazardly in shelves and layered in grime, most looking unusable. A stash of food packets was swollen, and some had split, adding to the general odour of decay in the bunker. Another cabinet and the food packets were just remnants of packaging and dark smears. From the lack of rankness, she guessed the spoilage of this compartment of food had happened a long time ago.

After checking a few packets, she doubted any of it could be salvaged. Then she noticed that there was another room behind the cabinets and decided to check it out. She rounded the corner, discovering a warehouse-sized compartment with large doors at the opposite end. Large, fabric-draped mounds obscured whatever was beneath. She peeked under one and saw it was a vehicle. Before she could investigate further, the low hum of the cryo unit opening drew her attention back to Rik.

The door clanged shut behind her as she headed back to the cryo unit. The cover of the sarcophagus slid back, followed by a loud inhalation. A dark-skinned hand gripped the side. Next came the head and the upper torso of the biggest woman Deleen had ever seen. Mostly naked, with glowing ebony skin, thick-muscled arms, she had short cropped black hair and deep coffee-coloured eyes—eyes glittering with nanotech.

Deleen thought Mac was of mixed descent—Chinese, African and something else—which didn't account for her size. Perhaps these cold soldiers had been genetically modified as well as implanted with tech.

Genetic modification was banned on Five, and all the other colonies as far as she knew. No cross-species meddling, no mixing or enhancing for the sake of experimentation. Instinctively, she recoiled at the thought of these soldiers and what they represented, then she relaxed her jaw, realising she was reacting to prejudice. These guys were human and from Earth. She knew that. Rik was a warm-blooded, thinking and feeling human being.

Mac took a moment, blinked, sucked in large, audible breaths and shook her head as if trying to clear her mind. She visibly shuddered, then noticed Rik. She looked at him, just looked and then a smile grew, transforming her face with joy. She reached out a hand and he took it, clasping with a weird grip, something military she suspected. He handed Mac the clothes he'd prepared. These she quickly donned.

With a nod from Mac, Rik helped his comrade to climb out of the sarcophagus. She was shaky at first, but when she steadied, they embraced, slapping each other on the back. Rik stroked her back and spoke hurriedly to her in a low voice. Deleen caught enough to know he was giving her a quick, urgent sit rep. Mac let out a sob and exclaimed, "no!" before controlling her outburst and taking on a stoic expression as Rik spoke to her soothingly but firmly. "It's all right. You're back," Rik said. "You're safe. Alive."

MacKenzie remained impassive and stepped back, assumed a formal posture. No salute or any of the other types of obeisance she'd read about it books that featured Earth military.

Unlike Rik, MacKenzie had not been fully naked. She had been wearing a covering over her breasts and genital area. Perhaps clothing in those contraptions was optional. It did not surprise her that Rik might have wanted to be naked on waking. Or maybe they didn't have a choice, or the procedures changed if they went in at different times.

"How long?" MacKenzie asked in a surprisingly light voice.

Rik went back to the cabinet and pulled out military fatigues similar to his own. These he handed to her. She put on the button-down shirt over her T-shirt. Her limbs, Deleen noticed, were heavily tattooed, as well as muscled. Each muscular leg thrust into the trousers and she did them up. He handed her a belt.

MacKenzie was full of contradictions. Her focus had been entirely on Rik. She hadn't looked around the bunker or at Deleen. He had been a bit that way at first, as if it took time for his body to wake up and for his tech to kick in.

Rik told her how long and Mac whistled as she punched her feet into the boots Rik had put out for her. Looking down, she straightened her clothes but otherwise gave no other reaction to what Rik was telling her. There were no tears, no talk of ones that had been lost. Deleen wondered how long they had expected to sleep. Did they leave anyone they cared about behind?

Once dressed and standing next to Rik, Mac seemed less enormous than on first appearances. Shorter by a hand, but easily over six foot, she was broad and muscled, with a slim waist and generous behind. Rik was much more solid, and bulkier all round, but still

Mac was impressive. Deleen had never seen a woman like her in her life.

Turning her head slightly, Mac noticed her and nodded an acknowledgment. "Ma'am." She turned back to Rik. "A civilian?" She flexed one inked arm before tugging down her sleeve and doing up the cuffs. Her expression showed mild surprise and thankfully no judgement.

Deleen was definitely a civilian, but hopefully not an impediment. She had helped, hadn't she?

"Yes, a civilian." He paused and glanced at Deleen. "My civilian."

Deleen blinked at that. If she was his civilian, did that mean he was her cold soldier? He had been on her land, had been her family's responsibility. Yet, there was something more there, a kind of possession rather than a notional attribution.

Now wasn't the time to point out a few things. However, the connotations of being owned sent a sliver of fear shooting through her middle. At first, she wondered why the notion had her feeling uneasy. Then she remembered that she was good at blocking out things, like the existence of Rik in the bunker, so she pushed the gut-churning unease back into the place where she never looked, where she hid the things she didn't want to look at or remember. The psychologists had buried the past incident deep. She knew that on an intellectual level. She didn't remember the details, or feel the emotional impact, but she knew in a general sense what had happened. She remembered enough to be wary. A relationship gone wrong in her late teens. A very bad experience. Now that she thought about it, maybe that was how she had forgotten about the bunker and the cold soldier, about Rik. Therapy had buried more than intended, perhaps.

A chill crept along her exposed skin as if someone had a target there. She turned slightly, just to make sure they were alone. Then, rubbing her arms, she tried to ignore the sensation. She didn't want any more memories leaking into her mind. She was already dealing with the consequences of one major leak: Rik!

"Deleen. Come here." Deleen took the few steps required for the introduction. Mac dwarfed her. Her skin was brown, with dark freckles across her nose. Her eyes were large with thin eyebrows arched above, her cheeks full, and her mouth was well-formed with red lips.

"As you know," Rik said conversationally. "This is Mackenzie MacKenzie, but she answers to Mac. She's our transport specialist." Facing MacKenzie, he indicated Deleen. "Citizen Milo."

Mac's eyes widened fractionally as she looked Deleen up and down. "Commander Milo's descendant?"

Deleen stepped up to the tall woman, trying not to be intimated by her size. Putting out her hand, she said, "Yes, I am. Pleased to meet you."

Mac grinned and shook her hand. "I like you. Most people step away when they see me."

"You are surprising, I'll say that. In a nice way."

"Good. I like that you're upfront." Mac grinned and it transformed her face into a merry giant's.

Deleen shot a look at Rik and then back at Mac. "Rik mentioned transport?"

Mac's thin brows lowered over her eyes. "Yes, the situation is not good I take it. I just need a minute for my tech to wake up."

Rik nodded. "I'll help you get ready and fill you in. Expect an attack soon."

"In that case, I'll go and check on the entrance. Have a peak. See what the residents are doing." Deleen turned to the corridor.

Before she'd taken a few steps the tell-tale sound of a flyer reached them through the open hatch.

"Wait, come back," Rik ordered her.

Deleen stopped in her tracks, heart thudding. They were doomed. She didn't need an order to understand that. She bolted over to where Rik and Mac were standing, Rik with gun ready, jaw clenched. "It's too late," he said. "We need to move. Go check the transport and get it ready, Mac."

Mac bounded away, kicking open the door to the next room and disappearing inside.

"Have they found us?" Deleen said, feeling her pulse racing and trying not to let the palpitations worry her.

Rik had that faraway look. "They've reached the farm. It won't take them long to circle around and find the bunker, now it's open. They won't even need to question the farmer."

Deleen counted to ten. The mound shuddered around them. Rik

grabbed her to him, sheltering her head under his arm. Dirt rained down on their heads and a crack creaked open in the ceiling. Deleen screamed, thinking this was it. She was going to buried alive.

"Move!" Rik shouted as he pushed her in the direction Mac had taken. Over the sound of the flyer came the whiz of a missile. Rik pulled her along by the hand and shoved her through the door MacKenzie had kicked through. The explosion blew the door open behind them. Deleen went sprawling and then Rik landed on top of her, holding his weight with his hands and sheltering her from falling debris. Her ears were ringing from the blast wave, but she detected the rumble of a motor through the floor underneath her. Mac had one of the machines working.

Rik grabbed her hand and tugged. "Come on."

For a moment, she resisted. "But how do we get out?"

Despite everything, he grinned at her. "Don't worry. Mac will deal with it." He inspected packets that had fallen from the supply shelves. "Here," he slapped the contents of a packet against her chest. Then he reached for another and tore the seal. "Put this on your head."

He put a disc on his own head. On contact it expanded and hardened to become a helmet. She did the same. He slapped another packet onto her shoulder and armour wrapped around her as it did on him. Less chance to be brained by falling debris. Rik rummaged through some more packets and then grabbed a couple more.

A flash and a gust of air knocked her from her feet. Rik landed on one knee and looked behind them. "They have found this room. It doesn't look like they are interested in negotiating." He stood and brought her with him, hand on elbow as he propelled her in front of him. "Hurry. They'll come through and fight hand to hand or finish the bunker with another missile."

Deleen was beyond screaming. Her mind couldn't take this in. The administration she knew did not blow people up.

Yet, even as she shook her head, she knew that this wasn't the administration she thought it was. Taking people away for questioning? Sure. But blowing people up? That was different. It was something else entirely. Killing people who were frozen and unable to defend themselves was bad. Attacking them once animated was outrageous. She was a citizen and Rik was alive and a walking, talking person as was Mac. This was indiscriminate killing. A total disregard for human rights.

A number of vehicles ranged out in front of them. Mac was charging something that looked like a giant motorbike. It had two large, fat wheels at the rear that were taller than Deleen and handlebar controls set over a large, earth-eating front wheel with deeply grooved tread. It looked like it could climb a mountain.

"Get on!" Mac yelled. Rik tossed her the armour and helmet packets. She ripped them open with her teeth and slapped them against her body and head. The armour unfurled around her body. Now they were all protected, but Deleen didn't think the armour would stand against a missile or being buried alive under a lot of dirt and rocks. The bunker was about to collapse.

Rik lifted her up onto the giant bike and climbed up behind her, nestling her between Mac and himself. She was dwarfed by their size and weapons. "Hold on," Rik shouted. "I'm going to mesh our armour together for greater protection and stability. The armour on her back hooked to Rik's and her front to Mac. A crackle sounded in her ear.

"Can you hear me?"

"Yes!" Her gaze locked with his.

He nodded in acknowledgment.

The deafening sound of more munitions fire scared the life out of her. She wanted to scream at them that they were trapped, that there was no way out, but a sudden jolt silenced her. From the smell and the debris pouring down on them, Mac had just punctured a hole in the opposite side of the bunker where doors had once been, making an exit at the rear of the bunker. She let loose another shot and then the bike screamed out after it. The doors had been buried under a thin layer of dirt so there wasn't much debris to ride over.

Rik held onto the vehicle by sheer strength as they leaped and surged forward out into the open air. Deleen managed a peek over her shoulder at Rik behind her. He was sheltering her with his body, his jaw clenched, lips a thin line.

He caught her eye and nodded, a certain confidence in his expression. She wasn't believing that. Deleen gave him a thin-lipped grimace that would never pass for a smile.

The exit from the bunker happened so fast that she didn't know if the flyer had moved to confront them head on or whether Mac had turned to position herself. Still wide-eyed, Deleen saw the flyer drop into view, a brief flash from the launcher signalled the attack.

"Incoming!" Mac yelled.

A rocket punctured the air around them as the flyer exploded in a ball of flame. Then they were off so fast Deleen hadn't quite digested the fact that they had killed the pilot of the flyer and whoever else was inside. Before she could raise a protest, the trike's huge wheels crushed through the formal garden and flattened the children's playground equipment. She heard Rik's voice, and they slowed as they passed the main house.

Okafor was in the yard, kneeling, mouth slack in shock. Rik's voice, amplified by the com link, pealed over the roar of the motor trike. "Take yourself to safety. Take your family and supplies and leave now. They will come back and they won't be merciful." He then gave him a thumbs up.

Dirt and smoke wafted over the homestead. The farmer lifted his head, tears threading the grime on his face. He lifted his hand and gave a thumbs up in return. As they passed the homestead, they saw a transport stationed there, stacked with supplies. Okafor had missed escaping before the attack by minutes. At least he and his family appeared unharmed.

Once clear of the yards and outhouses, Mac gunned the engine and the trike leaped away, churning up the ground beneath them. "Where are we going?" Deleen asked over her helmet com link. "We're leaving a very big trail."

"To find Bates." Rik looked behind them. "The trail can't be helped. We need to be quick about it. He hasn't got much time." He pointed to his wrist unit. The green light was amber now, a slow blink of fading hope.

"We're no good to him dead," Deleen commented as she lifted her helmeted chin to indicate the obvious signs of their passage.

Chapter Eight

BATTLE

Rik held tight as the combat trike ploughed through the landscape. If his armour wasn't meshed with Deleen's she would have been thrown off a number of times. He suspected she was as unused to armour as she was to combat but had the ability to adjust quickly. He turned back to glare at the wide trail they were leaving, shaking his head. It was no good. Deleen was right. If there was another flyer close by, they could be tracked too easily. "Mac, change course. We need cover."

"Acknowledged." The motor slowed and Mac changed modes. The wheels changed to a smother tread, the thick grooves sliding back into the tires. They were moving fast still, but their tracks were less obvious. The vehicle was too heavy to pass without leaving any trail.

The trike swerved and they were jostled as they sped over a rock-strewn stream. It was a good way to hide their trace.

"Engage the screen," he said into his link.

"Engaged," she replied. "Seeking cover and disguising tracks."

She veered off to the left, revving the engine and cutting up a track. Then doubling back on the same track, she re-entered the stream. Ahead was a heavily wooded area. The vehicle slowed and Rik felt the screen engage as Mac cut the engine back and put the trike into hover mode. The trike skimmed over the field and then ducked around the first of the trees. As the woods thickened, Mac slowed further, so that they floated around the obstacles. Hover would be good for a short while, but it was only ever a short-term solution as it ate into the power cells.

"How long before we need to reengage traction?" Rik asked.

"I reckon we'll last ten minutes before we need to switch to conserve power."

Rik nodded. "Good." He touched Deleen on the shoulder to get her attention, then switched channels. "Del, are you okay? No injuries?"

Del grimaced and replied, "Besides a headache and ringing ears, I'm fine. What the hell was that manoeuvre? It was awesome!"

Mac chuckled. "There is a bit more this old girl can do."

Rik grinned tightly. He knew Mac words had a double meaning. The trike. Her. She was tough. Strong. Dependable. He was happy that Deleen was excited, rather than afraid. It had been a close call after all.

"So," Mac's voice filtered over the link. Her breathing was laboured, which was to be expected seeing as her body was still coming online and everything had happened so fast. No wonder her adrenaline was up. "Anyone want to tell me what we're up against?"

Rik filled her in on what he knew. Deleen added a few details. Mac whistled.

"Dead? Those guys were burned while they slept? Thank the universe it wasn't me. I know that's an awful thing to say, but when I die I want to go out fighting, not murdered in my bed. Who'd do that?"

"Old enemy, I think." He'd need to watch the gravity in his voice; he didn't want to unsettle his companions any more than he had to. His memories of the time before he went into cryosleep were still hazy. He was certain that the orders that came through said they were alien. Rik was also sure he had seen one of them once and what he'd witnessed looked human, or part human. The trouble was he didn't know for sure because of the state of his memory. He'd never had this much trouble remembering the time just before cryo before. It made him uneasy and angry, because he suspected tampering and that was wrong on so many levels.

"Gogola? But I thought they were gone into the cold of space."

Rik sighed. "Me too, but unless there's a new type of enemy out there, I'd say it's them. Until we are certain, we take care."

"Deadly force?" Mac asked.

It hurt him to say this. "Yes, until we have further information."

"But didn't we already kill someone—the pilot in the flyer?" Deleen interrupted.

Rik shook his head. "It was remote piloted. We didn't kill anyone."

Deleen sagged and let out a sigh. "Oh, thank heavens for that. I thought ... well you know what I thought."

"From now on, though, it's us or them." The battle lines had been drawn. Their enemy was out to kill and in return they had to kill to stay alive.

"What did you mean by cold of space?" Deleen asked.

"When the battle, war if you like, was over, the government shipped them out into space."

"Did you see that happen?" Deleen asked.

"No. It was reported to us before ... before we ..."

"Went into cold sleep," supplied Mac.

He saw Deleen bite her lip and frown.

"What?" he asked.

Deleen angled her head to the left, obviously thinking. "I'm wondering what they shipped them out in. That early on, there weren't that many ships and the big lumbering, colony ship is the administration now, repurposed into buildings."

Rik lifted his chin and met her eye. "It's what we were told. I do have that report in my memory."

"Me too," Mac added.

Deleen nodded, but it wasn't in agreement, just acknowledgement of what he'd said. "I hate to ask this, but can your tech be meddled with, your memories altered?"

Rik's mouth drew into a tight line. He knew the answer and as much as it challenged his loyalty to Deleen's great-grandfather, she was right. His memory could be faulty, as could Mac's. But she wasn't done undermining his certainty in the past.

"If they were sent home," she continued, "wouldn't they bring back reinforcements? I mean why would you send the aliens back out into space?"

Her logic floored him. It was so simple and yet he hadn't seen it, not then, and he was finding it hard to accept now. Rik let the memories of that time come forward, assisted by his nanobots, which stored information efficiently. "The commander," he began. Then corrected himself. "Your great-grandfather brokered a deal. He let them go. There had been enough bloodshed. Then the commander called for volunteers for cold sleep, in case we were needed again in the future. The rest of the service people, like your grandfather, blended with the settlers and the rest is history."

"Or not history," Deleen added.

Mac grunted as she re-established traction and reduced speed once they were in the woods.

"There is no record of the short war you fought, the cold soldiers, or these Gogola. Did you actually see their spaceship?"

Rik shook his head and then ducked a low-lying branch. Green flashed by. The green of leaves, of foliage and of ground ferns. "I never saw their spaceship. Not much was known about them," Rik replied, a feeling of unease in his gut. "We were just told what we needed to know."

"They came from nowhere," Mac said, voicing a thought that was growing in his mind. "They just wanted to kill us."

"That's true," Rik agreed. "It wasn't what we were expecting. This section of space was devoid of life. Terraformers had changed and adjusted the suitable worlds and requested the colony ships be dispatched. They'd seen no sign of aliens out here. No one objected to our presence until we were here, maybe fifteen years into settlement."

"You said they wanted to kill you. Do you mean us?" Deleen asked.

Rik paused and thought about it. "I'm not sure I understand the quest—"

"She means did they kill the colonists, or just the soldiers, the special forces," Mac explained.

Deleen nodded. "Yes. That's what I mean."

Rik tried to remember, but there was a blank there. He recalled the fighting, but not statistics or reports of casualties among the civilian population. "I don't know. We definitely had orders to kill them."

"I heard rumours that women were taken," Mac added.

Deleen let out another big sigh. "Right then, have either of you seen these aliens up close," she asked. "Do you know what they look like?"

"Not up close," Mac replied, as she steered the trike around a large tree and over a fallen log to plunge over the other side. "What about you, sergeant?"

Rik let the memory come forward, inviting it in but hesitant just the same. "Only ghost-like glimpses through flames. They look humanoid but I wasn't sure if that was wishful thinking or brain fog. I had the impression they looked like cats maybe or lizards. The memory is so vague though. Cryo does that sometimes. There was definitely something different about them, something other."

"So," Deleen said in a calm voice. "We know an unknown alien force, which could be these Gogola, have taken over Five, infiltrated the administration and set about killing cold soldiers while you slept. Is this what they tried to do last time?"

Rik pursed his lips. "No, the attack was much more straightforward than that when they attacked our camp. This kind of coup had to take time and planning."

"A long time!" Deleen said. "You've been out of it over, what, a hundred years? It would take a lot of patience to wait that long. The changes were subtle. History altered and so on."

"That's true. If, as you said, they went home for reinforcements, the time would work. I mean if they went back to their planet."

Deleen groaned. "But that makes no sense either. I've not heard of any threats to Five and as I'm in security I should have. No intelligence reports from the other colonies discuss an alien threat, past or present. I'm not buying that this is the work of aliens.

"On the other hand, it makes sense that it must be the enemy you fought before, because who else knew you were there? The colony archives have no mention of you. I didn't know and I should have. I'm not the only one who didn't remember about the cold soldiers or why you were hidden."

Mac snorted. "You're saying I'm not famous? That no one knows how we saved the colony? That's crap. Geez."

"Someone hid the truth," Rik said with certainty. "Someone we knew and trusted. Had to be. But why? That's what I don't understand. Why wipe us from memory if the threat was going to return?"

"Decision time," Mac reported. "Wooded area is thinning. We will become visible again."

Mac sped up as the ground became clearer. Rik checked his wrist. "You reading Bates's signal, Mac?"

"Yes, and Oyuda too, who is reading steady."

Rik was pleased that another cold soldier's signal was reading now they were in range. He felt less alone and more able to deal with the threat. "Roger that. Bates first, I think. Prepare for trouble. His signal has been weakening steadily."

"I know. Changing direction in five minutes. We are closing in."

They travelled on steadily for an hour. Deleen grew quiet. Rik listened hard and then detected her breathing pattern. His civilian had dozed off. He checked his wrist and then calculated time and distance. He could go for two or three days on little sleep. His clocked-up biology was made for that. Del, though, was not going to be able to stay awake more than a day. He nudged her head and let her rest against his chest. While she slept, he filled Corporal Mac MacKenzie in on what he was thinking.

Mac could out cuss the best of them. She was none too impressed. "Why the civilian?" she asked after she had let off a stream of very descriptive and anatomically impossible instructions to aliens, civilians and the universe in general.

He pursed his lips as he thought over the answer. "She's important. I wouldn't be here without her. She knows this place, too. Society has changed since we went to sleep. We need someone like her."

"Yeah, I know all that. But, Rik ... you know ... liability ... distraction ..."

"Yeah, I know, but ... she's really strong. Strong in ways that are important to me."

Despite not really understanding why Deleen liked him and was attracted to him, he accepted it because he was feeling the same about her. Her thinking was a bit alien to him. The current social mores had altered, and he had to account for that. But she was important to him in all the right ways. He wanted—no needed—to protect her.

* * *

Deleen woke up from a doze. She didn't even know she'd been sleeping. One minute she was listening to Rik and Mac talk, the next she had slumped. She had come alert with her head resting beneath Rik's chin, their linked armour securing her in place. The trike travelled at a sedate pace, along a field and up over a number of low-slung hills that hemmed in a lake. She tried to call up the topography of this place from her study of Five's geography. By the size of the lake, they were near Lake Arika. They'd covered a lot of distance. Green fields spread out around them. She'd never been this far south.

"You okay?" Rik's voice sounded in her ear.

"Yes, sorry. I ... er slept."

"No need to apologise. We are nearing Bates's bunker."

Deleen nodded and then noticed something strange and peered around Mac's body to get a better view. Black angry smoke spewed into the sky like an angry finger. "That doesn't look good."

"Scans indicate no activity," Mac reported.

"Does that mean who ever attacked is gone?" Deleen asked.

"Maybe," Rik commented. "We will keep eyes open for incoming. They could be using shields. We have them, so we have to assume they do too. Bates's signal is flashing. If they used remotes they might have missed him."

"What can I do?" Deleen asked.

"Keep your eyes open and stay out of trouble," Mac said, in a not-too-friendly way as she slowed down on the approach to the farm. The whole place looked wrecked, as if there had been a full-on battle.

"Follow orders," Rik added.

The trike pulled to a stop in a copse of trees about a half a click from the scene of destruction. "You reading Bates?" Rik asked Mac.

"Minimal readings. Could be a malfunction," Mac suggested, a touch of hope in her voice.

"He could be dead." This came from Rik with little emotion, but when Deleen glanced at him, she detected sadness in his expression through the plate of his helmet. "Disengaging armour mesh." Deleen was now free to move independently.

The two soldiers grabbed weapons that had been resting in slots by their feet. Deleen hopped off the trike with a lift from Rik. He passed her a handgun. "Just in case you need it."

Deleen checked the safety and the charge.

Mac grunted. "Be careful where you point that thing. I don't want another hole in my butt."

Deleen lowered the weapon and took her finger away from the trigger, a bit annoyed at the comment from the cold soldier. Deleen was not that incompetent.

"That's better." Mac said. "I feel more comfortable already."

"Cut the chatter," Rik commanded.

Deleen lifted the visor on the helmet and could see better. Rik and Mac kept theirs down but they had tech to enhance their senses.

Comms went silent. Deleen shadowed Rik, who motioned Mac to approach from the other side. Deleen coughed as smoke billowed over her. It smelt like burnt flesh and fuel. Someone had died here.

She blinked and wiped her eyes, not sure that it was only the smoke that caused her tears. Some innocent colonist had died here, maybe with their family. What about the soldier? The friend of these two with her. How was she going to deal with them and possible bad news? Her head reeled at the thought.

Smoke cleared up ahead and she saw the old man, the remains of him at least. He reminded her of her grandfather, similar age and build. Half his body was burnt away or blown off. She averted her gaze, as she didn't want to puke, and kept walking. Not since she'd found her grandfather passed away had she seen a dead body up close.

The burning bodies of the cold soldiers she had seen were from a distance, so not so immediate. There was no point in losing it now because it had finally hit home. She punched down the hysteria that had been rising up her throat and focused. She'd have time enough for grief when this thing was done. If she lived long enough to mourn.

Rik crouched down and she sheltered behind him, trying to glimpse what he'd seen. The bunker was exposed, punctuated with holes. Rik lifted his hand and motioned for them to follow. He gestured to his eyes and Deleen kept her head moving around, her eyes on anything that moved. She didn't have the luxury of sensors, but she had eyes and instincts. Nothing seemed to be living. No activity, Mac had said.

Deleen could hardly breathe from the smoke and fumes when they entered the tunnel. Light flickered ahead, red and gold like flames. Inside the chamber, they lowered to their bellies. The air was clearer. The sarcophagus was there, but looked like it was open. The light panel beside it was dead.

Rik motioned Mac ahead and pulled out his weapon, sighting along it. Mac elbow-crawled, large weapon in her big hands in front. Deleen was impressed with her speed and agility. She made it to the cryo unit. Paused, checked the vicinity and then darted upright, looked inside and then ducked down.

Deleen held her breath. Was he dead? Mac made a thumbs down sign, then crawled around the back of the unit. Perhaps this bunker had another room, another place to hide.

Rik's breathing sounded through the com link. She wanted to speak, but kept her mouth shut. She wasn't about to risk alerting whoever did this to their presence. Mac was out of sight. The wait made her mouth water and her stomach churn.

Minutes went by. She could sense Rik's tension as they waited. Then Mac appeared and waved them forward. Rik moved, keeping to his belly. Deleen crawled along behind, her breathing harsh. She wasn't trained for this and the movement only made her feel the aches and pains from the trek. She wasn't about to complain about it. Not now.

They reached Mac on the other side of the wall. She was kneeling beside a man, five-ten with a lean build. Deleen sucked in a breath. She didn't know if he was alive or dead.

"Report," Rik said, his voice coming through her helmet.

"He's alive, just. He's not talking, but it looks like he's been out of the unit for a day or two. Probably a malfunction or he was defrosted by the owners."

"Injuries?"

"None that I can see. I need the med pack."

Rik nodded. "You stay here. Keep down." Deleen gave him a thumbs up that she understood and lay down. Rik was gone for about five minutes, but it seemed longer. The med pack slid along the ground before he arrived. He was half crawling with supplies on his back. He pushed a backpack ahead of him.

"Del, fill these packs with food supplies." He tossed a few empty packs her way.

It was then Deleen saw the burst open cabinets were full of supplies. She leaped on them, keeping an eye on Mac as she worked on Bates. She drew out a scary-looking device and placed it over Bates's chest. She read the monitor. "He's fibrillating. Stand clear."

Bates's body jerked, once, twice. Mac checked his life signs then removed the device. It hadn't revived the man. She whacked him with a big, pressurised injection pack. Bates reacted.

"Adrenaline," Mac supplied.

Deleen opened an empty pack and shoved the food sachets in. They were near expiry date but looked intact and useable. Other assortment of supplies, she filled in the side pack—bandages, medicines, ammo and flat discs in sealed packages, which Rik and put there to be packed. The discs reminded her of the tech they'd been using, a kind of memory tech, which wasn't used routinely in the colony.

Bates revived and spoke in a slurred voice. Mac was giving him a brief and simple situation report. Bates's head turned towards Rik. He blinked a few times and lifted a hand. "Sergeant."

Rik nodded. "Private."

Rik grabbed the pack that Deleen had filled. "Bates is our comms man."

Deleen looked back over the trashed machinery. Bates's tools of trade had been put out of commission.

"Can you move, private?"

Bates waved a hand. "In a minute."

Mac shot Rik a nasty look. Deleen wondered what was going on. Mac grabbed some clothes for Bates and helped him dress. She whacked a disc on his head and it moulded itself into a helmet. The smoke was worsening so Del engaged her helmet visor.

Mac grabbed her weapon and a pack from the shelf behind her. Deleen tossed meal packs to her until she signalled, she had enough. Deleen grabbed some more meals and stuffed them into her shirt, and then found another pack and started to fill it too. It seemed like the right thing to do.

"Del, good thinking. I'll assemble a pack too. Corporal MacKenzie is going to take Bates on the trike. We're heading out on foot."

Her eyes widened. "But ..."

"The trike can't take all of us. Bates needs time to recover. Mac can grab some charged cells on her way out. They can reach the next bunker before we can. Mac can handle the situation there.

"Where's the other bunker?"

Rik helped Mac with Bates and Deleen carried two packs to where the trike was parked. "Another twenty clicks to the north and west," Rik supplied.

They said brief goodbyes and then Mac fired up the vehicle. The trike bulled its way over the terrain with barely controlled power, leaving Deleen with Rik in the middle of nowhere. Deleen repressed a groan. Trekking again.

Rik lifted his wrist. It was blinking green. "Oyuda is still showing green. We'll meet them there."

Rik disappeared into a shed and came out with a shovel.

"What are you doing?" Deleen asked, casting her gaze after the departed trike.

"I need to bury the old man."

After he buried the old man, Rik constructed a cairn. Deleen helped by fetching rocks from the destruction of the bunker. It had taken time, but Deleen was glad that they had. Rik demonstrated that he cared about life and people, more than those who were out to kill the cold soldiers. It was really important to her that he had this softer side to his nature. It helped her realise that she was absolutely doing the right thing and that he deserved her trust and loyalty. Particularly when she realised that his old commander was her great-grandfather Milo and how that might affect how he thought about her.

* * *

Under cover of night, they set out. The pack weighed against Deleen's back. She ached from carting rocks for the cairn, but it was a righteous sort of pain.

Rik scanned the horizon. "Move fast. We need to get under cover."

"Do you think another flyer will come?"

He met her gaze and shook his head. "No, given the amount of damage they did to the bunker, they likely believe they have cleaned it out. We were lucky we got here in time, but we don't want to hang around. We need to get to Oyuda."

"Will he make it?"

Rik didn't pretend he didn't know who she was referring to. Bates was alive but it looked dicey. The newly awakened cold soldier was pale, sweating and lacked energy. "I hope so," Rik replied. "If they can retrieve Oyuda safely, then I can work with four of us. Three is not much. Not really. It's not the one hundred and fifty I would ordinarily need to seek out who is doing this and remedy the situation."

Deleen studied his face and then looked down at the weapon now secured to her belt. "You have me, too."

At his reassuring look, all her fear washed away. She was ready to fight and save what she knew of Five. More than that, she wanted to know why there were secrets hidden from the populace. It was part of their legacy and they'd been robbed of that. She was also afraid of the answers, because that could reflect badly on General Milo, a revered First Family member. Her family. He was long dead, but her family had put great store in his bravery, his administration of the early days of the colony. She had been proud to be his descendant. Now, though, that pride was shaken. It was looking more and more likely that he had duped these cold soldiers.

Rik touched her arm. "Come on."

Deleen's muscles were already aching from helping with the cairn. Now with the pack and the quick pace of Rik's march, she was in agony. She licked her lips as she thought of the road ahead. It was another long trek and she'd had little sleep. Fatigue sent her mind into numbness and her heavy body just followed Rik, each step heavy and slow and slowing.

They entered the shadows beneath the trees and she retracted her helmet visor to look at the sky and the branches waving in the light breeze. Smoke still lingered here, but the air was clearing. She took a sip of water, wondering if she'd ever get the stench out of her nostrils and whether her body would ever feel normal again.

Even though she was exhausted, she fought her weariness to keep putting one heavy foot in front of the other. Rik passed her some dried meat, which she chewed as they walked. Some hours later, he called a halt. She was so mind numb she walked into him. He turned quickly, steadied her and then helped her sit on the ground and eased the straps of the pack off her shoulders. She sat and tried to keep her eyes open as he set up the shelter. Her chin kept resting on her chest as sleep tried to claim her. Then when the shelter was up and he'd laid out the bedding, he didn't need to ask. She went on all fours, heading to the opening.

"You first," he said handing her the portable bath unit. Nodding dumbly, she crawled through the opening and then turned around to take off her boots. Her feet were still outside the tent because she had enough awareness not to track dirt into their bedding. She blinked at the boots, for a moment not even knowing how to undo them or even when she'd acquired them.

Seeing her problem, Rik knelt down, undid the clips and slid them off her aching and swollen feet. She nodded wordlessly and drew them inside. Then, closing the shelter, she stripped off her clothes and ran the unit over herself from the top of her head to the bottom of her sore, red feet. She leaned down to sniff herself, relieved she no longer smelt of smoke and sweat. Then she called out to Rik as she covered herself with a sheet. He came in, retrieved her clothes and then took the bath unit. She wondered if he was cleaning her clothes as well. He was military neat, and she was too tired to care if her clothes stank to the high heavens. Later when he entered, dressed in underclothes, a skin-tight T-shirt and shorts that moulded to his butt, he put her folded clothes by the door. That answered that question. Deleen was so tired, she was too tired to sleep. Rik reached outside the door and brought his pile of neatly folded clothes and placed them next to hers.

"That's so nice," she murmured.

"Deleen?" Rik asked, but his voice sounded far away. That was the last thing she remembered before her eyes closed and her body, heavy with fatigue, sank into the bedding, perhaps even the earth below as she had the sensation of sinking into the ground. She was asleep.

* * *

Rik watched Deleen's sleeping face and wondered at her stamina. She was not trained for this gig. He didn't know why, but she hadn't complained once in their three-hour trek. It was just acceptance and diligence. Admiration for her filled him. He turned his head and watched her breathe. Normally he'd be wary of such sentiment, of attachment. He shrugged. They could all be dead tomorrow or the next day. What was the point of ignoring emotion, the feelings inside? He'd put his life on hold for over one hundred and thirty years for this moment.

What had that cold sleep taught him? That there was nothing there. Just a black endless nothing with no sense of self or time passing. It was like closing your eyes and waking up again with nothing in between.

Life was for living. He was living and breathing—a miracle of technology—and this woman who slept with such abandon in front of him was amazing. He studied his hand and opened and closed it. Since he'd been awake, his life had been in danger. Just the thought of those who died while asleep made his stomach clench. It could have been him, if not for Deleen. That was selfish he knew. Yet he could do nothing for them except save who remained and put an end to those who had orchestrated this slaughter. None of the men and women who had died had been given a chance to fight, to choose their destiny.

Closing his eyes, he thanked whatever fate had preserved him. Unravelling the mystery of the past was essential to understanding the present situation. For Rik they were inexplicably linked. If the colony had forgotten them, then it had been a deliberate manipulation. Somehow, Deleen had retained a memory of him. They hadn't had time to figure that out. When he looked at her, her red hair and freckles, he thought of Dr Siobhan McPhee. She'd captured Commander Milo's heart and the result of their legacy was here in front of him.

He'd give his life for this woman. Was it some kind of programming, some deep-seated instinct, or something else—a realisation of what was important after being dormant so long? He didn't know.

What he did know was that Deleen was his. His awakener, his soldier, warrior woman. And she was deeply asleep. He nudged her and she didn't even move. He nudged her again when she started snoring, her hands out to the side as she lay on her back taking up the whole bed.

He knelt down and then climbed in under the covers, moving her to her side and basking in her warmth. He was lying next to someone who wasn't revolted by him, someone who even liked him. He drank in the heat of her, the sweet clean smell of her. Her flesh touching his. Tears rolled down his cheeks and he buried his head in her hair. She was what it was all about. Being human. Protecting humans. It had been a long time since he'd experienced such a connection with another person. Shaking his head, he decided he better get some sleep. His sensors went quiet, set only to wake him if they detected a threat. He slept with his arms locked around her.

* * *

Deleen woke up warm, arms of steel around her. She turned to face Rik, wiggling under the arm that didn't budge. Rik's eyes were open.

"You're awake?" she asked.

"Yes," he whispered. The sound of his voice was so intimate that she caught her breath.

"What is it? What's wrong?" she asked, her gaze taking in the shelter and that everything seemed as it should.

"Please, Del," he said, again in a whisper, but his eyes tracked over her face as if committing every nuance to memory.

Her arms came around him and she squeezed. He sighed as she relaxed her grip. It didn't escape her notice that he was naked and lying close to her.

"Is this more hormones?" she asked.

"No. I just need ..." he said and then trailed off.

"Need what?" she asked softly, a forefinger trailing across his jaw.

"You," he replied. Something in what he said and how sent a thrill into her. Her breath caught and her eyes widened. He moved closer and caught her lips in a deep kiss. Now wasn't the time to analyse this, she thought. Just go with it.

Again, they kissed, exploring each other, squeezing together as if there was too much distance between them, as if they would suddenly be torn apart. Limbs entwined. Arms embracing. Mouths locked tight. Her fingers dug into his scalp and his fingers combed through her hair. Kissing was magical. It transported her. How did she not notice how wonderful kissing could be?

"That was amazing," Rik said softly as he pulled back. "Thank you."

Deleen wanted more but Rik just stopped. "What's wrong?"

"Nothing. I just need to concentrate on the task at hand."

"You're picking something up on the sensors?" She'd seen the elsewhere look in his tech-filled eyes.

He nodded. "It's just an animal. It reminded me not to get distracted."

Deleen just nodded. "Good night then." She closed her eyes and fought to process what just happened. It wasn't news to her that she was attracted to Rik. Until she had kissed him, she hadn't known he was attracted to her on deeper level. If they had sexual intercourse, maybe she could have dismissed the encounter like she did at the Liaison clinic. The slow, deep kissing though had engaged something deep, her emotions, her heart. It was a good thing he pulled back she decided. She didn't need romantic complications.

* * *

When she woke up, she was under the covers, alone. At first, she thought she'd dreamed their kissing session, but knew with certainty it had been real and that her emotions were engaged now. She remembered his entreaty. *Please.* It had come from the very heart of him, from the deep need to connect. For many years, she thought she didn't have the capacity to bare herself emotionally. Now she knew she did. There was desperation in their kisses, like there was no tomorrow and that every moment was precious, building to a black and deadly climax. Then, duty intervened. They had to focus on the task at hand. Throwing off the covers, she got herself ready to continue their trek.

Chapter Nine

OYUDA

As they neared the farm that housed Oyuda, they approached with caution. Rik motioned Deleen to drop to the ground. Smoke curled lazily from behind the homestead. That didn't bode well for the bunker being intact. As they continued to crawl closer, they could see the fat wheel of the trike sticking out from behind one of the sheds. Rik shook his head. He couldn't raise Mac or Bates on comms. The vehicle might appear intact from their angle of approach, but they couldn't be certain.

As they neared, Deleen could see signs of neglect on the property. The windows of the main house were broken, the wood on the verandah broken or missing. There was no livestock and she checked behind her and realised that the fields were overrun with weeds, the wheat gone wild. It was abandoned.

Her comm unit cracked. "Mac, report." Rik's voice was quiet but still full of command. No response.

Rik rolled toward her. "It doesn't feel right. Mac should have secured the place by now. Get your weapon ready."

She nodded once and unclipped the snub-nosed weapon she carried. She had no idea if she would be able to hit anything. She held it out in front of her.

"Keep the safety on. When I signal 'action' take the safety off. Your weapon will be live. Be careful."

Deleen licked her lips. "Okay." She wasn't happy about it. She didn't want to kill anyone. This was as close to a lethal weapon as she ever wanted to be. It was a small firearm, but deadly in a pinch.

When they reached the side of the main house they stood and walked out of shelter. The place was eerily quiet. A light breeze fluttered the wild wheat and weeds. A bit of trash rattled against the rail fence. Rik stepped ahead of her and checked the house through a window. He lowered a thin wire, one of his sensors, inside the house and plugged it into his wrist. She kept her gaze fixed on him and he shook his head slightly, signalling nothing was there.

He reeled the wire back in, looping it over his belt.

At a nod, he edged along the side of the house closer to the bike. She flattened herself against the side of the house and followed along behind.

Rik stuck his head around the corner and pulled back. A loud report killed the silence. She sucked in a breath at the close call. He lowered his sensor wire and made it crawl around the corner. The expression of his face became slack as he focused on the feed.

"Action," he said, and she unlatched the safety on her gun. He did the same for his larger rifle. It made a soft purring sound.

Rik dove to the ground, aimed and fired off a shot and then rolled. There was no return fire. She dropped to the ground, right behind Rik's booted feet. Rik rolled further, reaching the bike, which looked whole. There were no bodies to be seen. She stayed in the shelter of the house and looked behind her. There was something.

"Rik," she hissed into her com link.

He turned over, gun aimed behind her, but he didn't fire. "Oyuda!"

The man was shortish, five six. He was full Asian, she thought. He hadn't lowered his weapon. Rik ripped off his helmet. "Oyuda! Kazu, it's me."

There was no sign of recognition in the man's face. His skin was pale and his hand shook. Had he taken out Mac and Bates?

"Don't move, Del." Rik said to her. His voice was muffled through the helmet, but she nodded. Her weapon was held in both hands between waist and chest. Even if she was aiming for him, she didn't think she could hit the man.

Rik put his weapon down. "Kazu. You were in cold sleep. Corporal MacKenzie came to wake you up."

The words didn't appear to register. Oyuda was dressed, but in a haphazard way. The trembling in his hands increased. He started to babble. Something had gone wrong with the defrost, she suspected.

She kept her eyes on Oyuda, but she had detected movement behind him. It wasn't that she saw anyone, just a change in the shadows.

Oyuda aimed his gun. Not at Rik, but at Deleen. She breathed in and held it. Oyuda's gun went off. Wood chips showered her, and she lifted her arm instinctively. A growl out of nowhere and there were teeth coming for her arm. A goddam dog! She accidentally squeezed the trigger. Her scream of warning was way too late.

Mac barrelled into Oyuda, before he could squeeze off his next shot. Rik had bounded forward, too late to help Deleen, but close enough to get clipped by her wild shot. He shot the dog who was readying to attack her again. It happened so quickly.

Rik was on the ground, his breath hissing in her ear through the helmet comms. Mac cussed, swearing while she wrestled with Oyuda, who punched and kicked at her.

Deleen tossed her weapon away, leaped over to Rik in a flash, "Rik?"

His face was flushed, and his neck was red. He was holding his shoulder. "Winged me."

Hands over her mouth, tears filled her eyes. "I'm sorry. So sorry!" Fear made her blood pump and regret made her useless.

A noise made her look up as Mac thumped Oyuda in the side of the head and he went limp. "Stop whining, you fool. Deal with it," Mac hissed at her, eyes flashing with anger. "And pick up your weapon!"

It was enough to snap Deleen out of her panic. She snatched at her weapon and slapped at her leg pockets, as she had stuffed some bandages in there. "Just hang on," Deleen cried, sounding desperate.

Rik's body relaxed, he closed his eyes and sighed. "It's not bad." When she touched his shoulder, he hissed in pain. His tech-filled eyes snapped open. "Not your fault."

"Lie back," she begged, fumbling with a bandage. The protective seal was stubborn.

"I warned you she was a liability. Bloody civilian!" Mac growled.

Rik hissed. "Shut up. Protect our backs."

Deleen helped him pull his shirt and armour away and saw that she'd taken out a small chunk of his shoulder, flesh and muscle. It was a flesh wound, blood and black singe marks framed it. Her stomach roiled. She had hurt him. Never had she felt more like a liability than at that moment. "Mac is right."

"It's okay," Rik said, sounding more relaxed. "Meds releasing to ease the pain."

There was no time for self-pity. She toughened up and focused. "Nano?" She asked as she staunched the blood and then groped around her pockets for some cleaning solution. It was in her other leg pocket.

He nodded, jaw clenched. It still hurt all the same. She held a small spray. "This might sting."

She sprayed the wound. A shadow blocked the light. She took off her helmet to see better.

"Of all the stupid things to do. Giving a bloody weapon to a civilian," Mac said, scathingly.

This comment was aimed at Rik. "She needed a means to protect herself," he hissed back. Defiant, Deleen thought.

"Right. What about protecting us?"

"You have the job of teaching her. Now report."

"Bates is dead. Oyuda popped him while my back was turned. Looks like some kind of malfunction in his cryo unit sent him loopy. I haven't been able to read the stats on it."

"Sedate him and then get on it."

Mac swung around and eyed the still form of Oyuda. "I don't think he'll wake up soon."

"Doesn't matter. I want him under. He still has healing tech and that makes him unpredictable. He could wake up any time. You get a read out on his unit and then the recommended counter measures."

Mac frowned and then nodded. She spat on the ground, then rifled through the med kit on the bike, grabbing various items. She then knelt down, dosing Oyuda from a pressure syringe before heading back in the direction of the bunker.

Deleen sprayed more saline solution into Rik's wound. He stiffened and then relaxed. Next, she applied some antiseptic sealant. Undoing the package of bandaging she placed some wadding over the wound. Wincing as she did. "Can you hold that?" she asked him quietly.

He didn't answer but his left hand came up and held the wadding by the edges. She wound the bandage around his shoulder, securing the wadding. The bandage sealed itself. Rik would need a sling until the wound healed. She climbed to her feet and went to the bike. Taking a clue from watching Mac, she searched the med kit and found what she was looking for.

When she turned around, Rik was sitting up. "Wait. You'll rip the wound open." He paused, studying her as she put her arms around him to tie the sling. It was barely big enough to fit around his neck. When she was happy with the placement, she nodded. Rik took her hand in his left and squeezed gently. "Thank you."

She looked at him and then did the most embarrassing thing she could think of. She burst into tears. "I'm … I'm so … so sorry."

He drew her to him and nestled her in his other shoulder. That was how Corporal MacKenzie found them.

"Oh, how touching," she said in a sickeningly sweet voice. "She nearly kills you and you're comforting her. I think I've seen everything. Rik Chesson in love."

Rik's head shot up. He didn't speak, but Mac went quiet. Deleen removed herself from his embrace, wiping her face with the back of her hand.

Rik got to his feet. MacKenzie stood up straight, waiting. "Report," Rik said, his voice hard-edged. It was the first time Deleen had heard annoyance in his voice.

"There was a malfunction in his revival routines."

"Can it be fixed?" he asked.

"Yes, I'm compiling a fix. It should be ready in fifteen minutes."

"How did Bates die?" Rik asked, his voice still giving no ground.

Mac looked up and then away. "Bates was weak and his tech had not engaged as expected. I left him by the cryo unit while I hit the revive on Oyuda and I went to look at supplies." She rolled her shoulders and then looked back to Rik. "By the time I got back, Oyuda was awake and out of the unit. I think Bates must have helped him. Looks like Oyuda strangled him, took his weapon and went into hiding. I've been ... I was unable to re-establish control of the situation until you showed up."

"It seems to me, Corporal MacKenzie, you owe this civilian an apology. She was not expecting to be shot at by one of my men and this situation is completely your fault. You should have remained by the unit until you ascertained Oyuda's condition."

Mac's faced hardened but she kept her gaze fixed on Rik. "Yes, sir. I know, sir."

"You aren't to blame yourself for the equipment malfunction and you weren't to know that Bates couldn't handle the situation. We'll say no more about it."

Mac slouched and lowered her head. "I should've known. Bates wasn't pulling up as well as expected. I over—"

"Enough, Mac We can't save Bates, but we can save Oyuda. We need him. Any other signals?"

Mac straightened again, once again in control. "I can't detect any more in this area," she replied.

Rik nodded once. "We need to go to ground and plan our next course of action."

"Yes, sir," Mac answered, her voice stiff. Deleen felt a stirring of pity for Mac.

Rik jerked his chin. "Kill that fire. The smoke will attract attention."

Mac sprang into action, grabbing some fire retardant to put out the flames.

"I'm sorry about Bates," Deleen said to Rik.

Rik's cheek muscle moved, and he nodded once and then looked away from her. The loss of one of his men had to be a blow, particularly killed by a friendly.

Mac came back. "Fire out. The remedy dose should be ready about now."

"Good. When you've given Oyuda the shot, you'll take Deleen and me back to the woods. Then you will return and fetch Oyuda."

Deleen was about to interrupt and say she could walk back herself, but one glance from Rik and she shut her mouth. There was no way he was leaving her alone while they retreated.

"Deleen, keep an eye out, will you?" Rik said. "And pass me my helmet and put yours back on. I want to be using comms."

Deleen picked up his helmet and handed it to him. He put it on and then gingerly replaced the armour she had removed and put his arm back in the sling when he was done.

Mac gave her a hard stare and moved toward the bunker. Deleen replaced her helmet and kept her eye on the horizon, moving around slowly so she didn't get dizzy, but also didn't leave any part of the sky unobserved for too long. If the enemy attacked them now, she didn't think they'd make it out. Not with morale so low and Rik injured. She shook her head and kicked at the dirt. *Stupid. Stupid. Stupid.*

Mac carried Oyuda to the edge of the woods and covered him with a camouflage blanket and some light debris. Next, she carried out more packs. A couple she stowed in the trike and the rest she dumped next to Oyuda. Deleen supposed, then, that there wasn't another vehicle in this bunker. That lowered her spirits. They weren't going to rid the colony of the people who'd taken over administration. Not any time soon.

* * *

Rik's jaw ached. Not because he was injured there, but because he was clenching it so hard. Frustrated. Angry. Annoyed and downhearted. He couldn't afford to lose people. There were so few of them left. With Bates down that left three of them and Deleen. Rik didn't blame his civilian for shooting him. The wild dog was an added complexity, not easily foreseen. It was his own fault. He'd told her to take it off safety. Oyuda had fired at her. He closed his eyes trying to block out that moment. The moment when his heart was in his mouth and he thought she would die. But she hadn't and, although his shoulder ached, he wasn't permanently harmed. The nanobots in his blood would rebuild the damaged tissue. He did feel vulnerable though. For the next day or two, he wasn't going to be able to function at full capacity.

Mac had to be hurting bad. She and Bates had had a thing once, when Mac experimented with relationships. Bates had supported Mac through the gender identity thing. They hadn't been lovers any longer, but good solid friends. More importantly, they were unit kin. Family.

He knew Mac would be taking on the blame and hating the world right now. Dammit, he needed Mac to pull herself together. He needed Oyuda too. As a tech, Oyuda could give them an edge. A full complement of soldiers would have improved his mood and the odds, but he knew it was too late for that. Not if Deleen's account was true. There might be more soldiers out there somewhere, but he'd run out of time to save them now. They had to plan how to stop the takeover of the administration and stop the killing of the rest of the special forces personnel hidden around the city.

Mac had finished moving gear and stomped up to him. Deleen had been sitting silently while he brooded. Rik climbed to his feet and Mac edged under his good arm for support.

"Thanks, Mac," he said softly.

She squeezed his forearm in acknowledgment and then helped him onto the trike. Deleen stuck to his side but kept some distance between them to protect his shoulder and the arm that was in the sling. "Take it nice and slow, corporal" he said. Deleen took up a position next to him.

Mac fired up the trike. "Yes, sir."

True to her word, MacKenzie gave them a smooth ride, barely leaving a trail in the wild wheat and between the occasional copse of trees. She even paused to help set up their shelter and engage the shield. Deleen tried to help, but jumped at Mac's every abrupt movement. No easy truce there. It would take Mac a while to calm down. He'd read the disapproval in her eyes. He knew she hated that he was fraternising with a civilian. She had even joked that he was in love. Stars, is that what it felt like? It was his duty to protect civilians. Deleen was a civilian and a descendant of his commander. In that she had a special place without even earning it. He thought about the previous night, and how he had all these emotions and feelings for her. Yeah, he was in deep. He lay down on their bed things. Deleen crawled over to him. "You need pain meds?" she asked.

Rik shook his head. "No."

"I'd better take a look." He relaxed as she undid the bandages. The wound gaped. The bleeding had slowed and the wound itched, mostly due to the activity of the nanobots. Deleen leaned in, her brows puzzled, then her face paled and her mouth opened.

"What is it?" he asked, touching her hand with his good one. Her horrified gaze moved to his. "It's moving. I can see the muscle tissue mending." Her hand went to her head and her lips whitened. He thought she was going to puke. Turning away abruptly she crawled outside. Sounds of retching followed.

"Chesson?" Mac called before entering. "What's going on?"

Rik chewed his lip, not quite sure what was going on. "She took a look at the wound and lost it."

Mac struggled into the shelter to take a look. "It's healing fine. Repair is in progress." She wrapped it back up in the bandage and sealed it. "You want me to check on her?"

Rik nodded, but he was worried by her gut reaction, worried about what was behind it.

He heard Mac quiz Deleen. After a brief exchange, his corporal fired up the trike to fetch Oyuda.

Rik fell asleep waiting for Deleen to return. He couldn't suppress the feeling that something was terribly wrong. That he had revolted her in some way. She knew he had tech inserts, knew he had nanotech. Yet the sight of him healing unravelled her somehow. Not for the first time he wished he'd been able to log into the colony's archive and catch up on history. Although, by Deleen's account, that had been altered to exclude their existence and the war, so maybe it wouldn't have been reliable or helpful.

What had replaced that history? As he dozed his thoughts reordered themselves, shuffling and reshuffling information. Deleen's apparent unfamiliarity with memory tech like the helmets and armour and the shelter, which had been common at settlement. Surely the colony hadn't had time to go retrograde. What else was there? Deliberate denial of tech? His eyes snapped open.

Deleen slept on top of the covers at his feet. He screwed up his face at the arrangement. Since he'd been revived, he'd slept with her by his side. Something was definitely wrong.

At his movement, she started awake. She didn't look him in the eye. "How are you feeling?" she asked, while staring at the walls of the shelter.

"Better," he replied truthfully. "Del, what is it? What's wrong?"

"Nothing's wrong," she said, shifting her gaze to her tangle of fingers, which wrestled with each other, the ones of the left hand not quite conquering the right.

He sat up carefully. "Ms Milo, you are a terrible liar."

Her gaze flew up to his, her jaw dropped, eyebrows knitting together. "I'm not lying."

"Tell me something. What is the colony's attitude to tech, to technical enhancement, to someone like me?"

Tears filled her bright eyes, shimmering on the edges like gold peelings. "It's ... it's ... not done. Just not done."

He lowered his eyebrows. "Not done? You mean you don't have the means or it's not condoned."

She shook her head, a tear falling down one cheek. "Not condoned. Like genetic manipulation, changing the human form with tech is ... a perversion."

Her gaze flicked up at him, then down. Her pale skin colouring. "So when you saw my nanobots healing me, you were sickened?"

Her skin grew pale again. "I didn't mean it. I can't explain my reaction. It triggered something ... from somewhere, something I can't control. I don't understand it. I knew you had implants, some tech ... but ..." Her green eyes pleaded with him.

"Can you bring yourself to touch me now, Del?" he asked, watching her for any further sign of revulsion.

She nodded and then wiped the tip of her nose with the back of her hand. "Come then," he said holding out a hand. Crawling toward him, she took his hand and buried her face in his good shoulder and bawled her eyes out, huge racking sobs.

Helpless, he just spoke to her softly and hugged her with his good arm. What had happened on Colony Five? Were the other colonies the same? Had they become human purists while he slept, and he and others like him had become the hated other? He tried to think back to those early days. The special forces had an open invite to settle on the colonies, but had there been an exemption because of the ethics of the new colony? Had that morphed into something stronger?

Chapter Ten

DELEEN'S SHAME

Shame flowed through Deleen. Rik appeared to have forgiven her, even though she knew he was concerned and hurt by her reaction. She honestly didn't know where it came from. It was like the revulsion to tech was programmed into her. Nothing that she actually remembered from her education could account for it. Her lessons in school did not teach her to hate tech. They focused on the pureness of the human form and how technology was only allowed to mend that which had deviated from perfection, that was faulty. One didn't try to improve upon the human form. Still dressed, she slept next to Rik, holding onto him as if such physical closeness would heal the rift between them. Not really able to understand how deep her reaction had wounded him, she could only imagine if such a slight had been offered to her and that would be profound indeed.

Thoughts of Rik filled her mind, taking her back to her earlier memories of him. The ones that had arisen with the burnings. Memories surged out as if through a broken rip in the back of her mind. Her grandfather holding her hand. Except she wasn't a child, not a young child, but a teenager, a young woman.

"Look there, Del. Here is a man who would never hurt you. A man who would protect you. Die protecting you."

Tears had been rolling down her cheeks. Her jaw had hurt and her eye had been swollen. Who had done that? Who had hurt her? The name came out of her memory: Mal. Her boyfriend Mal. Her memories wound back. To the assault. To the fear. The thought that she was going to die while the punches rained down. He wanted her dead. He wanted no one else to have her. How he had screamed as he assaulted her.

Next thing she knew she was sitting up straight. Rik panted beside her. Her ears were ringing, from a scream. Hers.

Mac called out. "Sergeant?"

Rik swallowed and answered in a shaky voice. "It's okay. Just a dream."

Deleen trembled. She wanted to be held, but Rik crawled to the packs and brought out a drink. "Take a swig." He pushed a canteen at her.

Nodding and brushing tears from her cheek, she tried to take a sip. Her hands shook so much, Rik gripped it and helped steady it. The drink was sweet and salty. Some kind of restorative. After a few mouthfuls she handed it back as the shaking had subsided. "I'm sorry," she whispered.

A small smile lit Rik's face, yet his expression was sad. "Don't be sorry." His voice was gentle and soft.

Deleen decided to be brave and speak about the dream, the buried memory that had burned so hard in her brain. "I remembered more— more about that time when I saw you frozen."

"Before now, you mean?" His eyebrows furrowed.

Deleen nodded once, acknowledging the point. "Yes, my grandfather brought me to see you. He was proud of you. Wanted me to see. Wanted me to see a good man. A man who wouldn't hurt me." Her face screwed up and tears slipped down her cheek. "There's more. The situation ... I can't quite piece it together."

"You don't remember it well?" He reached out to take her hand and rubbed her palm softly with his thumb.

Forget. Forget. Forget. The words sought to blanket her mind in black. "Remember! Remember! Remember!" she countered, using her free hand to slap the side of her head. A burst of frustration escaped her mouth. "Damn. It's blocked. It's blocked."

"How do you mean blocked?" Rik's breath was faster now, keen to hear what she had to say.

"Therapy." She said directly to him, meeting his curious gaze. "I had therapy. I don't know how much I've lost or how much is buried."

She saw him swallow again. "Seeing me made you need therapy?"

"No," she answered emphatically. "No. Definitely not that. It was a positive experience. A positive experience I needed. Losing the memory of you was a casualty of the therapy. It wasn't because of you. My grandfather thought seeing you would make me better, make me believe."

"Believe what?"

"That all men weren't brutes."

Rik let out a long breath. "Oh."

Deleen lay back down on the covers. "It's hard to remember clearly, but it's there ... It's coming back to me." She shrugged. "I don't know what it was like when you were young. Here, on Five, we are encouraged to explore what it's like to be human, to explore being male or female or non-binary, without ... you know ..."

"You mean sex?"

"Yes, I was sixteen. I started a bit later than my friends at school. I think it was because I came to the homestead with grandpa during the holidays." She sighed, her heart rate refusing to slow. She scrunched the edge of her T-shirt. "I had a few encounters with boys. Not very exciting encounters mind you, but enough to give me an idea of the mechanics. Anyway, when I was about seventeen I met Mal. He was older and was studying at Five's only university, well what passed for one. He was intense and I loved that. I remember it. But being seventeen, my passion didn't last. To cut a long story short, Mal didn't want the relationship to end. He started following me, turning up wherever I was. He threatened other boys whether I was with them or not. They just had to be near me. I blocked him on my personal so I couldn't see his messages. I talked to a counsellor at school who said that he would get over it, as we were both too young for a partnership."

Rik nodded, his gaze intent as his finger and thumb played with his bottom lip. He swallowed, his Adam's apple bobbing in his clean-shaven throat.

"But he didn't get over it. One day I was walking through the park near our apartment. I was alone, but I don't think anyone being there would have prevented what happened next." She could recall the actions but not the pain or the fear. There was a barrier there and she worried that it was a fragile one.

"What happened?" Rik asked after she'd been quiet while she wrestled with her memories.

"He hurt me. He said he wanted to make me ugly so no one else would want me. I tried to fight him off, but it was a casual passer-by who heard my screams who saved me."

"You were hurt badly?"

She met his gaze but couldn't speak.

"Del?"

"I can't tell you the extent of my injuries. In many ways I was lucky, but I was left damaged. I wouldn't go to school. I was afraid of sudden noises, of voices. My father was beside himself. Even after a year, long after the bruising had faded and the bones mended. I had intense therapy." *Forget. Forget. Forget.* "I didn't learn to deal with my issues. I buried them. Father brought me to the farm. I think that's when Grandpa showed me you. It's a bit fuzzy, but I think that's the series of events."

"Did you go out with boys ... I mean, men, again?"

Deleen blinked. It suddenly dawned on her the reason she acted the way she did. The reason she mocked—secretly hated—the idea of being in a partnership, of being owned, of being threatened. "Not on an emotional level. I have sex, I suppose when I wanted it. I went to a ..." She tried to put it into terms he might understand. She didn't think they had sex clinics when he was frozen. "Place where I could engage in sex without any emotional connection."

His chin lifted slightly as if he was trying to understand what she was referring to. "I ... er ..."

"A sex clinic. I paid for sex with men when I had the inclination. Admittedly not as often as some. It's normal on Five."

Rik bit his lip. Then looked at her again. "You're telling me that it's normal for a beautiful woman to pay for sex at a clinic because she's too afraid to date a man or get emotionally involved in case he hurts her. Sorry but that's screwed. In anybody's reality."

"Obviously it's not screwed. People go to sex clinics for all types of reasons. Men and women."

"You're saying none of your friends are in ... what did you call it ... partnerships?"

Deleen searched her mind for an honest answer. "No. A couple of my friends are in partnerships and are filing for reproduction rights."

"And that's never interested you?"

Deleen shook her head. "No, not then. I didn't understand. I didn't remember what had happened to me. Now, though, I understand that about myself. I don't know how I feel about all that yet."

Rik nodded. "That's something, I suppose. Something good that came out of this situation."

"What do you mean?"

Did he mean them? Their relationship? But they didn't have a relationship ... yet. She couldn't have a partnership with him; he had tech in him. It would be too strange. But was he implying that he wanted to?

"I mean that you understand more about yourself and your motivations. Once you do that then it's an easy step to conquer your fears."

She nodded. "Right. Conquer my fears."

Maybe he was right about that. She looked him over, noticed the heavy eyelids. "You better get some sleep."

"Yes, I better." He lay back on the pillows.

She looked around their shelter. "I'll bring the other pack inside."

His eyes were already closed and his breathing slower by the time she pulled herself to her feet and left.

Deleen exited the shelter, shaking her head at herself. She'd shot her weapon, nearly taking out Rik, and had gained a major insight to what made her tick, piecing together lost sections of her memory. She was mentally exhausted.

What a whirlwind few days. Just the thought that she could have killed Rik made butterflies take flight in her gut. A new thought imposed itself, flashing back to her retching her guts out. She'd reacted queerly to those nanos in action. Was that more conditioning? She'd never witnessed such a thing before. In fact, although she knew about nanotech and genetic manipulation in an intellectual sense, she'd never been exposed to it in person. Seeing the obvious tech in the cold soldiers hadn't bothered her at all. She'd been aware of it and had not reacted viscerally like she had to the tiny nanos.

It was as if someone had taken her mind and bunched it up into a ball and tossed it to the wind. It was like she had no control over herself, her memories, her reactions, her mind. That made her sweat. It made her distrust everything she knew. Finding records had been changed was one thing. Finding out her memory had been manipulated was another. As far as she knew, psychological counselling was about accepting and dealing with the situation, not burying it.

How did she end up burying her memories? There was something she was missing here. Something that wasn't right. Had she been hypnotised, rather than assisted in dealing with the assault? If so, who had done that and why?

Sealing up one of the packs, she was intending to move it into her shelter where it would be closer to access and more secure, when Mac burst out of her shelter, startling her.

"You've got a nerve," Mac said, standing on the edge of the camp, her body radiating tension.

"I'm sorry?" Deleen replied, at first not paying much attention due to fatigue. Then with growing concern she saw that the other woman's lips were drawn into a severe thin line and her eyes were narrowed. It dawned on Deleen that she was the focus of the soldier's anger.

Oyuda must still be resting, because a quick glance around didn't reveal him anywhere close. There was no chance of someone walking in and breaking up this little party.

"You're a liability. What is Rik thinking working with a civilian? He may as well take a gun to our heads now and pop us one," she said, jerking her hand, which was in the shape of a gun.

Already suffering from guilt Deleen accepted the accusation thrust at her. "I'm sorry." Deleen looked at the ground, feeling the burn of tears and trying against hope to stop herself from blubbering in front of the soldier woman. It would only confirm the other woman's opinion.

"Yeah, don't sorry me. Sorry doesn't cut it. Waste of bloody space. You disgust me. Go back to your civilian life and leave us alone to do our job."

Deleen's head came up. If it wasn't for her, this cold soldier would still be sleeping, maybe dead. Yet, she held back the words. It wouldn't help, not with Mac's angry mood.

Mac's jaw clenched and her fingers bunched into fists.

"I'll do better next time," she replied, softly, meekly, hoping that Mac would back off, settle it down.

"Damn straight you will." She lifted her shoulders. "You'll keep your weapon on safety until you are staring the enemy in the face. Got that?"

Deleen nodded like a salute.

"Right. You do that and we'll keep ourselves together and not be burying more dead."

Deleen lowered her head. "I'm sorry about Bates," she said carefully and sincerely. She wanted to deny that it was her fault, but that wasn't the point. She wasn't part of their unit. She was an outsider and unknown quantity and had to earn their trust.

Mac was suffering, that much she could sense. Bates was dead. Mac blamed herself, that much was obvious. Rik was hurt, Deleen's fault. Rik was in charge. Their leader. Him being nearly taken out by accident was bound to be upsetting. Deleen was in the way, too. If she wasn't there, Rik's attention would be more on Mac and the unit. Yet it wasn't jealousy so much as frustration. It had to be that.

Lifting her head, she studied Mac, seeing the signs of fatigue and worry. "How's Oyuda?" she asked.

Mac's eyes widened as if she didn't expect to be spoken to. "What's it to you? One look at us, at what we are, has you puking your guts out. You're not worth helping."

Deleen recoiled that Mac knew; that meant Rik knew too. She couldn't respond, couldn't speak around the lump of guilt clogging her throat. She was meant to be tolerant and inclusive. That's what Colony Five represented and here she was physically sick at the sight of difference. She was ashamed. She had only been worried about how Rik would take her reaction because she ... she cared about him. Cared? Oh dear.

Rik's voice bellowed through the opening of the shelter. "Can it, Mac."

Mac's chin came up, her jaw working. "You should listen to me," she yelled into the shelter. "We should dump the civilian and plan our assault."

"I said, can it." He emerged white-faced from the opening of the shelter. He'd dragged himself from his bed because of the altercation. He had stripped down to his T-shirt and shorts.

Mac's face paled, and she bit her bottom lip. Stubborn to the last, she was spoiling for a fight.

Rik didn't back down, though, didn't let his exhaustion stop him. "Don't take it out on her. Losing Bates wasn't her fault."

He rubbed at his head and shook it as if willing himself to wellness. "We wouldn't be here if it wasn't for her." He waited until Mac nodded before continuing. "We need her to plan the assault. She knows the security in the administration. Think on that. She knows the colony too, knows where things are, where information is. If we log onto the network, we're done for. They are looking for us. Killing us off. We need to stick together."

"But, if ..."

"There are no ifs, buts or maybes, Mac. Just reality and the future. I'm sorry about Bates. I'm sorry it couldn't be different. I'm sorry most of our unit have been lost without even being given a chance to fight back. Just thinking about it brings on dark thoughts that I don't want to dwell on. I understand—more than understand—how you feel, but Deleen is not the target."

"Why not? She's one of them, not one of us. You have a bloody soft spot for her, and it colours your thinking."

Deleen held her breath. It had been her reaction to the nanos that sparked this incident. It made them nervous about how they would be accepted in this society that was trying to kill them.

Rik just stared at his corporal. Mac shifted her shoulders, bunched her fists. Breaking eye contact with Rik, her gaze flickered and redirected to Deleen, then she turned away, shoulders hunched. Mac wasn't going to forget in a hurry.

Deleen felt saddened because she wanted to be friends with the other woman and she had traits she admired. She was strong, she was smart and she gave as good as she got, yet still had heart. Deleen couldn't aspire to that and maybe she couldn't fully understand Mac and her motivations, but that didn't mean she couldn't appreciate what Corporal Mackenzie MacKenzie had achieved and what she'd sacrificed to get there.

Deleen stood there, still coiled and tense after Mac returned to her shelter.

"Del, come back inside." Rik put out a shaky hand. He was weak. Not that she had a chance of supporting his weight, but she was happy to give any assistance, even if it was token. "About MacKenzie ..." he began as they slowly re-entered the shelter.

Rik made small sounds of protest as he moved, and Deleen locked her knees together as he braced himself against her when it came to turning around. "I know. You don't have to explain. She's hurting."

Rik let out a loud sigh as he lowered himself back to the bed. He wore a blood-stained T-shirt but she noticed the mark fading as the enzymes—or was it nanos?—slowly digested the organic material. Some more tech she had never seen. "You ready for a wash up?" she asked as she searched in the pack for the portable bath. She considered whether he was able to wash himself. He had one good arm, so after he nodded, she handed it to him. This he ran over his body while she watched. It was disconcerting watching him and not being able to look away. He had a casual sensuality, each movement precise, slow and measured. Probably playing this moment up for all it was worth, she thought. Yep. He knew she was interested. The discomfort of her reaction to his healing was over. He was offering her a way to connect with him again. Non-judgemental. Inviting.

He passed back the portable bath. She ran it over his clothes and folded them in the precise neat way he usually did. Then she unbuttoned her shirt and slid it off her shoulders. She knew he was watching. Her skin was burning and it wasn't from shame, it was excitement. She took her time, conscious of his interest, but going for maximum effect.

She'd stuffed things up badly. He'd forgiven her and offered her a way to reconnect. Turning her back on him, she removed her underclothes then ran the muzzle of the portable bath over herself. Rik's breathing was audible over the hum of the machine.

Looking up quickly, she thought he might have dropped off to sleep, but he was still awake with his gaze fixed on her, gold lights glittering in his dark eyes. She cleaned her clothes and then piled them up next to his, before sliding into the bed, a wall of his body heat welcoming her.

Chapter Eleven

PLANS

Deleen stood next to Rik, listening to Oyuda who had a tracking device on his wrist. He had recovered remarkably well and she was impressed. "This," he said, tapping it, "shows the next bunker and also the list the supplies stored there. No life signs, but the data on the bunkers indicates there is another vehicle there and a weapons cache. Also, a high-end communications system, as well as parts and components. I should be able to patch into the colony's network—not the secure network, mind you, but the public one—without being tracked. It will be something."

Rik nodded. "Better than nothing. We've been flying blind here. I have no idea why we were all hidden in people's houses and some out in here in the wilds. We went into cryo in the main lab. Something strange happened in the intervening years. At least, Deleen knows a lot about the colony, but her knowledge of the current situation is stale now after a few days away. Tapping into the public network and any broadcasts will assist."

He glanced Deleen's way and she spoke up. "You should be able to connect without being detected. My personal identifies me, but you're right some of the network is broadcast on a digital signal to reach the outer settlements. No tracking there, except for counting how many tap in as part of a performance measure."

Oyuda acknowledged her point, with a fierce look and pursed lips. She noted his colour had improved. He had lightly tanned skin, handsome dark eyes shaded with eyelids from his Asian heritage. Straight nose over a pink, slightly plump mouth.

He squatted down to draw a map in the dirt. "The bunker is due east from here. Can you tell us a bit about the terrain between there and here, Ms Milo?"

Deleen blinked at being consulted. She chewed her bottom lip and considered the rough map. They were on the outskirts of where she had travelled in her youth. But she had studied Five's geography, so could recollect key points. Pointing on the map she noted that the lake was behind them. She explained there were no mountains as such, but from memory there was a series of gullies and hills gradually lifting to the uplands. Not quite a plateau but a popular place in the hot season due to the cool winds that blew in from the ocean about twenty clicks further on. When she looked up from marking the dirt, Rik nodded. "Homesteads?"

Pulling on her bottom lip with her fingers, she considered and then pointed. "There is a holiday camp around here. A hotel of sorts, but only open in the hot season. I don't think it's manned in the off-season. But there are a series of buildings in that spot, so it's possible that's where the bunker might be."

"What's that place called?" Rik asked her, pointing to the place where she had marked the hotel.

She shrugged. "Black's Pinnacle. That's what we called it."

Rik nodded and then looked up. The sky had been quiet, no flyers searching. "We'll move out now while we have woods for cover. We'll reassess how to proceed when we reach the next clear area."

"About time we moved." Mac spoke but there was no humour on her face. She was still pissed, but her mood seemed to be less dark. Having something to focus on was having some effect.

Their eyes locked and Deleen looked away. There was nothing but derision in the other woman's gaze. Perhaps it was because she shared Rik's shelter and that created assumptions. At first it was out of necessity and now, with the passage of time, she'd come to expect it. But Mac and Oyuda had separate shelters. Rik was showing a preference for a civilian and that potentially irked his comrades. As they packed up their gear, Rik was back to being a soldier—precise, unemotional and focused on their mission—but she had seen a more tender side to him. She nodded to herself, understanding finally that his unit depended on him. They needed his strength and leadership, and throwing a civilian into the mix not only upped the unpredictability it also caused them to doubt his judgement. He had a soft spot for her, as she did for him.

* * *

They could smell the smoke before they could see it. Rik's stomach turned, knowing one of his men had died there. He wished he didn't have to see it, see the remains of a long-ago comrade. Face it he must, he decided as he surveyed the group.

Oyuda was much improved. Not quite his old self, but at least his system had rebalanced. He wasn't sure what had gone wrong with his unit, but the analysis indicated that his hormones and nanos had gotten out of balance. While Rik had been injured and recuperating, Oyuda had been recovering as well.

To Rik, Mac appeared better settled too. He saw the lines of tension in her cheeks relax as they planned this mission. Although Mac still snarled at him. He understood her fears, her attitude. He'd been fraternising openly with Deleen. Normally he wouldn't have done that. He'd have restraint. But something had changed in him, because he'd been given a second chance at life and he revelled in that life. The old life was gone and he had to forge a new one. Maybe it was short-sighted to do that, as that meant he wasn't focused on the end game. Avoidance probably. He shrugged. He hadn't thought of the end game when he became a cold soldier, as he'd been caught up in the now. Something had changed now, because he wanted a future. He never wanted to be in cold sleep again.

Smoke billowed, tapering to a thin, high trail in the sky. As they drew nearer, the evening sun made the sky redder than usual and long shadows crept from the partially destroyed homestead. Oyuda nodded and then kept moving through the debris field—chunks of rock and lumps of earth, torn-apart machinery, masonry and broken furniture.

Rik followed, Deleen slightly in front of him, her small body walking around a larger object—the burnt skeleton of a harvester by the look of it. Mac brought up the rear. He could almost feel her gaze on his back, her vigilance a comfort.

The opening to the bunker was partially collapsed, a testament to the violence of the breach. Rik's eye sensors kicked in, assessing the structure. Oyuda lifted a hand and they stopped in their positions. The other man's gaze swept up and around the bunker opening.

"It's sound," Oyuda said through comms. "Supports holding. Sir?"

"Proceed," Rik said. "Stay vigilant."

Then Oyuda stepped into the dark hollow and out of sight.

Rik's breath hitched as Oyuda's stepped from view, a sudden gut feeling that something wasn't right. "Oyuda, report!" he said into his helmet mic.

"Clear," Oyuda replied.

"Del, get behind me," he spoke and saw her pause and look over her shoulder at him. She nodded and waited for him to catch up, a mere two steps. Her weapon was in its holster with the safety on. Despite her anger, Mac had taken the trouble to teach Deleen how to care for, clean and use her weapon. That did not make Mac's mood lift, but it helped Deleen's for certain. A wary truce had existed between them since the argument. Rik gritted his teeth and shook his head. Looking over his shoulder, he saw Mac, weapon held across her chest, her eyes ranging all around them.

"Clear," she said, lifting her head slightly. He nodded and stepped into the darkness.

Despite Oyuda's assurance that the opening was structurally sound, Rik was nervous. While his own sensors confirmed that it would take a big hit to bring it down, a large section of the roof to one side had collapsed.

He guided Deleen over the dirt and fallen rocks and into the chamber. The cryo unit stood dark and daunting in front of him. Oyuda was not in this chamber, having moved further beyond. Rik had to look. He owed it to Nfador to see him buried if he was still in there. He stepped up to the unit and peered down. He closed his eyes and stepped back. Nfador was still in there, what was left of him. Blood smeared the inside of the sarcophagus. This cold soldier had been blown apart before he had a chance to defend himself. A terrible way to repay the sacrifice, the duty to the colony.

Opening his eyes again, Rik forced himself to look, to see how he had been killed. Nfador had been decapitated. The head wasn't there. It wasn't on the floor. Rik's fist clenched and anger burned his blood. The head of this cold soldier had been taken for a trophy. The Gogola must be involved in this. The Gogola had acted this way before. Not caring for the humans in the colony, rampaging and mindless.

"Rik," Oyuda said into his ear. "You better get here now."

Rik turned to Deleen. "Wait here. Don't look in there. Help Mac to gather supplies." He jerked his head in the direction of the supply stores. Some were strewn on the floor, some were gone and others destroyed. They would have to sort through them to find what they needed. Mac gave him a definitive nod. "It's clear outside," she said.

Mac opened an empty pack that had been secured in one of her leg pockets and jerked it in Deleen's direction. Rik left them and made his way to the chamber that housed the transport, hoping it had not been destroyed. Oyuda was checking a bank of monitors. Rik's attention was snared by the wreckage strewn about the cavern. "Damn!"

The hoped-for transport was trashed. Oyuda didn't turn around, so Rik walked up to him. "What else?"

"This is chamber number one. I'm looking for chamber number two."

"There was more than one? In here?"

"I'm not sure. Logic would indicate that, but I can't see where it would be. This seems to be it. Nothing below us."

Rik thought it through. "Under the main building?"

Oyuda glanced at him. "Yes, it's big enough. It's pretty destroyed. Not sure we'd find the access point in that rubble."

"What about the exit point?"

"On it."

While Oyuda conducted his analysis, Rik went through the rubble, looking for anything that they could scavenge or reuse. He piled up the equipment, requesting Mac to secure it on their transport. The trike was hidden for the moment under a makeshift camouflage cover. They all couldn't ride it at the same time so they had leap frogged it. Some walking, some riding and with Mac doubling back to collect the stragglers. It was tough on the energy cells, hence him searching for another transport. The charging socket in the hangar had been destroyed so they only had solar power, which took a while to build.

Mac took the first load of salvage, using a hand pushed lifter that she'd managed to find. That left Deleen on her own. Rik wasn't comfortable with that.

"Deleen?" he called to her through the helmet link. "Where are you?"

"Here," she replied. "Main hangar stacking supplies."

He headed there. She and Mac had done a good job of assembling good, medical supplies and a couple of charging units for the smaller weapons. "Well done." He grinned at her. Her cheeks and the tip of her nose were blackened from the layer of dust and soot. Her teeth glowed whitely with her smile. She pushed some hair back under her helmet. "Thanks. A lot was wasted, though. Too bad."

"It's enough to keep us going for a few weeks." She glanced up at him suddenly, a frown denting in the skin between her eyebrows. "Weeks? I hoped this would be over soon."

"We can only do our best. No guarantees." This mission was to get transport. They hadn't moved on to the ultimate game of taking back the city and putting down the usurpers. That reminded him, he'd forgotten to check whether Oyuda had been able to listen in on Five's public network. "Excuse me for a minute, I forgot to check on something. Will you be okay?"

"Sure. I'll carry some of this stuff outside so we can put it on the trike."

He nodded and strode off.

* * *

Deleen watched Rik walk away into the dark chamber, through to where Oyuda was connected to the communications station. She glanced down at the stacked supplies and picked up the first pack. It wasn't too heavy, even though it was stuffed with food. She may as well make herself useful and deliver it to near where the corporal was staging the supplies to stack on the trike.

Deleen didn't think she'd like to walk them all the way to where it lay hidden. Their caution was understandable. The trike was a key asset and they didn't want to lose it or damage it. Yet it was a good ten-minute march from the homestead.

After their two-day journey, Deleen was ready to lie down and stay down. Her muscles no longer ached as much as they had, but she was still tired and noticed that her borrowed fatigues were looser than before. She was eating three meals a day, and snacks in between, but her energy output was way more than she'd ever experienced.

The first pack of food weighed heavily on her back as she came out into the yard, waving smoke from in front of her face. She wished it would clear so she could see and breathe better. A cough seized her and she dropped the pack to the ground as she struggled for breath. She should reengage the helmet visor, even though it restricted her vision.

Mac was visible up ahead, coming back with her mini loader. Deleen waved and then stooped to pick up the pack. They passed each other and she called out. "So where shall I pack the supplies?"

Mac opened her mouth and shut it. They stared at each other, then Mac said, "The trike."

Deleen flashed a fake smile. "Oh, if you insist. I thought to stack them somewhere and then move them on from there in stages." Deleen was also counting on assistance from the other members of the team. They were more built for labour than she was.

Mac sniffed. "Sure, do that. When I'm done with the heavy stuff, we can use the loader for the rest." She pointed. "Assemble them over there."

With her weapon strapped to her back, Mac pushed the loader in the direction of the bunker.

"Will do," Deleen said to her back, repressing the urge to poke out her tongue. She wished Mac would give just a little. Barring what was required to communicate to get things done, the corporal blanked her. Deleen couldn't help that she was a civilian. She was what she was.

With the first pack deposited by the boundary fence, she made her way back to the bunker. A strange sound made her pause. Slowly she turned, eyes peeled. As well as smoke obscuring the view, they were losing the light. Night approached. Shadows that had been lengthening were now stretched out, joining together as if they were the source of the blackness invading. The noise didn't repeat so she straightened, and then kept walking. When she entered the bunker, Mac was nowhere to be seen. She had probably gone to the other chamber to load up more machinery. Deleen picked up the next pack and grabbed a handful of extras memory tech disks before returning the way she came.

Once free of the bunker, she had to tread carefully because of the low visibility. Twilight was deceptive. It was quiet except for the sounds of her steps. She stopped and hitched the strap of the pack higher and looked around. Something made her feel uneasy.

"Rik?" she called on the helmet.

"Yes," came his reply. "Where are you?" There was a crackle of static.

"Just outside the bunker. You all okay in there?"

"Yes," he replied.

Oyuda's voice intruded on the channel and then static obscured the words.

She started walking again, tapping the side of the helmet as she did. "Damn thing," she muttered.

The crackle of static became a deafening screech making her tear off the helmet so she could turn down the volume. To no avail, comms still emitted a high-pitched wail and she slipped the helmet strap over her wrist and recommenced walking to where she was stacking supplies. The noise was giving her a headache and it was best if one of the others checked it over when she returned to the bunker.

Away from the building, there was a sound again, a wheeze. She turned, the hairs on her neck rising as she thought she was no longer alone. Narrowing her eyes, her gaze swept the area around the main homestead. A small fire still burned, sending an orange-red haze over the ground and a flickering light overshadowed recesses in walls. Nothing.

She faced the spot where she had stacked the supplies. The pack she had placed the previous trip was gone. Had Mac already swung by and taken it? Yet, the soldier hadn't passed her with the lifter.

Wary she angled the helmet so she could speak into the mic. The whine of interference still issued from the earpiece. She had to hope the mic would pick up her words. "Hello? Corporal MacKenzie?"

There was no response. "Rik?" she tried again.

A burst of static greeted her. Lowering the helmet, she cursed and then tensed. Something moved out of the corner of her eye. She kept still and slowly moved her head to get a better look. A man-like shape was there one minute and then gone.

A chill broke out on her skin and her heartbeat thudded in her ears. It wasn't as big as Rik or even Mac. She shook her head. Had that been a tail? Sweat broke out and her hands grew clammy. *Oh shit!*

The sound of a step to the other side had her swinging around. She almost saw something. Dropping the pack, she was ready to bolt back into the bunker, when a form materialised in front of her. She let out a strangled sound and groped for her weapon. The creature was hideous, hairy and tall. Before she could scream, pain sent her flying backwards. A wall of black swallowed her consciousness.

* * *

"Oyuda, what's happening with comms?" Rik demanded. Oyuda was meant to be patching into public broadcast and web. "Not sure. I'm checking now."

Rik spat a curse and spoke into the mic. "Mac? Del?"

Static greeted him. He walked over to where he'd seen Mac go for more heavy equipment salvage. Relieved, he saw her piling supplies onto the loader. At his approach, she looked up.

He tapped his helmet and pulled it off. Mac did the same. "Comms are out. You seen Deleen?"

Mac nodded. "Next door filling packs."

"Right. I'll check it out." Rik put his helmet on as he left her and went into the main bunker. The packs and other supplies were there, but Deleen wasn't. He thought that the pile was two packs down, so maybe Deleen had left to head outside. "Deleen?" he spoke into his helmet, even though he knew comms were down. "Come in."

Nothing. Through the dark passage, he headed outside. From the entry he couldn't see her. He waited five minutes, thinking she would be on her way back. It was dark out.

Licking his lips, he cast his gaze around, then he left the bunker and walked across the yard, skirting debris, and turned around the side of the main house. Ahead a pack was lying on the ground. A few packs of memory tech spread out like they had been thrown. He squinted and then crouched down, casting his gaze about carefully. He switched to infrared. There didn't appear to be anyone around. That's what his sensors told him.

He darted forward and reached the pack. Deleen's helmet lay nearby and when he squatted down to pick it up, he noticed the drops of blood on the ground.

His heart thundered suddenly. "Deleen!" his yell echoed around him. Not a good tactic if the enemy was nearby.

But it was Deleen. A civilian. His civilian. She could be injured, nearby and not able to communicate.

"Oyuda? MacKenzie?"

Some static sounded in his ear and then cleared. "Rik?" It was Mac.

"Deleen is gone."

"Gone where?"

"Taken." Rik's heart thudded when he spoke the word. His sensors didn't lie. Deleen was not here. Deleen was gone.

"I'm coming."

"Oyuda?"

"Yes?"

"Why are comms working now?"

"I checked everything over. The problem wasn't coming from here. Some interference, I think."

Rik swallowed. MacKenzie was in sight. "From where?"

"External, it looks like."

Rik was still cursing as Mac jogged up. She saw Deleen's helmet and then the blood.

"The enemy?" he asked.

She inhaled, met his gaze and shrugged. "Too much smoke to smell their scent now. But, yeah, looks like she's been snatched."

"Check the trike is okay. We may have been sabotaged."

"Right, but why take a civilian, instead of taking us out?"

"Why indeed." Rik's mouth was drawn into a tight line. "She was easy pickings. But why is she the prize and not us." The why bothered him. Knowing that he had put her in danger rankled more. If they took her she was valuable to them, otherwise they would have outright killed her. It gave him hope that he could get to her before something worse happened.

After Mac ran off, Rik ran his eye over the compound, his sensors not revealing anything. Oyuda jogged up and Rik acknowledged him with a nod. "Let's secure our supplies and rendezvous at the trike," he said.

Oyuda nodded and as the other man ran off, Rick added, "Bring the portable comms unit; we have to know what's going on." Oyuda waved in acknowledgement and then disappeared from view. Rik cursed up a storm while he waited. Del was gone. Just like that. He had to get her back and soon. Who knew what the Gogola would do to her?

Chapter Twelve

ALIEN

The throbbing pain in her jaw drew Deleen to wakefulness. Mentally confused and with slitted eyes, she didn't feel awake. She groaned and then tensed as the sudden awareness that something had happened slammed into the front of her brain. She had had an encounter with something big and hairy.

There was a sound close by. She froze, knowing that she was no longer alone. Blinking a few times helped her eyesight come into focus. Nausea was having a party in her gut, but now was not the time to puke.

She moved her head fractionally and the pain increased, so she stilled and tried to pretend she was out cold. Yet, curiosity was driving her crazy. She had to know who or what had her.

With eyes closed, she tried to assess where she was. She was lying on something cold and hard. Her hand rested on metal. A floor, she thought, or an operating table. Nausea surged, spurred on by fear. She breathed slowly, fighting her reactions. She continued her stocktake of her surroundings and her body. Her back ached, and her right leg was numb. Injury, or had she been lying prone for some time? She wriggled her toes and pins and needles throbbed along her leg. Inactivity more than injury, she thought. Then she moved ever so slightly and her right shoulder shot pain into her neck and down into her hand. Injury.

Perhaps she had been thrown. It sure felt like it. Yet, while it was painful, she was still functional.

The sound in the room did not repeat and she must have drifted off, even though she was curious about where she was, with who and why.

When she cracked open her eyes the next time, she could see a whole lot better. A small room—a storeroom perhaps. Supplies were held to the walls with netting. She recalled supplies. She'd been helping move supplies.

There was no one else in the room, so she was free to move.

The pain increased as she checked herself for injuries. The pins and needles in her leg peaked and then lessened with the change in posture. Her head throbbed too. She eased her jaw. Massaging her right shoulder with her left hand, she worked the stiffness, which helped eased the pain. When she was able, she pushed herself upright using the wall to lean on. Flexing her arms and her legs, she winced at the pain. Bruising, perhaps, and maybe some soft tissue injuries, but no breaks. That was a relief.

A noise alerted her to someone approaching. It was too late to lay back down and pretend unconsciousness. Her eyebrows lowered and a trickle of blood snuck down her check and into the corner of her mouth. She nearly choked when the creature stepped into view.

The memories came rushing back. The compound. The comms difficulties. The alien.

It was male. He was humanoid, very much so, but with an animal aspect. The long tail twitched behind him, a tuft on the end like a lion. Her eyes took in the hair, brown-red but thick like a mane growing out from his forehead to sweep down his back and over his shoulders. His irises were amber, his nose slightly flat and two long fangs peeked out from both sides of his human-looking mouth.

"Awake?" he asked, voice raspy and slightly accented.

Her mouth hung open as she was not quite able to answer. He spoke standard. She rubbed her jaw instead. He'd struck her and then brought her here. She wasn't about to make small talk.

He took a few steps further into the room and her gaze was drawn to the shape of him, how he walked. He had thick thighs, muscled but slim calves that tapered to narrow ankles. His feet were small in comparison to the rest of him and were encased in soft boots, which looked to her to be handmade. His clothing appeared to be a uniform but bore no distinguishing marks, such as badges or rank pins.

He made a noise like a sniff and she saw he had whiskers, though it was more like a hybrid moustache.

"Why were you with the Tainted?" he asked her gruffly, amber eyes assessing.

"The Tainted?" her voice was croaky and it hurt to swallow. She rubbed at her throat. Had the alien throttled her?

He gave a shrug. "Those that you were with." He jerked his head, presumably to where he had found her. "The tech infested." His fangs got in the way of his tongue when he spoke, giving him a slight lisp, but she could understand him clearly.

She closed her eyes and rubbed her forehead. He meant the cold soldiers. Must be. Nausea rose again and her mouth went dry. "Can I have some water?"

His inhaled loudly and then nodded, an oddly human gesture. "Yes."

She slid down the wall she'd been leaning on and sank into a squat, rubbing her head, trying to ease the ache.

Disappearing for a moment, the alien returned with a clear container. He held it out to her, but not near enough for her to take it easily. She would have to move to grab it. Blinking at the pain, she crawled forward, reaching for the water. When she took it, his thick black fingernails scraped against the container. She repressed a shudder at the sight of his claws. Were the aliens felines of some kind? Rik had mentioned something about them resembling animals, but he was short on details. The cool liquid touched her lips, wet her tongue and soothed her throat.

"I will return. Stay here."

He backed out of the room and used a keypad to secure the door. Gulping the rest of the water brought instant relief. With a gasp, she inhaled as she wiped her mouth with her sleeve. She sniffed herself and wrinkled her nose. She smelt of smoke and something else—an animal smell. Crinkling up her nose, she tried not to think how she had got the alien's musk on her clothes.

She crawled around the space to see if there was another way out. After peering through a small round window, and taking in the metal walls and door, she understood she was inside a small flyer that was currently stationary. Poking her head up a little higher, she caught a glimpse of the woods and light traces of smoke that lingered in the trees like mist. The movement made her feel ill. A surge of hope that she was still at the homestead or close by eased the sickness. Rik might find her, rescue her. Then, checking the position of the sun, she did a mental calculation. She'd been taken at nightfall and it was now daylight. Reality sunk in. Rik and the others would have found her by now if she was close by. If they were alive. Her heart sank at the thought and she had to battle with herself to keep positive.

They may not be dead. This could be a different wood, different smoke. A muffled sound of a someone speaking made her jerk away from the window.

It was the alien speaking to someone. Speaking standard. Her language. That didn't seem right. Unless he was talking to her people. The room spun and she lowered herself to the floor and groped to where she had been resting before. She sat and leaned her head back against the metal wall. Nothing was making much sense and thinking hurt.

The floor began to vibrate. The alien approached. The door slid open again. She looked up, waiting for what was coming next.

"I am ordered to make certain you are Pure and not one of the Tainted."

Deleen pursed her lips. "What do you mean Pure?" She didn't know how he was going to determine anything. He didn't have a scanner or anything else obvious. Her body shook as she stood up, using the wall for support, and not entirely due to weakness. She was scared.

He moved closer. "You look like a Pure one, but you smell unclean, Tainted."

"Oh!" Was that Rik's scent on her? It was rather disconcerting. She could only smell the alien. He drew closer and the smell grew stronger. She didn't like the look in his eyes or the look of those black claws.

He paused two feet in front of her. "You will remove your clothing."

Her head came up, heart in her throat. "My clothing?" She gulped. "Why?"

He lifted his chin a notch. "I will inspect you." His lisp grew more pronounced.

Horrified but not thinking straight she tried to think up a solution to the problem. Glancing sideways, she weighed up whether she could dart around him and escape. Her heart thudded and her head ached like a hammer was smashing against the inside of her skull. "Um, I don't have tech in me."

"I have my orders. I cannot bring tech into the compound. Undress or I will undress you."

Deleen lifted her head. What the hell. Her armour was already gone, removed probably when she was captured. Normally she would have fought this. But this wasn't normal. This was all kinds of alien and strange. Pursing her lips, she unbuttoned her shirt and slid it off her shoulders. She undid her shoes, dropped her pants. She was left in her underwear. Looking up, he inclined his head. She slid off the singlet top and then her underpants so that she was completely naked.

"Turn," he commanded.

Deleen did as she was bid but hated the idea of turning her back on him. A sense of movement alerted her. He pounced, pressing her flat against the wall with his body. With a handful of her hair in his grip, he twisted her head so that her cheek was flush with the wall. His fingers gripped her jaw, forcing her mouth open and he inspected her mouth and throat with his clawed finger, then he sniffed her mouth, nose and ears. He let her go when she started to retch. Dazed, she dropped to her hands and knees. Before she could move, he was on her again, arm around her waist, tipping her upside down. Writhing and yelling protests, he repeated his inspection but this time with her other orifices.

Her scream was cut short when he dropped her to the ground. She rolled to the wall and he walked away, sniffing loudly, wiping at his nose. Turning back, he said, "You appear to be Pure, but you have been fraternising with the Tainted. The scent of their tech is heavy on your clothes."

"It's no business of yours who I've been fraternising with. I'm a civilian. I demand you let me go."

He huffed. "A civilian? Then you are the property of the Enhanced."

"I have no idea what you mean, you alien freak. Let me go right now."

His amber-coloured eyes assessed her. "No. You are to come with me." He paused as considered her. "You are quite right in your description of me. I am a freak, the hated 'other' even. But you will learn to respect me and mine."

Deleen snatched up her clothes and slipped her underclothes back on, trying to pretend he didn't exist. Her hands shook, but she was not going to break down in front of this creature. Shoving her legs in her pants, she did them up and then punched her arms into her shirt, all the while ignoring him.

His tail twitched. "We will be leaving shortly. You should secure yourself with the other cargo." He grinned at her. It was a scary sight.

"Screw you."

His head angled from side to side as he studied her. "You mean to insult me, yes? Yet you are wary to give the Enhanced ideas regarding mating habits. They may consider it an invitation."

Doing up her buttons, she glared at him. She wanted to deliver the appropriate gesture but didn't think he'd understand it. Clenching her jaw, she clamped down on a response.

A sound buzzed around him, like a purr. His fangs protruded as he attempted a smile. "You have some wisdom to refrain from provoking me."

She concentrated on her shoes, doing up the catches.

"As this flyer is at present incapable of flight, a larger transport will lift us." He gave a wuff. "If you do not secure yourself as I advise, you may be further damaged." His amber eyes glowed in the reflected light. "I do not want my Pure one further injured."

A fist of fear turned in her gut. *His* Pure one?

She rubbed her chin, certain that there was bruising now. He understood her gesture.

"Yes, apologies. You were more fragile than expected. I thought perhaps you were one of the Tainted. I erred."

With that he turned from her and began talking into his comm link, leaving the door open. There was no way out, except through that door, which lead to the cockpit of the flyer. Now that she could see out the viewport, she saw she was in a short-range, snub-nosed flyer. The roar of an engine vibrated against the outer skin of the fuselage. The mother ship was obviously here. The flyer lurched beneath her feet as she hastily grabbed hold of the netting, winding her arm through it, and then one of her legs, to anchor herself like cargo. Although it hurt, she secured her other arm too. A wave of sickness hit her as the flyer jerked up and continued to rise.

Thoughts of Rik arose as she saw the ground fall away through the viewport. There was no sign of the homestead. Her captor looked over at her and sniffed. Keening on the inside, she wondered why Rik hadn't come for her. There was something not quite right with the situation. Were the cold soldiers still alive even? What happened after she was knocked out? Was there anyone alive to rescue her? She had to keep her wits about her, and she'd have to escape by herself. She had no idea how but hoped that inspiration and opportunity would come soon.

To Deleen's disappointment, the flyer did not return her to the city. They did not appear to be the ones who had taken control as she had assumed. Their relationship to the current administration remained unclear.

The small flyer had been taken into the hold of a larger transport. Her alien stayed in the cockpit for the duration of the flight and she hung in the restraints, occasionally jostled like the rest of the cargo. Her outrage at being rough handled by the alien had transmuted into fear. He said they were the Enhanced and obviously Rik was one of the Tainted; she had been relegated to something called Pure. She'd never heard anyone in Five refer to themselves as pure or a purist, so she wasn't sure what kind of faction that was or whether the blow to her head had rearranged her thinking. Her jaw throbbed and the pain in her head came and went with sharp stabbing pains receding only to be replaced by even stronger aches. Why hadn't her captor given her medical treatment? More importantly, why had he taken her in the first place? Her brain didn't want to speculate on why. The thought of being a trophy or hostage or spoils did not appeal. She was the deputy head of security, that was something she supposed. Without identification she couldn't prove it. Neither could her captors. That was the ace up her sleeve if she could use it wisely.

The alien came through the doorway. Her gaze dropped to his hands, which held chains. Her heart sank at the sight. So much for opportunity. This situation was getting worse. Her face heated at the remembrance of having to strip and be inspected. The chains were a new outrage and problem.

"I won't give you any trouble," she said as she untangled herself from the webbing she had been clinging to. "You don't need to chain me."

He lifted them in his clawed hands, presenting them for inspection. "The chains demonstrate your captivity. Your status will be clear."

Stretching the kinks out of her neck, she eyed the way he held the chain. "Status?"

"If you leave this ship without these then your status will be open to challenge. That would not be good for either of us." He rasped out the last, his lisp more prominent.

"Wouldn't it have been easier to leave me behind?" she asked innocently.

"One does not leave valuable loot behind. Ever." He lifted the chains. "Come willingly. I do not wish to damage you further."

Coming forward with her hands out, she gasped at the weight of the chain as he looped it around her wrists and her neck and then sealed it. Gaping down at it she couldn't see where the lock was. It looked like one continuous chain. Damn it, she thought. It's a genetic lock.

Nodding, he turned and headed for the door. "Follow me, stay behind my left shoulder. Keep your eyes down."

He gave these instructions so ominously that her heart skipped a beat. What kind of people were these Enhanced?

The hatchway slid down, forming a ramp. She had to keep her gaze down anyway because she didn't want to fall down the steep ramp, so she had to keep her eyes on where she put her feet, but she did glance around covertly. They were in a large hangar. It was hard to see whether they were underground or above ground, but shards of light arrowing through small windows gave a hint. It was a large construction. Her mind began to buzz. This place wasn't in her memory as a landmark.

Nothing as large as this had been built this far out as far as she knew. Admittedly, she was a bit zoned from being knocked out, but the trip didn't seem to be that long and the flyer didn't seem to go that fast, as far as she could tell. If only she knew the direction. Chewing her lips, she fretted. Obviously, this building was away from Five's city, but there wasn't anywhere else in Five that wasn't either the city or the surrounding farms. The population wasn't big enough yet to support that. Yet, this place existed. It was a large planet, and mostly undeveloped, but surely there would have been word of such a large construction. How could it have remained hidden, without help? Her brain tried to put it together but it just throbbed and she tried to relax instead of think.

Sounds intruded on her thoughts. Wheezings, grunts and other strange sounds. Footsteps and strange scents. Some rather pleasant, others not.

"Harzell," a high-pitched voice intruded. It was directed at her captor, and he halted, bringing her to a stop too. She stood behind his left shoulder. Her eyes only lifted to the knees of the alien speaking, wary of breaking Harzell's dictates. She was assuming that was his name and not a title.

"Turro," her captor replied, that slight purr evident in the air.

"What is this ... prize you bring?" The voice was almost a squeak.

Harzell purr-growled. "One of the Pure."

"Where did you find it?" The voice rose in pitch. Excitement? she wondered.

"On one of the farms. Northwest of the lake."

"Do you claim it?" Turro said, voice lowering slightly, perhaps in awe.

"Indeed, I do. It is my property."

A growl sounded, suddenly savage. Instinct made her look up. She recoiled and hastily looked down. It wasn't another feline creature like Harzell, but something else. It was a part-lizard thing. Trying to cover her mistake she groaned and pretended to waver as if sick. It wasn't far from the truth. She did feel like fainting.

Turro was different to Harzell but had similar traits. A human aspect combined with animal traits. The skin of Turro's neck was scaly, somewhere between grey and green. His scalp was also scaled, though the hue was richer, more bright blue with a definite stripe rising from between his eyes, which were yellow-green and made her stomach turn. It was the vertical pupil, like a slash through the eye that had unnerved her. His jaw was long and narrow, with thin teeth and lips that seemed to blend into his flesh. The rest of him looked human, but when she studied his feet she saw the thick tail, resting, seeming to balance him. The sight of him seriously upset her. She wanted to recoil, but the chains held her. Harzell she could cope with, but this lizard hybrid? Her skin grew cold at the thought. What other horrors awaited her?

"You need to school it in proper respect," Turro said, his voice jagged with outrage. His accent was different to Harzell's, probably due, she thought, to the shape of his mouth and teeth.

"I will," Harzell replied calmly. "Is Mako in his office?"

"Yes," Turro replied in a bored tone, as if he was no longer interested. Deleen thought the disinterest was fake.

Harzell tugged on her chain, making her stumble after him. There were other aliens around and she tried peeking to the side, without being obvious. Odd shapes. Hair, scales, claws, feathers, beaks. A cold sweat inched down her back. The chains prevented her from scratching the moist itch on her scalp and lower back. This was the weirdest set of aliens. Not that she had ever imagined meeting any, outside the vids and grapho novels.

They entered a large office. Harzell put out his hand to halt her. "Kneel," he commanded. Trembling, Deleen went to obey but overbalanced from the chains weighing her down. She faceplanted instead, just stopping her nose from being pounded with chain-bound hands.

A hiss emitted from another alien's mouth. Deleen looked up and then back down again. "What is the meaning of this?" A harsh voice washed over her.

Mako had triangular ears that twitched, altering the direction like a kind of nervous habit. They stuck out of the side of his head near the crown, where a mass of white and russet tufts of fur sat. His face angled to a sharp nose, sort of like a snout, with little dark eyes on either side and a small, tight mouth with hardly any chin. His arms looked over-long and the claws on his hands were black and sharp.

Harzell bowed. "Forgiveness. I found this," he indicated Deleen. "While on equipment recovery."

Mako's voice was low and gruff. "Why is she chained like property?"

Harzell cleared his throat. "I claim her."

"Nonsense!" The word came out like a bark or laugh. "That thing is unclaimable." Mako came out from behind his desk. Deleen eyed him warily. "It is common stock, like the salvaged machinery to be used as required."

"No," Harzell said. "I claim it."

Mako backed away to retreat behind his desk. "Why would you do this? You will make trouble."

"She is one of the Pure—a breeding female."

Mako slapped a hand on the desk. "Make it stand up. I want to inspect."

Deleen responded to the tug on the chains reluctantly. She wasn't keen on being inspected. She wanted to thump Harzell and choke Mako with her chains, but she had trouble focusing. What kind of outfit was this? Breeding female? Not on his life.

Mako peered into her face, his breath pungent. She tried not to breathe as he walked around her sniffing and examining. "How do you know it is a female?"

"Inspection and," Harzell paused for a moment, "scent."

Mako scratched his chin with a forefinger, while studying her. "It appears healthy, if slightly damaged."

Mako reached out a clawed finger and poked her shoulder as if checking she was real. Then he shook his head. "The High will not like this. He claims all the Pure for himself."

Hazell half growled. "Only those in the city. She was not in the city."

Mako sat back behind his desk and took out a document. "Very well, I will record her as your property, but expect to be challenged ..."

"By whom, the High?" Harzell's surprise was evident.

"Yes, and by anyone who seeks your prize. You might find the market is your best option for material gain."

Harzell stood rigid. "Market?"

Mako might have smiled. Deleen couldn't tell. Only that a row of thin pointy teeth appeared below his top lip. "The High has created a market for goods. Goods in exchange for land and settlement rights."

A purring sound came from Harzell's throat. "I did not know the occupation had started already. I will think on this." He tugged on her chains abruptly, nearly toppling her. "I will return to my quarters."

Mako had already picked up another document and was paging through it. An aide shut the door behind them. "Come," Harzell said. "The more difficult part lies ahead. Do not speak to anyone and keep your eyes down. Really down. No sneaky looks. Others are not as moderate as those who you have seen so far. Many may find insult in your very existence. Understand?"

"Yes," she said with her head down. She kept to his left shoulder, trying to stop her fear from spiralling out of control. Part of her mind wanted to scream and run for the nearest exit to get as far as she could from Harzell and his 'breeding female' comment. The other part hinted that he was protecting her, but from what she did not know. Who was the 'High' and was he now running Five?

One thing was certain, this was definitely an invasion. A lot of Enhanced appeared to be living in this place. Land on Five was begging for settlement and development, as the colony was only young. The human settlement was confined to one region, around the equator on the major continent where the weather was mild and the rainfall plentiful enough for them to keep crops and animals. Further out, no one had bothered to settle there. Not yet. The population needed to increase to quota before another large settlement would be allocated and resources shared, infrastructure built.

These invaders had already begun carving up her home. The compound was larger than a village from what she could tell through sight and sound. They went down a long, dark corridor, turned left twice. Deleen committed that to memory, just in case she got the chance to escape. A futile thought at present. She didn't know the extent of her danger. She didn't even know where she was. The thought of Rik came to mind again and she pushed it down. He had no idea where she was, even if he was inclined to save her. Based on the number of the Enhanced she'd seen, the remainder of his squad didn't have a chance. Currently it could be three against fifty or five hundred. She didn't know, but she'd like to find that out. Maybe she could gather some intelligence while she was here. Maybe there was a way to turn the tables on this invasion.

Harzell stopped and opened a door. "In," he said.

She went in. He stepped in after her, shutting the door. Deleen's mouth dropped open.

Chapter Thirteen

CAPTIVE

Harzell's room was surprisingly large and luxurious, not at all what Deleen was expecting. It looked lived in, which indicated that the Enhanced had been here for some time. Invasion to her hinted at newly arrived. Deleen could not work it out and dared not ask outright. Maybe she wouldn't like the answer.

A large round pool sat in the centre of the room surrounded by three backless couches. Further in there was a large bed, also round. Artefacts covered the walls. Paintings, mostly. Ceramics sat on small side tables and there was a food preparation area, complete with large pots overflowing with vegetables and fruit. Harzell's room was twice the size of her city apartment.

Harzell nudged her forward into the room, stepping in front of her after securing the door. He unkeyed the chain with his forefinger and the weight of it slid away. Again he had surprised her. "Welcome to my home." He pointed to the bath. "You should bathe. I will get food and some pain killers."

Closing her mouth, because it was hanging open, she then nodded. She didn't move but stood there taking in her surroundings and waiting for Harzell to leave. He'd done enough inspecting for one day. Actually, for a lifetime.

Even though he had treated her roughly and taken her prisoner, she knew it could have been worse. The thought of the lizard Enhanced or the other fox Enhanced chilled her.

Harzell eyed her expectantly and then with a nod, turned to the door and left. There was something in his eyes she didn't quite like. The words 'breeding female' swirled in the forefront of her mind and sickened her stomach. Even if she was inclined to breed, there was no way she was attracted to Harzell, so whatever he had in mind, she wasn't going to be a willing participant.

There was way too much she didn't know about Harzell or his people. The door remained shut, so she confirmed it was locked. No telling when he would return. She quickly stripped off and climbed into the bath, using the three steps on the near side to get in. The water was not as hot as she liked but that meant she wasn't going to linger even though the warm water felt good on her bruised skin.

Checking around the rim of the round tub, she found a tap and turned it on. Warmer water spurted out. A slight sulphur smell made her think it was from a natural hot spring. It was filtered, but there was still an odour. Her tortured muscles eased in the heat. As she lay her head back on the side of the bath and floated for a time, her muscles unknotted, and her pain lessened. Massaging the back of her neck, she worked out the kinks there too. Sighing, she let her eyes close, and time seemed to stop.

When her eyes snapped open, she knew she wasn't alone. A noise had woken her. Harzell stood on the opposite side of the bath, studying her floating naked form. She dropped her legs and glared at him. "Had a good look, did you?" she asked.

"Not even beginning." He smiled, or smirked, she wasn't quite sure. He tapped a pile on a small table. "Drying cloths and a shift."

"For wearing?"

"For sleeping. You need rest. There is food there and some analgesics." He lifted his chin. "Your jaw. It looks painful."

"Someone doesn't know their own strength."

He wuffed, a sound she took for a laugh, but it came out strange, more animal sounding. "Someone does. Don't you forget that. You live because I desired your life. I exerted enough force as was required to keep you quiet, still and transportable." His fangs caught the light, emphasising his alienness.

Her mouth formed an 'oh'. She stayed in the water and stilled himself watching her. "Your food is getting cold. You must rise from the water to dress."

Deleen pursed her lips. She could stay in here, just to see what he would do. Or she could get up, dry herself and dress in front of his prying eyes and then eat. She shrugged. He'd already seen her body. No news there. While he had intruded during his inspection, there'd been nothing overtly sexual about it. Not yet at least.

She waded to the other side of the bath. Conscious that he was watching her, she snatched up a towel and draped it over herself as she climbed the steps and then dried as best she could without showing more skin than necessary. His eyes followed her movements. Her heart rate increased. Was he curious or aroused? The shift opened out when she lifted it. It was a pale yellow. Not really her colour but it was simple and loose and short. Slipping it over her head she was appalled that it ended a bare five inches below her butt. Casting her gaze around, she looked for her underwear. The clothes she'd removed to bathe were gone. Her head jerked up. "My things?"

"They have been sent to be cleaned. They may be returned to you, if you are compliant."

She screwed up her face and jerked her head, ready to argue and then deciding against it. Her stomach rumbled noisily.

He squinted at her. That's what it looked like. His eyes half closed and his mouth formed a grin. "Food?"

She walked past him to where he pointed. A covered dish was there with two bowls next to it with spoons. "Are you eating too?"

"Yes. You will serve me."

Deleen chewed the inside of her lip, biting down a retort. The way he said serve indicated a whole raft of meanings other than putting some food in a bowl. She opened the lid and a wonderful aroma hit her nostrils. Floating on the surface were fragrant chopped herbs. She stirred through the mixture and saw it was all vegetable. Roots and fungi and some kind of seed, with soft dumplings. A glance at Harzell indicated no surprise at this vegetarian offering.

"Why do you look at me like that? Is the food not to your liking?"

"I was surprised, that's all. I thought you would eat meat."

His hair bristled, the mane rising like hackles on a dog and an angry growl erupted from his mouth as he sprung to his feet. His whole body tensed, ready to spring.

She dropped the spoon and stepped back. "What? What did I say ... do?"

"You offer me insult. I am no cannibal!"

She put up her hand, urging him to sit back down. "Oh ... I didn't mean ... I'm sorry. I didn't know that to suggest you ate meat was an insult. The food looks great and smells wonderful." She hastily stepped forward and filled the bowls. A jug filled with water was next to it, so she poured some out. The pills were by the glass so she shoved them in her mouth, her anxious gaze fixed on Harzell as she swallowed some water to wash them down. Then she picked up a bowl and hesitantly brought it over to him. Lifting it up in offering, she said, "Here."

While his hackles had settled somewhat, she sensed he was still affronted. His amber gaze focused on her. "I didn't mean to offend you. Eating meat is accepted where I come from." Did they not notice the livestock on the farms? She lowered her gaze and he left out a wuff of air. He took the bowl from her and she backed up, ready to claim hers.

He took a seat on one of the chaises. He patted the fabric next to him. "Come eat with me."

Deleen picked up her bowl, wanting to be elsewhere but completely out of her depth and unwilling to rock the boat further by refusing. Besides she just wanted to eat and sleep, preferably under the haze of the analgesics she'd just taken.

Although she was starving, she waited until Harzell took his first spoonful. Then she lowered her gaze to the food, hating the way her hand shook. Her captor made no move to touch her and she was conscious of his scent, stronger now they were in this room.

The food was salty and very tasty, and the soft dumplings were divine. Even though she was hungry, she ate slowly, chewing each mouthful carefully. In doing this she was able to keep a sideways eye on her captor. He sipped the liquid slowly and then when it was finished, he ate the chunks of vegetables and slowly bit into the dumplings. When his meal was complete, he held out his bowl.

"Did you want more?" She was tempted to laugh at this game.

"Yes, if there is any."

"I'll check," she said with false niceness. Having lived on her own mostly, she didn't fetch and carry for anyone. At the farm when she was young everybody helped each other, everyone was equal.

The serving bowl held more of the vegetable stew so she upended it into his bowl. She was quite full and was no longer hungry. She brought it back to him.

He took it. "Kneel before me," he said.

Deleen didn't like the sound of that. "No."

He glanced up at her. "At first so biddable and now refusing a polite request."

"There was nothing polite about it."

He put his bowl aside and Deleen watching him warily. He leaped up so quickly she didn't even register the movement until she was stretched over his lap. Remembering the skimpy shift, she tried to hold it in place and wriggle away.

A quick slap across her rump silenced her. Her body went rigid and she didn't even cry out, even though it stung. "Is that a sufficient reminder of your predicament?" he asked her.

Deleen was reeling.

"Answer!" He slapped her again. Harder this time.

"Yes!"

He released her and she scrambled away and then to her feet.

"Kneel," he repeated, taking up his bowl.

Biting her lip, she knelt between his legs. She eyed his groin, having malicious thoughts about punching him there. If only she could be certain that he had testicles to mash.

He finished his food, put the bowl to the side. "Move closer."

Deleen repressed an angry shake of her head and leaned closer. His fingers touched her forehead and she started, then relaxed as his fingers trailed over her skull, then along her jaw, pressing cautiously. "You have no serious damage. Do you agree?"

"I agree. Rest and painkillers will help."

"Then it is best that I not summon a medic."

She nodded and he let out a breath. "Is there something wrong with the medic?" she asked him.

He purred. A sound that vibrated from his throat. "You are clever. I like that. Yes, involving the medic may complicate things."

"I don't think I want to know. Can I sleep now?"

"Yes," he replied, showing his fangs.

After a thoroughly exhausting day, a headache, aching body and the stress of being a captive in an alien camp, Deleen thought it would take a while to sleep. Her body had other things in mind. She crashed out, just after she crawled into the bed. She sniffed and smelt Harzell, but the lure of the pillow and being horizontal got the better of her. It did cross her mind in sleep that she should be scared, too scared to sleep, but her mind wasn't listening to anything.

Something woke her in the morning. A touch, a pinch, she wasn't sure. She elbowed up a little in the bed. Harzell blinked at her. "You slept well?"

Deleen had to admit that she had. A deep, dreamless sleep. She couldn't actually attest to feeling better for it. Her legs hurt when she flexed them, her back had developed a spasm and her mouth was dry. "I did," she replied wearily.

"You may rest further today." He passed her a tray. Cooked grain in a bowl. Some water in a jug with a cup.

"Thank you," she said taking a deep drink.

"What will you be doing?" she asked, deceptively nonchalant.

He got up and the mattress flexed beneath her. To her surprise, he'd been sitting on the bed next to her. She wondered where he'd slept. This had to be his bed. As she had no recollection of anything after closing her eyes, she didn't care. Even if he'd slept with her, he had not assaulted her.

Deleen refilled her cup and looked up at him. "I have work to do. I will return in a few hours to check on you. You may wash and move about my rooms. The door will be locked."

"Oh?"

"If there is an emergency the door will unlock. Follow the amber lights to the nearest exit."

Deleen grinned. It sounded like induction at the administration to ensure optimum occupational health and safety. "Is there likely to be an emergency?"

He wuffed. "If I knew that, it would not be an emergency but a situation. I tell you this in case being locked in distresses you. It is for your safety."

The image of Mako came to mind and the lizard man, Turro. She would not make the mistake of thinking she'd be safe around them. And from what she could estimate there were more of the Enhanced around, ready to pounce on her.

Deleen took a taste of her grain. It was rather bland and lukewarm but it was soft and went down easily. She wondered what sort of society this was and how they came to be here. "I understand."

"No one should bother you, but if they do, lock yourself in the storeroom." He pointed to the door off the food preparation area. "There are extra locks in there."

Her head shot up, mouth agape. He nodded and then turned to leave. After finishing off the food, she lay back down. Her headache was better, but her jaw ached, throbbing to a peak and then easing off. Harzell was very strong. She should be grateful he didn't break her jaw.

When next she woke, she got up to wash and noticed that her clothes were back. She wasted no time in putting them on. The skimpy shift did not do much for her confidence, particularly when dealing with the Enhanced, the aliens.

A rattling at the door made her tense. Was it Harzell returning? When he didn't come through, she got to her feet, watching the door. Scratching became pummelling. Someone or something was desperate to get in. Get to her.

A howl leaked under the door. Putting on her shoes, she crept closer to the storeroom. Whoever was trying to get in was making a racket and one or two times the noise was so disturbing that Deleen hid in the storeroom, ready to lock herself in.

The assault on the door subsided. It was quiet again for a few minutes. Then a thump hit the door and another disturbance began as someone tried to break the door down. Whether it was the same one or a new alien, Deleen didn't know. The thought did occur to her that

Harzell was playing with her mind, trying to break her and that this was some orchestration to erode her resistance, to make her turn to him and be pliable. Yet, from what she judged about him she didn't think that was so. It was possible, but not probable, as far as she was concerned.

After about an hour of incessant noise, it stopped suddenly. Her ears rang and the quiet was so noticeable that Deleen crept out of the storeroom. She stood poised ready to hide again but it remained quiet. Gradually she relaxed and lay down on the bed. It was there Harzell found her.

"You are well?" he asked, placing more food down for her. This tray had a steaming bowl on it. When she looked down, she saw it was soup and there was bread too.

"I'm okay, thanks."

His amber gaze studied her, then he wuffed. "Were you disturbed in my absence?"

She took the proffered bowl. "Yes. They came to the door. It was noisy and a few times I thought they would get through, but they didn't."

He shook his head and stroked his chin. "Word of you must have spread."

Her skin chilled. If it was just word of her, what would actually seeing her do? "That's not good, I take it." She took a sip of the soup. It was hot and plain but had chunks of tasty vegetables in it.

Harzell inclined his head. "There are issues."

Deleen swallowed a mouthful. "Such as?"

He looked her straight in the eye and then shrugged, an entirely human gesture and weird on the alien. "I may be required to sell you."

She coughed, spluttered and then wiped soup from her nose. "Sell me? No way."

He angled his head from side to side. "I said *may*, and perhaps it will not come to that. I found you and claimed you. That should be sufficient, but everything is in a state of flux. My claim over you may be challenged."

"Actually, you didn't find me. You knocked me out and kidnapped me. There is a difference."

"Not much of one. You were alone and unprotected."

Deleen finished the soup, which had helped to settle her stomach. She knew that he knew she hadn't been alone. He called Rik, and the others, the Tainted. Obviously, the Tainted didn't count as people as far as Harzell and the Enhanced were concerned.

She was in turmoil. Ever since the administration made that announcement about bringing out the cold soldiers and burning them, her life had been turned upside down. Life as she knew it had changed. Colony Five had changed. Killing innocents was against all that the colony stood for and it was too hard to reconcile. Now the Enhanced too. What was really going on? There was a layer of lies everywhere and she had to trust strangers and her own heart to find a way forward.

Rik may have been big and slightly overbearing, but he had looked after her, cared for her. But these Enhanced people, these aliens, were another ball game altogether. Their culture and ways seemed bizarre to her. Rik and his companions looked like her. Harzell and his kind did not. Something deep in her reacted to that difference.

Harzell paced the room, his tail twitching, apparently deep in thought.

"Can't you take me back to where you found me? Then you won't need to sell me. The problem will disappear."

He wuffed slowly, like a sigh. "That is not an option. In any case, you should not wish for this thing."

A feeling of dread began in her gut. "Oh? What should I wish for?"

He turned to face her. "You should wish to stay with me. I will care for you and ..."

Deleen gave him a cheeky grin. "I can look after myself."

"Without my protection you would not last a day here." He jerked his head to the hallway outside. "Not all my kin are like me. Not all of them would care for your wellbeing. They would care only for what you represent."

"And that is?"

"One of the Pure."

"You've mentioned that word before, but I don't understand the relevance. What would your people want with me if I was one of these Pure?"

"Some would kill you outright for what you represent." He spoke harshly and she flinched. "Others would mistreat you, make you suffer for the same reason. Others would try to breed from you, to purify their line."

Deleen swallowed. "Breed from me? As in in-vitro?"

He shook his head. "No, in-vitro breeding is banned. Direct mating until you are full with offspring. And then again and again until you die."

The dread in her gut surged and she could barely swallow. "And what do you want me for?"

A purr escaped from his throat. "I find you pleasing to look upon. I would have you be the mother of my children."

Deleen sized him up. She was in serious shit. Not only did he want to have sex with her, he wanted to breed ... kittens? There was no way that was going to happen. Harzell was trying to make it sound like the good option and the alternatives did sound awful.

She had only kissed Rik and had been left wanting more. He was a big hunk of a man and she cared for him. They had a rapport and now she missed him. Was it because she had developed an emotional attachment? Or because she was in danger and he could save her? She couldn't really make up her mind about that.

Faced with this new threat from Harzell, she just wanted out. If she was going to escape, she'd have to start thinking up a plan. That meant getting out of this room. If she believed Harzell, her chances of doing that without being killed or caught were small. Yet staying here meant having sex with this large part-cat, or lion or whatever. Was it even possible they could breed? She wasn't going to ask him that because she had no intention of agreeing to such a thing.

"You did not respond to me in the way that I'd hoped," he said.

She'd been looking down at her hands, twisting her fingers together. Her head jerked up with the realisation that she'd been transparent. He could read her. "I'm sorry. I can't be what you want."

He pounced onto the bed, his face close to hers. "Why? You trust me. You slept by me all night. There was no fear. Is this not sufficient trust to mate with me?"

How could she explain that she was so dog-tired she'd have slept next to a bear and be damned? She didn't fear him, because she was out of her depth and had to rely on him. "It takes a bit more than that. I'm sorry."

He climbed back off the bed. His tail twitched, a sharp single movement. "I am sorry too."

He left the room and she hoped he had locked it. With a sinking feeling in her stomach, she considered that maybe she'd made the wrong choice. She could have laid back and thought about the colony while Harzell went for it … She cringed … maybe not.

He'd likely want to do it more than once. Likely all the time until she had kittens inside her. She shuddered at the thought.

Harzell wasn't human. It was a bit much to ask her to start breeding with an alien. She didn't want to breed with a human for stars' sake. She was definitely in the shit and didn't know how to get out of it.

She had to plan. After she finished off the now-cold soup, she paced the room, easing out the cricks and spasms in her back and neck and massaging the muscles in her legs and back. She needed to get ready for a fight and a flight.

No one came banging on the doors this time. Even so, there was tension in the air. Damn, she'd lost her only ally in this place. Harzell may have been her captor, but he had also been her protector and now she was going to lose that. All because of her fastidiousness.

Shaking her head, she tried to picture copulating with the alien and just couldn't. But if she was sold to the highest bidder? What then? She might be bereft of choice. Raped by some half-animal. How stupid was she? It all seemed so clear cut now.

The locked sounded. The door swung open. It wasn't Harzell who stood there, but the fox creature, Mako. He had chains in his hands and a feral grin on his pointed face.

"I belong to Harzell," she protested, holding up her hands in a defensive posture.

"Not anymore. His claim has been voided. Soon you'll belong to someone else … or many someones." He moved forward with the chains as she dove to the side to get around him and out the door.

He was quick. He had the chains looped around her before she'd taken two steps. "Do not resist," he growled into her ear, "or I'll be forced to drug you." He sounded almost gleeful at the prospect.

"Damn you!" She rammed her shoulder into him. Claws sank into the soft skin of her upper arms and then there was a sting. Her head drooped and her heartbeat slowed. He had drugged her. Words came out of her mouth, but they were slurred, made no sense. Her body hit the floor with a thump, the chains biting into her flesh.

* * *

The clamour of grunts, growls and deep voices filled her ears as she came to. Disoriented, her mouth was dry, head aching. Had she been to a party? Unsticking her eyes, she blinked as the blur of shapes came into focus. She licked her lips and pushed up off the floor into a sitting position. A set of bars encircled the round dais she was sitting on. On the other side of the bars stood an angry mob of nightmares. Aliens? She stared momentarily stunned by sight ofthe creatures, the Enhanced, who all appeared to be a mixture of human and an animal of some type. A bizarre combination that defied even her imagination. Some were more animal than human looking, while others wore more human aspects. Their growls had her pulse racing. If they got to her, she wouldn't have a chance.

After the initial panic receded, she saw some were drinking and others were already apparently intoxicated. It made her feel she was an exotic dancer in a bar, except she wasn't dancing.

Unfortunately, she'd made eye contact and now that she had moved, more of the attention centred her way. Close to the bars, two males with dark fur and twitching tails didn't appear to be wearing much in the way of clothes. They were bare except for some sort of loin cloth hiding their genitals, which she was glad of.

Females also made up a number of the audience. Well, she supposed they were females due to the breasts—some had four, but the norm appeared to be two. Like the males they had differing animal aspects. This puzzled Deleen. If they were an alien species, then why were there mammal and reptile varieties? The common element was the human-seeming part of them. Thinking about the answer made her feel very ill. These were human hybrids. Had to be. Her theory that the aliens weren't aliens was correct.

A voice speaking standard echoed around the room. "Thank you for joining us. As you see the first prize is on display. Get your money ready. We will be starting the bidding shortly."

Deleen's face heated. She peered into the crowd, seeking Harzell. Not that she expected him to save her. Obviously, she'd blown that idea out of the water when she refused to be owned by him, refused to be the mother of his children. A friendly face in this sea of strangeness would have been most welcome.

A clawed hand inched toward her through the bars. She didn't even want to see what was at the other end of it. She backed up and hit the bars behind her. Other hands reached for her, groping for her breasts and sliding beneath her clothes. With a yell she surged to her feet, circling to keep them all in view.

Life had been simple once, the thought. True, reviving Rik had made her life interesting, but she missed him right then. Why he wasn't there now saving her? she thought, rather desperately. It was smelling mighty stinky right then, animal scents and booze and a whiff of vomit. She worried she wasn't going to like the answers to the questions that raced around in her head.

The announcer came back, their voice inciting the crowd to whoop and scream. Deleen had to cover her ears as the sound grew to a crescendo. "We have today, ladies and gents, a Pure from Colony Five city. While she was found with some of the Tainted, she appears to have escaped unscathed. She's ripe and willing to be your companion and, perhaps, even the mother of your brood. Start your bidding, folks. Your next step to purity awaits you. You could have many near-Pure offspring with this female."

Deleen glanced nervously around her and hunched down to make herself small. They had to be kidding. They were selling her off like a brood mare. Taking in the assembled crowd, she almost puked. The announcer was back again. "Lots of good bids there, folks. But you can do better."

A speaker above her head barked. "Stand up, female. Look presentable."

She studdied the space above her, thinking there was someone there. "You can't do this!" As she yelled, the crowd roared, drowning her out.

More hands darted in trying to grab her. She backed up only to have her shirt grabbed and ripped down her back. Dark, hungry eyes studied her. The bidding commenced again. Doom rang like a bell in her ears.

Deleen lost most of her clothing before the bidding ended. Judging from the yelling and backslapping going on between a group of grey-furred men, she'd been purchased by a consortium. Gang rape was a very real possibility. The crowd parted as her new owners marched up to her little prison to claim their prize. Deleen thought that standing in the middle of the dais would keep her relatively safe. Except when the group of Enhanced males approached, two of the bars lifted.

Facing them, she leaned back against the remaining bars and wrapped her arms around them for an anchor. She wasn't going to go easily.

Two pairs of burly arms reached in and grabbed her by the legs and tugged. Deleen's fingers slipped from the bars as if they had been buttered. She was carried aloft over the men's heads and lots of cheers and fist pumping accompanied her passage.

There was a yell, and another, then a murmur as the crowd grew quiet. The men conveying her were late to an understanding of the change in the crowd and they continued bouncing her along on their conveyor belt of hands and cheering until they reached a break and empty area.

Deleen was very shaken by this time, even more so when they flipped her onto her hands and knees before a set of well-polished black boots. Taking a moment to catch her breath, she hazarded a glance upwards. A human male stood before her. Medium height, dark hair and eyes and a narrow mouth, frowning at her. She sat back on her heels, chest still heaving, trying to keep the scraps of her clothes covering her bits.

"What is the meaning of this?" he bellowed, the timbre of a growl at the edge of his voice. He was Enhanced too. Her eyes widened and she couldn't stop the flinch. The beasts who had been manhandling her stepped back. Glancing over her shoulder, she detected the space around her. Looking down, she could see streaks of blood all over her, claw marks and scrapes covering her visible skin. She had barely kept her underwear intact.

Quiet murmuring peppered the crowd. Heads turned, looking at each other with questioning gazes. Some had their heads down. A ripple in the crowd formed as someone made their way through. Mako came out, nose twitching and ears erect. He bowed flamboyantly. "Most High, I am at your service."

The High's gaze snapped to Mako. "Are you responsible for this?" He indicated Deleen. "This outrage?"

Mako bowed his head. "Oh no, most High. It was Harzell. He brought her here."

The High bit his lip and his gaze sped over the crowd. "Where is Harzell?"

Mako grinned and looked at her sideways. Deleen shuddered.

Someone, a guard maybe, came to inform the high that Harzell was in the lock-up and was being brought out.

Mako kept his head down, nails clicking idly on the material of his pants. His skin rippled now and then, and Deleen was sure he was anxious.

Time seemed to slow, until finally a chained Harzell was dragged before them. His face showed signs of a beating, yet he kept his head held high. "Most High," he said with an incline of his head.

"Are you responsible for this ..." He indicated Deleen. "Mako said this despicable event was your doing."

Harzell didn't even blink. "I brought the Pure here, that is true. It is Mako who orchestrated this auction," he indicated the room with his chin and let out a growl. "I had claimed her, but he took her from me by force."

The High's head snapped around to Mako. "You have tried to deceive me once too often."

"That's not true," Mako whined. "It is his fault.

The High flicked his hand. "Take him to a cell."

Guards emerged from the shadowed walls and grabbed the fox man. He tried to wiggle out of their grasp, but the guards had a firm hold of him with claws of their own digging into his flesh. Deleen grinned as they dragged him away. Dare she believe this ordeal was over?

The High knelt down in front of her and took one of her hands. "Can you stand?" he asked gently.

Trembling Deleen managed a nod. "Yes."

She stood up, the High supporting her by the elbow. Her attention went to Harzell, and his battered face. "I'm sorry they hurt you, Harzell."

She had no reason to say anything. He had captured her, but she was glad to know this was not what he'd intended for her. Apart from knocking her out, he'd treated her reasonably well for a prisoner. Mostly. She remembered the spanking. Maybe not treated her that well.

The High took her hand and stood beside her. The crowd was still milling around, murmurs now down to a whisper.

The High drew a breath and then addressed the crowd. "These auctions are beneath you, beneath us. You seek to be civilised. You seek acceptance and a place in the wider world, yet actions like these demonstrate you are not worthy."

Louder murmuring spread around the crowd like an infection. Undertones of anger rippled around her. Heads bowed in shame. "You show yourselves to be animals, sub-human. Is that what you want?"

'No!' Someone shouted and more voices joined in. Soon they were yelling and punching the air. "No! NO!"

"We are human!" someone in the back yelled.

Deleen flinched, then blinked around her. Human? The possibilities converted to probabilities and then to facts in a fraction of a second. Definitely not alien. Human. How was that possible, given Colony Five's creed? Theoretically possible, yes ... but. Denial set in, taking a hold of her. Not true. Can't be true. Must not be true. Lies. Lies. Lies. Panic seized her. If she accepted this truth, all other truths would be destroyed.

It just couldn't be.

When the crowd quietened, the High continued his address. "Then you know what you must do. Respect each other." He turned his head to engage more of this audience. "Respect those who are different." With a pause for effect. "Then you will be worthy of greater things."

Silence greeted his last words. No applause. No cheers. Just quiet. A whisper sound of shuffling feet began as the crowd began to disperse.

He turned to her and nodded to Harzell. Easing her along by her elbow, he said, "Come, we will get your injuries seen to. Then you will tell me what you do here."

Deleen looked over her shoulder at the dispersing crowd. They were not going as quietly as she'd first thought. A frightened shout pierced the quiet. Sobs broke out and then arguing. Blame was being tossed around like a volleyball. Deleen quickened her step.

Chapter Fourteen

TRUTH AND LIES

The medical centre appeared like any other, except the medic was an Enhanced. His head was cloaked in glossy black feathers like hair, which continued beneath his tunic top. His nose was aquiline, his chin pointed and eyes dark. If he had wings she couldn't see them. Who were these people? How did they get here? Deleen was still in denial. They couldn't be human or even aspire to be human. It made no sense.

Another medic appeared. A female one. Her skin was glossy and she had no hair. Deleen wondered whether she was part snake. She tended to Harzell while the bird man tended to Deleen's injuries. A few bruises were sprayed with lotion to accelerate healing, her cuts and abrasions cleaned and sealed. Her eyes were checked and her brain scanned.

The medic nodded to the High. "Nothing serious, most High."

The High looked her in the eye, his face serious. "Jay here will see to your comfort until I return." He glanced around the room at the three guards stationed there. "Best you wait here until I get back."

Deleen nodded. The High nodded to Harzell. "You too." He turned on his heel and left the room.

Deleen lay back on the bunk she'd been sitting on while Harzell was treated. Worn out, she was still hazy from the drugs and exhausted. Her captor needed a bit more than skin seal to treat his wounds. It looked

177

like sutures were in order. Deleen overheard the snake woman, Celine, talking about a concussion. Jay joined her in analysing the results of a scan. Harzell caught her eye and angled his head down at his body as if to say *look at us*.

When her stomach started growling, she couldn't hide the fact she was hungry. She had no idea when she had last eaten. Jay moved away from the others and went to a small cubicle. He returned with a steaming cup. "Some sustaining soup," he said by way of explanation when he held it out to her.

She took it, tried to smile and winced. "Thank you."

She took hesitant sips. The soup tasted like it was made from field rations—rehydrated vegetables and stock. She frowned and took in the room. How did these people get their supplies? Where did they get dried food? The puzzle just kept getting more complicated and the ideas they generated in her mind became increasingly frightening.

Before Harzell was released from the medics, the High returned. He inquired after her and then waited patiently for Harzell to be released from care.

A pair of guards followed him. Their outward animal characteristics were not obvious. She realised that they didn't have to be. One could have Enhanced characteristics of an animal but it might be reflected in sense of smell, reflexes, strength and so on. She couldn't repress the shudder. Her reaction was similar to seeing Rik's nanotech healing his flesh—a kind of inbuilt revulsion. A reaction she couldn't account for logically.

As they walked through the corridors, she studied the back of the High's head, not sure what she was looking for. Horns perhaps. She rolled her eyes. That was beneath her, but then again, her thoughts were addled so she was entitled to a little hysteria-inspired bigotry, wasn't she?

The High led them down a corridor and then across a suspended walkway into what appeared to be another building. The windows of the walkway were opaque so she couldn't see the terrain or the layout of the facility.

Door locks responded to the High's DNA when he pressed his finger to the lock. Then, on opening, they proceeded through and into a hallway, the end of which contained a large office complete with desk and a set of lounges to the side.

Muted light leaked through the opaque windows that adorned the room. Deleen had wished for a view so that she might pinpoint her location. Not that she was a geographer by any stretch. Wanting to know where she was being held was like an itch needing to be scratched. If she could figure it out, would that give her hope that Rik and the others may find her? She wondered what Rik would think about this secret enclave of the Enhanced. It wasn't an alien spaceship, which she figured was the usual transport arrangement. As she looked around the room, she noticed the architecture was familiar. It was human. The walls and ceiling were made from Colony Five material. The furniture too was worn and showed some age. Either the Enhanced had taken it over when invading or they had been living here for some time. Her gut told her it was the latter.

The High indicated the lounges with an open hand. Harzell sat on a backless chair, his tail swishing leisurely. Deleen took comfort in that. At least he wasn't agitated by this meeting, so maybe she had nothing to worry about.

Some of the pain meds were wearing off. Twinges niggled where her skin was mending.

"Refreshment?" the High asked. Deleen was still hungry and thirsty. The soup had only taken the edge off. Besides, she needed fuel for her body if she was going to escape.

"Thank you," she replied. Harzell just nodded and grinned in a cat-like way. He dropped the grin quickly though and rubbed at a bruise on his right cheek.

An aide came in carrying a plate. He placed it down and then brought cups and a jug of water. "Please eat and drink. Then we will talk," the High said, indicating the food in front of her.

The High went to his desk and dealt with something at a computer monitor. Harzell inclined his head, indicating she have first choice of the food. It looked like bread with salad so she took some and began to munch, wishing for a nice hot burger. The colony ate meat, either real meat farmed or synthesised in great vats. The water was warm but it didn't matter to Deleen. She drank two big cupfuls before the High returned to them.

He took a seat. "Once again, let me apologise for what happened to you, Ms …"

"Milo," she supplied. "And you are?"

An eyebrow rose, as he appeared to recognise the name, then he inclined his head. "Ms Milo. I am referred to as the High, which is all you need to know."

His gaze turned to Harzell. "You should not have brought her here, Harz. Why did you?"

Harzell's amber eyes focused on her. "She was with the Tainted. It seemed like a good idea. Some protective instinct perhaps."

Deleen cleared her throat. "Some protection."

The High glanced her way, then returned his attention to Harzell. "And your other motives?"

Harzell looked down at his feet. "I wished to claim her for my own."

"Hmm," the High said. "A bit precipitous. I thought you more intelligent than that."

"So did I," Harzell agreed. "I apologise. She is very Pure."

The High tented his fingers against his chin and studied her. "So, what do we do with you now?" The High said over his fingers. "That's my dilemma. Believe me I wish you no harm, but the knowledge of our existence could be a danger to you, and it is most definitely a danger to us."

"Let me go," Deleen said flatly. "You cannot expect to keep this place secret much longer."

"We are doing a reasonable job," the High said calmly, moving his hands to indicate the room.

Deleen had never been a gambler and was not much of risk taker. "Rik will come for me." Deleen met his gaze.

The High's eyes flicked to Harzell and then he dropped his hands to his knees, leaned slightly forward. "Rik?"

"I was with some cold soldiers when I was snatched. They will search for me and I'm confident they will find me."

The High's pale complexion flushed, particularly around the neck. He stood up and walked to the opaque window. With his back to them, he replied, "I wouldn't be so sure. Almost all the Tainted are accounted for." He turned back, his gaze fierce now and his expression hard. A tingle of fear crept up her legs. "Their extermination is a foregone conclusion. They will not be able to help you. They can't help themselves."

Deleen chewed the inside of her cheek to bite back a response. There was nothing to be gained by arguing. If the High thought Rik and the others were dead, then all the better. They wouldn't look for them and wouldn't be on their guard against them. That had to work in her favour.

Yet, his words had affected her. The thought of Rik's dead face filled her mind, but she scrunched the image up and threw it out. If Rik and the others didn't find her, then she'd escape by herself.

"Why?" she asked, changing the direction of the conversation. "Why are you doing this? Why are you killing the cold soldiers?"

The High studied her. "I think you know the answer as to why the cold soldiers must go. If you wait until our task is complete, then you will know the rest."

"I'd rather be ahead of the game." She looked up to the ceiling and then to the walls. "This is an admin facility. How did you get it?"

He let out a short sigh. "It was given to us."

Deleen chewed her lips for a moment before asking, "Who gave it to you?"

The High smiled thinly. "That is a complicated question. One which requires a detailed explanation." His smile widened. "One that I'm not prepared to give at this time."

His aide came in. "Most High."

"Yes?"

He stood rigid at the door. "A crew returned to the site of the Pure's capture. There was no sign of the Tainted."

"Sign?" the High asked. "What do you mean *sign*? Had they been there or not? Has a thorough search been undertaken?"

The aide swallowed. "I will double-check the report."

"Do it quickly."

The High's genial demeanour dropped away as he leaped to his feet and strode to his desk. He flicked a few documents from his screen. Deleen slid her glance to Harzell, who was staring at her, studying her.

The High returned, standing behind the chair he'd been seated on. "Your presence here, Ms Milo, is not conducive to peaceful relations among my people. I will organise for you to be returned to the city."

Deleen sucked in a surprised breath. "You're letting me go home?"

The High drew his mouth into a thin line, brows dropping. "No. You will be held in the secure section of the administration building until this operation is over."

"You can't do that. I know my rights. On what charge?"

"I *can* do that, Ms Milo. I am the Administrator of Colony Five."

Deleen surged to her feet. "No! That can't be right. You are one of ..." She turned to Harzell, eyes pleading for a denial.

The High lifted his chin and regarded her. "Yes. I am one of the Enhanced. However, I pass easily for one of the Pure. I've been working behind the scenes, manipulating events so that I could step in as administrator."

That meant the Enhanced were currently in control of Colony Five. That knowledge was like a physical blow. "I don't understand ... how ..." The question of why she could probably piece together. Why does any power conquer another?

The events she experienced swirled in her memory. The horror of the burnings. The strange orders. The undercurrent of fear in the city; even she had experienced it. It was as if she could put her finger on the very moment it happened.

Puzzlement gave way to anger. "Then you are responsible for the deaths of all those ... soldiers? Killed before they could even wake."

"It was necessary."

There was no repentance in him. No sign of remorse or compassion.

"What kind of creature are you?" she demanded, hands clenched at her sides.

"I am an Enhanced. So enhanced I can pass for a Pure. Do not fear. We do not wish to hurt the Pure, only to live among them. We aspire to be like them, like you. Be equal with them."

"I don't understand. Why kill those soldiers if that's all that you want? They were human too."

He shook his head decisively. "No, they were not. Do not be fooled. They are the Tainted." He walked away from her, rubbing his chin as he considered his next words. "After they nearly wiped us out, they were put into cold storage to prevent them from telling anyone about our existence."

"How would you know that?" she asked, horrified.

"We have the records of decisions made during the early days. Precious Earth didn't want our enhancements in the human gene strain. The Tainted orders were to kill us on sight. Don't you understand? It is either us or them. There is no choice. We saw our chance and took it."

Deleen shook her head. "I don't understand. Rik said you were aliens. He said you were Gogola." Her voice was but a whisper. The truth, or the subjective truth, opened up like a chasm. She was afraid of falling in. Afraid of what she'd find.

"Perhaps they believe that is so, because that is what they have been told, but I think you understand the truth."

Deleen shook her head. "Understand? No, I don't understand. I can see a glimpse of it, but it is hard to break through all the ... the ..." A sudden pain in her head robbed her of speech, pain shot down her spine and her knees crumpled. Harzell leaped to his feet and tried to hold her. Clinging to his arms and then her head, as blackness rolled in. Her body felt distant, she slumped, knees buckling, head falling down, down, down.

A rough carpet pressed against her cheek. She tried to talk to hang on. The black at the edge of her vision stalked forward, cloaking her vision in darkness. Her name was being called, but she couldn't respond. Sight gone, sound fading. Awareness winked out.

Chapter Fifteen

DELEEN AND THE THRUTH

Deleen awoke in a dark room, her mind fuzzy. Moving her head brought on a savage headache and she groaned at the strength of it. She felt a pinch against her arm and the pain eased after a few inhalations. When she opened her eyes, the room spun. She closed them quickly, breathed shallowly as drugs flowed through her system. The pain lessened. Analgesics she surmised. She tried again, fluttering her eyelids until her vision focused. A blurry large form sat close to her. She focused and the figure crystalised into Harzell.

"Deleen?" He bounded from the chair to her side, his paw-hand stroking her arm.

Her mouth was dry. Her tongue thick. "Yes. What happened to me?"

A sigh escaped him. "Thank the maker. I thought ... I thought you ..."

"Died? I feel like death ... slightly warmed." She groaned again, as she tried to sit higher in the bed. "Can I have some water?"

"Of course," Harzell said. He disappeared from her side. Water gurgled into a cup. Then he was back, placing pillows behind her. She tried to sit higher in the bed so she could drink. He helped her move easily and placed the tumbler into her grip. Her hands shook disconcert-

185

ingly. Harzell placed his hand over hers to steady the cup so she could drink.

"What happened to me?" she asked him, after swallowing a few mouthfuls. Her composure was returning. She sipped more water.

Heat radiated off his body. He stood so close she could inhale his musk. "The medic said there was a kind of psychological block in your mind. The knowledge that the High spoke to you, broke it down. The medic surmised that it overwhelmed you. Fortunately, scans do not indicate any physical damage."

She tried to nod, but just managed to lower her head before the pain increased. "Easy for him to say. He's not on the inside."

He took her empty cup and refilled it. "More?"

"No, thank you. Can you tell me what is going on? Am I still in the compound?"

"Yes, the High has delayed moving you."

"Who is the High?" She pushed the hair out of her eyes. "What is the High?"

Harzell wrinkled his nose in thought. "You took him for one of the Pure?"

Deleen let out a groan as her head throbbed. The recollection of the High being the current administrator of Colony Five was bad enough. How to stop him. She rubbed at her temple. "I did, yes."

He grinned. "The High was elected by us because he is the most Enhanced. There is no outward sign of his talents." Again, Harzell lisped on the 's' sound. "He can pass for Pure. You would not be able to tell has wolf in him."

"And that is important? That you look like one of us?"

Harzell's brows drew down. "Yes, it is important. It is what we aspire to."

"I see." She focused on him, watched his face. "Harzell, why did you really take me? What value did I represent?"

Harzell growled, his lips turning down. "I am ashamed."

"Please," she asked, lifting her hand and placing it on his. "I want to know."

He coughed, an awfully human gesture. "I thought perhaps our offspring ... My offspring fathered on you would mean my descendants would be closer to becoming Pure. That they would have a better life, would be equal."

Deleen's head throbbed again and she gasped at a sudden surge in the pain. She leaned over and vomited noisily onto the floor, then fell back against pillows. "Oh stars, I'm sick," she said wearily.

"Understandably." He took a step back. "What I intended would make a Pure like yourself ill." He looked down at the floor. "I should leave you."

"What? No. Stay here." She reached out a hand to him. His head shot up, eyes bright. "I'm physically sick from this headache. It wasn't ... what you said." His eyes widened, suddenly hopeful. "But that's a damn stupid idea. I am not up for breeding. Never wanted to with anyone, Pure or otherwise."

He paused. "Truly? I'm not offensive to your eyes?"

Deleen sighed. "I'm not repulsed by the idea of you, only by being kidnapped, taken away against my will and then sold. That ... that, made me very pissed off."

His expressive brow wrinkled again. "I see that now. Hence my shame. The High is ... was very angry with me."

"I've forgiven you, at least. When will he send me back to Five?"

"I do not know what he has determined. I do know that knowledge of us ... of this place must remain a secret for the moment."

She raised herself on her elbows. "So you can keep killing the cold soldiers and take over the city?"

"The Tainted are unclean and they are the enemy. They must be destroyed."

She shook her head. "Harzell. They are people too. Just like you and me."

"No, they are not like us."

Deleen had the urge to thump him. "Yes. They are very much like us. They think, they feel, they love. The core of them is the same." She pinched her skin. "They have this. They hurt and bleed." She reached out to him, brushed her fingers on his forearm. "They started life from human, just as whoever made your ancestors, started from the same base."

A sharp pang throbbed in her chest at the thought of her cold soldier. Rik! Stars, she cared about Rik and she thought he cared about her too. At that moment she wanted him so badly it was a physical ache. What must he be going through, knowing she'd been taken?

Harzell's eyes widened. "How do you know this?"

Deleen swallowed, suddenly fearful of how he'd react to her words. "I know because I have lived among them and I love one of them."

"By they are Tainted. Full of unnatural tech. It contaminates them. It could contaminate you."

Deleen ran her hands through her hair. She could understand his fear. The colony generally despised tech. On understanding the situation better, she knew that to be a kind of social manipulation. The colony existed because of tech. Technology and science were what brought the colonists across space to this planet. To all twelve of the colony planets. Technology allowed them to survive and to build this place, to manipulate the environment of the planet. Some of the humans had to be altered to fit the environment, too. Five prided itself on its purity because Five was so Earth-like and the changes to the humans were minimal. She tried to remember her early school lessons. Yes, they had to be inoculated—or was that genetically altered?—to withstand the planet's pathogens. The Special Forces that protected them had tech enhancements and that didn't make them less human.

There was also the embryo bank. Each breeding right included the obligation to gestate one of the colony's stored embryos. Until the embryo bank was empty, each family had to have a child. Her elder brother, Josh, was one. Not related in blood but related in family. As a bank child, he was allocated land for free as his birthright and funds to assist him in life. He had always known that he was a child from the embryo bank , brought to Five to continue the human race.

She tapped his arm. "Rik isn't an *it*. He's a man, a friend."

Harzell's mouth dropped open. "No."

"Yes. He's all man."

Harzell stepped back and then walked away from the bed, hand rubbing his chin. "I cannot believe that." He almost spat the words and his fangs peeped out over his bottom lip.

Deleen was warming to this argument, which meant the meds were working and she was feeling better. "Have you even spoken to one of them? Even looked at them."

He swung around, something wild in his eyes. "No! They are the Tainted, unclean. They are marked so. Marked as perversions."

Deleen remembered the mask placed over Rik's face and Mac had had one too. The scary masks designed to look like death and devilry. Those masks had been placed there for a reason. Maybe to scare a casual observer. To mark them in some way. It was only the memory she had of Rik from childhood that had enabled her to remove that death mask. What a foul trick to play on people. It would certainly boost Harzell's argument.

"I don't know who put the death masks on the cold soldiers, but underneath that mask they look like me or any other Pure. Just bigger."

Harzell's eyes widened and his mouth turned down. "I find that hard to believe."

"Maybe next time look before you kill. I've seen them."

A sob or something akin to it escaped his mouth. His shoulders tensed. Then with a breath he said softly, "I am sorry, Deleen. It is too late. They are all gone."

Silence hung between them. She didn't want to believe, refused to believe. Not Rik! "No! My friends can't be dead." A big ball of grief was stuck in her throat.

He moved forward, using his uplifted hand to placate her. "Not your friends. We have not eliminated them yet. But we think we have destroyed the rest that were hidden away."

Deleen shook her head and then bit her lip, the lump of grief not quite gone. Rik and the others weren't dead. But the others? Poor Rik. He would be devastated by the loss. "Isn't there a better way to get what you want? Negotiation instead of murder?"

Even as she spoke the words, she wondered to what end. Were the Enhanced better than her fellow colonists? Were the cold soldiers better, more powerful? Or were the colonists the best of them? Or were they just people with different personalities, looks and talents. Equal in the law. Equal by right.

"No. Negotiation won't work," Harzell said. "We must take our chance now and seize what is rightfully ours. We have waited to be offered a place among you, to be recognised and accepted. It never has happened. It will never be given freely. The Tainted are proof of that."

Laying back against her pillow, Deleen frowned and shook her head. "I still don't understand. Offered a place by who? I have never heard of your people before. There is no mention of you in our history. How can you be invited to join us if we don't know you are there?"

A voice spoke from the doorway, giving her a start. "You must read our version of the archive. It was sourced from files that had been hidden, even deleted." It was the High. He walked into the room, looking as pristine as he had before. "It will explain a lot of the history of Five. It is a truer record than the official colony record."

Deleen sat up in the bed, fist clenched on her lap. "The colony's archive has been altered. Deliberately."

The High's eyes widened, but he didn't argue against her assertion. "Intriguing. How did you figure that out? It is true. I know it to be so."

"I worked it out. There was no mention of a war or the cold soldiers. I have no idea who changed it or why."

"I think the existence of us will logically lead you to understand the why. As to who, I think that is best for you to discover yourself. I have my suspicions." He narrowed his eyes. "Or perhaps I should call it evidence-based deduction."

He walked up to the wall and slid open a panel. The light from a reader screen ebbed into the room. "When you are ready, you may read it here. I have granted you access."

"Thank you. I will read it with interest."

The High inclined his head to acknowledge her thanks. He then turned to her visitor. "Harzell? You should leave Ms Milo to rest."

Harzell nodded. "Forgive me, I have stayed too long."

She managed a weak smile. The High wanted Harzell away from her for reasons that probably had nothing to do with her health. There was a glitter in the High's eyes, an assessment of the situation. Deleen couldn't guess what he suspected. His revelations had her mind reeling. Now she had access to an archive. Would it prove to be a construct like the colony's had? Or would it reveal the whole truth. How would she know, in any case?

"I will leave you to your rest. When you are more restored, I will visit again." The High spoke formally. He walked to door and waited for Harzell to precede him. Then they were gone.

A minute later a medic entered, her ginger-coloured tail curling elegantly. Her amber eyes were set close together and she had fur on her chin and on the backs of her hands. Her fingernails were long and thin, a mix of cat claw and human finger.

"I am Citrus. I have brought you some analgesics."

As she took the proffered pills, Deleen noted that the medic's ears had tufts of fur along the back edge. Citrus left the room and returned a few moments with lunch on a tray. She cleaned up the mess on the floor and then left.

As Deleen ate the salad she'd been provided, a mixture of green leaves, dried fruit with a sprinkling of ground nuts, liberally covered in a tangy dressing, she contemplated the reader screen across the room.

The second lot of analgesics and lunch helped restore her. Soon she was up reading, the last of the headache fading away, leaving just a crease in her forehead. The archive contained a similar account of the settlement of Five and the twelve colony ships that left Earth. It contained a geographic and climate survey of the Colony Five planet, the five-hundred-year plan for the planet's development, as well as mineral assays of the planet's crust and long-term development plans for other cities to be built when economic and population targets had been reached.

Deleen chewed her lip as she read these pages. So far, the history and other information matched what she knew. There was nothing new there and no great changes from what she recalled of her schooling and general knowledge of Five's origins and plans for the future.

The First Settlers were also discussed in detail. Her great-grandfather, General Frank Milo, was pictured, his history described in succinct paragraphs. Pictures of her great-grandmother, Siobhan McPhee, tending the embryo bank followed on after and then an account of her genetics specialty.

The other family names were featured in the account too. She read them, thinking them almost word for word with the official, but obviously compromised, record. Then she scrolled along to a face and a name that she didn't recognise—Professor Scott Lenane, research scientist, with a specialty in genetics. She read a bit further along, wondering why the colony needed two geneticists. Her own great-grandmother had been caretaker of the human embryo bank that would be brought up as part of the population, thus providing the genetic diversity required to build a healthy population. As she continued to read, she saw that Lenane's biography included a number of his interests. The word that snagged her attention was hybridisation. The fusion and manipulation of human and animal genes. This scientist was not mentioned in the official record, she was sure of it. Her own ancestor was the colony's geneticist and that was the history she knew.

Her heart thudded. She searched other contemporaneous information about the embryo bank at that time. There was a list of restored files, reports, logs and journals. This must be the hidden and deleted ones that the High had mentioned. One title in particular caught her attention—*Theft of embryos from the bank*. A picture of her great-grandmother and empty storage units. "Oh heavens," she said to the screen. What was becoming clear to her was very disturbing. Someone, possibly this Lenane, had stolen embryos from the store and manipulated them. She could understand that the First Settlers would want to keep that quiet. Those were soon to be humans that had been stolen away. Their lives as valued as any other member of the colony. They were considered citizens-in-waiting.

Narrowing her gaze, Deleen keyed up a search for the war or anything on the cold soldiers. The first three combination of terms brought up nothing. *Alien invasion* brought up nothing. *Embryo bank* and *hybrid experiments* brought up one journal entry. *Emergency* and *soldier* brought up four results. The first article had a picture of General Milo walking along with a team of soldiers. They were dressed in armour and quite large. She enlarged the picture and saw Rik's face. The article discussed the threat to Five's security. There was the link.

She read on. It seemed that Lenane's experiments had been successful as well as unsanctioned. The next journal entry appeared to be a draft report about military action that repelled an unsavoury alien element. Although the journal didn't spell it out, it appeared that the soldiers had put down the threat and everything had returned to normal. The next file, dated a year later, discussed the interring of the soldiers in cryosleep until a new threat arose. Her great-grandfather had written a personal log entry: "It is with regret that I order my special force back into cryo sleep. Hopefully their interment will be of short duration." Deleen wondered what happened, why they were kept in cryo sleep for so long. There was no mention of the extra-terrestrials or hybrids. Was this as true an account as she was going to find? Obviously, someone back then, maybe even her own ancestors, had disguised the truth. *Was it you, grandmama? Did you hide the truth?* She flicked back to the picture of General Milo, her great-grandfather and studied it. Both of them maybe hid the truth. She could understand why they might have done that, because the truth would have been fatal to the colony. In the early days, the colonies were under the jurisdiction of Earth Colony Control. A colony could be closed down in those days if they strayed from the strict parameters set for them.

Out of curiosity she perused further files in the archive from subsequent years. She read and then scanned more documents. It appears Lenane was never apprehended. How could he hide in those early days? The planet was big, of course, but there were hardly any people. He must have had help.

Another file was a compilation of news articles from Colony Five as if the person collecting was studying something in particular. As she read, she grew more and more concerned. One article dated S22 began by discussing the soldiers and how they had tech incorporated into them. The author went on to talk about purity of the race and the recent threats to humans' very existence and how humans had migrated to keep the species going and to expand their dominion to the stars. Another article published about five years later called for no genetic manipulation, or very limited intervention in the case of life and health and argued vehemently for no technical enhancements. As the years progressed, the articles continued to post articles calling for the colony to embrace the natural aspects to life and turn its back on technology. Here, she could see the origins of the current cultural dictates and it scared her. It smacked of manipulation. Admittedly it was only one publication but there were likely to be others that either agreed or disagreed. She suspected that this information would be available in the archives of Colony Five but these had been preserved as active files in this version of the record, probably because the Enhanced had an interest in the social climate of the colony and how they would be treated if they made themselves known.

It seems certain these Enhanced were the progeny of those earlier experiments, Lenane's legacy? It seemed logical to her. Just because the archives contains reports that the issue had been dealt with, didn't make it true. She only had to look around the room she was in, at the colony-built structure, to know there was more to it. Over the years, someone high up had helped the Enhanced to flourish unseen. But why so against the cold soldiers?

She stared unseeing at the screen as she thought. If the hybrids had been attacked and almost wiped out by the cold soldiers who had been ordered to eradicate them, then that would certainly support the idea of the Enhanced viewing them as a threat. What if this anti-tech movement was even stronger than espoused in the publication she had read? What if there was an element among her own kind that despised the concept of the cold soldiers? Successful social manipulation at its worst? She recalled how readily citizens surrendered and even burned alive the tech enhanced soldiers and shuddered. It was murky to say the least. Was that the High manipulating citizens or something that went way back?

Logically it made little sense to her. They wouldn't be on Five without tech or technical enhancements. She didn't know the details, but to survive the journey their progenitors had to undergo genetic and technological alteration and intervention. She called up more files on the First Settlers. There were a lot about Earth, about what they went through to get the colony ships into space and to the twelve colony planets. It took just under a hundred years and the colonists slept through most of it. Some of it she had studied in school. This compilation of files though was more extensive than she had seen before.

She sat back and closed her eyes. Rik was born on Earth and the nanotech in his system and those of his comrades was Earth-based. From what she knew it had been more and more common for science to intervene in the daily lives of all Earth inhabitants. Augmentation for communication, for example. Medical monitoring devices for the sick. Treatment for infections during pandemics. Supporting a dwindling workforce as the population aged. For the so called *Super Soldiers*. Tech was necessary for them to survive battle, to protect settlers, to live longer and stronger. She didn't see tech as bad or good. It was neutral. It was how it was used. Humans throughout history always found means to kill, and to kill efficiently. She thought that was one of the reasons the colonies were made. To move beyond base nature and embrace higher reasoning. She frowned again and rubbed at the crease between her eyebrows. Was it possible for her to be objective about any of this? She liked—or better still, believed in—the ethos of Colony Five. Or what she thought the ethos was.

Nothing, though, could convince her that killing cold soldiers was the right thing to do. And nothing could convince her that leaving the Enhanced out of society was the right thing to do. They derived from the colony's embryo bank. That meant they were human.

When she read a selection of articles from the colony's two main news streams dated around S50, the narrative grew reactionary to say the least. The narrative appeared to be against any enhancements to humans, technological or biological. She realised Five had become purist. Deleen blinked, taken aback. That was why she reacted so viscerally to Rik's tech and the Enhanced hybridisation. She had been conditioned to be a purist. To value the human form in its natural, or close to natural, state. At first she was angry, then that rage focused. That had to change.

The Pure, that's what Harzell called them. It started to make sense to her now. There were no aliens, not in the sense that there were non-terrestrials wanting to settle on Five. There were human-animal hybrids who were thought to have been eradicated but had obviously not been. They had survived and someone had helped them. There was no record of what happened to Lenane. No evidence of capture, punishment or death. Did he survive and go on to help the survivors? Did he have a faction, people who continued his work in secret? She couldn't answer that question, yet. What did remain though that the Enhanced, through no fault of their own—they were what they were, existed and were excluded from the mainstream colony. A pure human had made them for his own purposes. Those that knew about it had covered it up and with no official record of the Enhanced, time had forgotten about them. In exactly the same way, the soldiers with their tech and superior weapons had been forgotten.

To hide the existence of the Enhanced, they had hidden the cold soldiers too. They had condemned the soldiers to sleep on, never to participate in colony life. Either it was because they knew about the Enhanced or because they represented technical pollution of the human form. Neither was a valid excuse to her mind. She tried to picture how it had been. The soldiers could heal themselves, were strong, trained, hard to defeat. No wonder the attack on them had been while they were dormant and vulnerable. Could she blame the Enhanced for that? Or were those who had written them out of history—denying them equality or the right to live as was their human birthright—the ones to blame?

Standing up, she staggered toward the bed, headache suddenly pounding again and heartache tightening her chest. She tried to rest, but was seized by a sudden idea, she dashed back to the computer terminal and looked for specs on this facility. It wasn't known in the city, but there could be information in this system, buried deep. She had a sneaking suspicion that this place had been built around the time the city had been.

A few beeps and she was blocked. She tried again and got hints. Lenane had set up a facility away from the settlement. He had petitioned and had been granted a large segment of the colony ship's hull and supplies. The colony ships had been designed to be repurposed for construction, once settlement had taken place. So this place was as old as the administration buildings in Five.

The door slid open. "I see you took up my offer," the High said to her, an amused expression on his face.

She pushed away from the monitor. "Yes, your archive does have different information in it."

"Which is the truer do you think?"

She swallowed and nodded to him. "Yours."

She studied him. "Are you descended from Lenane?"

The High's eyes widened. "That has a dual meaning. I am descended from his creations, yes. As to whether his DNA is mixed with mine, he never said."

"You knew him? Surely he died before you were born."

The High smirked. "He lived a very long life and only recently left us. He used cryo sleep and gene therapy to extend his life."

Deleen digested this information. If Lenane had only recently passed away, then that answered part of the question about how the Enhanced remained hidden. "You suspect you are his offspring, though," she added, going with her gut feeling. "You could find out."

"If it mattered to me, I could find out but at this moment in time, it matters little to my plans." He inclined his head. "As you are feeling better, I am afraid I must move you to more secure apartments."

"Oh! Are you taking me back to Harzell?"

He glanced at her, eyebrows lifting. "Oh no. His quarters are not sufficiently secure, as you have experienced. I'm afraid I must put you somewhere where you can't escape."

Deleen lifted her chin. "You have no right to detain me."

The High laughed at her. "Since when did the world revolve about what is right and fair?" He pressed his finger to the lock. "Come along."

Deleen looked at the lock, really looked. It was a similar system to that at admin. A system she was very familiar with. "All right I'll come."

Chapter Sixteen

FORTRESS

Rik had been looking for Deleen for days. At first, he thought that she'd been taken to the city, but after tracking in that direction for two days, he changed his mind. There'd been no signs of aircraft. The public transport system had been shut down. "Oyuda. Can you use scan for other settlements? I know Deleen said everything centred on the city and the outlying areas but I have a feeling she may be wrong about that."

"On it," Oyuda said and set the scanner up. Mac sat outside her tent, finishing off her meal.

Rik sat down opposite her and pulled out a packet, unzipping it so that the aroma of the food teased his nose. Mac glanced up at him, but remained sullen and silent.

"What's your problem?" he asked her and then took a bite.

"You?"

"Me?"

"Yes. Why are we tracking this girl, this civilian? You keen to get your cock wet? Man, she must be good."

"That's got nothing to do with it. She's a civilian and she's important. And don't get so freaking righteous. She saved me and helped me save you. If she hadn't, you'd be dead like the others."

Mac eyed him and then shook her head slightly. "I get that, but what's our mission?"

Rik took another bite. "First was to secure as many of our unit as possible. Then end the threat."

"So, what are we doing here, looking for what's her name?"

"Deleen Milo. General Milo's descendant. And if you must know, she is important to our mission. She has security access to the administration. We have to liberate the city from the threat. I think you know what the threat is. I think one of them took her."

Mac's eyes widened. "The enemy?"

"Yes, the aliens. They're back."

"How do you know she was taken by one of them? It could have been the new administration that grabbed her."

Rik shook his head. "No. It was them. I smelt it."

"It?"

"The one that took her."

"Aw gee," Mac said. "Surely it's too late. Do you really want her back after she's been with them?"

Rik frowned at her. "What do you mean? Of course, I want her back."

"But won't she be tainted, changed by being with them ... maybe even used."

Rik shuddered. "What do you know?"

Mac crushed her food packet and it started to decompose. "There were reports during the action. Being a woman, I was briefed about what had happened to those who were captured, including female civilians. It wasn't pretty. They said there wasn't much left to salvage once the aliens got you."

Rik's stomach turned. He crushed his own food packet and it started to decompose as well. "I'm not abandoning her."

"You're stuck on her, aren't you? It's pointless, you know that, right? We're soldiers. We can never be like them, never fit in. Why do you think they froze us for so long?"

Rik rubbed his chin. "Maybe ... I don't know ... she makes me feel like I'm normal. Like I fit right in. Like I'm just a regular guy. After all this time, all my service, it's time I retired. Why can't I be normal like everyone else? Why do I, or for that matter, why do you have to keep apart? Tell me, do you want to go back into cold sleep?"

Mac spat into the dirt and wiped her lips with the back of one hand. "I'd rather die. Why should we be frozen to be brought out when needed. Why should we fix these colonists' problems? They should learn to manage them on their own. Take their own bloody risks."

A grin broke out. "You get it then? What I mean about wanting to fit in."

Mac grunted. "Maybe, but I don't have some delicious civilian to make me all warm inside."

Rik grinned and winked. "Once we fix this you might."

She scoffed and ran her hands through her hair. "What makes you think that they are going to let us live amongst them if we do survive? Besides I will never fit in. I'm a six-foot-two female of dubious gender and ambiguous sexual preferences."

Rik met her direct gaze. "You are amazing. You will find someone, I'm sure."

Mac harrumphed and got to her feet. "I'm going to prep for departure."

Rik sat there and frowned. He tried thinking about how he'd come to be frozen. His memory was hazy. Were they given a choice? Was it an order? He recalled that it was something to do with the greater good, a future threat. Whatever, it hadn't been well managed. Now, the ranks of the cold soldiers were all but destroyed. If by chance others survived, he didn't have time to go looking for them. He had two left out of his squad. It wasn't much, but it was the best he had.

"I found something," Oyuda said from the other side of the camp. "Some particles from a heavy aircraft going off in this direction." He pointed to a map.

"We have to double back." Rik's heart sank. He had wasted precious time going off in the wrong direction. He surveyed the two bikes. "Mac, run a check on the vehicles, make sure they are charged up. We are heading out. ASAP."

Mac sent him a mocking salute and collapsed her tent as she walked past to head for the bikes. Rik bent down to clean his weapon before retrieving his pack.

Oyuda entered coordinates into his wrist band and commented. "I don't know why the craft has gone in that direction. Nothing on the colony's public network says anything is there. Just savannah lands as far as I can tell from these maps."

Rik recollected discussions with Deleen about how the colony's archives had been altered. Obviously, the information from Five could not be completely trusted. "Can you tap into the satellite?"

Oyuda looked up and frowned. "I forgot about that. It's an old installation. Not sure it's even functional."

Rik finished packing up his gear and securing his weapons. "Try it anyway. We know it's there, because we deployed it. If the city admin aren't using it, well good."

Oyuda nodded. "On it. I'll try our standard military codes. If it hasn't been changed, they should still work."

"You do that." Rik had the camp packed and ready before Oyuda finished downloading the relevant satellite imagery. He shook his head.

"What is it?" Rik asked. "You found something."

Oyuda nodded. "A building or a large settlement."

"What else?"

"Lots of heat signatures."

"How many?"

"About five hundred, give or take. If they are armed, we don't stand a chance."

* * *

Before the High could have her escorted to more secure lodgings, there was a commotion down the corridor. He shut her back in the medical centre with a curt apology. After staring at the door for a few minutes, Deleen shook her head. No way was she staying in here. She knelt down and inspected the lock. He'd used his finger to open the door. The lock type was a familiar DNA lock, just like the ones in admin. If he was the administrator, then his DNA was on file. Then just maybe ...

She pressed her finger to it. Nothing happened. Rats! Her profile wasn't in the database. She was screwed.

Her gaze shifted to the computer terminal. "I wonder." She raced over and started navigating the system to access security. It had been her job after all and the last thing she did was implement the new security protocols, which presumably were in use on this computer too. She couldn't get in directly to the operating system, but she was able to see the date of the latest update. The system had updated last year. She looked at the audit trail. The update had come from Five's admin. That's how they had infiltrated admin. They had a mirror system.

She had been in security last year and that meant that her security profile was there, but not active. She tried a few ways to get into the access file, without luck. She was running out of time. He'd be back.

She had this one opportunity. Sitting back, she breathed a few times to calm herself down. There had to be a way. She was the deputy head of security, but she didn't have the security admin interface. What could she do? Go in the back way, to the file itself. She found the right screen and the list of security profiles flashed up. She isolated hers and made it active.

Voices outside her door meant she was out of time. She hit update and blanked the screen.

"Ready?" the High asked. He lifted his eyebrow as he saw she was near the terminal. "Reading more history?"

"Just a bit. I was bored."

He ushered her ahead of him and then directed her down the hall. Furiously she considered if she could make her break. She contemplated the idea of hitting the High in the head and making a run for it. That idea was taking shape, when two guards joined them and derailed it completely. The lift door opened and they ushered her in, caging her. Sweat broke out on her forehead and itched along her lower back. She was running out of options. They were headed below ground. The chances of escape dwindled before her eyes.

No. She mustn't think like that. Sending herself calming thoughts, she bided her time. If that update went through as planned, she could escape, provided she had access to a DNA lock. If they put her away in a room without one, there would be little chance.

The lift opened. The idea to stall came to mind but one of the guards shoved her between her shoulder blades and she stumbled out of the doors. She managed to keep upright and turned back to sneer. The

High inclined his head; a tight smile flashed then disappeared. "I will leave you here," he said and gave a nod for the other guard to key another lift. "Perhaps we will meet again soon."

Taking a step toward him, she said quickly. "Are you leaving?"

"Yes, to the city. I'm expected." A slight bow before he stepped into the lift and the doors shut, cutting off her view.

"Move!" the guard said, giving her another shove.

Deleen preceded them down the corridor. They came to an intersection that was busy with pedestrian traffic. Some Enhanced turned their heads to look at her, mouths, beaks, snouts gaping open before they turned away and pretended to mind their own business.

A trolley sped by. A noise behind them made one of the guards turn his head.

The sudden impact of metal hitting bone made Deleen flinch. The guard slumped to the floor, blood in a halo around his head. The other guard tried to raise his weapon. He too was bludgeoned and near toppled her on his way to the floor.

Stumbling free of the two bodies, Deleen glared, open mouthed at the three Enhanced who were closing in on her. They didn't look like liberators. Big, ugly and hairy, they had scarves over their lower faces and their clothes were shabby and ripped in places. Two held metal poles and the other just rubbed his hairy paws together in apparent delight. The latter swung a paw at her and she ducked under the arm, pivoted and kicked. With an *oof* of surprise he doubled over. The second one, his hands clawed and scaly, tried to swipe her with the pole. She ducked and came up with a two-handed strike straight to the groin. He wasn't expecting a fight. The screech of pain and outrage near deafened her. He rolled on the ground, out of the fight for now. The third growled threateningly but didn't attack. He waved the pole in front of himself as is he was holding off her attack. The traffic in the corridor slowed as the pedestrians began to notice what was going on. Deleen fake lunged at the third Enhanced and then darted off into the growing crowd, the first few bystanders falling back at her approach.

The attack had been so quick that no one seemed to react fast enough. She pushed and shoved and before anyone chased her, peeled off into another corridor, dark and uninhabited. Panting, she flattened herself against the wall to hide in the shadows. No one came after her immediately, but she had to move because they would. These people had enhanced senses, particularly smell. Perspiration and fear was probably a cloud around her. It wouldn't take long for them to gather their forces and pursue her.

A few calming breaths and she was inching away from the main corridor and the light. She had to find a lift or stairs to regain the surface. After a few minutes, she bumped up against a closed door. In the dim light, she patted the side of the door, trying to find a lock. A surge of hope swelled inside when her fingers detected the outline. Now to see if her update had done the trick. Holding her breath, she stuck her finger against the lock and the door slid open. The relief nearly toppled her. She let out a whoosh of breath as warm, moist air wafted out. She darted inside the room. Water trickled through an extensive irrigation system and lights shone over rows of plants. She had stumbled on the hydroponics bay. Stepping quietly, she hoped not to alert the attendants if there were any. Close by were some herbs. She grabbed a few and rubbed them into her skin and clothes. It probably wouldn't do much to disguise her scent but it was better than nothing.

The sound of chatter alerted her to the presence of workers. Darting under the rows of plants, she spied two Enhanced. One male and the other female. They were loading a trolley with harvested vegetables. When they finished, they slid it on to a purpose-built elevator. It swallowed the trolley and went on its way with a whine. The two workers went back to their harvesting selecting another empty trolley to take with them. They talked to each other as they worked. It seemed such a normal activity.

While she stayed out of sight, Deleen looked overhead and around, noting the hydroponics shed was huge. It was like a large warehouse that stretched a couple of hundred metres in each direction. The two workers moved well away from her position. When the coast was clear, she crawled over to the elevator and pressed the call button. Then she looked around for one of the large trollies to hide in. There wasn't one. The workers had taken the last one.

The elevator door pinged and she was out of time. No choice but to get in and hope for the best at the other end. Flattening herself against the wall, she hoped she was sufficiently hidden by the frame of the door and the shadows as she started her ascent.

The lift was slow. It stopped with a jolt and then the doors slid open. No one was waiting for it. She popped her head out of the opening and saw the coast was clear. She darted out and hid in some shadows against the far wall. It was another corridor. Scents lingered there. Cooking aromas. She was near the kitchens. At a run, she bounded down the corridor beneath bright artificial lighting. The corridor had a wide room at the end with big windows and a deck beyond. Filled with tables and chairs and Enhanced: it was a refectory.

She strode toward the exit, but the transparent door was locked. To the side, she saw another lock. She pressed her finger to it and the door swished open.

The outside was so close now. Soon the High would discover what she had done and delete her access. She had to move quickly, stay ahead of them. She headed to the doorway to the deck. It was open, letting in sunlight and a light breeze. A few Enhanced sat out there eating. Outside was a hill and maybe a ravine. In the distance, grass rippled in a light breeze. She saw a glint, light off metal. Hope surged as the metal object moved and appeared larger. It had to be Rik and rescue, but she needed to get free of the building.

A quick glance over her shoulder and she stilled as an almost pure-looking female with white skin and small brown patches stopped wiping the table and looked directly at her. They regarded at each other for a heartbeat and then Deleen made a break for it.

The female barked in alarm. Deleen dove through the open window, stumbled and righted herself as headed straight for the deck railing. The other Enhanced who were eating, stood up, knocked over chairs and cried in alarm. She kept her focus and ran on. Freedom was so close, and she had to take a leap of faith as she swung over the rail and let go.

The ground was further away than she expected, with an outcrop of jagged rocks. Flailing her arms and screaming, she realise she could die or break every bone in her body and pulp her flesh. She closed her eyes. Next, the air whooshed out of her as she hit. It took a second to notice that she had hit too soon and that she wasn't sludge smeared against rock. Struggling for breath, she noticed she was moving through air. Not downwards but up and away.

Encircling her waist was a thick arm. She screamed, thinking she'd been captured again. She hit out, punched and squirmed, trying to break free.

It was better to fall than to be taken back.

"Deleen. Stop!" A deep voice boomed over her head. Her head jerked, trying to see who had her. She saw a helmet and a familiar set of eyes peeking out. He was hovering in the air.

"Rik?" Her voice was raspy from screaming.

He nodded decisively. "Stay still, I don't want to drop you." She clung to his arm while he steered the little hovercraft away from the compound. As she secured herself to the craft with a tie, she caught a look at the building, which looked like a historical monastery, but constructed from slate grey ship material rather than stone.

The little hovercraft veered and accelerated away. She held on tight, feeling the centrifugal force trying to drag her off the small platform. She reeled from the fact of her reprieve and that Rik had come for her. Emotion began to fill the spaces where fear had taken root. She'd thought she would never see him again and here he was.

Rik adjusted the orientation so it swung the other way, and she got her legs locked around the seat, did up the belt, before he hit the accelerator and powered away.

Deleen checked behind them for pursuit. No one seemed to be coming after her. Maybe she'd made it out after all. Maybe they thought she plummeted to her death. They'd be surprised then when there was no body smashed up on the rocks below.

Resting her head against Rik's back, she tried to calm herself. He was alive. He'd found her. He'd come for her. She'd thought she'd never see him again, feel his warmth, and now here he was. They flew on for ten minutes. Another manoeuvre and he lowered the hover into a copse. Three small tents stood in a loose circle.

He keyed off the engine and sat there panting. Deleen undid the seat belt and slid off the seat, landing on her butt, too shocked and relieved to do more than breathe. Despite the three tents erected there was no sign of Mac and Oyuda. Rik spoke rapidly into the mic in his helmet. "Abort. I have her. I repeat, abort."

Then he undid his helmet and chucked it onto the hover console and turned to her. His eyes were bright and seemed to see right through her. "Del?" he said softly as he came to kneel beside her.

Tears stung her eyes. She sat up, flinging her arms around his neck, clinging to him and feeling so much emotion that she couldn't put into words. "Oh, Rik. Rik. I thought ..."

He held her head against his chest, stroking her hair. "I thought the same." He bent his head and kissed her hair. "Are you hurt?"

Looking up at him, she shook her head and sniffed back the tears. "All good now."

Her gaze travelled over his face. His eyes narrowed and his nostrils flared. "Aren't you going to kiss me?" she asked.

Before she could draw breath, his lips crushed against hers and his embrace left no room to move. She kissed him as hard and fast as she could and didn't stop. The kisses become more and soon they were in Rik's shelter.

Later, as they held each other, she said, "Thank you for coming for me."

"You didn't think I would?" he paused in kissing the top of her breast, eyebrows furrowed.

"I hoped, but it seemed impossible."

"I'd die for you, Del."

"I don't want you to die for me. I want you to live for me." She reached forward and he caught her mouth in a deep kiss. She couldn't tell where he ended and she began. It felt so right to be with him. She didn't care about the tech, she just cared about him.

Her eyelids grew heavy after a while. Rik leaned forward and kissed her forehead. "Sleep now. I'll bring you food in a bit."

As she sank down into sleep, she heard him leave the tent. It felt so good to be in his bed again. It felt extra good to be free and not a sex slave to a hybrid human/animal. She didn't think Harzell was that bad, even though she was irked by his plans for her. Although, considering the way they had been treated, she could understand the desire to be accepted, to be recognised as human.

Chapter Seventeen

THE REUNION

Someone shook her by the shoulder. "Come on. Get up, dressed."

It was Rik's voice, all hard and authoritative.

"What is it?" she asked, pulling on her shirt.

"Company. Oyuda picked up a trace on his scanner. We need to move."

She darted out of the tent, still pulling on her clothes as he collapsed it. "Get on the hover. We're splitting up. Hope to lose them that way."

With a nod, she bolted for the hover. Mac flicked her a salute from the peak of her helmet. Oyuda just looked at her. Deleen gritted her teeth. They resented her and would never accept her. She had to face up to it. Luckily, all that mattered was what Rik thought and felt. The rest she would have to live with.

After fixing the rest of the gear onto the vehicle, Rik leaped on and keyed it. The three vehicles went off in parallel and then diverged paths. The pressure of gravity dragged at her as he pulled up and to the left. Then Rik dove down below the tree line and wove in and out of thick trunks and hanging vines. Next, he began darting out and doing a turn before tearing off to the right. She guessed he was piloting in this way to disguise their direction. It worked on her as she had no idea where they were going and, looking over her shoulder, she had no idea where they'd come from. Ahead was the lake. It looked familiar. There was no sign of Mac and Oyuda. Rik landed and they sat there waiting.

"What are we doing?" she asked in a whisper.

"Listening ... waiting ..."

There was a noise in the distance. "What's that?" she queried.

"Weapons fire." He brought the machine to life again and they sped off, angling off the ground in a way that resembled more the launch of a rocket than a controlled take-off.

She spoke into the helmet mic. "Are we going to help?"

"No. Not the plan."

"But you're not going to let them die for me, are you?" She hit his shoulder.

"I don't think it will come to that. They follow orders and we stick to the plan. They know we are coming now. They are expecting us and we are prepared."

Deleen shook her head, perplexed. She bit her lip as they wended their way around rocky outcrops and back into green cover. Mac didn't even like her. Why should she be fighting for *her*? She was a civilian—a useless chunk of flesh that caused nothing but trouble. But then she realised it was bigger than her— it was the humans and the colony that was important and also any of the cold soldiers that may remain.

Once they landed Rik set up the camp and wouldn't let her help. Mac and Oyuda hadn't turned up, but he didn't seem worried. When she eyed him expectantly, he tapped his wristband and she understood. He could see their vitals. He knew they were alive. He didn't keep in communication with them, but he knew they were okay. The less chatter, the less chance there was of them being found. Now she understood.

Rik handed her a bag of food. She took it and broke the seal. This one was a flavoursome curry and the scent of spice wafted around her head. Who knew field rations could be so tasty? She was very hungry and began to shovel the food into her mouth.

"How did you get out?" Rik asked her as he inspected his own food, poking it with a fork as if looking for some especially tasty morsel. His tone was casual, but his eyes were intense.

She filled him in on how she'd been given access to the archive and that she'd used the security access to give her a way to unlock the doors.

"The aliens didn't harm you?"

She lowered her gaze. "I was a bit bruised and stuff, but no. Not really harmed. You see, Rik ..."

Hesitating, she licked curry sauce off her bottom lip. She wasn't sure what he knew or what impact the news she had would have on him.

"What?"

"They aren't aliens, Rik. They are humans who have been genetically altered using animal DNA. They call themselves the Enhanced."

His head jerked up and his eyes narrowed. "You know this how?"

She thought of The High's words. "Evidence-based deduction."

He didn't speak, just waited for more.

"They call you 'the Tainted' and people like me, without tech, 'the Pure'. From what I saw they want to be like us, more pure. Accepted into society. Obviously, given the past history, they see you as a threat to them, so they have dealt with the cold soldiers."

"You agree with their tactics?" His voice was suddenly harsh.

"Of course not. But something underhand has been going on here on Five, Rik, since before you went into sleep, and in the years since then."

He opened his mouth to speak but she touched his lips gently, silencing him. "A subtle erasure of the past, a changing of our culture. Five is anti-tech. It prides itself on doing things without high tech. Machinery exists and is used, of course, and some high-tech medicine, but genetic engineering, tech enhancements? Hardly anything. Only if there is some catastrophic deficiency detrimental to life is tech allowed to be used. Nothing to make us more than we were born to be. Nanotech. Definitely not. While you slept, the colony changed around you. You weren't forgotten due to the lapse of time. You were deliberately written out of our history, along with the Enhanced.

"You seem very sure of this."

She nodded and then narrowed her eyes. These things started in Rik's time. She decided to feel him out on what she thought had happened. "Do you remember a guy called Lenane?"

"The geneticist?"

Her heart leaped. He knew of the geneticist. That was a start. "That's the one."

"What of him?" Rik shoved some food in his mouth and swallowed. He didn't seem to be enjoying it.

Deleen swallowed a morsel of curry. "Well, there is no mention of him in the colony's archives, now. I've a pretty good memory and as you know my great-grandmother was a geneticist. The colony's geneticist."

He opened his mouth to speak, but she rushed on. "Lenane is mentioned in the Enhanced archives. I think he created them."

Rik closed his eyes and breathed deeply. "So you're saying that the colony's archives were changed. What about the war? Did the Enhanced's archive mention that?"

She shook her head. "Yes, but no mention of aliens. They aren't aliens. They are people."

"No that can't be. We killed aliens. Not people."

Deleen licked her lips and sniffed because she could feel the tears. "No, Rik. They are people."

"So we were lied to? Manipulated?" He threw his food container and the contents splattered on the ground. "It's not like it's the first time in history. And the people who are at fault are long dead." He rubbed his hand over his close-shaved head. "You're sure?"

"I'm convinced. The Enhanced are human, not alien. People, like you are people."

His head jerked up. "You think I'm people—like you?"

She blinked. "Of course, I do. Why wouldn't I think you are people ..."

He grinned and it was infectious. "Not everyone feels that way about us. Even on Earth, people feared tech enhancements."

She sobered. "I understand there is prejudice, but that's just an excuse to label people as different. Colony Five ethos included equality regardless of race, gender or religion. That's why we are so blended. But even we have our blind spots about what it means to be human and they are going to be challenged."

"I caught a glimpse of one of the Enhanced once. I told you I thought they were animal-like. Their camps were targets to be destroyed. Before we went into cryo sleep we were told that the aliens had been rounded up and sent out into space in their own ships to find their own planet. Obviously, that wasn't true."

"I didn't read anything about that in the archive." She shrugged. "If they—and I am thinking of my own relatives here—wanted to hide the truth from Earth then they had to hide it from the soldiers too."

He nodded, forehead furrowed. "Yeah, cold sleep can mess with recall, particularly about events just before you go under." He met her gaze. "You're saying Lenane created these Enhanced here. That would take a lot of know-how and tech. He would have to either started his experiments on the colony ship or had some way to mature his creations quickly. I was created on Earth and dispatched with the colony ships. I remember Lenane. I spoke to him once. He quizzed me on my tech."

"We don't have the tech to make soldiers like you here, even if it was permitted. There is probably more to this story than we will ever know. Obviously, Lenane had tech, either brought with him or developed here. It was very early in the colony's history."

"You know even on Earth there was a ... how can I say this ... a distaste for us. We were superior to ordinary humans, to civilians, and that created tensions. I think that is why they sent us out with the colony ships—to get rid of us."

Deleen felt sad. Why had the people who had created these soldiers then despised what they had created? Humans were so strange. Deleen didn't think she would ever understand. "Did you know that would happen? I mean, when you agreed to be changed?"

Rik shook his head. "No, I didn't think through the consequences. I was young. All I thought of was glory and battles and becoming more than ordinary. I remember what it felt like to be powerful." He sighed. "Now, though, that's not important to me."

Deleen nodded and crushed up her food container and watched it begin to dissolve. She studied Rik. "And now, what is important to you?"

He leaned back, his eyes assessing her. "It was overrated. There's nothing like more than a hundred years in cold sleep to give you a perspective. I find I want to be normal again. Just everyday Rik."

Deleen lifted her lips in a small smile. "You'd never be ordinary."

His eyebrow lifted and then he smiled in return. "I want—"

The sound of a vehicle approaching had them ducking for cover and the conversation was over.

* * *

A whistle allowed them to come out of hiding. It was Mac and Oyuda.

"We lost them," Oyuda said.

"We killed a couple of them, too," Mac added, seemingly happy about that.

Rik rested a hand on Deleen's back as he urged her forward. "Now we plan."

They sat on the ground. Rik filled them in on what Deleen had told him. Mac angled her head, sizing Deleen up. "You saved us a heap of trouble, escaping like that."

Deleen frowned. "What do you mean?"

Rik shifted his gaze toward her. "We were going to attack that facility and break you out."

"But that's madness," she replied aghast. "There were hundreds of Enhanced in there and the building is well protected. It's made from the hull of one of the colony ships.

Mac snorted. "My thought exactly. Oyuda counted five hundred or more warm bodies. We were hoping an analysis of the structure would give us an edge. Having you outside saved so much time."

Deleen's mouth hung open. She shut it and opened it again. "You'd risk yourselves for me? I don't know what to say."

Oyuda grinned. "You're a civilian. It's our job."

"Is that like programmed into you or something?" Deleen shot back, feeling out of her depth.

Oyuda shrugged and said, "Not really, but our bodies can stand a lot more punishment than you and you happen to know your way around."

"Oh, you're saying I'm useful? That's a relief. For a moment I thought you cared."

Mac grunted out a laugh. "We don't," she said pointing to herself and Oyuda. "He does." She jerked her thumb at Rik.

Rik grunted and avoided eye contact. "Let's get on with it. The city is full of civilians, and we don't know what's going to happen to them. Particularly if the Enhanced want to be accepted among the humans they call the Pure. We could have a war on our hands. In the fighting we could lose many colonists and we can't let that happen. We know our ranks have been destroyed. Del's intelligence is that the rest of us Cold Soldiers are dead."

Deleen studied their faces. No wild fluctuations in emotions, but she noticed the grimace, the sad nod. They'd lost friends and comrades. It couldn't have been easy. What about her friends? What were the Enhanced intending? An unsettled feeling grew in her gut. What had Harzell said? The Enhanced want their offspring to be pure. They want to be integrated. What if that integration was a forced thing? That meant forced mating. She closed her eyes and shuddered. Would they do that? She remembered the market where she was sold. Some of them would do that and more. The High might have nice notions of behaviour, but even he would have to give in to the desires of his supporters or they would oust him in the long run.

The Enhanced would take by force what had been denied them. They'd had no scruples killing the cold soldiers while they couldn't defend themselves. She tried to remember that nagging feeling she'd had about the High. He was the new administrator. He could manipulate the whole city, and he was on his way there. She could imagine all the horrible things that could happen if they didn't fix this now. Deleen sat forward and thumped the ground to get their attention. "Okay. Here's the deal. The supreme leader of the Enhanced looks like a normal human, and he's the new administrator of Colony Five. Don't ask me how that happened, because I don't know. But he's the one pulling the strings behind the new administration.

"I don't believe people should be discriminated against for things that they have no control over, but I also don't believe that they should force their ideology onto others or do things that change other people's genetic identity without their consent."

Mac's head rock up. "What are you saying?"

"The Enhanced want to breed with the pure humans so their offspring will be more like the pure. They believe their offspring will have a better life and more equality. My captor said they did not want to be the hated other anymore. They believe they are the hated and excluded so that must have been taught to them.Which is weird because I didn't even know about the Enhanced before now. I didn't get the option of hating them or liking them."

Mac sat up and fixed her with a stare. "And would your society have accepted these animal-human hybrids? Would they have treated them fairly ... equally, if you had known?"

Deleen's heart sank. How could she answer truthfully? "Not at first because Earth had control of the colony and back them there was to be no deviation in the human DNA strain. However, the colony's ethos was one of tolerance so after the colony became self governing, maybe. Now, though, after the way the colony's attitudes have changed or have been manipulated over time, it would take work, education, a change in culture, and that takes time."

"They were hidden, just like we were," Rik added. "I can understand why we would not be accepted. We are weapons. We are more than human and that is something to fear. These creatures, though, these Enhanced they are people. Right?" Rik said.

"Yes, I believe they are people because they think, they feel. They know right from wrong. But they look different and some act more like their animal aspects so it isn't as straightforward as all that. Some of them will be feared too."

Oyuda squeezed his lower lip between his fingers and let go. "But they were created through genetic engineering, by mixing animal genes."

"Yes, that's right. But that's not their fault, is it?" Deleen argued. "The embryos were stolen. Part of our heritage was taken and altered. They didn't ask to be created. Their existence was hidden, probably by the leaders back then, wanting to cover up Lenane's experiments, his very betrayal of what Five stood for. It seems like after you battled them —and I don't know how many you killed—their compound was forcibly locked down and knowledge of them wiped from the record. You thought you were battling aliens, but you weren't."

Rik sat back, his gaze taking on a faraway look. After a while he commented, "I'm trying to review orders from the war. I can't seem to find any in the database." His brow furrowed. "Mac? Oyuda? You got anything?"

Mac took on the same look and then shook her head. "No," she said after a few seconds. "Nothing. Audit log says the file was flushed about the same time we were reinterred into cold sleep."

Rik nodded, his expression changing. "My file is empty too. Screw that. That means command had to be complicit in this. Why else would they erase our orders?"

"Was General Milo your commander?" Deleen asked, even though she already thought she knew. She hoped it would be someone else.

"General Milo was our commander when we landed. We helped set up the colony. It's a bit fuzzy. I'm not sure if I went into cold sleep for a while or not, but the next memory is the war. He was still the general then.."

"What do you remember about Lenane?"

He cocked his head. "A little bit. Only from the early days of setting up the colony. He worked with your great-grandmother tending the embryo bank." He lifted his lips in a half-hearted smile. "I think I recall that they didn't get on, but I wouldn't put money on it."

"Who cares what happened then? What do we do now?" Mac asked. "I'm telling you, I want to fry those bastards that tried to end us and ended up killing all my buddies. We weren't a big unit. I knew them all."

Deleen touched her forearm and squeezed gently. Mac glared at her. "I understand how you feel, but we can't just kill all the Enhanced. Not all of them are bad, or responsible for what went on. Right now, I think our target has to be The High and anyone else he's controlling. We need to neutralise his power."

"Even if they're civilians?"

"Even if they're civilians, but only if they are in on it. You know the difference? Most of the administration probably don't know what's going on. And I mean neutralise, not kill, unless your life is in danger."

Mac snorted and Rik gave her the evil eye. "We'll do our best to be discriminating, but we aren't judge and jury. We don't have time to weigh up guilt and innocence. We act in the moment. If our lives are at risk, we are going to protect ourselves, protect you and the other civilians. Got it."

Deleen had to accept that. They needed to act before the situation got worse. "Got it. So, now to plan the attack. We have the trikes." She reached down to draw a rough map of the city in the dirt. She explained the transportation hubs, the railway, which was now shut down, the pedestrian walkways and the warehousing district where food and other supplies came in from the outer regions. "There's also the space port, but I don't think there's much point in sneaking in there. Security is always high. Spacefaring ships only come every six months or so. From memory, none are expected for about three months."

Rik studied the map. "Warehouse hub seems the best way in. Food still has to be transported to the city from the outlying areas, otherwise people would starve. I can't see them shutting that down. Dead civilians can't breed."

Mac nodded. "I suppose the men are as vulnerable as the women to this breeding program."

Deleen's eyes flicked up and met Mac's dark gaze. "Yes. There were many females among the males. Either they are going to rape the males." She shrugged. "Or milk them for sperm. Not nice either way, if you aren't willing and don't want to have your offspring be a hybrid."

"Are they good looking, these hybrids?" Oyuda asked.

Rik barked out laugh. "Be serious."

"I am. I mean a civilian wouldn't want me to father any children or even get intimate." He tapped his chest. "Maybe one of these little beasties would be more accommodating."

Rik's eyes widened. Deleen opened her mouth to protest, but Rik touched her arm gently and shook his head at her.

"From what I understand," Rik began, "these Enhanced hate us because we tried to wipe them out as well as the idea that we have tech in our bodies. The civilian reaction to us is based on fear because we are superior in many ways—"

"And," interjected Deleen, "because someone within the colony has been running an anti tech campaign."

Rik nodded. "This is a new world from the one we left. Deleen here doesn't find us repulsive, does she?"

Mac eyed her and snorted. "I figured she was an anomaly."

"She might be," he said with a chuckle. "Regardless is it our duty to give the rest of the civilians a chance to live free and make their own decisions."

Mac frowned, cast a glance at Oyuda and then nodded. Deleen felt the woman's gaze on her and avoided eye contact. Deleen couldn't hide that she had been intimate with Rik. Also, Deleen had acted to save them, not harm them. That didn't equate to instant trust, but it helped.

They all looked to her. She met each of their gazes in turn. "Right. Once we get there, we need to get in. If I can get to a terminal, I should be able to get us through security and inside the city."

"Should?" Mac quipped.

Deleen grinned. "Can, then. If my access is blocked, I know the back way in. That's how I escaped from the Enhanced. They are using a mirror system."

For the next hour they discussed detailed tactics, approaches to key centres of power within the administration building, rules of engagement, such as locking large groups of civilians in rather than trying to herd them or guard them, fall-back positions. If things went wrong, they had three places to meet, each a little further way from the administration building.

"You're with me, Deleen. We hit the admin building. I'll get you there, you get us in. Mac and Oyuda, you take Del's codes and break through these access points." Rik pointed to her dirt map. "Here, here and here. Then secure the civilians you encounter and take over the communications hub. Once linked in you will be able to feed intel through the helmet comms and re-establish contact with us. You will also be able to broadcast to the colony and update them on the current situation."

Deleen's job was to change the security profiles and lock the High out of key systems, and also track him down along with any other key collaborators if she could identify them. Her body was coated in a cold sweat. For someone who was a desk jockey, her life had become very action oriented.

"We leave right away, so we are well placed at sunrise. Any suggestions where we could take cover?" Rik lifted an eyebrow.

Deleen considered her rough map and then pointed. "This old section of the warehouse district is unused and scheduled for recycling. A newer building took over all warehousing two years ago. If I remember rightly, admin couldn't decide between converting the building in situ or pulling it down and repurposing the materials for another building. We should be able to access the admin building from there."

"Right then. That's what we'll do. But first, I want you to wear this." He clipped a wrist band on her.

"What this?" Deleen asked.

"Protection of a kind. Humour me."

Chapter Eighteen

THE BACK WAY INTO THE CITY

Once the party drew closer to the city, Oyuda could pick up the news broadcasts. He relayed it through their helmets. "It's him," Deleen said.

On the screen was the High, the sub-title listing his name as Neil Kameer. "The state of emergency is still in place. The attacks on the embryo bank were severe and our losses are great. We're still hunting the warmongering soldiers who perpetuated this atrocity, this attack on our legacy from Earth. The heart of who we are and why we are here."

"They destroyed the gene bank?" Deleen exclaimed, then covered her face with her hands, fighting the desire to sob. It was a great loss. All the potential citizens gone. She could see the Enhanced logic there. No competition from pure Earth embryos. "The bastard! He's blaming you guys."

"Sssshhh!" Mac hissed. Deleen quieted herself down to listen to the rest of the broadcast.

"... we are doing our best to salvage what embryos we can and will keep you advised. Those allocated an embryo from the store should be able to have their order filled. Implantations are proceeding as normal."

Deleen swallowed fear. "Holy fuck! That can't be good."

Rik's brows drew down. "You think they'll use their own Enhanced embryos?"

Deleen nodded, her finger and thumb pinching her lip as she continued to listen to the broadcast. What better way to take over than to impregnate the unknowing people who were doing their civic duty?

Kameer's unctuous voice continued. "As the new administrator, I am bringing in some new policies. Five's population is growing too slowly to accommodate the expansion we need to take our rightful place among the Twelve. From this moment, everyone over the age of twenty-one will be fertility assessed and assigned a breeding license. It is your duty to have children to take the place of those we have lost in the gene bank and to further the success of the colony.

"Furthermore, leisure clinics will be closed. Sexual intercourse outside of the pursuit of breeding is to be regulated. We cannot have our precious reproductive capability squandered."

Deleen was shaking. What about Vi and her marriage plans? They were having a baby together.

"All domestic partnerships will require an assessment and endorsement from the administration. Do not be alarmed. We're not looking to prevent you making a union. We only wish to assess the health of the candidates to ensure our population remains pure."

"Bullshit," Deleen spat. "He's going to put Enhanced embryos in everyone. He's going to contaminate them all to make sure the whole population has a stake in the Enhanced's survival."

"That's a bit harsh. Contaminate?" Mac said, her gaze flicking to Rik.

Deleen sobered. "Okay, maybe that was a bit harsh. But impregnating people without knowledge or consent is a great evil. If they went about it differently, then it would be more acceptable."

"How would it be more acceptable?" Oyuda asked.

Deleen cast her gaze up, thinking hard. "By letting the Enhanced mix with the general population. Demonstrating that they are people too. Letting individuals choose to breed, live with or love them."

"You think civilians would choose to mate with a half-animal hybrid?" Mac asked, unable to hide her incredulity.

"Under the right circumstances, I do," Deleen replied, her cheeks heating up a little at the scrutiny.

Rik sat back, his tech-filled eyes assessing her. "What circumstances?"

Deleen looked him square in the eye. "When people get a chance to fall in love. They can choose to have sex or marry or what have you."

"Would you choose someone different to you?" he asked.

Deleen shrugged and dropped her gaze. "Yes." Rik was what she wanted. He was different. He had tech running through him. That might repulse some people, but not her.

Rik let out a sigh. "Let's call it a night. Oyuda, set up your scanners to alert for intruders. We should bunk in. I'll wake you before dawn."

He stood up and Deleen followed suit. He gazed at her and she had trouble looking him in the eye. "Where do you wish to sleep tonight, Del?"

Her gaze flew to his. "With you, of course."

His grin was entirely feral.

* * *

Rik followed Deleen into their shelter. The tent wasn't necessary to keep the weather out, as they were in a warehouse but it was useful for privacy, particularly if it gave him space to be with Deleen. He had nearly lost her, and he didn't want to waste a minute of time with her. The situation was in flux, so he had to seize the moment because who knew what would happen. He was half-buoyed by her response to his question. At first, he'd been alarmed by the phrasing of her initial objections to what the Enhanced appeared to have planned for the civilians. He could not help thinking about himself. He was not pure human. In the past, the enhancements he'd had to his body meant he was outcast, and he had accepted that and was happy about it, until now. He loved Deleen and being what he was could seriously impact any future they might have. Although she was sometimes wary of him, he knew she trusted him. She responded to him physically. Their lovemaking had been amazing. But something more permanent? Offspring? He couldn't see that happening.

"Do you have the portable bath?"

He nodded.

"May I have it?"

He cocked his head dramatically. "I'll consider it, but first we have business."

"Business?" her eyes met his and something in him quivered in response. It wasn't some nanotech repairing damage. It was his heart thrilling to the sight of her, and full of fear that this might be their last time together.

Kissing her was always a delight. Once their lips touched, his mind was caught in the moment, in the heat of her. Hands in her hair, he savoured her lips, her tongue and also how she tried to press herself into him, to entwine herself with him. His clothing was too tight. She was pulling on his T-shirt, trying to pull it off. "I want your skin on mine," she said, her voice deep and eyes heated. They paused long enough to shuck clothes and then enjoy the friction of skin on skin. Her hands grabbed his biceps. "Stars, I love how strong you are. How big ..."

He lifted her up and rolled so she was on top of him. "That does things to me," she said, and they began to move together. They were in the throes of ecstasy when a familiar and scorn-filled voice sounded outside. "For stars' sake. Can't you two keep it down? There are celibate people out here." It was Mac.

Deleen made eye contact, biting her lip. Rik laughed out loud. "Use ear plugs, Mac!"

"Bastard," Mac replied, and they could hear her moving off, cursing as she did.

Deleen burst out laughing. "Sorry," she called out to Mac.

Rik went back to the business of enjoying every moment he could with Deleen.

* * *

Deleen was in Rik's shadow. So far, their incursion had been quiet and as stealthy as planned. Two security guards had been eased into unconsciousness, then hidden in a storage cupboard. They were human as far as Deleen could tell. They hadn't been replaced with Enhanced. A good sign, she thought. Maybe the invasion hadn't progressed too far and Kameer had not moved against the civilians yet. She screwed up her nose at the memory of the broadcast he had made. Kameer didn't need to make a move. He was going to do it by stealth, seeding them all with Enhanced offspring. Most parents wouldn't reject their offspring, even if they had a few strange characteristics. Those that did would be dealt with. Of that she was sure.

A security access port was just ahead along the corridor. Rik's broad frame protected her while she worked, yet she checked over her shoulder. Nothing there, but she was worried. She had identified the surveillance cameras and either killed them or they passed through their blind spots. But there could be more now with Kameer and knowledge of her escape. She tried to recall the different security logs that she'd consigned to the archive as a matter of course, worrying there was one she had overlooked for the access from the warehouse to the main administration building.

Mac and Oyuda had taken a different path in. As well as taking control of communications, they would be ready to create a diversion in case Rik and Deleen were discovered and needed a fast exit. If that didn't work, they had to launch a rescue, if they could. Deleen hoped rescue wouldn't be required.

Rik had been strangely quiet and wouldn't be drawn out on why, just saying they needed to concentrate on their mission. Could it be that he thought he wouldn't make it? Her hand quivered at the thought. Closing her eyes, she tried to block out the image of him bloodied and dead. It wasn't the right time for distraction. She needed to override the security, so they could enter the supply corridors into the administration.

It was not as straightforward as she had originally planned. If she used her DNA print, Kameer might have put an alert on it. That meant she entered her security officer codes and responded to the challenges via the back end of the system. While she'd set up the challenge questions a few years ago, she'd never had to use them. Getting one wrong could lock her out and set up an alert. That alert was likely to go straight to the administrator of the colony. Currently, Kameer. That couldn't happen.

After tapping in the code, she waited until the challenge question came up. Her birthdate. Simple. Next challenge flashed up. She squinted at it. It was a series of numbers. What was it? Oh, now she remembered. It was her student number from university. She rearranged the numbers and the system accepted it. One more challenge. Another series of numbers. A date. What was it again? Her mind was blank. Damn. She breathed slowly and closed her eyes. What had been on her mind when she had set that. Her first time. She opened her eyes to peer at the figures. It was her age and the date of when she lost her virginity. She moved to type it in, then paused. That was wrong.

The response was … was … her address. She keyed that in. Unit number, building number, street number and block ID. She rested her head on the monitor, feeling faint. The lock flashed green. She had done it.

She hit open.

Something flew past her helmet, startling her. Rik grabbed her and tumbled her through the door at an angle so that they were inside as the projectile detonated. "Move!" he shouted and they both scrambled under a desk. Another projectile pinged up the corridor. "Okay," she said through gritted teeth. "It looks like they know we're here."

She cast a look over to him and met his steely stare. "You don't say." Then he aimed his weapon and squeezed off a shot. He spoke into his comm link. "They know we're here. Engage, plan B."

Chapter Nineteen

THE SINS OF THE PAST

An explosion rocked the building. Deleen's eyes widened as she pressed herself against the wall. Rik crouched protectively beside her, his focus on the security force at the end of the corridor. He shot off another round and downed one of the men.

"Come on. Time to move." Rik's voice sounded in her helmet.

She waved away smoke and dust to clear her line of sight, not really liking the idea of moving but grateful for her military kit. She was armoured and protected for the most part. Rik dragged her to her feet and shoved her behind him. Rik fired another shot through the smoke at the remaining guard.

There was no return fire so they ran. They reached the intersection. "You got them," Deleen said as she gaped at the bodies of two admin security. She didn't recognise them and was grateful for that.

Rik spoke into the helmet mic. "Yes. Not proud of it. They weren't very well trained. With Mac and Oyuda creating a diversion, we should be able to get into the bowels of admin before we encounter any firm resistance."

"Just get me to a computer room. I can lock key people out. If we can get Oyuda and Mac in place, we can let people know what's going on."

"But there's no evidence in the city's databases to back up what you tell them."

Deleen thinned her mouth into a grim line. "I know, but there is in the Enhanced's archive. I just have to figure out ... Let me see." She did some mental mapping. "We should be able to run an update between the systems, as they are connected. Updates from Five go there, so I just need to get it to update the other way. Then our archives will reflect the truth."

Rik nodded. "Which way?"

Deleen checked the corridor ID number. "That way. We have to go down a level to use the access corridor to main admin building."

"Barriers?"

Deleen let the memory come forward. She had been involved with security drills. Sure, they weren't conducted with military precision, but they were useful. "Normally, DNA entry and a security guard. Alert status, DNA lock protocols in place, double the guard."

Deleen wondered if she could bluff her way past the guards. Then she assessed Rik and figured she couldn't bluff him into anywhere. He was in his battle rig and that only made him look bigger and deadlier. She glanced down. She was also dressed for battle. Not really the attire to fool anyone into thinking she was an administrative clerk on the way to a meeting.

She chewed her lip. "There are also weapon sensors now that I think about it. You're going to have to take the guard without shooting him. Otherwise, the corridor will fill with gas."

Rik grunted. "Gas? Worst case we can survive gas if you close the intake on your helmet and close your visor."

She put down her visor and switched the intake.

"If you want to do it your way, you'll have to distract him," he said.

"My way? I didn't put the gas solution in there. That was my predecessor. How do you suggest I distract him?"

They continued on, slipping down a stairwell. Rik opened the door a crack, peered out and then pulled back and held up two fingers. "You'll think of something."

"Two guards?" she hissed.

He confirmed with a nod.

"Okay, then. I'll distract both of them. You'll just have to be quick."

His lips twitched upward. She couldn't quite call it a smile.

Rik checked the door and then gave Deleen the go ahead with a decisive nod.

She straightened her shoulders and walked purposefully down the corridor, her weapon held across her body. At the sound of her footsteps, the guards turned around. It was then she noticed they were armed. The muzzles of two flash guns pointed at her.

"Stay where you are, or we'll shoot." The taller one said. She didn't know him either. "Identify yourself."

She stopped, keeping her weapon in front of her. "I'm the Access Security Administrator, Deleen Milo."

One of the guards straightened. The other was less impressed. "What are you doing down here in the middle of an alert?" he asked.

Good question, thought Deleen. "I was checking up on a malfunctioning DNA reader when I heard there was an explosion. I need to get access to a terminal and reinforce internal protections." She looked down at her military gear. "Because we are at alert status, I am dressed in the new uniform to give it a test run."

He hesitated, not quite believing her. If she didn't convince them both to move to the DNA lock with her, they were going to get shot rather than being put out of commission by a thump on the head from Rik.

"Look, you can point your weapon at me if you like, but I need to get going." She looked meaningfully at her own weapon. "I'm armed too and I'm on your side." She made a step toward the DNA lock, making out as if she was going to use it. Maybe they didn't know it would be deactivated. Both of the guards turned with her.

Confidently she pressed her finger to the lock. It flashed red for a few seconds, and she had a moment of alarm in case they reacted. She needn't have worried because the guards collapsed to the ground before she had time to blink. Rik towered over her.

The DNA protocol required voice recognition as well as a finger DNA match to prevent unconscious personnel being used to gain access. She spoke into the mic.

One of the guards at her feet moaned.

"It's green. Move," Rik said.

The door slid open. He darted after her before it closed. They ran down the corridor. There was another DNA lock at the other end. She hadn't remembered that one.

"Hey!" a voice called to them. Deleen jabbed her finger and spoke into the mic, hoping it would flash green. She couldn't look around. They hadn't moved the fallen men.

"Wait," she said to Rik. "Don't shoot or we'll go into lock down and the gas."

Running footsteps trembled along the floor. The lock flashed green and the door slid open. She was through, then Rik. He darted out of sight. Not that the person following them could pretend he wasn't there.

A guard ran up, weapon at the ready. "Quick," she said. "He forced me to open the door. He's getting away."

The man's eyes narrowed and then he darted around her to give chase. Rik's blow flipped onto him back and knocked him out. Rik dragged him down the corridor while Deleen found a toilet door. Together they dumped the downed guard inside and shut the door. Out of sight, out of mind.

"That was close," she commented as Rik assessed the passageway. Flat against the wall, she searched for the corridor ID and found it. "This way."

Two more DNA locks and they were just across from the computer room. There was no point in trying to access her workstation. Too many admin people there. Another explosion rocked the building and the lights dimmed. That had to be Mac and Oyuda with their diversion. It was certainly getting her attention.

She shared a look with Rik. "Not caught then," he said.

"You've had no word?" she asked.

"We decided to maintain comms silence once we started plan B so it would appear they were alone. We'll communicate in an emergency only.'

Deleen nodded. "Well, here goes."

The corridor was dim, but the computer room had its own power supply. The lights behind the framed glass door were bright.

Not just anyone's DNA could get them through this door. It was for technicians and her as the deputy head of security. Not that she'd had cause to be here before now. Once the door was open an ominous ping started as they entered. Instinctively, she startled, not knowing the alarm would sound at their entry. Rik dropped to the ground beside her, taking his approach low so he couldn't be seen from desk height. Deleen looked around. There was a camera, perched in the corner of the ceiling. She walked along the towers of servers, looking for a terminal. Down one line and then another. The terminals she found were for stand-alone systems for different support functions. Water control. Sewerage. Power. Transport. "Shit! There has to be one somewhere."

The ping and the camera meant it wouldn't be long before they had company, as the IT systems were a crucial function. Next corner, a terminal winked at her and it was the one she was after. She refreshed the screen. No point in using voice control for entering code. She started typing in the commands to bring up the security software.

The list of names with system's access flashed up on screen. She scrolled through it again, chewing her bottom lip.

"What are you doing?" Rik asked from where he squatted on the floor by her knee.

"I'm looking for his profile. Obviously it isn't 'the High' and I'm not sure if it's this Neil Kameer either. I'll have to do a match with access hierarchy."

"The most access equals the boss?" Rik asked.

"Not really. But the colony administrator has a particular set of permissions. He approves law changes for a start."

A list of names came up on the screen. One was the old administrator who'd been deposed. His system access had been de-activated but his profile remained intact. She noted one or two of his high-level security clearances and permissions and searched on those. Meanwhile she opened up another screen and began copying over her profile to a dummy account using her DNA lock. Then she did that again. "Rik?"

"Yes," he replied looking up at her, a particularly soft look in his eyes.

"Put your finger on that reader over there."

He nodded and drew off a glove. "What are you doing?"

"Giving you access, in case anything happens to me. As Deputy Head of Security, I have access to everything. Although now they have my image on camera they might kill my access."

His eyebrows rose. "I'm not going to let anything happen to you."

She flashed him a grin. "I know. Just call it *my* plan B."

The sound of weapons fire made its way into the room. She switched to the other screen. There were three names. "Rats. I'm going to have to erase all three of them."

"I think someone is coming." Rik supplied as he readied his weapon.

"I know. I have to do the update from the Enhanced's archive to here. I can kick that off now and we don't have to wait for it to complete because it can run in the background. Better still is that I don't think they'll be looking for it."

"I suppose there isn't a back way out of here."

"Why?" she asked, initiating the update with a tap of a key.

"We've got company." Rik's voice was low and serious.

Deleen looked around, knowing there were no other doors. She looked up and then to the back wall. "There are air conditioning vents that keep this room cool." She eyed him. "I'm not sure you'd fit, but let's try."

"Never mind. Show me."

Before moving off, she cleared the screen in case someone came to investigate what she'd been doing.

Thumps from fists pounding on the door reached them, along with muffled yells that were clearly demands to come out. A few random shots. It wouldn't be long before they got serious and came through.

Deleen crawled with Rik along the floor to the vent at the back of the room. Rik extracted a tool from his belt and started unscrewing the cover. "You're going through here. Tell me where it comes out." Deleen snuck a peek at the door, noting that those trying to get in hadn't found someone with access yet and didn't seem to know where she and Rik were. Good for now but it was a minor delay.

She scrambled into the vent and looked over her shoulder. "What about you?" Melt holes were forming on the inside of the door.

Rik frowned and jerked his head at the door. "I'm going out the other way."

"But ..." The look on his face didn't invite argument. "I don't know where it comes out," she said. "The cooling system runs through the whole building. From memory this one is separate because of the computer system."

The commotion by the door grew louder. "Go, go!" Rik urged giving her butt a shove.

"I'll try to meet you on the level above," she said and she crawled as fast as she could.

"Hurry."

"Be careful. Don't kill too many people. They don't know what's going on."

He nodded and lifted the cover to hide her exit.

Deleen was in near darkness. The sound of weapons fire was muted, but smoke started to obscure her vision. They must have hit a server tower or something. Carefully, she patted her way along the vent making sure she wasn't going to drop into a hole or stick her head into a fan. She didn't get very far before the vent bent around and narrowed. It didn't look big enough for her and her armour. She'd have to slide along on her belly. Not her idea of fun.

With no idea what was happening in the computer room, she had to trust that Rik knew what he was doing and would stay safe. Light shone ahead of her and as she slid closer, she saw there was a mesh screen blocking off her vent to a small junction, about two metres square. She pried the screen off and then elbowed her way out of the narrow tube. It was then she noticed the barrier. She climbed to her feet and patted the space in front of her. A transparent seal of hard plastic formed a block between the computer room's cooling system and the rest of admin's system. This took a while to break through as the brackets holding it in place were hard to undo.

A series of loud weapon discharges made her freeze. They were distant, but distinct. Rik. She moved faster and finally managed to edge the barrier aside and slip into the admin building's vent system. Sliding feet first down a slope in the vent, she came to a stop at a three-way junction. At least this section had enough head room for her to stand. She was disoriented, though and needed to figure out how to get back into a main corridor or room. She was currently going downward, but she needed to go up two levels. She passed over a grating in the floor and glanced down. It was an opening in a ceiling in a hallway.

Not ideal, but she needed to get out of here.

With her fingers through the grate she tugged once, then again. It opened and she lowered herself down, letting the grating rest against her head so it would drop down when she slid through. It didn't close properly, but it would be less obvious than an open hatch. As far as she knew no one was looking for her. Rik had made sure of that by taking the attack front on.

Her arm muscles ached. She ran to the corner seeking the corridor ID number. Booted feet thumped down the adjoining corridor. She backtracked and flattened herself in a door recess. As she stood there, she looked up, seeing the light through the grate made it obvious that it was open.

Her heart beat like a drum, feeling like it was going to burst out of her chest. They were going to find her. She waited and her heart rate calmed some. It was quiet. No one came running down the corridor. No one had called out for her to surrender. No shots had been fired in her direction.

She waited a bit longer, trying to calm her breathing. Quickly, she poked her head out to look up the corridor and then drew back. She almost fainted with relief. There was no one there. They had turned off before they got to her.

She recalled the corridor number, and she was stumped. She didn't know where she was. Being lost wasn't the worst part of her situation. It seemed that she had to follow after that small squad of guards, hoping that they took her to a stairwell. Protocol meant the lifts wouldn't be working during an alert, unless there was a physical override key. That would be with the head of security currently on duty. She crept along the corridor, stopping now and then to check behind.

She found a lift, and on both sides were stairs. Heart in mouth, she cracked the door open and peered inside. No one was in the stairwell. She couldn't believe her good luck. Taking each riser as fast as she could, she paused on the next landing and peered up the stairwell, just to check it was as deserted as it seemed.

When she was two levels up, she slowly edged the door open and peered through the crack. No obvious sounds of battle, but there was a scent in the air like burnt skin. Not good. She slid out and then crawled along the ground. If she was going to be a target, she didn't want to be a large one.

From around the corner, the sound of panting grew distinct. She flattened herself on the ground and took a peek. A sliver of fear cut right into her gut. Two bodies lay sprawled on the ground.

She blinked, let out a breath. "Rik?" she whispered loudly. "It's me."

A sound like a wheeze reached her. Getting on all fours, she peered around the corner again to check there were no active shooters. Rik was looking her way, blood splatter decorating his shoulder. His gun lay across his lap.

She scrambled over. "How bad?" she said into her helmet mic.

"Not too bad," came his pain-filled voice. "It's healing already. I was taken from behind. I was fighting one and didn't see the other. Didn't get my weapon up in time."

She glanced at the dead men. "I think you managed fine. Can you move? We need to go up two more floors."

He nodded and lurched to his feet, breath hissing out with the pain. "Let's move."

The stairwell wasn't far. She took point and checked inside. Voices floated around the empty space. It was occupied. She listened as a door opened and then slammed. No more voices. "Clear," she said.

Rik acknowledged her. She entered first and ran, taking the steps two at a time. She was amazed she was able to do that. The trek across country had obviously toughened her up. Rik followed like liquid, no hint that he'd been injured. His nanos probably pumped out exceptional pain killers.

Two floors up, they stood on either side of the door. Rik nodded and she opened the door, just a sliver. There were admin personnel walking around. Now, it was going to get hard. She wasn't dressed like an admin person. She thought the emergency might have cleared them out of the building.

"Give me a few minutes," she said. "I've got an idea."

Rik glared at her. She held up a hand and then gave the thumbs up. Slipping out, she walked along as if she was heading somewhere. She caught a few odd looks but no hint of fear. She found a fire alarm. There was a little hammer stuck to the wall. She took it and smashed the case. The alarm blared.

She knew the drill. The staff would think it was just a test. She had to make it more convincing. She slid into a storage unit, took out her weapon and fired at the cleaning equipment. Smoke billowed; flames leaped. She opened the door to let out the smoke. Then lifting her visor, she yelled up the corridor. "Fire!" she yelled. "Evacuate."

Smoke started to fill the corridor. The alert tone switched over to the evacuate signal. "Hurry. It's spreading."

A man with a fire warden's helmet ran toward her. "Is there a fire?" he asked in a panicked voice.

"Yes. It's spreading. You need to get people out."

He nodded and ran back. She heard him chivvying people along. Within a heartbeat, Rik was beside her. "Good thinking."

"I better put it out. I don't want to burn down the whole building." The fire extinguisher on the wall nearby did the job, but the smell of soot and smoke was still in the air.

"Is this the floor?" Rik asked.

"Yes. The administrator's office is in the far corner."

A crackle of static leaked from Rik's helmet. He put his hand out for her to wait. A voice came through, but the signal was weak.

"We're pinned down," Mac said.

"You both okay?" Rik asked.

"Oyuda has a small leg wound, but yeah, we're good."

"Then get out now. Nothing more you can do. We are close to target."

"Acknowledged. Bugging out."

Rik's suit still showed signs of blood and scorch marks. "What about you?" she said, with a chin nod to his wound. "Shouldn't you wait here?"

He shook his head. "You aren't going in there without me. Now's our best shot."

"I know, but I'm having second thoughts."

He lifted his eyebrow. "Why?"

"So much could go wrong."

He shook his head and hefted his weapon. "Move out, Del."

The door to the administrator's office was closed. Deleen thought that was strange. The alarm ceased blaring and they waited. Surely someone was still in there. It would be terrible bad luck if Kameer had left the building.

Footsteps approached. Rik and Deleen ducked further down the hall to avoid being seen. Peeking out, she caught a glimpse and sucked in a surprised breath. Harzell and three other Enhanced pushed the administrator's door open. It couldn't be good that they were comfortable being out in the open. It also indicated that Kameer might be in.

Voices sounded down the corridor. She could hear some of the words, but Rik with his enhanced hearing could probably understand better. "Can you hear what they're saying?"

Rik's brow furrowed. "They're reporting that the fire was a false alarm. Also, that two insurgents have been prevented from entering the building." He listened further, then swung around. Too late. A large-pawed hand swatted him into the wall. Deleen screamed as she was grabbed. Bloody Enhanced and their superior senses. Her helmet was removed and tossed aside, and she was hauled down the hallway towards the office by her hair. She tried to fight, holding onto her hair and kicking out. Her captor changed grips. A large arm encircled her ribs, right under her breasts and then she was flung through the door and onto the floor.

Dazed, Deleen pushed up off the carpet and shook her head. Her back hurt and there was a shooting pain down her right leg. "Bastards!"

"We meet again, Ms Milo. You have been very enterprising."

Kameer looked unruffled as he peered at her over the top of his desk.

A ruckus heralded the arrival of Rik. His helmet was absent too. At least he was still alive, but his face had swollen lumps on his cheek and blood leaked from his nose and mouth. His shoulder leaked fresh blood. They hadn't been gentle.

"On your knees, hands behind your back," said the Enhanced who prodded Rik with his own weapon. Rik assumed the position and the muzzle of his gun rested against the back of his bare head. His gaze flicked sideways in her direction, but his expression was neutral.

"Once again you are with the Tainted. I do believe you prefer them.

See, Harzell, you should not have fretted about her. Your little friend is unharmed."

Deleen's gazed settled on Harzell, who stood at attention against the wall. Only the flicker of his tail betrayed any emotion.

"What were you planning?" Kameer asked. "Breaking in here and killing me? Did you think that would solve your problems?"

Deleen shrugged. "It might have prevented you from succeeding."

"Place her there."

He pointed to a chair. She was lifted and then shoved down in the chair. Kameer's eyes glittered with anger. "You would have made things worse. I am what keeps the Enhanced in control, keeps them civilised. Do you think they are going to sit idly by and be ignored and forgotten again? They want their place in society. They are going to take it one way or another."

"But you can't do what you are planning. Impregnating people with hybrid sperm without their knowledge or implanting them with hybrid embryos. Or taking people's sperm and eggs without their knowledge. People need to give consent."

"Do they?" His eyebrow lifted as if surprised by the concept. "Do you think the ancestors of these Enhanced gave consent?" His gaze burned bright with a fanatical light.

She dropped her gaze. "No." Her voice was quiet. But anger filled her. "But that doesn't make what you plan to do right either. Just because someone did an awful thing in the past to you, to your kind, doesn't mean the people of Five should be punished for it. They didn't even know."

"We are people of Five," he said icily.

She acknowledged his point with a nod. "I mean the civilians, the pure."

Kameer sat back in his chair, making a bridge with his fingertips. "They will never willingly accept us. Having them give birth to Enhanced offspring will change their minds."

Deleen relaxed her shoulders. If Kameer was going to kill her, he would have done so. "Perhaps. It's a dangerous social experiment, though. What if you're wrong? What if the offspring never become pure? Wouldn't science be better? Some gene therapy?"

He lifted his eyebrow and inclined his head, as if in respect for her opinion. "I looked into that. We would have to request help from the other colonies. Given the prevailing aversion to what we are, we can't risk that they will try to sterilise us—or worse, sterilise this world."

Deleen went cold. That had never occurred to her. "But there is a population here. They can't do that."

Kameer nodded slowly, keeping his gaze on her. "Yes, they can. Economics, my dear. This planet is rich in resources. The population here is small, easily discounted, easily dismissed. They can settle a whole new colony ship here and get rid of the taint of us."

Deleen shook her head. "No. I don't believe that would happen. Humankind has progressed. They couldn't and they wouldn't."

"Perhaps ..." He stepped out from behind his desk to inspect Rik. "You are an impressive specimen ... what's your name?"

"Rik Chesson."

"Harzell, come here."

Harzell detached himself from the wall. "This is what your precious pure prefers to you. What do you think?"

Harzell's gaze met hers and then looked at Rik. "He looks impressive on the outside. She does not see the taint, the rot on the inside."

"Rik is a person, just like you. Leave him out of it."

Kameer *tsk tsked*. "But that's our point, Ms Milo. On the outside, Rik can pass for human. You obviously prefer him over Harzell, who is obviously hybrid, less human. Harzell was good to you, but you spurned him. Others would do the same. There can be no choice, if we are to coexist. We must all be forced to be equal."

"No! Don't. That's not the way. Tell the citizens of Five the truth. Let them know what was done to you. I'm sure they will try to right the wrongs. Give them a chance to prove themselves."

Kameer lifted his head. "There's no point. We are hunting your companions. The other Tainted. Your friend Rik will join his frozen companions. We will not let them exist with us. Will not let them harm us."

He nodded and guns came to the ready.

"Please, no!"

"No point in begging, Ms Milo. This will be cleaner for you. Harzell will have you—as his reward. There will be no hiding your union. I have a public relations campaign at the ready to announce your partnership and also for the birth of your first child."

Deleen launched herself out of the chair. A weapon fired. Time froze for her. Someone screamed her name. Rik. Harzell.

* * *

Rik hunched over Deleen's inert form. Blood welled out of the wound in her chest. A sob broke out of him as he rocked her back and forth. His trembling fingers brushed her hair out of her eyes. Soft, ginger locks that he'd loved to look at. Tears dripped from his chin to her face. "Del?"

She was mute. Movement beside him. "Is she dead?" the part-feline asked. Harzell was his name.

Rik couldn't form the words. He just clutched her closer to his chest. Mine, he thought. Mine.

"Fools," Kameer said. "You were meant to shoot him, not her."

Harzell's clawed finger traced the shape of Deleen's brow. A growl grew in Rik's throat. They had no right to touch her. It was because of them she was dead. It was because of them his whole unit was dead. Maybe Mac and Oyuda had already been taken and killed. What had it all been for? Lies and lies. All of it. Everything.

An argument broke out behind him, full of curses and growls. "Enough. Call medical. I need confirmation she is dead. Take him outside and finish him. See if you can do that competently."

"No," Rik said in a quiet voice.

Rik had nothing to lose now. He met Harzell's gaze and nodded to him. The Enhanced reached out to take Deleen from him. "Take care of her."

Harzell nodded and took Deleen's inert form.

Rik rose to his full height. Kameer blinked and before he could issue an order, Rik moved. He disarmed one of his assailants with a quick grab for the weapon and a head butt that sent the creature flying back against the wall, where he slid down unconscious, blood trickling from his head. A reverse kick felled the other before he could bring its weapon to bear. Rik grabbed up his weapon and downed another two before they could flee.

Kameer scrambled behind his desk, pressing the intercom. Rik had him by the throat before he could summon more guards. Kameer's eyes bugged out. "Get your filthy hands off me," he rasped, face suffused with blood.

Rik squeezed. He wanted to kill him. Wanted to erase him from existence. But not only did he have Deleen's words in his ears, he knew that Kameer had spoken truth about his control of the Enhanced. "You have a lot to answer for."

He threw the leader of the Enhanced back into his chair and stepped back. Kameer rubbed his throat. "We are the victims here, Tainted."

Rik tried not to think of Deleen lying lifeless in his arms. Although deep down he wanted to destroy Kameer, he had to think ... think more like Deleen. "Then why not explore a different way forward? Why make *everyone* a victim? Why this path?"

Kameer kept his gaze on Rik, but seemed to sense that Rik was not going to kill him. "This way is the most certain. Over time, the pure will accept us. Mingling the blood lines will give them an incentive."

Rik squared his shoulders. "There are other ways—"

"What do you know?" Kameer interrupted. "Your kind are condemned and outcast, as we are. The ethos of the colony has always been focussed on the Pure—anti-hybrid, anti-tech."

Rik shrugged. "Maybe I once thought as you did. But then I loved one of the pure, as you call them. It was real and true, and it didn't matter what I was. She didn't care about that. She only saw the person I was underneath."

Kameer swallowed, cheeks flushed pale pink. "So?"

Rik jerked his chin toward Kameer. "Your people could do the same. Let the rest of the colony know you are here, let them look upon the sins of the past and offer you a life."

Kameer shook his head, his mouth twisting with bitterness as if he was about to spit. "You have great faith in these pure, these civilians."

Rik lowered his eyelids and breathed out slowly. "I do." And he knew this to be true.

* * *

Pain paralysed Deleen. She could scarcely draw breath. Her brain was full of fog and sludge. Her thoughts would not move. She was being carried. Her sense of smell was acute. It was Harzell.

He kicked open a door and then rested her on the edge of a desk while he swept the computer monitor and papers to the floor and then laid her down. A sniff sounded in her ear and his fingers brushed across her brow. "I will mourn you," he whispered.

A moan escaped her mouth.

Harzell stilled and then drew back.

Her eyes fluttered open. Harzell stared at her in horror. "You live? Not possible. It was a death strike. I smelt death on you."

Deleen looked down, saw the blood, inhaled its metallic tang. The site of her injury itched. She frowned. "I died?"

Harzell nodded. "Yes. You couldn't have lived through that."

"But I'm talking ... or are you dead, too?"

"No, I am not." He surged forward, ripped her armour apart and peered into her injury. A look of horror came over his face. "You are infected by tech. I can see things repairing your tissues. You are like the Tainted. You are tainted."

She screwed her face up and tried to look down, but any movement hurt too much. "How?" she whispered.

"The soldier. He's your lover?"

Deleen stilled. "Lover?" That sounded just right and not enough. "Yes. I love him."

"I've read about this. You must have had unprotected intercourse? That is one of the ways contamination occurs." He stepped away. The room spun and Deleen tried to maintain consciousness and her concentration. "The nanobots in his seed have infiltrated your body," Harzell said, "They have seeped into your tissues and multiplied."

Deleen relaxed somewhat. "Then I'm like him now. Tainted?"

Harzell hissed a reply. "Yes."

A smile spread across her face. It hurt to smile, but she didn't care. "Excellent."

Harzell loomed over her prone form. "Not excellent. Don't you understand? The High has probably executed him already. When he finds out about what you have inside you, he will do the same to you."

Deleen considered this. She couldn't engage with the thought that Rik might be dead. She had to have faith in him. He was a super soldier, a cold soldier. "But I'm already dead, right?"

Harzell's golden eyes brightened. He gazed into her eyes and then ran a hand down her arm. "Yes. You are already dead."

Harzell understood and she liked that about him. He appreciated the subtleties.

He picked up her hand and brushed his lips across her knuckles. "Farewell, Deleen. Think kindly of us."

Then he was gone. He'd left her, knowing she was not dead but understanding that Kameer thought she was. He'd helped her in the end.

Deleen wasn't in any condition to move, but at least she was breathing. She stayed still while the nanotech worked its magic on her body. The wound hurt like the seven hells. Pain had to be a good sign. It meant she was alive.

But she had tech inside her.

Chapter Twenty

THE HIGH'S DILEMMA

Two guards burst through the door, weapons at the ready. "Take him to a cell," Kameer demanded.

Rik inclined his head, not moving an inch. He didn't want to appear aggressive or give them an excuse to kill him with their energy weapons.

He took comfort that at least Kameer wasn't ordering him shot like before.

"There aren't any cells in this building, most High," a monkey-faced Enhanced said.

"Well find somewhere else to secure him. I need to think." His two guards shared a puzzled look and then moved to his side.

The intercom buzzed. "Yes," Kameer snapped.

"Most High. We are being inundated with enquiries. Apparently, there is something wrong with the colony's archives. The pure are sending in queries, in the hundreds. They are asking about the early experimentation on stolen embryos. They are asking about us."

Rik and the two guards turned to stare at Kameer.

"What?" Kameer dived to his terminal and called up the archives. "How the hell did that happen?" His gaze flicked to Rik. "It was her, wasn't it?"

Rik nodded and relaxed his stance. His attendant guards stepped back to let him speak. "She thought that everyone should know about Lenane's experiments. That everyone should take responsibility."

Kameer scrolled down the screen and then thumped the desk. Rik could see that Deleen had included an article about the Enhanced. Also, she had sourced the Enhanced medical records, which included images of all of them. An array of faces filled the screen.

Kameer sat back. "No. No. It's not possible. How could she do this? We are exposed."

Harzell came back into the room. Rik's heart clenched. Was Deleen truly dead? He knew the wound was mortal, but something in his mind, his heart wouldn't let him accept that fact. The lion man didn't appear very distressed and that made Rik angry. He balled his fists but before he could lash out, Kameer stood up and bellowed. "It's all your fault. You brought that Milo woman to us, you, you soft-centred ball of fluff."

Harzell froze, his gaze slipped over Rik, who dominated the room, to focus on Kameer. "What happened?"

Rik thought Harzell looked guilty and wondered why.

Kameer filled him in about the sharing of the database. "I didn't know," Harzell said. "It wasn't me that gave her access to the archive."

"No." Kameer breathed out slowly, leaned back into his chair and then nodded. "I did." Kameer's head jerked up as if he had suddenly remembered Rik was still there. He flicked his hand in Rik's direction. "Harzell, do something useful and take this Tainted and put him somewhere secure." His gaze focused on Rik, and his anger suddenly flared. "I don't want him seen. If he gives you any trouble, kill him." Dismissively, he waved a hand at the door.

Rik and Harzell shared a look but didn't move.

"Now!" Kameer bellowed. "Before I grab a weapon and kill you both."

Harzell near leaped to Rik's side, making the two guards step back in their haste to get out of the way.

"But there are no cells," one of the guards hissed to Harzell. "What are we meant to do with him?"

Rik weighed up whether to fight the lion man. He was smaller built, but Rik guessed what lay underneath that soft fuzz was all muscle. It wouldn't pay to underestimate the gifts from the animal genes. He didn't know much about the experiments performed on these hybrids, but enough of what he'd read of the article Deleen had shared made him wary.

He let Harzell take him by the arm. The two other guards got out of the way but made to follow. "Where are you taking me?" Rik asked.

"Quiet, Tainted." They moved to the door, Harzell squeezing his arm.

"Why don't you just kill me?" Rik hissed at him.

They entered the hall and the two Enhanced guards followed behind, weapons at the ready. Two more joined them. They looked deadly. One had tusks coming up from his jaw and the other had a horn growing out of his forehead.

"Here will do," Harzell said. They all stopped in front of a door. Harzell put his finger to the DNA lock. The door snapped open. It was a board room.

"Empty it," Harzell instructed two of the guards. The other two scary looking guards took up position by the door, their weapons trained on Rik.

The guards started bringing out the chairs. "Leave the table," Harzell ordered. "It is too big to fit through the door. Besides, I haven't got all day."

Only the table and one chair were left in the room. The rest were stacked in the hallway.

Harzell jerked his head in the direction of the room when his assistants were done. "Get in."

Rik stepped inside. The door *thunked* closed behind him and the lock engaged. He let out a breath. He was alive and he was grateful for that. He shook his head and eased his shoulders. Now that he had time to contemplate things, sadness welled up. Deleen had sacrificed herself for him. He leaned against the table and rubbed his stubbled chin. She'd cared for him. Loved him. The realisation floored him.

Their attraction to each other was well understood, but love? He didn't think it was possible for him to feel such a deep emotion, but he knew deep down he did care. Did love. What had held him back was the expectation—no, the belief—that it was impossible. He was Tainted. He had been outcast from normal life the moment the nanobots had been placed into his blood stream. The role he'd been asked to fill was cemented by the tech placed in his body, the enhancements made to his musculature.

Tears gathered in his eyes when he replayed that moment when she had dived between him and the gun. His shock. His disbelief. His loss. Tears flooded his eyes. "Oh, Deleen."

Her acceptance opened up a world of possibilities that hadn't existed in his mind for hundreds of years. A small sliver of hope, of a future, had been neatly cut away before it had time to grow. There was nothing left now but to die, doing what she had set out to do. Save Five.

He walked to the window and gazed down. The room he was in overlooked a plaza. He wasn't that high up. He'd survive the jump. Rik assessed the glass, and it was easily smashed. That made him think. Why had Harzell put him in such a room? One that could not contain him. Harzell wasn't stupid. What was the hybrid up to?

The door swished open. Rik spun around, ready to burst through the glass if they had come to take him. But it wasn't a kill squad. There was just a lone, unarmed figure.

"Quickly," Harzell beckoned to him from the door.

Rik assessed him with the scanner in his eye. Nothing too untoward there. No hidden weapons or explosives.

"Hurry, you fool."

One more glance at the plaza below and Rik was moving to the door. He wasn't sure what Harzell was up to, but he was grateful for another opportunity to escape or destroy Kameer's plans. Preferably both.

Harzell mistook Rik's speed and held up his hands. "Do not attack me. I'm here to help you."

Rik slowed and relaxed his stance. "Help me? How?"

"Be patient." Harzell stepped back, checked the corridor and said, "Come." Then he turned on his heel and darted down the corridor with his tail bobbing behind.

Rik loped along, still uncertain about whether he wanted to strangle the man or thank him.

Round the corner he came upon Harzell standing flush against the wall and peering around the corner. Rik didn't need prompting. He found a doorway to crouch in, reaching up to kill the light so that he was wrapped in shadows.

Harzell backtracked and then pretended to walk purposefully along the hall. A small squad of four guards marched past him, apparently without taking exception to his presence. When their steps had receded, Harzell waved Rik forward. "We must be quick."

Then they darted down the corridor and turned left as Harzell hurried into a room. Rik followed and stood dumbfounded by what was before him.

Deleen lay in state on a bed. Pale and still in death. He stumbled forward, not expecting the opportunity to say goodbye to her. "Thank you," he said softly to Harzell.

"Do not thank me," Harzell responded. "Not much time, so be quick."

"Quick?" Rik ran his forefinger along her nose. Her face was surprising unmarked after what they'd been through. Her lips were full and red, and he dropped his touch there, a featherlight brush. He jerked his hand back.

"She's breathing." He wondered if he was imagining things.

"I know. She is alive. That is why I brought you here. You need to tend her and then you need to leave."

"Leave?"

"Yes, I can cover for you. The High believes she is dead. All I have to do is say I killed you too. Leave the city. Find your own place and live out your life there."

Rik ran his hands over Deleen, pulling down the cover that hid her chest. Her injury was almost healed. "How?"

"She is Tainted like you now. Your tech is in her body. It is repairing her."

Disbelief and joy warred for control of his emotions. It was all happening too fast. He had a choice. Take her and leave and live out his life with her.

Deleen's eyelids flickered and a small murmur escaped her mouth. He didn't think she'd like that. Her connections to the city and to the civilians was too strong. He might take her out of this building now, but as soon as she was better, she'd be back to fight once more.

"We can't leave," he said to Harzell quietly. "There has to be another way."

Harzell gripped his arm, squeezing the vambrace. "Do not be a fool. Save yourselves."

"It won't be foolish. Not if you help us."

Harzell fell back and shook his head. "I am helping now, much to my own risk. If you care for this woman, you should take her far from here. It is a big planet. You could be safe."

"No ..." It was Deleen's voice.

They both turned to her.

Rik understood. She did not wish to live with him, to make a life. Not with an unworthy Tainted.

She reached for his hand and then squeezed his fingers and opened her eyes. "Rik ... it really is you."

He nodded. Her gaze travelled to Harzell. "Thank you for bringing him to me. Can you help us get to central broadcast?"

Harzell's yellow skin paled and he shook his head vigorously. "I cannot."

Deleen tried to sit up. "Don't you see? It's the best way. It will open this whole situation up."

"You ask too much."

Deleen nodded. "Okay then. I understand. You would rather there be death on both sides." To Rik she said. "Help me up. It's time to move."

Harzell growled. "Why do you persist in doing this? It is much easier to escape now. Be free."

Deleen groaned as Rik helped her to sit up. She faced Harzell. "What about the colony? Will they be free? Free to choose their own genetic future?"

Harzell licked his lips, catching briefly on a fang. "They will destroy us."

Deleen's expression stilled. "Perhaps. I can't say for sure. You have murdered innocent cold soldiers. For that I think there must be justice. But you are people and the rest of the colony have to accept that."

"You gamble a lot on our future," Harzell said. "The High will kill you for this."

"I'm already dead. You said so yourself."

* * *

Deleen felt like absolute shit. Her body was a sack of metal filings that dragged her down. If it wasn't for Rik and Harzell she wouldn't have made it this far. Rik had transfused more nanobots into her system. He had a small tube fitted into his vambrace and inserted one end into the opening of her wound. He said it was for topping up other soldiers during battle, if they were badly wounded.

While she imagined she could feel them crawling around inside her, she didn't actually notice that they were busy repairing the damage to her body. The wound was one thing, but she did die, and the bots were working on oxygen deprived areas of her body and repairing the damage.

She couldn't keep her gaze from Rik and he in turn seemed to look at her differently, as if he wanted to say something but couldn't.

Perhaps he had been surprised by her death and sudden return. He hadn't told her off—yet—for putting herself in harm's way. He hadn't acted surprised that she had been infected with his tech. In the circumstances she wasn't complaining. She was actually pleased. Being killed wasn't much chop.

Harzell pushed open the doors to the communications centre. There were two staff members there. They turned, screamed at the site of Harzell and scrambled for the emergency exit. It happened so quickly that only the alarm on the exit provided evidence that they had been there. Harzell eyes widened. "I should leave you now. I've done enough."

"Not yet, Harzell. I need you." She felt pity for him that the 'pure' had acted that way at the sight of him.

Rik spoke into his helmet mic. "Mac. Oyuda?" Harzell had retrieved what remained of Rik's kit.

Deleen looked at him expectantly. He shook his head. There was no word from them.

"It's probably the insulation here blocking the signal. Don't give up hope. I can't see Mac letting anyone get the better of her.

Rik grinned. "Mac will be pleased to hear you say so. What's the plan?"

"The plan is we broadcast our own newscast. We've updated the archives to reflect the truer version of events and that's a start, but it will take time for that to filter through. We need something more immediate."

"Okay. What do you need us to do? I can probably manage the camera."

"I need you both to be in the newscast. The cameras are automatic. Preprogramed. Give me a minute."

Deleen went up to the bank of equipment. She'd primed this many times when assisting the administrator to make announcements. She'd only helped out when she was unlucky enough to be still at her desk at a late hour. Besides, it was policy for support staff to be trained in multiple functions. Deleen could pay accounts, write a policy brief or prepare a meal in the refectory. She was management.

While she keyed in the parameters of the broadcast, she started thinking about what she was going to say and how to put the segment together. It was important to have both Harzell and Rik talking and also sitting in peace together. It was the only way to prove that there was a way forward. It wasn't going to solve all their problems, but this broadcast was going to put a huge spanner in the plans of Kameer. No way was the colony going to be duped.

"This is an emergency newscast for Colony Five. I am Deleen Milo, Deputy Head of Security. Firstly, I want to alert you to the circumstances of the sudden change in administrator and the events that have followed. There has been a coup. I repeat there has been a coup.

"Second, I want to talk to you about the history of the colony. Some of you may have seen the update to the colony's data files. It speaks of forbidden experiments, of human embryos that were interfered with, illegally changed by one of the scientists that arrived with the first ship. Those embryos were mixed with animal genes in unsanctioned experiments. The new archive that you are reading is closer to the truth. Our own city archives were tampered with long ago to hide what happened."

The camera zoomed in for a close up. "You might ask why I am telling you this now, when the colony is under threat? Well, the results of those experiments were not destroyed, nor were those experiments a failure. Unknown to us, a group of humans with animal genes have been living on Five, but kept apart from us. They call themselves the Enhanced. They are in this city now. They have taken over."

"Someone in our past hid the truth from us deliberately. Just like they hid the knowledge of the cold soldiers. The ones you recently surrendered to their deaths. The soldiers were there to protect us."

"We haven't been here long, not in terms of history. We should not have forgotten so easily, so quickly. This forgetting was deliberate. I remember how I forgot. I was programmed to forget under the guise of psychological counselling. I'd seen our family's cold soldier when I was a child. The administration tried to erase that memory, but I didn't forget. I saved my cold soldier."

The camera zoomed to Rik, who sat quietly, not even blinking. "My cold soldier, Rik Chesson, saved my life today. He worked to save Five in the past and he is protecting us again today by undermining the coup.

"The Enhanced have behaved badly. They have tried to take over the city. To change us. Do not allow yourselves to participate in any health assessments or fertility screening. The plan is to impregnate females with a hybrid child, an Enhanced child, without your consent. If you are male, your sperm will be used to fertilise an Enhanced female. It was the Enhanced who ordered the cold soldiers be murdered. But there is a reason for this. The cold soldiers were tasked with destroying them in the early days of the colony and so the Enhanced feared them, feared what they could do. They saw them as their enemies." She took a breath and caught Rik's eye and smiled.

"I believe that the Enhanced have been denied justice, denied a place in our society, even denied their own existence. They were created without their or our consent. Their children didn't ask to be Enhanced. That's not our fault, I know. We didn't even know about them. We didn't know about this injustice. Someone in our past hid them. Now it is time to acknowledge them, accept them, treat them equally. They are people too. They are as much a part of the history of Five as the rest of us."

A thumping on the door indicated that the broadcast was being received and someone was desperate to stop it. Voices raised in outrage penetrated the sound of thumping against the door. "I have with me Harzell of the Enhanced. He's a reasonable man. He helped us bring you this story today. Tell us about yourself."

The camera zoomed in on Harzell. She nodded. "Hello, people of Five." Harzell was nervous. "I was ... was born in Jerrytown thirty years ago. My parents were Harrison and Zelda of the clan Felidae. My parents were natural born, as were their parents before them."

Deleen lifted her forefinger and the camera diverted to her. "Jerrytown is an enclave to the north of us. It has been here as long as Central City. Harzell, how do you feel about living in Jerrytown?"

He smiled. "I like it well enough. It is home. We have the colony archive and all the literature and information available in it, plenty to read and study. The food can be a bit boring but it is plentiful."

"What do you eat normally?"

Harzell peered at her, as if trying to figure out what was in her mind. "We Enhanced are vegan. We do not eat animal products. We are civilised. We are not cannibals."

"What do the Enhanced want? Why have you come to the city?"

Harzell licked his lips and the pink flesh passed over his protruding fangs. He lowered his eyes. "We want to be equal to the Pure. We want to live among you in peace."

The camera cut to her. "You will see the Enhanced in the administration buildings. I'm sure after this broadcast you will see them everywhere. Some of them look like us and you cannot tell they are Enhanced. We cannot punish these people for who they are. We must accept them into our lives, into our hearts.

"The same can be said for—" She indicated Rik, but the camera dropped to the floor with a clunk. A quick glance at the console and she knew the power had been cut. The door yawned as it was forced open. The muzzles of many weapons pointed accusingly at them. Kameer burst through, hair dishevelled, face livid with anger.

"You are meant to be dead!" he screamed these words so ferociously that Deleen blinked. "You have ruined everything!"

He surged closer, fists balled up tight. Pausing, he backhanded Harzell, near tipping him backwards in the chair. "Traitor! You will die for this."

A growl escaped Harzell's mouth, but he didn't attack. Deleen wouldn't have been so calm about being struck like that.

Harzell sucked in a breath. "I did it for us," he said in a rush. "Deleen is right. We should announce ourselves openly."

Kameer shook his head. "We can't, you fool! We've gone too far." Kameer pointed. "Guards, kill the tainted."

Deleen moved quickly and placed herself in front of Rik. Rik grabbed her by the waist and shoved her bodily aside. "I won't let you take fire for me again."

She wrestled with him. "I won't let you die for me. You can die if they wound you enough."

No shots were fired, even though the muzzles kept moving as they tried to target Rik.

"For stars' sake kill them both!"

"Why do they have to die?" Harzell asked Kameer, moving to stand in the path of potential weapons fire. "From what I can see Deleen has tried to help us, the Tainted ... Rik too. Despite the harm that we have done. She has shown forgiveness and compassion. If she could do that, surely others could too."

Kameer rubbed his forehead. "You're a fool."

"Hello, admin?" A voice piped through.

Kameer wrinkled his brow. "What is that?"

Deleen looked around, nonplussed. It was a direct call on the emergency line. One that was independently powered. She hit the key. "Yes?"

"This is Jason Pekson at Station C Five. We wanted to let you know your broadcast has generated a lot of interest. The survey results are in."

"Survey?" Kameer asked, his pale face had two spots of colour on his cheeks. Idly, Deleen wondered what animal genes he possessed.

"What survey?" Deleen asked, her heart racing. She reached for Rik's hand and squeezed.

"We asked whether we should embrace the Enhanced?"

"And the result?"

"The survey's still running, but so far with seventy per cent response rate it's around eighty per cent yes."

"That's a clear majority, right?"

"Yes. We thought you should know."

Deleen watched Kameer. His eyebrows furrowed over his dark, disbelieving eyes. "Not possible."

She responded to Jason. "Thank you. Great news." To Kameer she said, "It is possible, but this is only the first step. It's not going to be easy. I don't suppose you left the real administrator alive."

Kameer's head shot up. "Of course we did! He is Pure."

"That's a good start," Deleen said. She would have smiled, but she felt ill all of a sudden and slumped into a chair. Rik came to her side, his expression anxious as he smoothed her hair.

Kameer signalled to his men and they lowered their weapons. "We surrender."

Jason piped up again. "We have broadcast the audio of the surrender. I expect security will be with you shortly."

The Enhanced guards in the room slowly put their weapons on the floor and then raised their hands.

Deleen fought the nausea and sat up straighter. "I'm okay," she said to Rik. "Maybe gather up the weapons and store them over there. Harzell, can you restore power?"

Harzell nodded and slid past the guards and out the door.

Power came on not long after. Deleen felt improved.

Within ten minutes, more booted feet heralded the arrival of admin security. "Milo!" It was Cooper Pound from her section. "Are you okay?"

"Yes, I'm fine. Kameer here will tell you where to find the real administrator."

Cooper nodded and had his men escort the Enhanced away. Harzell was spared such an escort because Rik stood beside him, arms folded and looking deadly.

Cooper watched the others depart and then faced Deleen. "Your broadcast certainly explained a lot. It's been chaos here. No information getting out." His gaze reached Rik. "How did you do it?"

"I had help. I'm not sure how the administrator's going to handle this situation when he is released. I seem to recall that there is an emergency protocol that brings all heads of department in to run things. Do you think that we should initiate that?"

Cooper nodded. "Yes. It would give you power to set up on an interim government."

"Me?"

"Yes, under the emergency arrangement security is the chair of the committee."

"But I'm only the deputy."

He shook his head. "Your boss is dead. You succeeded him."

Deleen's heart sank. "Then you better get me sit reps for the city and I'll start working on plans. Also, general amnesty for the Enhanced now. Cease hostilities."

"You need to rest," Rik said, putting a hand on her shoulder.

"I will. Cooper, can you provide an escort for Rik here. There are two more cold soldiers out there and we want to make sure they're safe."

Rik squeezed her shoulder. "Del?"

"I'll be okay. You make sure Mac and Oyuda are safe, then report back here."

"Very well." He gave her a nod and left.

* * *

"Kameer has escaped. There is fighting in the streets." Cooper reported to her at seven in the morning. She'd managed to get some sleep and her wound was almost healed. Her body ached in strange places, but her energy levels were well up on normal. She could probably run fifty miles.

"Fatalities?" she asked.

"Two. One Enhanced and one civilian."

"Bugger! This isn't going to be easy, is it? We needed cultural change, education programs aimed at the young so that they can openly accept the Enhanced. Not this instant amalgamation. Make a note for the education department. We should start on that right away. Also, Station C Five—get them working on some advertising. And, damn, we need to find somewhere to house over five hundred new settlers. We can't leave them in Jerrytown forever. We'll have a riot on our hands."

They walked into the administrators' office, which had a wall map, a large window and a desk full of ereaders lined up, each representing an agenda item. The administrator was alive, but his mind was gone. They had commenced therapy but the prognosis wasn't good. In the meantime, Deleen had taken over as chair. Although the emergency committee had convened, most of the decisions were Deleen's to make. Cooper was an excellent right-hand man.

Cooper pointed to the wall map. "The new subdivision is nearly complete. It was a rehousing project so that Inner-City, high-density apartments could be torn down. We could put about a hundred households in there and they'd be contained."

"Contained? We don't want to contain them, we want to integrate them. If we put them all in the one place they'll form an enclave." She chewed her lip. "Maybe set up a draw, using the people who were going to be relocated and Enhanced candidates. Harzell has the priority list. Take one from each list and then backfill the vacancies in central with Enhanced. That way they'll be nose to jaw with civilians."

Cooper's expression changed. "That's a dangerous move."

Deleen looked up, puzzled by the comment. So far Cooper had been supportive, backing her up, being in on all the plans. "Everything we do is dangerous. We either endanger racial purity, security, or economic welfare. There is no easy path.

"We just have to be smart about this. We have to promote the vision, the end game."

Cooper kept his gaze fixed on her, bit his lip and then nodded. She didn't have time to hold his hand. Housing was an immediate issue. "The priority list is made up of those civilians who want to integrate and the Enhanced who have proved not to have aggressive tendencies and were not actively involved in the coup."

Cooper stood next to her. "It's not the Enhanced I'm worried about. It's our people."

Deleen sighed. She was tired of arguing, of explaining, and in the back of her mind she was surprised she was having this conversation with Cooper. "They are all our people. We came from the same place. You need to believe that if we are going to make this work."

Cooper nodded. "I understand. We will get the housing allocations working. Now about the instigators. The city's prosecutor has asked for more time to compile the list of charges against Kameer and his team."

"That's fine. Tell him I want to meet with him before we commence court proceedings."

She picked up the next ereader, the agenda item came to life. "What about the food situation? Has the transport network been re-established with the outlying areas?"

"It's slow, but yes. Food supplies should be back to normal in two days."

Her eyes dwelt on the next item and her heart fluttered.

"And Carlo Levington?"

"The administrator is still receiving treatment. He's made some progress; full recovery is not expected. You will have to stay in the hot seat until we can run an election."

She acknowledged his words with a nod and looked at the next item.

"Any word on the cold soldiers?"

"Your friends have disappeared. No more have been found within city dwellings. Accounts in from the rural areas indicate destruction of about seven bunkers. No news of any further soldiers found alive."

Deleen tapped a pen against her chin. *Rik, where the hell are you?* She missed him. "That's awful. I can't get over the guilt I feel that those soldiers died without even been given a chance. They gave their lives for us."

Cooper frowned. "They were dangerous. Not only to the Enhanced. They were killers. There had to be a reason why they were frozen and hidden away."

"Yes, there was a reason and that reason is tied up in the Enhanced. Two secrets rolled into one. They were hidden to protect the secret."

"Maybe, but there are other explanations."

"Like what?"

"That they were too unstable to live among us, but too powerful to destroy. Freezing them was the only way to solve the situation. The Enhanced saved us the trouble of dealing with them."

"Are you out of your mind?" Deleen found herself feeling very angry and did her best to control it. Logic should win this argument, not emotion.

"No," Cooper said calmly. "We left Earth and its filthy tech behind. We don't want it here on Five."

"But we wouldn't be here without tech. That statement makes no sense."

The door *swooshed* open. Armed security came in. Deleen gave them a curious glance, looked back at Cooper and then gasped when they raised their weapons and pointed them at her.

Cooper took her agenda out of her hand and placed it on the desk. "You're under arrest, Deleen Milo, for consorting with the Tainted."

"Don't be ridiculous." Deleen tried to splutter, but she was still reeling from the shock. From the betrayal. Cooper had been so support-ive. It made no sense.

"You are to be put into isolation until your hearing."

She narrowed her gaze. "Why isolation? I don't understand."

"Because you are Tainted as well as a traitor."

Chapter Twenty-One

FINALE

Deleen paced the small space, anxious for news. She'd not seen anyone or heard anything for days. What had happened to Rik? Had he given up on her?

She slapped the wall. Damn. Why was she even here? Who told Cooper that she had nanotech? It could have been any of them. Kameer, Harzell, Rik or even one of the med techs that tended her. She had no one to blame but herself. She should have seen it coming; should have understood the subtle hints. Cooper had played her.

While she hadn't known that fraternising with Rik could lead to contamination, she certainly should have considered the possibility. But she didn't care. She didn't think anyone else would care either.

Her studies included history. There was a political twist to history and this view on tech. She had tried to root it out, but was prevented before she had achieved progress. She'd been concentrating on the colony accepting the Enhanced, who were animal hybrids, and she hadn't even got to cold soldiers and their technical enhancements, their tiny nanotech. The unseen and the unknown frightened people. That was it, she thought. You could accept an Enhanced. You weren't likely to catch their condition. But a cold soldier could infect you or destroy you utterly if they chose.

Now she had tech in her veins and in her tissues. She had bits of Rik

261

inside her. If the colony was still in a spaceship, they might have flushed her out of the airlocks, but as it wasn't the colony had to deal with her differently.

There had been a lot of change, a lot of uncertainty. It started with the administrator being replaced and the call to bring out the cold soldiers. She'd ripped the scab off the wound, exposing the Enhanced, hoping it would diffuse the situation and give Five the chance to embrace the colony's hidden inhabitants. She'd had too much faith in people. Now she was left not knowing what was going on, and her own future and place on Five uncertain.

A ping at the door heralded the arrival of food. The aroma of hot roasted vegetables reached her. At least they weren't starving her; that was something to be thankful for.

She went to the wall niche to pick up the tray and froze. There was a note on the tray. She put down the tray and took the note and turned it over. Opening it up, she read it twice. Harzell wrote: *We are doing the best we can. Sit tight.*

She turned it over. Who was we? Other Enhanced? She had no option but to sit tight. After eating her meal and replacing the tray in the slot she crouched against the wall, even falling asleep with her head rested against the cool metal.

A sound startled her. She looked around, listening hard. Another clang. What was that? Unexpectedly, the door slid open. Her eyes widened. Were they coming to take her for sentencing? There'd been no word of a trial or charges.

She blinked, not quite sure what was going on. Rik stood there. "Come on!" he ordered and then jerked his head in the direction of the corridor.

Deleen sprung up. "Rik?" She narrowed her eyes. "How did you get here?"

"Talking, talking. Always talking. Just move now. Talk later."

A whirl of emotions made her speechless. He was alive. He was here to rescue her. "I hope you didn't hurt anyone getting in here."

"No need. You programmed my thumb print into the security system, remember?"

That's right, she had. She also had a dummy ID set up for herself so she couldn't be tracked.

"You're working with Harzell?"

He looked briefly over his shoulder. "You don't know when to be quiet."

Rik keyed a lock and led her up a flight of stairs. He exited two floors up and checked the passageway. "It's clear. Come on."

Why were they going up? Surely their escape route was down?

Rik pushed out onto a balcony, a large one where staff often had presentations and celebrations. He kept walking to the railing. Deleen worried he expected her to jump. She may be infected with nanotech but she didn't have his enhanced skeleton or muscles.

A soft burr sound reached her, the sound of a motor. Mac's helmeted head rose into view. "Your carriage awaits, Ms Milo."

"Mac! You're safe." Mac was on one of the small hovercraft.

"Hurry!" Rik nudged her and then practically threw her over the railing. Mac grabbed her and shoved her behind her on the seat.

"Room for you too, boss!"

Rik looked up. "Incoming. No time. Take her and go."

Deleen grabbed Mac on the arm and shook her head. "If he doesn't come with us, I'm staying."

Mac nodded. "I'll go. You drive."

"Oh, for heaven's sake. Just get in, Rik. We can work out who is most noble later."

Rik's eyes glittered with menace, but he leaped on, clinging to the side rails.

A shot flew past, singeing his helmet.

"Go!" Deleen yelled but Mac was already on it, sending the craft into a dive.

"Where are we going?" Deleen yelled.

Mac shrugged and yelled. "Can't hear you."

Rik's hand rested on her shoulder, and he squeezed lightly. They shot through the admin precinct like bob sled racers, the likes of which she'd only seen in historical vids. She'd given up screaming. Her hair zipped about her head, the tips biting into her flesh. It had been days since she'd been able to wash.

Shots whooshed past their vehicle. Amazingly, Mac sent them on an even more perilous path, swerving around buildings, diving under bridges and in among trees at the central park. Their pursuers were going to catch them. They had nowhere to go.

All of a sudden, Mac banked and then turned nearly three hundred and sixty degrees. Deleen squeaked in alarm.

They were landing in the playing field. The bleachers were crammed with people. What was going on? As they lowered down, she saw that Enhanced were sitting with civilians. A cheer went up. She looked from Mac, who was powering down the craft, to Rik, who kept his expression impassive. She thumped him in the chest. "What is going on?"

"Lots," he replied and plucked her out of the vehicle and placed her on her feet.

"Politics," Deleen muttered to herself.

"Ms Milo? I'm Jason from Station C Five ."

"Oh hello," she tried to smile and right her hair, painfully aware that her head looked inhabited by a nest of snakes, and she smelt as if she'd been unwashed for a week, which was true. "What's going on?"

"The people demanded your release. You're a popular figure and when it was announced that you were arrested for being infected by tech … well, there was an uproar. New elections are being called immediately and Cooper Pound has been removed from office. There are still some resisters in the prosecutor's office who are holding out against the popular movement, but now we have you, there's nothing they can do."

"You have me?" she shook her head. "I don't know what you mean?"

"We want you to stand for the Administrator position."

"But I am infected with tech. I'm in love with a cold soldier. I would gladly live as an outcast with Rik."

A great roar went up from the stands. "Are you broadcasting me?"

Jason nodded. "Why, yes. Did I not disclose? We've all come to see you rescued."

A strange noise, like choking came from behind her. She turned around and looked into Rik's startled face. "What is it?"

"You love me?"

Deleen frowned at him "Well, yes, of course."

"You would be an outcast with me? You'd leave all this, your life? Everything?"

She bit her lip. "Yes. I would."

A roar went up again. She turned to the broadcaster. "Will you stop broadcasting my private conversations?"

He had the nerve to laugh at her. "You don't understand. You don't have to be outcast, either of you. We want you to help us adjust to this new future. See?"

They looked up to the score board. It was another vote. Deleen and Rik. Yes. Ninety per cent.

She indicated to Jason to turn off his microphone. "I ..." she closed her eyes. "Is this some sort of revolution?"

"Yes ... and no ... we aren't overturning the Constitution. Just enforcing a vote now, rather than putting up with another coup from Cooper Pound."

"So who am I standing against for administrator?"

"The usurper, Kameer."

"Kameer? But I thought he was an escapee."

"Yes, technically he is. But it is a little hard to get to him in Jerry-town, and we are still awaiting formal charges to be laid. Technically, he is still allowed to stand for election, until convicted. Mirabelle Stanley, a school teacher, is also standing."

"A school teacher?" Deleen didn't know the name.

Jason appeared to understand her confusion. "Yes. She stands for the Purist party."

That didn't sound good either. Deleen waved to the crowd, who cheered. "Okay," she said to the broadcaster. "You need to get me out of here if you want me to live long enough to stand for election."

Jason had reactivated the microphone. "You are going to stand?" A cheer went up.

Deleen looked at the crowd. Politics was not her thing. She was management, good at administration, but it seemed that she was the only one willing to go down the middle path to integrate. Did she have a choice? Not really. "Yes, I'm going to stand for Colony Five."

Chapter Twenty-Two

MOPPING UP

The hype of that day and her rescue didn't die down. Cooper's control over security had not lessened. They were still looking for her. Hiding with supporters meant moving house each day. While she hadn't expected the politics to get deadly, Cooper's betrayal meant she now had to be on the alert for treachery.

Exhaustion drove her to the very edge over the next few weeks before the voting began. She'd hardly seen Rik or the other soldiers since she said yes to standing for office. She longed for a tent, with the sound of the wind in the trees outside, and Rik inside making love with her, careless of their audience. But that was not to be. She had to carry on.

Each day she struggled against her own reluctance to be involved in politics and her need to get on with her life. Yet even that was up in the air. Rik, despite expressing surprise, had not broached the subject with her or even discussed a possible future. What did that mean, exactly? She had thought he cared for her. Now she wasn't sure. And there had been no time to explore a possible future either, as she had been whisked away and hidden, only coming out to talk to supporters and then going into hiding again.

The ugly suspicion that Rik was incapable of love insinuated itself. Part of her wanted to dive into the archives and learn about the cold soldiers, their conditioning, their capacity for socialisation. The stronger part of her didn't. She had to face this without the prop of knowledge. If she accepted that Rik was an individual, she had to let him decide. Rik. Rik who she could trust. Rik who was strong and gentle. She had to believe and not give in to doubt.

After a shower and dressing in borrowed clothes, she waited.

"It's time," a voice said from behind. She turned and nodded to the woman who was sheltering her.

"Thank you, Shell." Slightly older than Deleen, Shell Fielding had long, sleek dark hair and eyes. Her skin was nut brown. A descendant of Greer Fielding, the first comers' agronomist, she surmised.

"Don't be nervous, Deleen. The rally will be wonderful. We already know through the polls that you're set to win. You need to be seen." Shell had been supporting her this last week, moving from hiding place to hiding place as they outwitted Cooper's patrols.

"I know. It's just …"

Shell touched her forearm lightly. "There are plenty of us willing to help you. You know that."

She looked up into Shell's concerned face. "I do, thank you. If I win this, I could use an aide. Would you be interested?"

The woman's dark eyes widened. "It would be a pleasure. Provided I can keep my normal job."

"Oh, and that is?" Deleen asked as she accompanied the woman to the ground car that was taking them to the rally.

"Town planning."

Deleen grinned. "Oh, definitely. We are going to need a bit of that if we are to integrate everyone. Have you been out to Jerrytown?"

"Yes. Just a fly over. I have some ideas about that." The doors opened and they got in. "First we need to get you elected."

The car sped up. Shell was checking through her personal unit when she looked out the window. Her sudden gasp had Deleen's heart thumping.

Shell banged on the window. "Stop! What are you doing?"

Deleen saw that they were heading out of the city, not to central park where the rally was taking place.

Shell began tapping on her personal unit. "Damn it. There's a dampening unit in this car."

Deleen breathed slowly, trying not to panic. "Where are they taking us?"

Shell thumped the dividing window with her fist. "Does it matter? Not to the rally. Wait until I get my hands on these guys. Don't they know you've won already? Kidnapping you will only give more sympathy to our cause. Once word gets out. It will be a landslide."

"That's the key issue, though. Will word get out?" Deleen asked.

"Of course, it will. You not being at the rally will alert everyone." The car entered a tunnel.

"They're taking us north," Deleen commented.

"Not much in the north, is there?" Shell replied, giving up trying to get a message out and sitting back and biting her lip.

"Mostly wheat fields. Some hemp farms for paper and such." Deleen sat back. It was no wonder she hated politics. Even in a small colony like this it sucked. It sucked in her great-grandfather's time, and it definitely sucked now. Except with the Enhanced in the mix it was just more complicated. She had no idea who had kidnapped her.

They were still in the vehicle as the sun went down on Second Day. Deleen peered into the night, wondering where their kidnappers were taking them. Shell couldn't stop raging. She said 'Shit' and 'fuck' once every five minutes. Shell's ranting echoed her own feelings.

"Which faction has us do you think?" Deleen asked.

Shell, who was about to curse again, met her gaze. "I don't know."

"Too many to choose from?"

Shell nodded and stared out the window at nothing.

There was Cooper and his crew, desperate to cling to power, Kameer who wanted to rule instead, and the Purist school teacher who wanted everything to stay the same. There were many Enhanced who were behind their glorious leader. The Purists took exception to welcoming anyone genetically compromised—in other words anyone different from them. They gave support to Cooper, even though he wasn't actually standing for administrator. He'd just taken over undemocratically. Deleen suspected he would be the power behind the purist school teacher if she won.

Now that Deleen's infected status was known, she was hated by both of those factions. Her supporters had formed a party called TAP or the Total Acceptance Party. This signified, among other things, the acceptance of difference and also acceptance of responsibility. This last thing, in particular, was important to Deleen. She didn't believe in blaming the innocent and she also had a soft spot for extenuating circumstances, which wasn't so widely shared among the populace. A lot of TAP's creed had been adopted from the original settlers. They had established Five to be an equal society and that is why the colony had no definite ethnicity, but a mixed one.

Deleen liked this creed, even though she didn't personally choose it. It represented values she held close to her heart. While they were driving away from the city in the hands of kidnappers, something changed for her. She wanted to win. It was a privilege to lead. There was nothing better for her to do. If she lost this election, she'd have to look for a new home, possibly a new planet. She couldn't stay here and see either of these opposition parties win.

The car swerved off the road, throwing Deleen into Shell's lap. "Shit!" Shell said.

Deleen laughed. Not a very appropriate response she knew, but tension was so high, she was losing it. Shell stiffened as the door behind Deleen lifted up. They waited, but their captors didn't show themselves.

There was a tang in the air. Deleen sniffed, finding that she could smell a whole raft of things. Perspiration. Detergent. A whiff of a drug. Electronic scents such as the car would emit. There were sounds too, receding into the distance. Footsteps. Boots crushing undergrowth. A twig snapping. A grunt. Rapid breaths.

Shell climbed out of the car and turned back. "There's no one here."

"They've gone," Deleen said, still sitting there dazedly. Was that the nano doing that? She didn't have the control implants that Rik and the others did, so she didn't think she'd notice any extra abilities, but she now realised she'd just had her first taste of enhanced hearing and smell.

Levering herself out of the car, she was about to send a message on her personal when she detected another smell—a metallic scent.

"Shell! Run!"

Deleen grabbed the other woman's hand and bolted into the shelter of the trees. Then a sound, a click, sounding so close made her dive for the ground, bringing Shell with her. The explosion blew debris over their heads, splintering the trunks of trees, and shredding upper branches and leaves. They covered their heads as the debris rained down.

Panting, Deleen lifted up and looked around. "You okay?" she asked Shell, feeling the burn of grazing on her knees.

Shell cradled her arm. "Okay. But I think my arm is broken."

Deleen was shaken and the pain in her knees started to ease. She had underestimated the situation and her adversaries. Lucky her nano-enhanced senses had alerted her to the explosives. Not that she had suspected a bomb. It was a combination of strange smells and sounds that alerted her to danger.

Now they were stuck in the middle of nowhere. She looked at her personal and it was busted. She tried to get it working but it would not engage. She thought about her captors. What if they came back to check that they had been killed? She climbed to her feet, dragging Shell up with her. "We need to move."

A fine sheen of sweat covered Shell's upper lip, yet her skin was cool to the touch. She was a bit shocky. There was no point in returning to the vehicle. Nothing but twisted burnt metal and flames were left. Wisps of smoke drifted off Shell's personal unit, which lay on the ground a few paces back, barely recognisable.

"We have to stay off the road," Deleen said. "But not far off it. There's plenty of cover if we need it." There were plantations and farms and wilderness in this part of Five.

"Do you have any idea where we are?" Shell asked. "Maybe we should stay with the wreck."

Deleen bit her lip. "Normally that would make sense, but that wasn't an accident. They will come back to search for our bodies and when they don't find them ..." She hated voicing her thought. Shell was pretty shaken up.

"Oh. I didn't think of that. About that job being your aide?"

"You want to pass?"

"No. Not pass. I want a raise."

Deleen smiled. "With danger money?"

"Absolutely."

Deleen found she liked her new offsider a lot. Not that they had even discussed salary and benefits.

They'd been walking slowly for about an hour when they heard a vehicle approaching. Deleen's hearing picked it up far sooner than Shell's. It was coming from the city. The purr of the motor was familiar to her ears, but she couldn't quite place it.

With Shell flagging, there was little point in running. When the sound grew too loud to ignore, they stopped. They sheltered among rows of corn, waiting to see if it was friend or foe.

With the light of First Day wisping through the mottled clouds, it would be harder to hide. More sounds filled her ears. A pattern of breathing, a light buzz of electronics. Deleen was still processing this, when out of the air above them, Rik dropped to the ground. His armour glinted in the early sunlight, his helmet highly polished and undented. He was wearing a full pack on his back. If she hadn't been so relieved to see him, she would have been dazzled.

Shell squeaked, but Deleen put out an arm around her and eased her to the ground to sit. "It's okay. It's Rik."

Mac dropped down next to him, her kit equally immaculate.

They stared at each other. After making such a public statement about her status and her love for him, he'd never mentioned a word about it.

"In trouble again, I see, Ms Milo," Rik said.

Deleen looked around exaggeratedly. "I believe we were doing fine without you."

Mac grunted, but it was to hide a laugh. "So you don't need a lift then?" she asked.

Deleen shrugged and then changed her mind. "Shell here is hurt. We could do with assistance."

Rik turned his head but spoke into his helmet mic. "Mac, assess the injured woman and prepare her for transport to medical."

A few minutes later, the flyer landed via remote control. Mac had a hand rig, which allowed her to bring the craft down. She grinned at Deleen and then went to examine Shell. Mac spoke softly to Shell, checking her vitals and offering her pain relief before putting a sling on her arm. "We can move you now, ma'am."

Mac helped Shell into the front passenger seat of the flyer. "I'm taking off."

Deleen looked around. "Wait!" Too late, Mac was off. She turned to Rik. "How are we going to get back?" She was not looking forward to walking.

"I thought we'd take our time returning to civilisation." His voice came through the helmet speaker.

Her anger began to boil. "What? But I've been kidnapped. I need to get back and let them know I'm all right."

Rik raised an eyebrow. "Mac will report that you are alive and well."

"But I have an election!"

He took off his helmet. "An election you will win, whether you are there or not."

Deleen reeled. "What makes you say that?"

"News of your kidnap, and the attempt on your life, has appalled the citizens of Five. The faction that was responsible foolishly claimed responsibility. I believe even more are going to fall into line after such a cowardly and horrific act." He grinned. "I believe there is a survey running that has you at eighty-five per cent."

"That's unheard of."

"Exactly." Rik held out a hand.

She stared at it and then looked up at him. "I don't understand. You went away."

Rik shook his head. "I didn't go away."

"But—"

He put a finger to her chin. "Your minders separated us."

Her eyebrows drew down in puzzlement. "But I asked after you and everyone gave me blank stares. I publicly announced how I felt about you and you ... well, you walked away."

"Ahh ... that it is how you see it."

He took her hand, and she didn't object as they started walking. He squeezed her hand, but she was deep in thought. "How did you find us?" she asked after brooding for a few minutes.

He tapped her forearm. "You're wearing the tracker bracelet. In a pinch I may have been able to track the nanos in you because they are clones of mine, with the right equipment and not very precisely. Luckily, we were looking for you close by when we detected the explosion on sensors."

She experienced a heart flutter. A part of him was in her. "That's a little bit kinky that part of you is in me."

"It is, I agree. But after Harzell kidnapped you, it was a relief to be able to find you, track you, this time." He tapped the bracelet on her wrist. "I'm glad no one convinced you to take it off."

She gazed into his face and saw the glint of light in his eye and the soft smile curving his lips. "Me too ... well I'm glad you found me."

The corn had given way to shrubs and then nut trees. "How about here for a camp site. I brought the tent."

Her lips twitched, amused that he thought she was keen to camp again. "How convenient. Did you bring the portable bath?"

"I certainly did."

His grin was very wide. Deleen laughed—laughed so hard she couldn't help him set up camp.

Luckily, Rik had the tent erected in no time at all. Deleen estimated that the rally was long over and that the dramas of the evening had run her into morning. She had thought she was exhausted, but when Rik brandished the portable bath her stamina revived. Laughing, she went to take it from him, but he moved it out of reach and shook his head.

"Before we get down to niceties. I think there's something we need to talk about," Rik said.

Rik undid his vest and peeled it off his shoulders. The sound was like an electric current tuning her senses to his every movement. Nature sounds were a background orchestra to his movements, his ballet of undressing.

Deleen forgot everything and just stared. He sat on the end of the inflated bed. A pleasant scent teased her nostrils—it was Rik, not quite a perfume but the essence of a man. Her man.

For some reason, she was frozen to the spot.

"Look, can you pay attention?" he asked as he peeled off his T-shirt, revealing his bare chest, arm muscles flexing.

Her face flushed. "I am."

"I have a lot to say to you."

"You do?" She looked down. Wasn't she wanting to talk to him? She was fully dressed and there was blood on her sleeve. It wasn't hers, so it must be Shell's. Rolling her eyes, she started to peel off her clothes. Rik was a man of extremes. When he wasn't trying to kill something, he was hot for sex. She was crazy to think that she was in love with him. Crazy to think he could feel anything for her.

"Good. Now lay down. I know you like this part." She was starting to let go her angst. Maybe a good sex session was what she needed to settle her emotions.

The hum of the portable bath was overloud. When Rik touched it to her skin, she nearly shrieked and started. "What the hell?"

"Relax."

"I can't. It ... it ..." She stared into his face

He lifted an eyebrow. "It's the nanos. It's what you feel."

He grinned and gave a slight nod. "I have a moderator, a control that regulates the sensory input. You don't."

"Will I have to have one put in?"

He sighed and ran a finger over her cheek, stopping at her chin. "No. You don't have to have one put in."

"Do it again."

He engaged the portable bath. When he ran it over her body, she trembled so hard and then an orgasm hit. Just like that. A powerful shudder and exploding lights in her head. Panting, she looked at him in wonder. "Oh my. That's ... um ... handy."

Rik threw his head back and laughed. "That's what I love about you. There's no guile in you. You just enjoy everything. I want to be like you."

"You love me?" She bit her lip. It was a risk, asking him outright.

Rik laughter fled, but that heat in his eyes remained. "More than life itself. You are my life. You are my reason for existence.

"If you didn't want me, then I don't know what I'd do. I've been beside myself this last week. Your announcement surprised me. I couldn't believe that such a dream could come true. That anyone could love me seemed impossible. I know what I am, but that you love me—you, Deleen Milo, beautiful, clever and brave, Deleen—well that was beyond even my unspoken wish."

"But ..."

"I hardly had time to digest it and you were being taken away and I was quickly dispatched, excluded. Shut out. I tried to contact you, but all my attempts were thwarted. Mac and I stayed close to the city, hoping, waiting. I was hoping to see you at the rally but then there was an announcement. You'd been taken. The rest you know."

"I had no idea. I feel a change in staff is in order."

He ran his finger between her breasts and her breath was stolen. It was beyond any other sensation. "Oh stars. Rik!"

"You don't have to keep the nanos. It's not a true infestation as the Enhanced would have you believe. You could have them removed. It might take a few sessions ..."

"Touch me again."

Deleen shuddered with delight. Her mind totally ensnared by the physical sensations. The nanos enhanced her senses, sight, hearing, touch, smell. Rik knew this. He knew how to maximise her pleasure. With realisations like these, the rest of the world could go to hell.

"I want to have sex right now," she said.

"I thought you might," he replied.

She lowered her head and captured his mouth, delving deep. He matched her, even though she tried to keep it light. "I want you," she said, when she broke the kiss.

"I know." His eyelids lowered.

Her eyes widened and she bit her lip.

"You are part of me, Del. More than anyone who has ever touched their life to mine."

Tears fell and it took a few breaths to say. "Can you let me be part of your life?"

He reached up to kiss her once more. "You are going to have a hard time keeping me out of yours."

Closing her eyes, she nodded. "Oh, Rik. We may end up on a ship to someplace else. Outcast."

"It doesn't matter where we are as long as you are there with me."

Her face crumpled and she buried her face in his chest. He brushed a hand down her spine and made gentle noises. He ran his fingers through her hair. After a few minutes, he ventured. "Del?"

Wiping the tears from her face, she said, swallowing hard first. "I love you so much, Rik. You're my cold soldier forever."

He swallowed too and studied her face as if she was a portrait he wanted to memorise. "And you are mine."

* * *

It took a few days for them to make their way back to the city. On the outskirts they were spotted, and a car came for them. By that time, Deleen was thanking providence for the nanotech in her body. They had had an energetic time of it.

They had talked about removing the nanotech from her body, but Deleen wasn't convinced of the need. They would need to take precautions to prevent transfer of more nanos and that seemed like too much hard work. They hadn't quite decided yet but they were keen on starting a family someday. Besides they were part of her, part of Rik in her. Maybe she was warped. She laughed and Rik squinted at her. "What is it?"

She shook her head. "Nothing really. Just a random thought."

"Like what?"

"It's silly."

"I'm all ears. Silly never stopped you before."

"Bastard! It's just that this nano stuff came from you, and it occurred to me that this madness, this mad devotion I have is because of the tech."

Rik grinned. "A good thought. I'll see what the software developers can do. I am having trouble too."

"Really?" she assessed him through narrowed eyes. "In what way?"

"I thought you were controlling me through the tech too."

Deleen was still laughing when the car pulled up and Shell got out. "There you are," she said and grinned. "Administrator Milo." She fake bowed.

"I won?" Deleen sobered up quickly.

Shell nodded. "The word landslide covers it."

Deleen blinked. Rik had said eighty-five per cent. "But?"

Shell's gaze flicked to Rik, a question in her eyes.

Rik stood there expectantly. Deleen understood and piped up. "This is my soon-to-be partner. I need you to arrange a partnership license and a small ceremony for friends."

Shell's eyes widened, shifted from Rik to Deleen and back again. "Um ... sure ... standard contract or extended."

"Extended," they said in unison. Deleen couldn't repress her smile. No one would be able to separate them once there was an official partnership on record.

* * *

Being the Administrator of Colony Five was even more tedious than being a public servant, Deleen decided. The tedious aspect was that her job was no longer just a seven-and-a-half-hour day. She was on call day and night. Only calls from Vi kept her grounded and sane.

"Hi hon, you getting laid enough?" Vi normally asked, which had Deleen coughing and laughing.

"Don't forget to come over and check out my bump!" Deleen smiled as she had indeed patted Vi's growing abdomen on a regular basis.

She did her best to keep her life normal but all sorts of mind-bending problems were flung her way. What day should the streets be cleaned? What rationale should be used to price energy? How much land should be approved for cultivation? How are unions between civilians and Enhanced to be conducted? Do we need newer medical facilities to develop gene therapy, fertility programs? And the most mind-bending one—should the Enhanced be required to raise a child from the gene bank, like everyone else? Although many embryos had been destroyed, there were still many deep in the bowels of the gene bank that had survived the attack. Accompanying that last question were several essays, petitions and position statements on the topic. They ranged from absolutely not, to most definitely they should. These she put aside in a folder for the next day. She was too brain dead to deal with the big issues. Perhaps if she chose a smaller issue.

With a sigh, she pondered what had been happening over the last month. The integration of the Enhanced with the civilians was not completely without mishap. A few skirmishes had required police action.

Rik was the new head of security and employed Mac and Oyuda in training new recruits to maintain order. Both Enhanced and civilians were included in the patrols. There was some hesitation regarding the nanotech, even though the science department had issued a statement that the nanotech could be cleansed out of a human body if unwanted cross contamination had occurred. However, there was also a rumour circulating that nanotech increased sexual stimulation and subsequent calls for the technology to be freely available. This was somewhat supported by the fact that none of the cold soldiers wanted to have theirs removed.

A new memo came across her desk, and she sat back in the chair and pondered it. *New name for Colony Five* was the title and it was something that Rik and she had been discussing for a few weeks. There was no doubt that discovering the existence of the Enhanced had been a profound occurrence that necessitated a significant gesture to acknowledge it. The cold soldiers were also an addition to the populace. Two more had been located unharmed and then revived—Commander Jen Wyatt and Lieutenant Dan Snowden. Now that was some party when they celebrated their animation.

Deleen recalled the hangover and the after-party sex with Rik with vivid clarity or was that pre-party sex? Even with her own enhanced abilities, she had been exhausted. With the good news that two more cold soldiers had been revived, Rik displayed amazing stamina and enthusiasm in the bedroom.

The door chime rang. "Come in," she said absently, still studying the memo. Next thing she knew a pair of rather large hands were massaging her shoulders. "You should call it a night." Rik leaned down to whisper in her ear.

She groaned in delight. "I know, but I can't rest until we find a new name for the colony."

"A toughie, that."

Deleen sighed. "We need something that speaks of what we are."

"Something other than Human Colony Number Five?"

"Yes, and something that the other colonies won't get too excited about."

"You know they are going to copy us."

"Why did you say that? I'm under enough pressure. I have to suggest something that no one can beat." She stood up and he picked her up, giving her a squeeze. "That's nice. I like that." All the kinks in her spine were spirited away.

"Not helpful, though." Rik said as he lowered her back to the floor.

"It has to be a name that all can identify with, that they feel they have equal rights. Something like 'Equality'.

"Yes, that works, I suppose. But we have gone beyond the norm now."

"You mean, like post-Human?"

"Not quite, but heading in that direction."

"Augment." She wrestled out of his arms and keyed that word in. "I need one more choice."

"It's a vote?"

"Of course."

"So are we voting on the name of the colony or the name of the city?"

"Both, I suppose. Plans are under way for a new city."

"What you really want is to name the planet, unless you plan on calling it Five. Once you do that then the names of cities can follow a similar theme."

She chewed her stylus. "Well, we want the colony to prosper, we want acceptance, both within our society and from other colonies. So *Prospera* for the planet name and for the city, *Acceptance* and the new city, *Equality*."

Rik grinned. "I like it. Now if you're finished, I have something to show you."

She sent off the memo and glanced up. "If it's something I've seen before then let's just get at it."

Rik chuckled. "You have no respect." He picked her up bodily and tossed her over his shoulder. "I'll teach you some."

Deleen couldn't protest, as she was laughing too hard. There was nothing cold about her soldier. Laughing together, she was delivered to their shared quarters. Luckily, the door managed to shut before they were completely naked.

<<<<>>>

Acknowledgments

This book has taken a long time to publish. I can't think how many years ago I started it and then stopped part way through a rewrite. I guess books are ready when they are ready.

Thank you for my Phd, the printed and bound thesis of which I handed in today. Waiting for the University administration to do their thing gave me time to get this book out the door.

Not so much thanks to house renovations, which delayed this book by another two months!

I owe immense gratitude to Nicole R Murphy, who read this book a couple of times in its early stages and gave me tips on what I should do and also encouraged me to keep going. Thank you Nicole, you wonderful woman.

To Lily Mulholland, thank you for the great critique and suggestions. You are so generous with your time and a talented critic.

To the dynamic duo at DP Plus, thanks for the edit and the nit picks. The story is so much better because of your efforts.

To my partner, Matthew Farrer, much appreciation for being my rock and for help with the blurb. Hint! Hint!

Donna Maree Hanson

December 2022

Afterword

We have been through some tough times lately, with Covid 19, lock downs, changed social conditions resulting in distance from friends and family. With the virus still circulating, I've come to value the time I have with family and friends. I also look back and compare how different things were, how freely we met in the years before the pandemic and how with everything going on in life, I haven't been able to keep in contact with friends as much as I wanted to. I have felt myself become more insular, more inwardly focussed. I have also found my ability to be creative curtailed.

I'm hoping that changes from now. My Phd is done. The house renovations are almost done. Excuses are done. I have loads I want to do on the writing front. But with everything, there are choices, a balancing act, do I write or do I hang with friends? do I write or be with family? do I write or do some weaving or other craft?

This is the hardest thing for me, for all writers I think, choosing to write when there are other demands on my time. Writing is done due to sacrifice but more importantly from the joy of creation. I love creating stories, I love being lost in other worlds and in the minds of fictional characters. I've heard writers say that writing keeps them sane. I'm right in the frame on that.

A theme that appears to be occurring in my writing is the question of difference and what makes us human. I hope you enjoyed Awakening.
Happy reading
Donna

Donna Maree Hanson is a traditionally and independently published author of fantasy, science fiction and horror. She also writes paranormal romance under the pseudonym of Dani Kristoff. In April 2015, she was awarded the A. Bertram Chandler Award for 'Outstanding Achievement in Australian Science Fiction' for her work in running science fiction conventions, publishing and broader SF community contribution. Donna writes dark fantasy (the Dragon Wine series), epic fantasy (the Silverlands series), steampunk (the Cry Havoc series) and young adult science fiction (Space Pirate Adventures) as well as short stories across the speculative fiction genre. Her short story collection, Beneath the Floating City was shortlisted for an Aurealis Award in 2017. Her new novel, Awakening (2022) is science fiction with romance and the first in a proposed series.

In 2022, Donna completed her PhD candidature, researching Feminism in Popular Romance at the University of Canberra, and is waiting on her degree to be conferred. Donna lives in Canberra with her partner and fellow writer Matthew Farrer.

Also by
Donna Maree Hanson

Cry Havoc Series (steampunk fantasy)

Ruby Heart, Cry Havoc Book One

Emerald Fire, Cry Havoc Book Two

Silverlands Series (Epic Fantasy)

Oathbound:Silverlands Book Two

Ungiven Land: Silverlands Book Three

Dragon Wine Series (Dark Fantasy)

Shatterwing: Dragon Wine Part One

Skywatcher: Dragon Wine Part Two

Deathwings: Dragon Wine Part Three

Bloodstorm: Dragon Wine Part Four

Skyfire: Dragon Wine Part Five

Moonfall: Dragon Wine Part Six

Love and Space Pirates (Science Fiction Romance-Sweet level)

Rayessa and the Space Pirates

Rae and Essa's Space Adventures

Opi Battles the Space Pirates

Short story collections

Beneath the Floating City: Short science fiction stories

Through These Eyes: Tales of Magic Realism and Fantasy